Sail Upon The Land

About the Author

Josa Young was born in Kent, England. She has worked as a commissioning editor and features writer on *Vogue, Country Living* and the *Times*. She now specialises in digital content and strategy. Her first novel *One Apple Tasted* was published in 2009 by Elliot & Thompson. *Sail Upon the Land* is her second novel. She lives in London.

Follow her on Twitter @JosaYoung

Find out more at www.josayoungauthor.com

Praise for *One Apple Tasted*:

'Following in the footsteps of once-popular novelists Rose Macaulay and Margaret Kennedy, Josa Young debuts with an entertaining and charming romance about love, sex and the upper-middle classes behaving badly.' THE INDEPENDENT

'Delicious froth combines with wit and insight in this romantic comedy of manners.' MARIKA COBBOLD

'One Apple Tasted is by far the best-written new romantic comedy I've read this year.' AMANDA CRAIG

'Funny, warm, touchingly eccentric and irresistibly readable.' JULIE MYERSON

'Compelling, original, cleverly plotted and funny, One Apple Tasted reads like a Virago Modern Classic.' ISABEL WOLFF

'It reminded me very much of Mary Wesley in its lack of sentimentality, the way a certain class of people all seem to know or know of each other and the slightly odd way the characters behave. The author obviously lived through the 1980s but the earlier setting also comes across as very authentic, which only usually happens in works by writers that have actually lived through the era such as Wesley, Elizabeth Jane Howard and Rosamunde Pilcher.' 'GINGER' FROM YORKSHIRE ON AMAZON

'… read it if you're in the market for something a bit more heavy than fluffy but not Wolf Hall challenging.' KIT HARMAN: GOODREADS

Praise for *Sail Upon the Land:*

'Josa Young writes with warmth and wisdom about the complexities of motherhood in this captivating tale of four generations of women that sweeps eighty years of English history. Her eye for period detail is masterly and her characters so vivid they dance from the page and into our hearts.' RACHEL HORE

To Gill

Sail Upon
The Land

JOSA YOUNG

KEYES INK

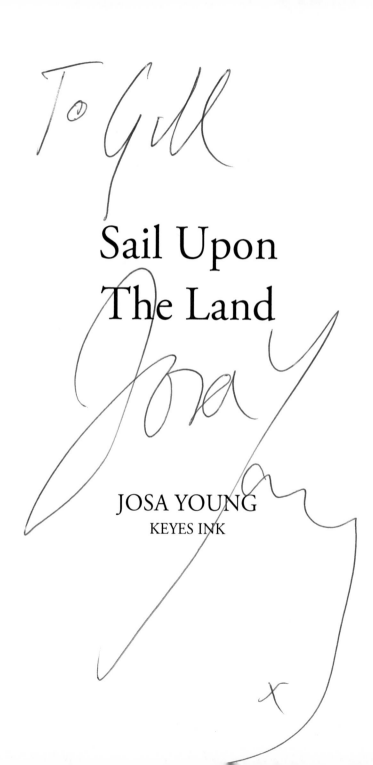

First published 2014 by Keyes Ink
London UK

ISBN: 978-0-9931248-0-8 (Print)
ISBN: 978-0-9931248-1-5 (Kindle)
ISBN: 978-0-9931248-2-2 (ePub)

Sail Upon the Land is a work of fiction. Names, characters, places and
incidents are the products of the author's imagination or are used
fictitiously. Any resemblance to actual events, locales, or persons, living
or dead, is entirely coincidental.

TITANIA: *Set your heart at rest.*
The Fairyland buys not the child of me.
His mother was a votaress of my order,
And in the spicèd Indian air by night
Full often hath she gossiped by my side,
And sat with me on Neptune's yellow sands,
Marking th'embarkèd traders on the flood,
When we have laughed to see the sails conceive
And grow big-bellied with the wanton wind;
Which she, with pretty and with swimming gait
Following, her womb then rich with my young squire
Would imitate, and sail upon the land
To fetch me trifles and return again
As from a voyage, rich with merchandise.
But she, being mortal, of that boy did die.
And for her sake do I rear up her boy,
And for her sake I will not part with him.

William Shakespeare, *A Midsummer Night's Dream*

Prologue

Ronny was a big man. His sheer weight was impossible to shift and he wasn't bothering to prop himself on his elbows. Very little straw between him and the stable floor so Damson couldn't blame him for that. But she'd said no repeatedly, pushing at his massive chest, hitting and slapping. He didn't seem to notice let alone care. She tried to scream but there wasn't enough air in her lungs and no one nearby to come running.

An hour earlier they'd been leaning from the saddle to kiss each other by the light of an Indian moon. Silver water hyacinth choked the half-ruined irrigation tank where they paused in their reckless midnight gallop.

The kissing went on after they rode back to the stables. Unsaddling the horses they kissed each time they brushed against each other in the dim light, moving between stall and tack room. After the horses were tied up with a meagre scoop of feed and fresh water he took her by the hand.

He'd stopped before they got to the door and pushed her quite gently into an empty stall. So sweet, as if he just wanted another kiss before they wandered through the yard and up the path, parting at the door of the Guest House – as they had on the two previous evenings. He was holding her too tight. He crushed

1

a breast in his huge hand where before he had not touched her body apart from holding her in his arms. With a twinge of doubt she pulled away to let him know he was going too far. He responded by tripping her over on to her back.

She gasped, banging her head, winded and struggling to get up. At first she imagined it was a joke or that he was playing, so confused was she by the swift change of mood. Then she caught sight of his eyes and any doubt was seared away by his blank gaze and lowered lids. Why was he shoving down so hard on her chest with his left hand? She couldn't breathe. Gripping his forearm with both hands, she shook it as if trying to dislodge fruit from a tree. He was far too strong for her, ignoring her resistance with frightening intensity. She twisted and squirmed and tried to bite. Scratching was pointless with her bitten nails. He didn't say anything. She realised he hadn't since they came back into the stables. At least he didn't hit her.

'No,' she said again. 'Please. I don't want this.'

He didn't seem to care. And the jovial man who'd wooed her so passionately every evening for the last three days was now a heaving rapist in the shit-scented dark.

They were miles from anywhere. She was alone. If she sank beneath the water hyacinth bound with the straps of her sodden rucksack stuffed with stones, who would ever know? She froze.

As soon as the mood had shifted, his size, which had seemed so reassuring, became hard and threatening. His muscles moved with lazy power. How charming he'd seemed, how handsome and masculine, how jolly. How beautiful she'd felt, dumpy Damson with her long mousy hair and fat bottom. He'd delighted in cinching her small waist with his big hands.

Ronny had constructed what she now realised were idiotic air castles so subtly in the drought-stricken garden of her mind: of dropping out, moving in and running the Vhilaki Guest House with him, making it a big success. Maybe even turning the Hunting Lodge into a smart hotel. He had such plans, seemed so civilised, so educated, so familiar. He'd hinted at her continuing her medical studies in India, maybe opening a charitable clinic. She'd lapped it up.

She was shot with a bolt of shame like an abject beast in the sudden shambles of her life. In the straw. That was slang for having a baby, wasn't it? She wasn't on the Pill. She'd never even had proper sex before. Oh hell.

Ronny had been a drug, so fast was the rush of infatuation to her head. Cambridge, for which she'd worked so hard, disappeared under his wooing into a hazy, meaningless distance. What was Cambridge compared to Ronny's big brown eyes staring into hers, telling her she was beautiful? And not just that, but talking to her about the birdlife in the forest all around, the history of the house, Partition – all kinds of stuff that fascinated her. He'd even elicited her sympathy and budding professional interest by discussing his type 1 diabetes. She'd felt so grown up.

No point in doing anything to stop him now. Even screaming was pointless. The stables were a good hundred yards from the Guest House. She couldn't make much noise anyway as there wasn't enough air in her lungs. She didn't dare. He hadn't been violent but his eyes were empty and she had no friends nearby. Just a bunch of stoned Australian strangers. The stable walls were thick and the door closed.

Mortified, she remembered Caroline who'd left that very

afternoon fed up with Damson's flirtation. Caroline the not-really-schoolfriend she'd met up with in Goa. Caroline, whose grandparents had 'served'. She bored Damson to tears with her tales of durbars and elephants and dire warnings about caste and manners and appropriate dress and keeping a distance and on and on. So many of her sentences had started with, 'I don't mean to be racist…'

She'd been company of a sort. They read about the Vhilaki Guest House in the backpackers' bible, and the free horse riding had hooked them in. The guidebook hinted that the owner was some relation of a local big wig's. No one knew much about it but Rhonap 'Ronny' Viphur was definitely a 'character'. Educated in England, he offered a taste of the Raj for nostalgic backpackers on a budget. The Guest House was difficult to reach, in the grounds of the Vhilaki Hunting Lodge up in the hills served only by a rack train. You got off at Hunters' Halt, a station built for grand hunting parties at some point during the reign of Queen Victoria. Determined and adventurous backpackers with a love of riding found their way up there, but there wasn't much detail and the guidebook requested more feedback. The girls detected that it might not be very comfortable, but they were young and used to discomfort and the prospect of riding in the hills was enough compensation.

Damson thought that Ronny didn't seem to mind one way or another whether he entertained a crowd or a trickle, and only ran his Guest House for the 'company'.

She'd rejected the older girl's warnings as jealous spite. She'd suspected that Caroline was a bit Raj-minded too and believed it demeaning to have a relationship with a 'native'. That made

Damson even more defiant. Shades of *The Jewel in the Crown*, which she'd watched on television, tinted her vision all the more rosily. Who wouldn't fall for Hari Kumar? She didn't let herself think about what had happened to Daphne.

Damson had watched while Caroline stuffed her clothes into her rucksack any old how, in contrast to her usual meticulous folding.

'You should come with me you know,' she'd said.

'But I'm happy here, I want to stay for the full week. We paid for it. I still don't understand why you're going so early.' Damson did know perfectly well. But she was harbouring her own secret fantasy of staying on much longer, of being a blonde princess in the Indian mountains – all very *Far Pavilions*. Maybe she could effect a reconciliation between Ronny and his mysterious important relations. They could leave the Hunting Lodge and live in the city.

'I'm not enjoying watching you making a fool of yourself with Ronny. It's so inappropriate, Damson. He's a big, fat, middle-aged, divorced chancer and you've got all your life ahead of you. You're meant to be going up to Cambridge in October aren't you? What on earth do you think you're doing?'

Caroline kept nagging at her to leave right up to the end, when Damson could see she was red in the face with irritation. Caroline had turned at the gate, 'Damson, please come with me. There's nothing for you here. It can't possibly be real. He doesn't care for you.'

'He does. He's lovely. I'm having a wonderful time.'

Damson had been wavering, had thought of running back, chucking her stuff into her rucksack and tagging on to the tiresome familiarity of Caroline.

'Why would he be interested in someone like you? Except for the obvious.'

It had been Caroline's spiteful last words that pushed a tender place already bruised with overuse.

'Please, Damson. I'll wait. You can go and get your stuff.'

Damson turned her back and walked away.

In their no-longer-shared room, lying in a sensuous stupor on the charpoy, it was easy to banish Caroline to the back of her mind. Nasty cat, she told herself, she's just jealous. And she gave herself up to dreaming. What should she wear for the promised moonlit ride? Perhaps she should have a bucket bath with that sandalwood soap from Mysore?

Now she was lying on her back once more and no one gave a damn how she smelled. She wondered for a moment if the stable's occupant might be ridden back in to her rescue but it was too late for anyone to be out.

Tears slid out of the sides of her eyes and into the hair on her temples and a crying headache started in her forehead. She hadn't wanted it, had she? Or was this what it was always like the first time? Uncomfortable, embarrassing and frightening? At least she was getting rid of her virginity – and she hadn't even had to make a decision about it.

Damson couldn't breathe properly. Her last thought before she blacked out was, 'How many others?'

Surfacing to find herself being carried, Damson's instincts kicked in and she stayed limp in his arms, hoping he wouldn't realise she was conscious. She felt sick as she inhaled Ronny's distinctive smell – spicy sweat mixed with eau de Cologne – that she'd found so attractive and reassuring.

She prayed that her brief tensing as she returned to consciousness had been undetectable. There was no sound apart from his breathing and the soft fall of his feet in the dust. Where to? Nothing seemed real, and she wondered in a detached way how he would do it. Strangle her? Those enormous hands with which he would try to encircle her waist, how much more easily would they fit around her neck? Her best chance was to appear unconscious. Then she must seize her moment when he put her down – as he must at some point, at least to shift his grip. If she could run towards the Guest House and scream, someone would surely notice and come to her aid.

Right at the bottom of the mess that was her mind lurked terror, but she couldn't allow that boiling slime to erupt or she would come apart. She needed to be in one piece if she was going to get out alive.

Ronny gasped and something wet dripped on to her face. She didn't dare react although it itched.

Then he stopped. Resting her weight on one raised knee, he turned a handle and opened a door.

Where were they? She didn't dare look.

It was cooler but stuffy and darker than the warm starlit navy of the night outside. Ronny wore riding boots and she could detect that he was walking on a hard surface. She was no lightweight, even for a man as strong as Ronny, and he was moving less cautiously now. Progress was quite slow as he had to stop and open doors. Wood sounded underfoot. Then they were going up carpeted stairs. Damson had stayed down in the Guest

House, which was a relatively modern bungalow in the grounds floored throughout with worn linoleum. She must be in the Hunting Lodge itself.

If he had taken her indoors, it was unlikely he was going to murder her, wasn't it? Better to play dead. Did he have servants living in? She had no idea. At the top of the stairs he turned right. He opened another door, walked across the floor and laid her gently down on a soft, quite high surface that smelt of the dust dislodged by the weight of her body.

She let her limbs flop as if still in a faint. To her surprise he seemed to be wrapping her in velvet. He whispered, 'Are you awake?'

She didn't answer. Lay deliberately limp, desperate for him to go away. He waited, probably looking down at her in the moonlight that streamed through the window. He touched her wrist as if checking her pulse and pushed away the hair that had fallen across her face. She hardly dared breathe. Then she heard him shift his balance and couldn't help tensing up. He sighed, and then he startled her by saying, 'I am so sorry, it's not what I meant. Sleep now. We'll talk in the morning.'

So he wasn't going to kill her. Relief washed through her, but she had no intention of answering and concentrated on relaxing her muscles. Said sorry? She didn't think that quite covered it. Had he been crying? More likely to be sweat dripping off his forehead. She sensed him move away from the bed and risked opening one eye. The moonlight revealed the door closing. She listened for a key in the lock but it didn't come. She lay still for a few heartbeats longer, thinking around her body for damage. There were no obviously sore places, and her *salwars* were pulled back up around her waist. She was just uncomfortable and panicky. What if he changed his mind and came back in? She had to move fast but when she stood up the room swam around her. She lay back down on the bed, thinking she'd just rest for a moment to get her strength back before escaping.

When Damson awoke, daylight flooded the room. She lay on an enormous mahogany four-poster bed in a Victorian time-warp. For a moment she struggled to remember what she was doing there. Every surface in the room was dimmed with neglect. It looked as if no one had been in there for decades. She caught a whiff of stale horse shit, eau de Cologne and sweat and fear detonated in her mind. She leapt off the bed and ran to the door. It wasn't locked.

Opening it very slowly, she peeped out, heart pounding. Nothing moved in the passage barred with dust-dimensioned sunlight. The corridor stretched away from her, the heads of tigers, sambar and other game mounted all the way along to the top of the stairs at the end. She glanced the other way and saw dark pictures on the walls, rugs and animal skins backed with pinked red felt on the wooden floor and more stuffed heads.

Ronny's 'guests' never set foot in the Hunting Lodge as far as she knew. She went back into the room and closed the door, crossing to look out of the window and find out exactly where she was. She must get herself over to the Guest House undetected.

Skin crawling and desperate to wash, she tied the cord of her *salwars* more tightly and pulled her *kameez* down decently over her bottom. There was nothing much she could do about her hair, which was loose and all over the place, stuck with grubby straw. She combed it as well as she could with her fingers, then plaited it tightly and looked around for something to tie the end, pulling a piece of cording off the edge of a velvet cushion. Tiptoeing to the door, she opened it a crack and listened. Nothing. She slipped out and padded barefoot, her sandals in her hand, to the top of the stairs. She stopped again. The house seemed deserted. Fear grabbed her. Heart banging she ran down the stairs as fast as she could towards the front door, skidding across the chequerboard floor, praying it was unlocked. She still had no idea what time it was or who would be about.

It wasn't locked. The dusty space outside was empty, so she slipped through the crack and ran across the overgrown carriage sweep, glancing back once at the windows. Some were broken, and there was a small peepal tree getting an invasive grip on one corner of the house.

She was out of breath when she got back to her room in the Guest House. Hoping no one had seen her, she locked the door behind her with her padlock and went straight into the squalid little bathroom shedding clothes as she went. She scolded the stupid deluded moron who had been herself before she left that room the night before. Still no point in wasting time beating herself up. She was very lucky no one else had.

She knew she'd get nowhere reporting him for rape to the local police. They would laugh and say she deserved everything she got, being an unmarried young woman flaunting herself and her long fair hair around India without a father or husband to protect her. Even in England, she wouldn't get far with a rape charge when she had been seen flirting with her assailant and going off with him in the dark.

Stripping herself naked and shuddering with disgust, she filled a bucket with water from the tap by the squatter loo and began to scrub herself all over her body and across her mouth with her flannel and the sandalwood soap. It hurt but she didn't stop, rubbing hard to get rid of what had happened to her. She opened her mouth to howl like a beast but something stopped her from making a noise. However stoned her fellow guests, they might hear and come to see what was the matter. Her instinct was to hide

She forced herself to calm down, taking huge sobbing breaths. Having roughly dried her stinging body, she got dressed from the pile of clothes delivered by the *dhobi wallah* outside her door that morning: faded jeans, plain white man's *kurta*. She laced on Indian army boots.

Groping in her body belt, she found her Swiss Army knife and opened the tiny scissors. Holding her thick wet plait in her left hand, pulling it as hard as she could, she began to cut it off, sawing and snipping and stabbing until her scalp screamed.

At last she was wrenching the last hairs out of her scalp and dropping the plait to the floor. Her head seemed to tilt forward, weightless. She sat down abruptly, her vision blurred and darkened.

Then she packed, upending her sponge bag and replacing only the toothbrush, toothpaste, sunblock and lip salve, her soap and deodorant. Lip gloss, eyeliner, mascara and Rive Gauche stayed on the bed. The one dress she had with her she left, along with the pink *salwar kameez* she'd been wearing last night. Her drop earrings, matching necklace and a strappy top and wraparound skirt were also discarded. She took the two greying cotton sports bras and left the lacy one. Only plain white knickers went back in, anything feminine she left on the charpoy for the sweeper to take. Then she strapped her body belt around her waist under the *kurta*, filled with her passport, her watch with its broken strap, travellers' cheques and money, all luckily still intact.

She went back into the bathroom for a last pee and caught a glimpse of herself in the little mirror. Her hair looked bizarre, longish bovver-girl strands hanging around her face. So she took the scissors out again and trimmed them off, trying to cut everything fairly close to her scalp. She sat down on the side of the charpoy to think what to do. Ronny or one of his servants took people who were leaving up to Hunters' Halt in the Jeep. There were two trains on the track. One cranked itself at walking pace up the mountain in the afternoon and spent the night at Girigarh, a cool and airy hill station built by the British Raj to spend their summers away from the blistering heat on the plains. It then reversed down again, stopping at Hunters' Halt around eight o'clock in the morning. The other moved a little faster and went up and down within the day, spending the night at the bottom. She fumbled for her watch in her body belt, hit by intense relief when she realised it was only seven. The Halt was less than half a mile away. She could walk, particularly as her rucksack was now so light. It was just a question of escaping without being seen.

It was far too early for heads sore from country wine and balls of off-white grubby opium to consider getting up. There was no one to say goodbye to. She swung her pack on to her shoulders and, having unlocked and unhooked her padlock, she left Ronny's compound.

From Rikipur at the end of the rack train line in the valley below she would get a train to New Delhi more than two hundred miles away. There she'd need to change her flight, but she planned to hole up for a week or two in a small clean hotel first before facing her father and stepmother in England. Then there was Cambridge. Thank God for Cambridge. She was more determined than ever to qualify as a doctor.

As she left, she glanced back at the house. Nothing moved in the early morning sunlight. She could hear a horse in the stable stamping its iron-clad hoof on the concrete floor. She turned and set off.

One

Sarah Bourne wanted to scream. It was a typical Monday morning and Mummy was pretending to be in charge as usual. The ghost of Abbots Bourne past seemed to have taken up residence in her mother's bones. It was less than fifty years since Sarah's great-grandfather Big George Bourne had built the great red-brick pile to celebrate his rise to nobility on the froth of his popular coloured raising agent. And Mummy – the current Countess of Elbourne – was infected by far grander ideas than her own background or circumstances would justify. The great house was already peeling and cracking.

What was Abbots Bourne now but a glorified private hotel? In place of grand pre-war house parties that went on for weeks, the house was full of paying guests. Originally refugees from Belgium and from zeppelin raids on London, they'd stayed on as a useful source of additional income after Armistice.

Mademoiselle Droge had arrived as a terrified sixteen-year-old without luggage from Belgium when her parents had sent her to England as the German Army advanced. With her witchy long nails and disdain for housework, she'd evolved into the children's governess. And Mummy, or Mama as she preferred, had fled there with her widowed mother in 1917 and married the heir –

14

excused from military service due to his extreme myopia – two years later. It was never mentioned, but Sarah knew that the place they had escaped from was called Penge. Her mother cultivated a vague air whenever anyone asked where she'd been born.

When she was cross with her mother, Sarah would mutter *Penge, Penge, Penge* under her breath until it was divorced of all meaning. She had no idea where Penge was, or why it should be something shaming. But she did know that Granny and Mummy (and Mummy's deceased Daddy) had lived in a small house with no one living in before they came to Abbots Bourne. Mummy would tell morning callers how Abbots Bourne had teemed with servants in Sarah's great-grandfather's day.

'They all got so spoilt,' she would grumble to some caller's eager listening ear half-concealed by an outmoded cloche hat. 'That ghastly war wrecked everything for people like us.'

She would try her hardest to carry on as if nothing had changed at all since Big George's day, even though her ideas about what that had been like were as vague as she was and mostly gleaned from *The Making of a Marchioness*.

For the former Claire Ditsworth catching the short-sighted eye of William Bourne – only son and heir to the second Earl Elbourne – had changed everything. Which was why Monday mornings in particular made Sarah fume.

'Sarah, darling, would you go and ring the bell? I need Cook to come up and discuss menus.'

Sarah would sigh and stamp over to the fireplace. She knew it was childish and she should practice her gliding, but stamping seemed to relieve her feelings about Mummy's silliness.

'Ladies don't stamp, dear,' said her mother automatically.

'Cook always cooks the same things, so what is there to discuss?'

'It's the done thing. I must discuss menus with Cook, darling, as it is Monday. Please go and ring the bell.'

The ringing of bells was a hit and miss affair. Often no one heard, let alone responded, and if someone did come up, a huffy atmosphere blew into the room with them. Her mother seemed impervious to it, but it made Sarah's skin crawl.

These days there were just daily women from the village to keep on top of the dirt, a gardener, an odd-job man (essential for the endless leaks) and a put-upon maid or two, distinguished mostly by giving notice after a couple of weeks. No butler or footmen of course – they'd never come back from the Great War.

Built at a time when servants had servants who had servants, Abbots Bourne had once been inhabited by a large and thriving community whose sole purpose was to wait upon the tiny family perched on top like a hut on a mountain. Now the remaining staff had abandoned the enormous servants' hall and the quality of their service had dropped off considerably, as had any sense of loyalty.

While Big George Bourne was still active and Queen Victoria on the throne, the family could not get by without a French chef, butler, housekeeper, lady's, house, parlour and chamber maids and six-foot liveried footmen who still powdered for gala occasions. There was even a between maid and boot boy, never perceived by the family, their role being solely to look after the upper servants. Their livery was still hanging in dark basement and attic wardrobes breathing ancient sweat like ghosts of an army that had passed through and vanished.

It was made discreetly clear to the paying guests that they were responsible for their own cleaning, and must bundle and box their laundry for the van that came on Thursdays. The latest kind of Hoover had been purchased, and this was parked in the upper corridor in the mornings, the idea being that the PGs would take it into their rooms and wield it vigorously. This happened only sometimes.

Then there was Cook, who – due to the absence of butler and housekeeper – was at the pinnacle of the dwindled servants' hierarchy. A necessarily stout woman without a creative bone in her bolster-like body, Mrs Jones wore her ceremonial wedding ring with pride. She managed to overcook all the produce from the farm and the kitchen garden, and everything was served cold because the kitchen was so far from the dining room. Sarah minded very much, although nobody else ever mentioned the food at all. It was rude to talk about eating, like mentioning where babies came from, or bottoms and lavatories.

In her great-grandfather's seldom visited library, she'd tried to assuage her childhood boredom with books. Most of them weren't very interesting – sermons, political works and geographical tracts. With no one to guide her, she read her way through everything that did catch her imagination. In social histories, old novels, diaries and memoirs, she was led outside the limits of her family home and into a realm where people ate for pleasure.

She suffered genuine stomach pangs at Pepys' description of a hot venison pasty, wondered what Beau Brummel's favourite capon stuffed with truffles had tasted like, swooned over dishes designed by Escoffier at the Carlton Hotel, and dined in her imagination with Oscar Wilde at the Café Royal. All far from the pale and chilly strips of translucent cabbage exuding a faint satanic whiff of sulphur, the lakes of fatty-globuled tasteless brown gravy with carrot lily pads, served every day except Friday. On Friday, in accordance with some half-forgotten religious urge, Cook boiled cod into a kind of white mattress stuffing. Sarah had to eat so she wasn't hungry, but she knew full well that there was a whole world of delicious food out there that did not resemble the Jones cuisine in any way at all.

When and if Cook came up to the drawing room, she would stand with her large flat feet in broken-backed slippers comfortably spread, arms folded and head on one side. Claire would ask vaguely about the coming week's meals with an air of being above all that sort of thing.

'Yes, my lady,' she would say. 'Yes, the leftovers of the joint. I've minced it and we are having rissoles as usual.'

Sarah shuddered. These indeterminate, tasteless cylinders were granular and greasy from being boiled in much re-used oil – beige on the inside, black on the outside. She had to put up with them every Monday.

Her father never seemed to notice the ruination of the vegetables cultivated by the gardener in the old walled kitchen garden. She preferred her Daddy, who looked and smelt like and indeed was a farmer, to her Mummy with her silly airs and graces. At least he never tried to get her to call him Papa. Daddy seemed quite sufficient for him. Before she was even awake, unless it was a very sunny morning and she went too, her father was out and about supervising the milking, even taking a hand if they were a milker short. Her mother just sat on a sofa all day.

He dressed indistinguishably from his men, right down to tying bits of binder twine around his trousers just below the knee to keep them out of the slurry in the byres. When Sarah went to stay with schoolfriends, their fathers looked very different as they set off in the mornings to travel into the City. They wore bowler hats, striped trousers and black coats for jobs as stockbrokers, lawyers or physicians. They carried umbrellas and copies of *The Times*. At weekends, a concept unknown to Abbots Bourne, they wore smart tweed jackets and flannels. Sarah had never been close enough to judge, but she was sure they did not smell of cowpats and cigars.

She wasn't sure she didn't prefer their neat, warm, well-run, well-lit houses on the edge of Home Counties villages to the vast and ramshackle chaos of Abbots Bourne. Her friends' mothers were brisk, their version of the done thing seemed a lot more practical. They were out serving on committees, playing bridge or golf, while Sarah's mother was marooned on a drawing-room sofa all day long: something about having four big babies so quickly Sarah had heard Nanny whispering to Cook. She didn't understand but it sounded shocking. Everything to do with having babies provoked the grown-ups into tutting and dropping their voices.

Sarah returned from visits to schoolfriends sighing with frustration and longing for a different kind of mother. Many of them had served in Flanders as nurses behind the front line. They didn't talk about it much, but she was inspired by her friend Alison's mother saying the best thing had been taking a filthy, mud-plastered casualty into the ward, stripping and washing him, dressing his wounds and making him comfortable in a clean white bed.

At home, the paying guests had decidedly pre-war ideas. Like Sarah's grandmother, many of the older ladies wore corsets and long skirts, toques perched on their curled front hair pieces, in the timeless style of their much admired Queen Mary. But Sarah wasn't interested in the past. At seventeen she burned and ached to escape into her future.

As a child she'd liked running about with her younger brothers in the more wooded parts of the extensive neglected park, building camps and climbing trees. Now, on her solitary walks, she came upon the tumbled remains of a cemetery that she and her brothers had set up among the rhododendrons. There they had buried anything dead they came across, however small or smelly. There was a good supply of slates that had fallen off the roof, and she and Diggory, the eldest of the three boys, would write with broken bits of slate the right sort of things, such as 'In Memoriam' and 'RIP' copied from the churchyard. The two little boys would scrawl their versions of skeletons and skulls.

There had been screams of guilty pleasure when they found a possibly dead beetle (although there was a scuttling reluctance among the beetle population to be buried), whiffy skeletal bird or poor naked nestling. They would fall upon the remains with glee, knowing a long afternoon of cheerful rituals lay ahead: the making of elaborate shrouds from leaves, the collecting of flowers for wreaths and the burial, in a grave dug with a stolen spoon. This was accompanied by the funeral service as heard when they were walking past the church wall one afternoon, and subsequently looked up in the prayer book.

'Dust to dust, ashes to ashes, bones to bones, mud to mud, earth to earth, grass to grass,' Sarah would intone.

She'd been six when Stephen, her youngest brother, was born. Old enough to remember with pleasure how tiny he had been. At the same time he had looked in his bath like the naked fledglings that fell from the sparrows' nests in the wisteria. Transparent, and a bit purple.

As Nanny, who'd looked after their father, was too ancient to venture into the more distant reaches of the park, Sarah wore a highly valued pair of breeches which she had found in a drawer in the old servants' hall, held up with a snake belt removed from her brothers' room. These treasures she kept in a hollow tree. She would slip off her skirt whenever she was out of sight of the grown-ups and into the dampish, slightly mouldy freedom of the breeches. Her father had spotted her once, she could see him hesitate peering through his thick glasses, but then he shrugged and walked on, gun broken over his arm.

When her brothers were small they had accepted her leadership without question. The four children had played games of Lost Boys to her Peter Pan. The youngest was, at the outset, hauled around with them in a wine crate filled with cushions and roped to an old pram chassis. In Sarah's memory it was a perfect, golden time. They were out in all weathers, only coming in for lessons with the Belgian governess or for meals. That was until the outside world intruded when Diggory turned eight. He was just a year younger than Sarah, and he was packed off with his trunk and tuck box to St George's Court prep school by the sea.

He swaggered in his grey uniform blazer and shorts, cap and shiny brown lace-ups. The shooting brake was ready to take him away, trunk roped to the wooden rumble seat. Sarah, as she stood waving uncertainly on the drive, could see he was trying not to cry. Before this moment she had always done things first as she was the eldest.

While Diggory was away, it was sort of all right, but he'd been her friend and she missed him. So many jokes and long days outside. The younger boys were not quite as close to her and started to go off by themselves, leaving her behind. The first inkling she had that things were not at all the same, was when her younger brother Michael told her that he was Peter Pan now and she should be Wendy. She was so angry that she stalked off in protest and never rejoined their games.

Diggory came home for an exeat. She could see at once that he'd changed. With uncertainty in her chest, she bounced at him and he recoiled. The awful sensation she'd had when she saw the shooting brake bear him away came back and she knew that, however much she pretended otherwise, she was different from the boys and would be treated differently. Not as well in fact. Boys went out into the world, girls stayed at home. Diggory was only home for two days. She overheard him say to his brothers, who flocked about him like sparrows: 'None of the chaps at school play with their sisters. You wait. School's good fun. No girls.'

She burst into the boys' bedroom and jumped on him, banging his head against the floor until Nanny came in and broke them up. Shame, disgrace and loneliness followed as the two younger ones were rapidly dispatched in their brother's wake. All the boys together at St George's Court and Sarah left behind. The woods were not the same without her brothers and there was no one else to play with. The cemetery was neglected. Even a blackbird on its back, yellow beak gaping in death, failed to rouse her interest. She would see the village children playing on the green and long to join them as she walked past with Mademoiselle practising her French conversation. She didn't understand why she wasn't allowed to play with the children who went to the village school, but there seemed to be a kind of barrier between her and them and she didn't know how to cross it.

When Diggory was about to leave St George's Court for Rugby, and Sarah was fourteen, her mother roused herself sufficiently to realise her daughter was bored and unhappy. A cousin of approximately the same age was invited to come and stay in the holidays as her parents served in India. Sarah was extremely suspicious to begin with, but Jemima, who went to a girls' public school, was friendly. Best of all she had a suitcase full of Angela Brazil's school stories which she was happy to share. Sarah was swept into a world from which parents were absent, and where there were lots of girls who shared her longing to be free from the stifling 'old days' that crept the dusty passages of Abbots Bourne.

In Brazil's world, the Dulcies and Irenes with their breathless enthusiasms and excitements, plans and pranks, made her feel normal. Constantly being hushed by her grandmother or told she was talking nonsense gave her an itch under her skin, a desire to break free and run away or – shockingly – to slap someone hard. The world of boarding school seemed like liberation and she longed for it. By the end of the holidays, Sarah was begging her parents to send her away too. Jemima had converted her to the joys of female company and the pain of her lost boys began to recede.

Now she was home again, seventeen-years-old and having passed her Higher School Certificate, which surprised everyone given her earlier lack of education. It hadn't been quite like Angela Brazil, she had never attained the status of Monitress or House Captain at St Cecilia's School for Girls. She'd made good friends, learned that lacrosse was not her kind of thing, surprised everyone by enjoying some of the school food (it was the contrast with Mrs Jones's offerings) and the pleasures of the adult world were just coming into focus.

Her parents had a vague idea that she might be presented in 1939, which at least meant she could leave Abbots Bourne for a bit. William's sister Phyllis was willing to do the honours as Claire had never been presented herself, even after her marriage. Aunt Phyllis had brought out her own daughters and knew the form to Claire's relief, and there was a plan that Sarah should go and stay with her aunt in London, and go to a few parties in the summer after the Drawing Room where she would perform her curtsey. There would be men at the parties and she might possibly have to marry one of them. That would be one way of escaping from Abbots Bourne but she wasn't enthusiastic.

That wasn't for a few more months. In the meantime Sarah was bored and lonely again, as her mother sporadically tried to interest her in arranging flowers and other ladylike ways of spending her time. There was some new freedom. Her bicycle, brought home from school, allowed her to cycle into Framham five miles away and go to the pictures. She did this regularly, devouring films that revealed to her a very different world from the one she inhabited. Every week she was drawn deep into a monochrome swirl of beautiful women taking control of their lives in exciting ways. They spoke with staccato certainty, ran 'automobile' factories, were writers and musicians travelling the world. They might fall swooning into the arms of the hero in the last reel, but before they got there they did a great deal more than arrange flowers and write letters. She was restless, wondering how she could grasp this new kind of life that seemed so impossible to achieve in England, when rumours of war started to penetrate even the self-sufficient world of Abbots Bourne.

She could see from the faces of the older generation how much they dreaded going through it all again. But for her at last it meant something was happening, and it wasn't to do with putting some ostrich feathers on your head and curtseying to a stuttering monarch. It might be like the last war when women had proper jobs. Even Aunt Phyllis had worn a uniform and sat behind a desk.

As the possibility of war began to manifest itself, they gave over the vast and hideous Bachelors' Wing to be a convalescent home for officers. It was unused for many years as the rooms were too small for the better class of PGs that Lady Elbourne preferred. For the family life went on pretty much as it had before.

The Red Cross started a First Aid course in the village hall, and Sarah volunteered, going on to the advanced level and considering joining the Voluntary Aid Detachment, so she could nurse casualties if and when she was called up. She was proud of her bandaging skills and enjoyed getting involved with the village and meeting up with the girls who, as children, she must have seen and envied playing on the village green. There was still a distance, and she felt shy, but when someone was bandaging you up as you lay on the floor, it was impossible not to giggle together.

One Monday morning in 1939 she found her mother in the drawing room pretending not to cry. Cook had just been in as usual to 'discuss menus' but she hadn't wanted to go through her usual dirge of rissoles, cottage pie, steak and kidney. She had simply resigned instead. She'd been offered a job cooking for the garrison at the new anti-aircraft artillery battery that had been set up on the coast.

'Poor soldiers,' thought Sarah, rejoicing at the opportunity. Her voracious reading and domestic science at school had taught her that there was more to life than eating the same menu every week.

It was clear to Sarah that her mother had no idea what to do, not even how to get the next meal on to the table, let alone feed a man properly.

Gaining access to the kitchen was a brief moment of great excitement and liberation for Sarah although, having studied hygiene, she was disgusted by the dirt and squalor she discovered below stairs. She couldn't understand why they weren't all dead from botulism long since. The Aga, purchased in a moment of enthusiasm by her parents five years before 'to make Cook's life easier', was caked in grease. The worn brick floor was slimy and damp. In the evening, when you turned on the light, numberless reddish cockroaches flowed like unwholesome fluid into the shadows. In drawers she found ancient butter papers, stinking and rancid. Most telling was the complete absence of any kind of cookery manual. Mrs Jones had simply applied the same principle to everything that came through the back door. Get the scullery maid to chop it up, bring to the boil, add plenty of salt and leave in the bottom oven until convenient.

Quickly before he was called up she asked Jim Collins the odd-job man to take the green baize door that separated the servants' realm from the family off its hinges and put it away in the old stables. Her mother didn't notice for a while but when she did said nothing. It was clear she'd decided to ignore it as she did anything uncomfortable.

By that time Sarah had taken the household's food requirements in hand. The war was still phoney and there were no officers in need of a convalescent home just yet. She started by scrubbing every inch of the kitchen with the help of the daily women. After a week of eating omelettes, cooked on an electric ring, every surface was as clean as they could get it smelling faintly of Jeyes fluid pinched from the cow sheds.

Instead of going up to London to be fitted for her presentation gown, ball dresses and cocktail frocks – that was all cancelled now – she went to Charing Cross Road to buy cookery books. In the dim depths of a second-hand book shop she flicked through a weighty *Mrs Beeton* published in 1912 that exhausted her with its pages of napkin folding and vast buffets. She seized upon a copy of Escoffier with excitement but was bewildered by the very short and undetailed recipes. An old copy of Eliza Acton's *Modern Cooking for Private Families* struck her as a practical first step. On her way home she dropped in at Penrose & Quinn, the smart grocer and florist at the bottom of St James's, and bought spices to make Mrs Acton's curries, a brown paper bag of peppercorns and a French cheese.

P&Q as it was known was a revelation of deliciousness and

she had to rein herself in hard to stop herself squandering her allowance. She could not resist a small chocolate cake topped with a crystallised violet and stood, her mouth watering, while a haughty young lady in regulation full-skirted black dress and mob cap, placed it in a small gold cardboard box and tied it up with scarlet ribbon. She scurried as fast as she could into St James's Square and sat down on a bench. Taking it out she bit off a corner guiltily, Mummy's words about ladies never eating in public ringing in her ears. The chocolatey sweet intensity was astonishing to her deprived palate and she vowed that she would make something similar very soon.

She went home on the evening train, and made a chocolate cake the next day, flavoured with cocoa. Baking in the Aga was much harder than she had imagined. She missed the convenient gas stoves in the domestic science labs at school. Realising that she needed something more modern than Mrs Acton for baking, she found in the Abbots Bourne library a pre-Great War promotional booklet written for Bourne's Golden Rise, the coloured raising agent that had been the making of her family's brief fortune.

Her father had told her that Big George had taken his product to the Crimean War in 1853, like so many entrepreneurs of the time. He'd toured the front line with a mobile kitchen supplying fresh, hot, bright yellow bread to the grateful troops. It was so much easier to make bread quickly with a chemical raising agent as they did in Ireland instead of yeast. The Army contracts for Golden Rise that had followed had raised not only the nation's cakes but Big George himself from the Cheapside dry salters where he had been born to the dizzy heights of the House of Lords.

The booklet was illustrated with golden cakes and breads and introduced slyly with the words: 'Cakes are no longer considered too rich for daily consumption. In fact, cake is now known to be an exceedingly well balanced food product.' There was an advertisement on the back showing a neat cook looking thrilled with her improbably bouncy yellow sponge which she'd just taken out of the oven. The steam whispering from the cake spelled out *No surprise it's Golden Rise!*

There was no stopping Sarah after that, although Bourne's was no longer available and she was forced to use its original and deadly rival Grinwald's Baking Powder. After Big George died, his only son Young George, having been brought up to be a gentleman and despising 'trade', had handed over the running of Bourne's Golden Rise to people who managed to destroy the family's golden goose within a couple of years. Something to do with cutting costs by selling it in paper packets – where it rapidly became damp and useless – instead of in airtight tins. A flop in all senses of the word.

Sarah's first properly raised Victoria sponge was a triumph, oozing with strawberry jam and cream from the farm dairy.

Her father was delighted with the upturn in his diet. He'd never complained in Sarah's hearing, but the gusto with which he attacked every Irish stew, beef curry, roast chicken and cottage pie fragrant with bay leaves, convinced Sarah that he had not been happy. Just the revelation of butter on vegetables that had not been boiled to sludge was enough to lighten the atmosphere of meals in the vast and gloomy dining room.

Within days, she started attempting something more haute cuisine, and her chicken à la crème, with mushrooms she had picked in the park, sent her family into raptures. All through the remains of 1939 and well into 1940 she cooked. Rationing didn't affect them so much as they produced their own butter and bacon but Sarah had to cut back on the baking when the sugar ration came in. There were no more tennis parties, impromptu dances or trips up to London and she didn't miss them. War rolled ever closer. Her father looked gloomier except during meals.

German troops marched into Belgium again and the tuning up was over, the opening bars of war began to sound. Now there was a clear and distinct route out of Abbots Bourne and into the wider world. As she was nineteen, and had done her Red Cross training and become a skilled cook, she decided to volunteer immediately for the Voluntary Aid Detachment as a nurse, even if it meant abandoning her hard-won kitchen. She had some hope that Mademoiselle was beginning to rediscover skills long left behind in her native land, handing over her beloved Eliza Acton before she went.

Her father looked crestfallen, and asked when was she coming back?

Two

Sarah
May 1940

Bumping along an unmade back road Sarah worried about the stretcher cases behind her in the ambulance. The roads were in terrible condition, not much more than farm tracks, deeply rutted and grooved by the tanks and armoured vehicles that had gone before. She had to keep moving north as fast as she could, map spread over the dashboard so she could plan the route using a compass. The last detachment of British troops she had encountered told her the Germans were moving rapidly as the Maginot Line had ripped like rotten muslin and there was no hope of holding France. It was vital to get casualties on to the boats and away before the Germans caught up.

She could hear distant gunfire from time to time and the odd plane roared overhead. So far the huge red cross on the roof of the ambulance had protected her but rounding a corner she saw a road block up ahead just in time to pull off the track into a small copse. She knew they would have seen her. Impossible not to in the vast flat expanse of Flanders. Heart sinking she turned off the engine, got out and went round to the back. She opened the doors to check her patients and make them as comfortable as she could. She rummaged for the piss bottle at the same time.

'OK, lads, how are we?' she enquired as cheerily as she could manage. 'Sorry about the bumps. These French roads are terrible. Now, does anyone need to piss? Also I've got water and glucose tablets, and we'll soon be at a station. You'll be much more comfortable on a train.'

Separated from the medical orderly and her fellow VAD earlier in the day, there was just her driving and making routine checks, which slowed her down. There were six stretchers in the back, strapped on to shelves up the sides of the ambulance. The men were quiet, two of them dozing. She didn't want to administer morphine syrettes unless their suffering was unbearable.

'Got a gasper, nurse?' said one, his arm in a sling and one leg heavily bandaged.

'Sorry, I've run out. When we get to the station and catch up with the rest of the convoy, I'm sure rations will be issued.'

Checking all their pulses, she was worried about the case top left. His pulse was racing, he felt hot and wasn't fully conscious. She heard another vehicle draw up behind the ambulance. Turning round, she saw a German officer in black climbing out of a camouflaged Mercedes and walking towards her. She moved across to block his view of her wounded.

'Get down from the ambulance,' he said.

'Oh dear God,' she thought. 'Give me strength.'

He turned to the two men who were with him, and issued orders in German. They came up smartly at a trot, and one of them seized her arm and pulled her down off the step, thrusting her away from the ambulance.

'What are you doing?' She stumbled and tried to shrug them off, brushing at her arm.

They didn't answer but had already seized hold of one of the lowermost stretchers, and were undoing the straps that held it to the shelf, pulling it on to the floor and towards the door. The man on the stretcher had been sleeping but woke and started crying out.

'You can't do that,' she yelled, running back towards them. 'Leave them alone.'

They pushed her away, and had already pulled one stretcher out and on to the ground. The man was firmly strapped down, and remained on it however roughly they handled him. Sarah turned on the officer.

'You cannot treat my men like this,' she shouted. 'Stop it.'

'We are going to requisition your ambulance,' he said. 'No need to worry about your wounded. They won't know anything about it soon enough.'

He stood there looking at her, his black jodhpurs so tight around the knee, his stupid cap with its arrogant rearing front on his head. Boiling rage roared through her, and she marched straight up to him and slapped him as hard as she could across the face. His men stopped to watch. Her patient was lying still strapped to his stretcher, sobbing with pain. The officer laughed, whipping a silvery blade out of the scabbard at his belt, holding it in his fist with the blade pointing downward. With a swift, vicious movement he jabbed the knife at her, stabbing her in the upper thigh. She wore a British Warm overcoat that a friend had given her and the blade did not get far through the thick woollen fabric, but there was a hot sting and she clutched at her leg, biting her lip. She was damned if she would cry out.

The German soldiers were inside the ambulance, and she

limped as fast as she could back towards it, stopping for a moment to comfort the man on the ground. As she bent over him, someone grabbed her hair through her cap and heaved her up and backwards.

There was a sharp crack in the air, and her head was free. She lost her balance and fell forward, trying to avoid landing on her patient. Instead she found herself face down beside the stretcher. There was another shot. She wriggled closer to her patient on the ground and flung an arm across him.

'Can you see what's happening?' she said, her face close to his.

'I think we're going to be OK. It's those crazy Scots,' he whispered. 'There's some troopers coming out of the trees. The other Germans have scarpered.'

'You all right, Miss?'

She rolled over on to her back and looked up into a kind face.

'Yes, absolutely fine, thanks. What about everyone else?'

'The German who was grabbing you is dead, Miss. Sandy got him. Crack shot, our Sand.'

She glanced up and saw one of the troopers, still holding his rifle under his arm, bending over the German officer. Oddly the first dead soldier she had seen so far in this muddle of a retreat.

She sat up, and her rescuer turned his face away as she lifted her coat and skirt to look at the damage. A little red mouth had opened in the front of her thigh but it was only oozing blood. He hadn't hit her femoral artery. She snapped off her suspenders and pushed her ruined lisle stocking down over her knee.

'Must get this cleaned,' she muttered, as she saw purple bruising where the knife had thudded into her. 'Can you pop into the back of the ambulance and grab my First Aid box? Better do something about this, before I get on with driving these men up to the station.'

'Will you be able to do that, Miss?'

'Oh, it's nothing. Just a puncture. It isn't even bleeding much, just aching a bit.' One of the other troopers handed her the kit. She popped out one of the glass phials of iodine, snapped off the top and poured the contents into the wound. Gasping, she felt her vision cloud over as the pain was worse than the stabbing.

She wasn't going to make a fuss when her men were so gravely wounded and hardly complained at all. She applied a pad dressing and quickly wound a bandage tightly around her thigh, pinning it and pulling up her stocking. She snapped the suspenders back on, and then pinned the bandage again several times to the thick cotton lisle to keep it in place. Then she sucked on a couple of aspirins, packed everything back in the box and asked the young trooper to help her to her feet.

He was a corporal, she saw from the single chevron on his battle-dress tunic.

'Here, one of you men, I want you to stay with Miss here, and accompany her in the ambulance, OK?'

Sandy stepped forward. He was limping slightly. The others all seemed intact.

'Yes, you Sandy. You could probably do with a lift.'

Sarah walked over to the German officer on the ground. He lay flat on his back, the black of his tunic concealing the spreading stain of blood that she knew must be there. His hat had fallen off, revealing chick-yellow hair and a young pink face – his blue eyes open to the blue summer sky. The knife, a dagger

35

with a black handle and sharp tip, had fallen away from his hand on to the rough grass. She stooped to pick it up, taking a handkerchief out of her pocket to wrap it in. The troopers pretended not to notice. She put the wrapped knife into the medical bag.

She supervised while her patient was reloaded gently into the ambulance, then limped round to the driver's seat and swung back into the cab.

'I'm Sarah by the way. Come on, Sandy, hop in. We've got to get these men evacuated. You can read the map.'

Three

Sarah's desk was at the far end of the Long Gallery, behind a screen to prevent her reading light from disturbing the sleeping officers. She was now quite used to nursing in her former family home. In another life, she and her brothers had played sliding games on the wide polished oak boards when it had been too wet to go outside. The portraits that had hung there of other people's relations, purchased by her great-grandfather Big George Bourne, were in storage. The oak panelling had been painted in hygienic green gloss and the boards covered in washable linoleum.

The smells she remembered from her childhood, of lavender and beeswax furniture polish, wood smoke and her father William's occasional cigar, had been replaced with carbolic and Virginia tobacco. Convalescing officers were not on the critical list and required only light nursing and supervision at night. In the day they were all up, dressed and having rehabilitation including occupational exercises. Many were limbless, but that didn't stop them from grabbing her if she came too close, and she was used to dodging the more persistent. She knew she just had to put up with the attempted groping and be nippy on her feet, but it did make her cross. She kept it very quiet that Abbots Bourne was her family home.

Her father and mother were living in an estate house for the duration, far enough away for her visits to them not to be obvious to the other VADs. She was keen to make friends and merge into the background. Secretly it gave her a lot of pleasure that the house was being put to such good use, instead of simply dwarfing the PGs and her parents. The high ceilings and enormous windows let healthy fresh air circulate, instead of seeming absurdly over-large. The park offered the officers plenty of opportunities for exercise.

The doctors, whose advances might be more welcome than the patients' lunges, treated the VADs with strict professionalism. There was one who attracted her, Dr Reeves, but his lordly way of sweeping through the wards was off-putting. When he did his rounds, it was up to her to follow him, taking instructions, updating charts and removing dressings for his examinations. He hardly seemed to notice her except when issuing orders. Once, they had both bent down to pick up a dropped clipboard at the same time, and bumped heads when they straightened up. Her cap slipped sideways, and her long straight fair hair, which always resisted hairpins when clean, came tumbling down around her face. He had stopped, looked at her and smiled, turning away politely as she twisted it up and pinned her cap back into place.

Reading in the peace of the night shift, she was relieved that she wasn't in London any more, where so many nights had been spent stuffing the patients under beds to protect them when the sirens went off. It might have helped them avoid flying glass, but she had doubted it would do any good if there was a direct hit, and it had been much more difficult to dodge the groping in the fevered rush. Even some of the most poorly seemed unduly stimulated by her starched bosom with its little red cross. She'd had to wear a tin hat during raids too, which had given her a headache.

She heard footsteps outside her curtain.

'Hello? Do you need something?' she whispered, thinking it was one of the officers. The more active convalescents were given a late pass and went to the pub.

'Good evening, nurse. Sorry to disturb you. It's Dr Reeves, I just need to check up on the new patient. I was a little worried about how his leg was healing, and I didn't find the time to look in earlier.'

The doctors never came near the ward at night. But she shrugged and stood up, pulling aside the curtain to greet him properly, prepared to help in any way she could. He was just outside, in uniform, looking quite unlike his usual busy, lofty, white-coated self. She could see that he was younger than she had thought and that he had a nice smile, which she'd noticed when they bumped heads.

'Do you need me?' she asked.

'Oh, no. I'll just go down there and see him, if you don't mind?'

Mind? None of the senior staff cared a jot what the VADs thought about anything. She was slightly flustered.

As he set off into the gloom of the enormous room, she found herself murmuring, 'Would you like a cup of tea? There's a drop of milk left from earlier and even some sugar.'

He stopped and turned back towards her.

'Yes, please. If it isn't too much trouble. But I don't want to use up your ration.'

'No, no trouble at all. I don't take sugar anyway.'

She went to the sluice that had been built into an old lavatory on the landing, where a gas ring had been fitted, and put the kettle on, watching it to make sure it didn't whistle and disturb any of the sleeping officers. There was a stir of excitement in her stomach at the thought of having tea with a doctor. Dr Reeves was by far the most attractive and eligible man on the staff. The other two doctors were a retired orthopaedic consultant, brought back to work by the war, and a tall, thin, sandy chap in his thirties, with a wife and three very small children. Of course, there were plenty of officers, but they were her patients, and though she knew other VADs went out with patients, there was an invisible wall between them and her.

She was relieved to see that there was enough of the tea ration left to make a large pot, so she wrapped it in a tea towel to keep it hot, and put it on a tray with cups, milk and sugar. Switching off the dim light, she walked back into the ward as quietly as she could. There he was, bending over her logbook and sitting in her chair. As he heard her come in, he stood up and looked down into her eyes. The effect of his gaze was unexpected. She had seen him every day on the ward, preoccupied and professional. Now he looked softer, a bit hopeful. He wasn't handsome like Gary Cooper, but pleasing to look at, with a nose that looked as if it had been broken, thick brown hair combed back from a high square forehead, pale grey eyes and a wide, smiling mouth.

'I'll go and get another chair,' he said, going off into the gloom of the ward. Putting the tea tray down, she poured and stirred. He came back and waited until she had sat down to do likewise, and she handed him his cup. Did his fingers touch the backs of hers as she passed him the saucer?

'Miss Bourne, isn't it?' He spoke as quietly as he could and she needed to bend near him to hear.

'Yes. But do call me Sarah.' The war had brought a welcome relaxation in formality.

'I have a confession to make. I didn't need to see a patient. I wanted to see you.'

'Oh.' She clapped a hand across her mouth, staring at him. She was not used to gentle politeness. Grab first, talk afterwards was the wartime protocol of the hospitals she had worked in. Going out with the other girls during the blackout had been equally hazardous. She assumed all men had abandoned the art of courtship in the rough atmosphere of 'I might be dead tomorrow, dear, so you must be kind to me now'. But even gentle courtship gained a sense of urgency in wartime.

He took her hand in his and she returned the pressure.

'Do you mind if I turn off the light? It's just if the night matron comes round, I don't want to get you into trouble.'

Her heart sank, but then all he did was sit and hold her hand, sipping his tea as they whispered to each other about what would happen when the war was over. For her, a proper nurse's training at St Saviour's Hospital in London. He told her his father was a successful GP in Dorking and there had always been a plan for him to enter the practice interrupted by the war. They made a date for when she was off the night shift in a week's time, and then he left her without even a kiss.

When she woke at dawn with her face creased by its logbook pillow, she was ashamed of dropping off, and wondered if it had all been a dream. But the next night he came to see her again.

She slipped gently down a soft hill into something like love, laughing at herself for being so susceptible. It had never happened before so she wasn't quite sure.

Four

Sarah
January 1949

Sarah stood on the quay with baby Melissa in her arms, trembling in the sea wind. Seagulls caught in the fitful sunlight overhead turned to silver as they dipped and swayed in the moving air. Melissa's blue velvet bonnet with its white frill kept the chill from her small ears. She wore a blue wool coat that Sarah had made for her, double-breasted with a velvet collar. On her legs were fawn woollen leggings, one soft foot perkily flexed, the other twisted inwards. Her right hand clutched her mother's lapel. She sucked her left thumb and gazed around with blue eyes. The breeze tugged at Sarah's small gold straw hat not secured quite as firmly as she'd hoped to her short permed hair. She dared not let go of Melissa to check its moorings.

Arthur had left them to see about a porter for their luggage and now returned, waving as he glimpsed his wife and child. 'We can board now if you like,' he said. Their trunks had gone into the hold the night before, plastered with bright yellow 'Not Wanted on Voyage' labels, and filled with anything Sarah and Melissa might conceivably need for their long stay in America.

The quay was crowded, for it was RMS *Caronia*'s maiden voyage. The Southampton Municipal Band played lively airs from the musicals, and a roped-off area corralled the mayor and corporation. Sarah caught a glimpse of stout men standing in a row, heads cocked, unnatural sideways handshakes at the ready, posing for the press photographer. The quay was a carnival of joyful faces and happy laughter. Sarah felt separated from it all, hoping only that they were doing right by crossing the ocean to seek help for their baby.

The Reeves and Bourne families had said goodbye at home, not wanting a great fuss. Others were not so restrained, and each passenger seemed attended by a horde of well-wishers keen to have a look round the Green Goddess, as they were calling the *Caronia*. Arthur walked slightly ahead of Sarah, to make room for her to move with the baby and not be jostled. They approached B Gangway, one of four penetrating the hull at different levels all along its flank, and allowing the first few passengers to disappear into the ship's decks. The great shining new hull rose up beside Sarah like a green wave punctuated by five tiers of portholes, an anchor crouched like a spider in the bows. She feared that the ship's flank might topple and crush her and held Melissa more closely in her arms. Daunted by the taut nerves that dogged her recent transformation from woman to mother, only Arthur's love made it all bearable. Her courage had peeled away leaving her raw. She needed her man to protect her now and yet they would have to be apart for so long while she was in America.

If she could choose, she would not be here on the quay at all but at home safely cocooned with her little Lissy Lamb. As he was a doctor, Arthur had been able to stay with her while Melissa was born. Holding her hand and kissing her forehead, he had reassured her immediately the baby was delivered.

'She's perfect, darling. A little girl.' The midwife had taken her up, wrapping her in a white cotton cloth, whisking her away to have all bloody, greasy clues to her origins inside her mother's body removed. Then she came back, washed, dressed and fit for society, to be placed in Sarah's arms.

'Melissa,' said Sarah, looking at the small pink face. 'My Lissy Lamb.'

Only later had Arthur formally diagnosed her talipes or club foot. And it was her left foot, her right was unaffected. Her Lissy Lamb's little hoof. She had been momentarily dismayed but so in love that nothing could shake her. But she could not bear to think of that tiny foot, with its dimpled sole and miniature toes like pink broad beans, being cut to straighten it out, and begged her husband to find some alternative to surgery. He took Sarah and Melissa up to London to consult an old friend from medical school who was now a professor of orthopaedics at University College Hospital. He produced a medical journal from the US describing the work of a Spanish doctor who had taken refuge in Iowa after the Spanish Civil War. Traditional surgical methods could lead to pain and stiffness in later life. Dr Ponseti manipulated the little feet to reposition them while they were still soft and malleable, setting them in plaster to hold the new and improved position. It was all completely novel, there were no guarantees, but Arthur said the physiological argument was sound and it could be the answer.

Arthur wrote to Dr Ponseti, who had received funding and was delighted to welcome the daughter of an English doctor on to his list. It seemed vital to both of them to tackle the problem before Melissa even tried to walk.

Arthur employed a locum to look after his practice for the necessary month while he took his wife and child to America and saw for himself what was to be done. If all went according to plan, he intended to leave Sarah and Melissa with Dr Ponseti for the required four months and come home. The clinic staff had offered free accommodation, as spreading the word internationally about the Ponseti method was important and there were severe restrictions on taking currency abroad.

The family had never been away on holiday, not even on a proper honeymoon. So Arthur had taken a first class cabin on the new liner to celebrate their marriage and the birth of their long-awaited first child.

At the top of the gangplank a young purser looked at their tickets and referred them to one of a row of smiling stewardesses, who stepped forward, saying she was there to escort them to their cabin and settle them in. Sarah was struck by how much her starched linen headdress resembled what she herself had worn as a VAD during the war. She looked like Matron, only friendly. Matron, in her many manifestations throughout Sarah's war, had always been a gorgon.

'We've organised a sea cot for little miss, as ordered. Shall I take her for you?'

Melissa took one look at the stewardess's outstretched arms and turned a wailing face into Sarah's bosom.

'There, darling. It's OK. I won't let you go, don't worry,' she cooed into her baby's neck, glancing apologetically at the stewardess. They had hardly been apart since the baby was born. Sarah had no intention of employing a nanny, preferring to lose herself in the all-consuming rituals of caring for her baby. Her mother had sighed more than once in her hearing: 'I always find women who look after their own children get rather untidy and disorganised. Boring for their husbands too.' She hadn't wanted to slap her mother for years but she did then.

'Yes, they do get shy at that age, don't they?' the stewardess was saying cosily. 'I'm Andrews, by the way. I'll be looking after you all on board for the duration of the voyage.' And she chatted on about babysitting 'little one' in the cabin so Mummy and Daddy could have dinner and maybe even a dance in peace.

Never! Sarah wanted to shriek, and she held on to Lissy all the more tightly. The idea of leaving her little girl alone in the belly of the great green ship while she frivolled with Arthur on the upper deck seemed terribly wrong.

Arthur moved steadily ahead through the mirrored atrium with its huge Constance Spry floral displays. The words 'flower arrangement' were simply too prosaic for these intricate fans of lilies, gladioli and gypsophila. He glanced around at the brand new opulent decor as they went down the companionway towards the first class cabin deck. Sarah thought it vulgar, but then decided to stop being such a snob and give in to the cheerful naked green mermaids on the walls and the wildly patterned carpets underfoot.

When they reached the cabin, their suitcases were already unpacked and all their things put away. Like the smarter houses she'd stayed in before the war, thought Sarah, it was nice to be looked after for a change. She turned, pleased, to Arthur, who said: 'Thank you, Andrews. This looks very comfortable, don't you think, darling?' He rubbed his hands together. 'It will be terrific to have you in here to look after our little Melissa while we go and dine. We'd love to try the haute cuisine, wouldn't we, darling? And we have an invitation to the Captain's cocktail party tomorrow.'

Sarah's heart sank. She was sure he would see that she couldn't possibly leave Melissa alone with a stranger. She started to protest but he cut her off.

'Oh, you'll love it, darling. Whole point of sailing on one of these big liners. Wonderful food and wine. Like going out to a smart restaurant every night. There's a band as well. We can dance. Treat for you.' He smiled, delighted to be on holiday. 'We haven't been out for ages.'

He glanced at his wife. His gaze made her uneasy as if they weren't in perfect agreement about her overwhelming need to stay close to her baby girl. They hadn't made love since the birth. Her body had folded in on itself and rejected his. Not that he ever pressured her in any way. They had fallen into a habit of turning their backs to each other and sliding into bed without touching, both firmly carapaced in winceyette. The white-hot passion of their early marriage, where they could not wait to be naked in bed together – and not just at night – seemed quite vanished.

With a niggle of guilt, she had a vision of herself moping dowdily dressing-gowned in the cabin while he went to the main deck looking eager in black tie. She imagined him wading into a sea of coiffed women with bright red lips in strapless frocks with great ration-defying swathes of skirt below and little or nothing on top. She saw their ankles in her mind's eye taut and tiny above very high heels. It was so vivid that it made her gasp. What on earth did she think she was doing, preparing to let him venture among the serpents all alone in that paradise?

'There are some lovely dress shops on board,' Andrews was saying. 'Lots of leisure to titivate your wardrobe.' Sarah would like to present her own naked shoulders like a bouquet bursting from strapless silver satin. She wasn't at home any more, she had three days on board and then a month with Arthur in America. It was up to her to make sure he remembered their wonderful time together while they were apart. That decided her. With a great tearing wrench inside, she said, 'Yes, darling, that does sound fun. Now, Melissa, you go to Andrews, and you can get to know each other a bit better.'

The baby whimpered, her blue eyes filling with tears. Treachery, Sarah's mind screamed, but she knew she would have to be brave. She handed her over, detaching miniature fingers that snatched at her like brambles on a country walk, and turned away when the small face went red with indignation and the rosebud lips opened to wail.

She said, 'Shall we go and have a stroll on deck, Arthur? See the last of England?'

She saw the delight in his face, and he made a comic little caper, taking her arm and leading her from the cabin. She decided not to look back, whatever the roaring, over which she heard Andrews saying, 'There there poppet, they'll soon be back, but we must let Mummy and Daddy have some fun too.'

Indeed we must.

She'd been very foolish to try Arthur's patience for so long, often sleeping in the nursery instead of with him. Being cool and unfriendly, making excuses about not trusting babysitters when he had tried to suggest going out dancing, or for dinner or even just to the local cinema. And he had gone to parties without her, his exasperation not always perfectly hidden.

Well, Melissa could manage without her, but Arthur wouldn't have to any more. The baby would have her mother to herself soon enough. There was warmth in the pit of her stomach, such as she had not felt for years, at the thought of what was to come. She welcomed it and strode forth laughing into the chilly January air at her husband's side.

Later that evening the ship began to roll, gently at first and then quite vigorously. Their table in the empty Balmoral Restaurant had a dampened cloth and raised sides to prevent their dinner from taking flight. The wine was served in a decanter with a broad, stable bottom. The menu was lengthy and in French, and Sarah enjoyed every mouthful. The wine warmed her.

Back in their cabin, they found Melissa fast asleep in her sea cot that swayed like a hammock with the movement of the vast sea, as Andrews sat in one of the armchairs knitting, oblivious to the rough weather. The stewardess rose to greet them and reassured them that Melissa had settled soon after they had left.

The bunks were as wide as a normal single bed, one above the other. Sarah lay waiting for her husband in one of her silk trousseau nighties. The winceyette would not see the light of day again until after he had gone back to England. After cleaning his teeth in the little bathroom, he checked that Melissa was asleep, before coming across and slipping off his dressing gown. She saw his body in the faint light of a shaded lamp, and wanted him with an intensity of love and desire that surprised her. He slipped in beside her and began to kiss her. Memories of how it had been

– before the tension of her failure to conceive immediately had spoilt their love making – flooded into her mind.

'Darling, I think we shouldn't risk a pregnancy, do you mind?' He dealt with the French letter, and then he was within her where he belonged and her body folding around his like a flower around a bee.

The ship lurched. They had failed to put up the safety rail and rolled right off the bunk on to the bedside rug with a thump. She gasped at the impact and froze, expecting Lissy to wake and wail but all was quiet. Arthur seemed unperturbed by the change in altitude, and they were together, riding the waves until she was trembling, feeling deep within a rolling boil of tingling bliss. Arthur held her tightly, sighing with relief that he had his wife back at last. They lay cooling on the shifting deck, legs tangled, arms flung out. Then they turned to face each other, laughing and kissing.

'Better get you back into bed,' said Arthur.

'Stay there, please, just for a moment.'

She wrapped her arms around him, looking into his grey eyes. 'I love you, Dr Reeves,' she said.

'And I love you too, Mrs Reeves.'

Five

Albert
March 1954

The letter arrived on Monday morning while Albert and his mother Pearl were having breakfast, before she went to work and he to school. It was official looking, and addressed to Albert Hayes Esq. Mrs Hayes suspected it was for her late husband, who had also been called Albert, as her son was only thirteen.

'Open it for me, would you, Bert? I think it's probably meant for your father.'

She pushed herself up from the table and walked across to the sink, looking out of the window over their small garden. Bert noticed that she moved more slowly than usual.

He tried to push his thumb under the envelope flap, but found it so stiff that he picked up a knife from the table to slit it open instead. Inside was a letter topped with the engraved name and address of a solicitors' partnership in Belgravia, London. This meant nothing to Bert, so he scanned down to see what it said.

'Who's it from?' his mother asked, still with her back to him.

'It says Jenkins and Jenkins, solicitors, at the top.'

She turned around, making as if to snatch it from him, and then hesitated. 'No,' she said, as if to herself. 'You read it to me.'

Dear Mr Hayes,

We are the solicitors and trustees for the title and estates of Baron Mount-Hey of Hey in the County of Sussex, and we wish to disclose some important information pertaining to yourself, following the death on the ninth of June 1953 of Baillie John Hayes, thirteenth Baron Mount-Hey.

As the situation is complicated and delicate, we would like you to attend our offices in London at your earliest convenience. Please telephone or write for an appointment.

If you have any family papers such as birth, marriage and death certificates to hand, please do bring them with you if it is not inconvenient.

> *I remain yours sincerely*
> *C. Jenkins*
> *Senior Partner*

Bert glanced up at his mother, who looked pale. It must be because the letter was addressed to his father, who had died when he was a baby.

'Well,' she said, slowly. 'That is the most extraordinary thing. I knew Albert had grand relations. But I never heard of any lords, or at least he never mentioned any.'

'What shall we do?' Bert was bewildered. He lived with his mother in Eastbourne, where he went to the local grammar school, pedalling around the town on a heavy old butcher's bicycle delivering groceries on Saturdays and in the holidays.

They kept very quiet. Even though she had been widowed for more than ten years, Mrs Hayes had never looked at anyone else and their social life was confined to the family and her fellow employees at her parents' grocery business.

'I suppose we'd better go up to London. You must come with me as you'll be the person they want to see. Get me the writing paper and my pen, and I'll reply for you.'

Bert went over to the little desk and fetched his mother's fountain pen and some sheets of blue Basildon Bond. As she used the hand-held press to indent their address into the top of the paper, he went and fetched his satchel, kissed his mother's cheek and left for school.

Mrs Hayes, left alone, wrote a brief note informing Mr Jenkins that her husband Albert had died in a bombing raid on Eastbourne on 8 December 1942. She explained that he had left a son, also called Albert, who was now thirteen. She added a convenient date and time that they could both come, once the Easter holidays had started, and that she would bring the family certificates with her.

Grief ambushed her when she remembered him dying like that. Albert, who worked as a buyer for her parents, had taken a day off to do the family's Christmas shopping. She was due to go with him but little Bert had the croup, so she was at home in the kitchen holding him near a steaming kettle to soothe his seal-like bark. When the sirens wailed there was the familiar hollow fear and then the sound of bombs falling. Grabbing the kettle, she had hurried her son and herself under the Morrison shelter that doubled as their dining table.

The police came after the all-clear had sounded. Her Albert

was one of nineteen killed. She had collapsed. And now this, a voice calling out to her from an unknown family hinterland. People she had never met and knew nothing about, but clearly very different from anyone she had ever imagined. Could it be an unexpected legacy? Pearl felt pleased on behalf of her son. She herself would be provided for by her parents.

Her Albert had just been a nice eligible man as far as she was concerned. Privately educated, but not too smart to court the grocer's daughter. His parents had lived in India, his father managing a tea plantation in Darjeeling. He'd been sent back to England to school, before returning to live in Calcutta, working as a trainee tea trader. But he'd become ill with tuberculosis and returned to England to be treated at the South Downs Sanatorium in the clean, salubrious air above Eastbourne. Pearl had met him at the annual Sanatorium Christmas dance before the war. While he was recovering in England, his parents had both died, leaving enough to buy the newly married couple a decent house in a nice area. He had been a kind man and Pearl Hayes had loved him dearly, but that was long ago now.

A week later, mother and son were on their way by train to London as early in the morning as they could manage. They walked up from Victoria to a tall white stuccoed house in Elizabeth Street. The brass plate on the area railings told them it was the offices of Jenkins & Jenkins, Solicitors. They went up the steps and rang the bell. A young woman dressed in a smart navy costume answered the door. Pearl gave their names and they were asked to wait in a room to the right of the hall.

After about ten minutes, during which Bert just had time to

take *The Golden Hawk* out of his satchel and read a couple of pages, and Pearl had a flick through *Modern Woman*, the young woman came back and said, 'You can come up now.'

They both stood and followed her up the stairs into an office that occupied the first floor front room. Pearl had always imagined a lawyer's office to be dark and full of old books, but this was quite different. The curtains were a bright abstract pattern of yellow, blue and white, and there was a warm blue fitted carpet covering the floor. A sea-green linen-covered sofa and armchairs were grouped around a coffee table in front of the white marble fireplace. The solicitor was a surprise too. Pearl saw a woman wearing tortoiseshell spectacles, elegant in a fitted black dress, her violet-rinsed grey hair smoothed into a French pleat, who rose from behind a modern desk of light-coloured wood. Picking up a file, she approached, smiling warmly.

'Mrs Hayes? Albert? I'm Mrs Jenkins. Good morning, do please come over and take a seat.'

Pearl led Bert over to the sofa. Mrs Jenkins waited until they were comfortable and then seated herself on one of the armchairs.

'Would you like tea, Mrs Hayes? And Albert? A soft drink?'

They nodded, and the young secretary who had been waiting by the door left the room.

'Now, Mrs Hayes, do I understood from your letter that you were not aware of your late husband's Mount-Hey connections?'

'No, Mrs Jenkins, I had never heard that name before. I met Mr Hayes in 1937 at the South Downs Sanatorium. He was one of the lucky ones who recovered from his TB. His parents were both dead by the time we married, and he never talked about his wider family. It didn't seem important.'

'I understand, and in fact if this century had not been plagued with war, you would have lived out your lives unaffected by his family connections in any way. But two wars in rapid succession decimated many of the old families, particularly ones like the Hayes which don't seem to have been good at producing male heirs in the direct line. Surprisingly common, I'm afraid.'

The secretary came in with a tray, and put it down on the low table in front of Pearl and Bert. There was a pot of tea, milk jug and one cup, and a glass bottle of Coca Cola with a straw sticking out of it.

Mrs Jenkins indicated that Pearl should help herself to tea and opened the file on her lap.

'Thank you for coming to see me today. I'm sorry for approaching you out of the blue like that, and I hope it hasn't been inconvenient to come to London, but I felt we needed to proceed quickly.'

Pearl murmured, 'No, it's fine now it's the holidays, thank you.'

Mrs Jenkins smiled again and consulted the notes in the file: 'Now this is a bit complicated, so bear with me.

'I mentioned in my letter that your husband was related to Baillie John Hayes, thirteenth Baron Mount-Hey? He died unmarried and in extreme old age last year having inherited the title during the war when his much younger cousin Robert Langdon Hayes, twelfth Baron, was killed at the Café de Paris in 1941. You may remember the case? A bomb came down through the ventilation shaft and exploded on the dance floor. Everyone believed they were safe underground. So sad.'

Pearl nodded.

'Anyway, the twelfth Baron had been young and was expected to marry and take over the house and estate, having inherited as a child during the Great War from his second cousin Robert Baillie Hayes, eleventh Baron Mount-Hey, who was killed at Arras in 1917. Robert's brother and heir, John Francis Hayes, was killed before him in 1916, during the Somme offensive. Neither of them had time to marry or have any children.'

Pearl nodded again, and Mrs Jenkins continued, 'Now, as far as we have traced it back, and as trustees we have been in touch with the College of Heralds, your husband was a distant cousin of the late Lord Mount-Hey, and almost definitely his heir by descent from a second son of the eighth Baron.'

'That's dreadfully sad, so many men being killed in one family. But how on earth do they work out who is related to whom and who gets the title?' Pearl asked.

'Well,' said Mrs Jenkins. 'The original Baillie Hayes was one of the people who helped Charles II escape after the battle of Worcester. The Royalists passed the young king between them like a hot potato until he managed to get across to France. He never forgot the experience, and any of his rescuers who were still alive in 1660 when he returned to the throne were rewarded with titles, coats of arms and so on. But not money, sadly.

'It's a good story. Albert might like to hear it?'

'Albert? Listen to Mrs Jenkins, please.' She could see that he wasn't paying attention but she knew he liked history stories as he borrowed them from the library all the time.

Mrs Jenkins continued: 'On his last night in England, Charles stopped at the village of Hey, a few miles inland from Shoreham where a boat was waiting to take him to France. A troop of

Parliamentary soldiers arrived at the inn where the King was hiding disguised as a servant. Baillie Hayes, who'd been wounded early in the war fighting as a Royalist, recognised the King while he was unsaddling his "master's" horse in the stables. He couldn't go back inside, so Baillie took him home to what was then Hey House, dressed them up as maidservants, and got him away to the sea both riding one of Baillie's cart horses to disguise their height. They couldn't stop laughing at each other which nearly got them caught.'

She paused while Bert snorted into his drink, and then continued, 'The Mount-Hey coat of arms includes three petticoats – the King liked a joke.'

She extracted a piece of paper from the folder and passed it to Pearl and Bert. 'Look, you can see it here.'

They looked at the picture of a shield with three stylised white petticoats on a blue background, two above and one below, separated by a silver chevron. Above the shield, there was a knight's helmet with a silver horse's head on top.

Pearl looked up, bemused. 'But how does all this concern Albert?'

Mrs Jenkins carried on explaining: 'It works like this: when a peer dies without a male heir of his own body, you hop back up the generations to see if any previous holder of the title had second or third sons with legitimate male descendants, and that's how we traced your husband. Although I do just need to see his birth certificate and also his parents' and your marriage certificates.'

'They should all be in this folder. These are the documents that Albert brought with him when we married, including papers sent back from India.'

Mrs Jenkins took the folder. 'Do you have any questions at this point?'

Pearl said, 'What does all this mean for us?'

'Well, as your husband is deceased, we believe your son Albert may be the fourteenth Baron Mount-Hey of Hey, which is important for two reasons. First, he will have a seat in the House of Lords, and secondly, and less usually, the estate goes with the title as there are no closer male heirs currently living, although the law of entail has changed and I will need to check everything very carefully.'

Pearl digested this, and then said, 'You mean Bert is a lord?'

'In effect, yes. But I'm afraid there is no fortune as such. The main problem with all this was the repeated death duties as one heir after another died unmarried. There were few or no concessions in tax law for death in war, so all the outlying farms and some other property had to be sold off to pay them.'

To Pearl, who lived in a semi-detached house in Eastbourne, anything that involved outlying farms sounded enormous. Bert looked quite indifferent.

'There isn't much left, but there is a house in Sussex called Castle Hey. It was commandeered by the Army as a listening post, and up until now they haven't relinquished it so you don't have to worry about it yet. You must be prepared for extensive damage, but there may be some compensation. Some families have had to pull their houses down as they were completely wrecked by wartime use.'

She turned and smiled at Bert, who was sucking his unaccustomed Coca Cola through the straw – his grandparents refused to stock American drinks – with a great deal of pleasure and clearly not listening. She asked him if he had any questions, but he just blushed and muttered, 'No, thank you.'

The meeting went on for an hour. When they got up to leave Pearl was still not at all sure what to think. The only immediate impression she received was that there was a fund available for the heir's education.

As soon as they got home to Eastbourne, Pearl went round to call on her parents and give them the news. She could see that they too had no idea how to react to the information that their only grandchild was now a lord. Pearl led the way in deciding to ignore Albert's elevation until the family was forced to build it into their world view. That happened faster than expected. Having ascertained the age of the Mount-Hey heir, and obtained all the proofs they needed, the trustees specified that Albert must go to public school, even though the academic year had already started. So stunned was the family that they simply complied, writing anxiously to Mrs Jenkins asking for recommendations.

She decided that Armishaw's, a guild foundation school up on the Downs above Eastbourne, was the best choice. Albert would not find the hurried transition from grammar to public school so difficult there as it was on home territory.

Six

Albert
September 1954

Whap – loud, painful and shocking, it came out of nowhere. Bert's head reeled with scattered sparks at the blow.

'Daydreaming, Hayes? Is that what they teach you to do at these *grammar* schools? You're at Armishaw's now, boy, you need to buck up.'

It was his housemaster Mr Featherstone known as Eggy for his shiny bare pate which he tried to hide like a fat man behind a sapling with a slick strand of hair. After more than a term of it Bert was used to the slaps and jibes about his previous schooling, but he still wasn't used to Greek. It was a passion for Eggy who couldn't bear to be ignored when teaching his pet subject. Incomprehensible squiggles instead of the usual Roman alphabet had simply switched off Bert's attention.

Bert found Eggy to be a peculiar man, but he had an accepting nature. He wasn't particularly used to men at all, not having a father, and Eggy seemed always to be about to explode, his face red, his eyes watering. Hoping to keep out of Eggy's way, Bert just kept his head down and did nothing to attract attention. The inmates of Reynolds House split neatly into two groups: a minority of sporty boys who hated and despised Eggy as a jumped-up little social climber (Bert thought he wasn't in a position to judge) versus those who revered his classical scholarship and wanted to follow him to Oxford. Reynolds boasted a disproportionate number of Oxford Greats entrants due to Eggy's dubious but unrelenting efforts.

Eggy loathed any kind of sport and tried to force the classics into all members of his little fiefdom, promoting his pet scholars as prefects and heads of house. Set apart from the main block, Reynolds House had a reputation for being peopled by swots and was thus ignored by the rest of the school.

Bert didn't fit into either group. He wasn't particularly sporty. He could hold his own at both football and cricket, although he disliked rugby. But it was too late for him to develop a passion for the classics. He much preferred history. Quite soon, he realised that he had been assigned to an unpopular house, replacing a boy who had left in the middle of the Lent term.

The abrupt disappearance of Tomkins had been preceded by a perfect hailstorm of slaps, according to Bert's new housemates. When Eggy erupted, which he frequently did, boys jumped out of the way. Beating was falling out of favour, but that didn't prevent an atmosphere of barely suppressed violence. Eggy had one redeeming feature, his plump and gentle wife Marjorie. She provided a haven of tea and ginger biscuits and organised a 'house-father' programme, where she picked a boy in the year above to help all new boys find their feet.

Bert had arrived at the beginning of the summer term. He'd been invited to get there early to meet his house-father and settle down a bit before the rest of Reynolds House barged in, high on testosterone and holiday-flavoured boasting. Mrs Featherstone had assigned as house-father to Bert a boy called Richard Payge.

Payge had comparatively liberal leanings and a benign nature. His mother was an artist and his father a vague and dilapidated landowner of ancient lineage and few material assets. There was in the Payge family none of the rampant snobbery that infected public schools like a rash. Mrs Featherstone had waited for Bert in the hall when he first arrived and greeted him kindly, introducing him to fourteen-year-old Payge who was hovering behind her well-briefed and ready to do his stuff.

The taxi driver, who had brought him up to school on his first day, having deposited his new trunk in the front hall, came back to help him carry his cumbersome food hamper into the House Study. Glancing round, paralysed with shyness, he saw in every cubbyhole a wooden box, some pristine and new, some shiny with use and engraved with graffiti, all with black metal hasps and corners. He remembered, from being shown round with his mother, that these were called 'tuck boxes' and contained the boys' treats. No one else had a hamper. He felt uneasy and exposed by this difference, when all he wanted to do was fade into the scarred panelling.

'What's that you've got, Hayes?' enquired Payge immediately.

Sugar rationing had ended, and the bulging hamper contained a large fruit cake, tartan biscuit tins of shortbread, a can opener to deal with all the ham, turkey in jelly, condensed milk and fruit salad. His grandparents had added packets of peanuts, wine gums, Murray mints, Smith's crisps, Bourneville and Cadbury's chocolate bars and White's lemonade and ginger beer – all barely subdued by the wicker lid's straining leather straps.

'Just some food and stuff from my grandparents,' he replied shyly.

'Tuck!' exclaimed Payge and, his eyes gleaming, immediately took charge. Bert had nothing to worry about. Difference in the area of tuck was wholly acceptable.

Soon the hamper was concealed under the travel blanket prescribed in his kit list, in the dark space beneath the battered and graffiti-gouged shelf that served as a desk in his cubbyhole.

After that, Payge let it be known to a few select companions that Hayes had unlimited access to tuck, and word spread. His new friends seemed ravenous and Bert noticed that they wished to be in his good books in order to feed their insatiable hunger. Born just before or during the war, none of them had ever known anything other than rationing. Even now treats were scarce.

And never mind that Hayes' grandparents were 'in trade'. The trade they were in was food, and that made up for everything. Moreover, Bert had a generous nature and, having been brought up with groceries, took the food for granted. He had no desire to hoard and it was no novelty for him. Each time he went home for an exeat, his grandparents replenished the hamper with a lack of caution that was their silent way of loving their only grandchild.

Armishaw's stood on the Downs above Eastbourne, its high clock tower dominating the skyline and causing resentment among certain elements in the town. Bert had always been aware of the school, but without taking any kind of personal interest. Before he had 'gone up the hill', he had seen the senior boys out of uniform and on their superior bicycles on Sundays, circling aimlessly, going to the pictures or looking at girls. Their accents gave them away. To begin with it was strange to be transported up there himself, leaving his old friends down below.

It was all so odd that Bert didn't dare open his mouth to begin with, but Payge was friendly and put him at his ease. He was what Bert imagined himself expected to be at some cloudy point in the future, used to the whole business of public school, a country house sitting there in the background not mattering too much. Bert had never seen his house, and had no clear ideas about what his random inheritance meant to him or his future. He didn't know how he was meant to behave in this new world, so he got on with copying Payge's manners and demeanour.

Payge's bottomless appetite for fruit cake was the mortar that cemented their friendship, but it was Bert's anguished confession that he had inherited a title, and that there was a house somewhere, that sealed their bond. Without fruit cake, Payge would undoubtedly have wandered back into his own year, having done a bit of perfunctory showing Bert where the lavs were in those first few weeks.

After a term of getting used to school, he felt he could trust Payge enough to confide. He waited until Payge was quite stupefied with food one autumn evening, and began stumblingly to explain himself.

'Not Albert Hayes then. Mount-Hey? We should call you by your real name. But it's a bit of a mouthful, is it pronounced like that?'

'I don't know. I never met any others. Everyone else is dead.'

He tried to recall what the solicitor had said, but only remembered the novel taste of cold Coca Cola sucked up a straw.

'Well they would have to be, wouldn't they? Otherwise you wouldn't have inherited. Much more straightforward in my family. Lots of sons in every generation, including mine.'

Payge stopped, thinking.

'We should shorten Mount-Hey, it's sort of awkward sounding. Knock off the corners, wear it in a bit. Like St John is always called "Sinjin".'

He rolled the name around his mouth, muttering the syllables over and over again. 'Mount-Hey, Mount-Hey, Munt Hey, Munt-hay, Muntay, Munt, Munty.'

Bert sat quietly, not wanting to interrupt the process of his re-christening.

'I think Munty,' pronounced Payge at last. 'It's easy to say, and sort of amusing sounding. Could be the making of you. Goodbye, Hayes. Hello Munty.'

And he shook the younger boy's hand, clapping him on the shoulder.

Munty, the cornucopia of decent tuck, now had a nickname too. His acceptance was assured. The name caught on as crazes run through closed communities, and it helped him to accept his new identity for himself. Shortened and tightened, it was less alarming, more friendly. He was grateful.

One evening, a couple of townies (as he had learned to call them) attacked a chap named Melville who had gone out for a smoke in the sheep pastures around the school. He was small but they had miscalculated, as Melville was the school's best flyweight. Both townies had to be unstitched from barbed wire by the neighbouring farmer.

This marked the beginning of a series of skirmishes. Boys from the town would come loping up the Downs intent on mayhem and a little light sabotage, breaking windows and attacking isolated groups of smokers, gathered in the evenings under cover of the scant woodland on the south-facing side of the school. Bert didn't smoke, but he liked to saunter down with the others. It was sociable, before it became exciting with the prospect of a battle in the ongoing war.

Boys who were used to them – usually farmers' and landowners' sons – had permission to keep shotguns in their housemaster's gun cupboard. They were allowed to sign out their guns and go after rabbits in the gloaming among the woods and fields around the school. Payge was one of them.

One June evening when he was sixteen, Munty was preparing to go out in the company of a loose alliance of shooters and smokers, as they chatted idly about the prospect of an attack by townies.

'It's getting worse, you know,' said Atkinson, displaying a healing split lip.

'What did you do to him?' Munty asked. He half dreaded meeting someone he knew up from the town in these encounters. Luckily it was unlikely, as the grammar school boys believed they were above 'going up the hill'. It was the technical college lot who were rowdier and always spoiling for a fight. There was still a chance that one of his fellows from Mixed Infants might appear. Not only that, but he had to live in Eastbourne during the holidays and was visible in his grandparents' shop. So far, no one had recognised him in the few years he had been at Armishaw's. But still he didn't have the confidence to go in, fists flailing, as he saw the other boys do.

'I couldn't get close enough, he had a longer reach,' Atkinson was saying. 'They don't seem to care what they do now.'

Payge, his gun resting on his forearm, chipped in: 'Perhaps we could give them a fright. Guns might be more effective than hockey sticks.'

Eggy, high-stepping in his nervy way past the group just outside the House Study doors, overheard.

'Ha!' He let out a barking laugh. 'Why don't you let off a couple of rounds over their heads? That'll show the beggars who's in charge.' Grinning, he lurched onwards, leaving a trail of winks and sniggers in his wake. Bert wandered off with the smokers, the shooters choosing to go in another direction.

It was getting darker, and after an hour of peaceful chatting, the boys spotted shapes moving up the steep fields that separated the southern extreme of the school grounds from the outskirts of Eastbourne.

'Here they come, lads,' said Atkinson, touching his lip. 'What shall we do tonight?'

Nothing, as it turned out – the pearly evening was rent by a series of loud bangs, followed by screams and yelps. The shadowy figures were galvanised and running very fast down the hill.

'What the hell are you doing?' yelled Munty. 'Stop! You might kill someone.'

Then he recognised Payge coming towards him through the gloom.

'No chance of that, old Munty,' grinned Payge. 'We swapped the shot in a few cartridges for rice and salt. My father told me about it, Burma police used to do it to disperse a crowd. Hurts like hell but can't kill you. But we only used it to remove any risk as we were strictly firing over their heads. Didn't hit anyone, I promise.'

He had a wild look in his eye and Munty recoiled. It had all been over in a matter of moments. The townies had scattered far and wide, and the shooters broke their guns and strode back towards Reynolds House with the smokers. In the distance could be heard the siren of first one, then more than one, police car. The boys climbed the stone steps to the veranda of the House Study, where they were met by an incandescent Eggy accompanied by several grave policemen.

'What the hell's been going on?' the housemaster raged at the boys.

The police officer beside him said simultaneously, 'What's been going on here? There are reports of shotguns being discharged.'

'But Sir,' said Payge to Eggy, 'We were only doing what you said, Sir. You told us to show 'em who's in charge, Sir, by letting off the guns over their heads. Sir.'

Eggy fell silent and his bright red face drained to putty. To Munty's relief, he was gone within days, taking his random violence and obsession with the classics with him. But also removing his sweet wife, who had befriended the fish-out-of-water new boy and encouraged him to come to her sitting room for tea in the early, homesick days.

The house settled down after that under a calm and quiet man called Mr Rawlings, and became much like the rest of the school – increasingly sporty and thoughtless, smelling of feet and armpits. Munty had long since adopted the Armishaw's camouflage of the drawling accent and special language. A football was a bladder, a bicycle a bagger, trousers toggers and exams zaggers. The townies never again came up the hill, and the smokers and their friends were left in peace.

Munty risked joining his two worlds together by taking Payge to meet Pearl and his grandparents. Payge was charming, and his appetite for high tea filled the family with awe. Then Payge began inviting Munty to stay with his parents Lord and Lady Grangemere in the holidays, and Munty discovered a comforting world of friendly grubby chaos that was nothing like his image of how the upper classes behaved. Payge's family home was a large, flat-fronted Georgian barracks of a house. Parts of it were uninhabitable with damp. It was full of animals and children, and everything was covered in a fine layer of dog hair. The food was inedible, and Munty understood why Payge loved his tuck so much. There was no particular formality, and certainly no luxuries, and Munty grew more comfortable with his inherited identity. He knew his mother would be horrified and bewildered by what she would see as squalor. Having a clean tidy house was a daily preoccupation for Pearl. Munty found the mess soothing.

Payge had asked Munty about Castle Hey, what it was like. Munty had no idea, and decided that he ought to find out. He wrote to his mother, who contacted Mrs Jenkins. The house was still under the jurisdiction of the military, although they had moved out. Mrs Jenkins' reply mentioned that the house was in poor condition and its future uncertain and that they would have to wait until the War Compensation Office decided on their award before they did anything at all.

Other families had cut their losses and pulled down the scarred remains left by military use, as compensation was not generous and dry rot had run riot during the war years. A visit was arranged for mother and son but they were warned that they would not be able to go inside. They took a taxi up from the station, asking it to wait and stepping out on the overgrown carriage sweep looked up at the crumbling façade with mixed feelings.

It was as if Castle Hey had died, probably killed in the war, thought Munty. The pink brick bled green from overflowing gutters. The windows looked blank. An uninvited buddleia flourished above the front door. He hesitated, the pull of history for him was very strong. He noticed the pretty ogee arched windows and the toy battlements. It was undoubtedly romantic but also overwhelming, so big and decayed. He wanted to go away and think about it, and soon succeeded in persuading his mother to leave. They caught the next train back along the coast to Eastbourne. When Payge asked him about it again, he just muttered that it was a ruin.

Munty did his school certificates and then his National Service, and came out at the other end with his shoulders back and his muscles toned, but without much idea of what he wanted to do next. He was Lord Mount-Hey of Castle Hey, but the trustees had still not told him what that entailed, if anything.

Pearl had remarried soon after he'd left school. Her new husband was Reg Grigson, who was also widowed and also worked for his grandparents. Munty went home to live with his mother and stepfather, and to work in the family business. He began to learn buying, and soon was doing well enough to please the family. The only change was that they stopped calling him Bert and started calling him Munty, as it suited him. But soon he found Eastbourne stifling. He wanted to move out of his home and start a more grown-up kind of life, but didn't know how or where.

Then Mrs Jenkins wrote to him, suggesting that, as there was some money available now he was twenty-one, he should move to London. She didn't have realistic suggestions about where to get the capital from to do up Castle Hey, and when he went to see her she had joked that he needed a rich wife. He didn't like the idea, but he agreed that it might be worth looking for a nice girl to marry, and the best place to find the right sort, according to Mrs Jenkins, was still the London Season.

Castle Hey was shut up and made as secure as it could be against further deterioration, using government compensation money. An ex-soldier caretaker moved into the North Lodge, and indoor plumbing was provided for him. Munty took a room in a little cramped court near St James's, and looked for a job to tide him over while he looked for a wealthy wife, won the Pools or found some other means to help him get a firm hold on his bewildering future. None of which seemed remotely likely.

Seven

Munty
May 1966

Man and boy, what Munty knew best was the grocery trade. From babyhood, his mother had taken him to work with her, and as soon as he could walk, his grandparents had encouraged him to help out in the stockrooms.

It was no good thinking he could be a stockbroker or something else suitable for his acquired station in life, when all he knew about was coffee and tea, cheese and bacon. Luckily close to his rooms was Penrose & Quinn, the grandest of grocers and florists, founded in 1820 after the death of George III. His plain queen, the royal princesses and all the ladies-in-waiting demanded daily wreaths and nosegays and, according to royal etiquette, they had to be fresh every day all the year round.

Mrs Quinn, from a grand but impoverished family and one of Queen Charlotte's women of the bedchamber, developed a secret formula for perking up wilted flowers. She and Penrose, her equally secret footman lover and eventual husband, made their fortune selling the royal florabundance second-hand. This provided the original capital for their business. Luckily for Munty, there were as many titles behind the counters as in front of them. Working at P&Q wouldn't damage his fragile and recently acquired caste at all.

Honourables straight out of Eton and on their way to Oxford, Cambridge or Sandhurst would walk the floors during the Christmas rush, and Ladies would serve rose and violet creams without ruining their marriage prospects. Royals came in all the time. Nobody tried to stop the debutantes on the staff from slipping into luxurious customers' cloakrooms to put on their cocktail frocks and ball dresses before leaving for the day.

The debs' delights who worked there dressed down after work, changing into suits or jeans. On the shop floor, they were required to wear full morning dress with a high black stock around their necks in perpetual mourning for George III. The traditions of deference might be slipping away elsewhere, but in the richly scented halls of P&Q things went on as a rigid reproduction of life at the very top end as it had been lived for more than a hundred years.

Outside in the streets there was another scene altogether. Debs these days slipped out of the staff entrance in ever shorter skirts, winked at by the owners, who were still members of the Penrose family. Gossip photographers hung around during the Season, covertly encouraged by the press relations department.

Starting off at P&Q as a floorwalker, Munty rose to ground floor manager. Tall, slim and fair, with prominent blue eyes, he looked distinguished in his tailcoat. The great shop was happy to let customers know discreetly that they had a real grown-up peer of the realm on the staff. They were poised to allow him time off to vote in the House of Lords, although he had not taken advantage of that privilege yet. The thought of it terrified him and he had nothing to say.

He was always deployed when anyone aristocratic came in,

and particularly royalty, for whom he became a kind of unofficial epicurean equerry. His experience with his grandparents' business stood him in very good stead, and he was able to support himself on his salary, while beginning to explore what London had to offer. He dipped into the Season half-heartedly, taking a few girls out, but none of them stirred his interest. Indeed he found them intimidating. They soon moved on to richer, more straightforward marriage material.

The fate of Castle Hey was not real enough to him to persuade him to marry a giggling colonial uranium heiress or rich sharp American on the lookout for a title. He wasn't attached to the house as he would have been if he had been brought up there. In his mind's eye, it was shrouded in mist and overgrown, like Sleeping Beauty's castle. Secretly it frightened him. The Ministry of Works had relinquished it only the year before but he had no urge to go and take possession. He wondered sometimes what it would take to drag him from his inertia and down to Sussex to do something about Castle Hey.

What was real to Munty was working and drifting in a London that was shrugging off the past as fast as it could. Not that he was comfortable with the speed of change. But the busyness made it easier not to think about Castle Hey, to let the trustees deal with the roof and the caretaker. So far they hadn't put any pressure on him to take responsibility.

One Friday afternoon in May, standing with his hands clasped behind his back on the English Racing Green carpet that covered the entire ground floor, Munty watched the ebb and flow of customers. He was adept at distinguishing those who needed help from those who were simply browsing for fun.

Everyone had lived through rationing and to see such abundance, luxury and variety on display was still a source of entertainment. The uniformed doormen, burly war veterans under their old-fashioned footmen's livery and powdered wigs, kept out any real undesirables.

He remembered after the war when there was only one kind of cheese in his grandparents' shop, and that was yellow and oblong and didn't appear to have a name other than Government cheese. The P&Q cheese counter was famous for its glorious range, imported from France daily as there were no interesting cheeses left in England. They even had a French *affineur* on the staff. To his left was the grocery department, with displays of all kinds of teas, coffees and tinned goods, from *petits pois* to *foie gras*. To his right, the vast and varied display of flowers and, in front of him, confectionery and chocolates laid out on glass shelves. Behind the sweet counter, the not-so-sweet Honourable Lydia Adair wore black cotton gloves and a white muslin apron over her mid-calf black uniform dress with its old-fashioned full skirt. On her head was a white mob cap, reduced to a ridiculous puff of muslin teetering on top of her shiny red hairdo.

She winked at him, and he pretended to ignore her, a blush starting behind his collar. The revolving doors moved in the corner of his vision, and a girl stepped into the shop. She was very slight, wearing a short cotton dress of pale yellow with a white belt, no sleeves and little white gloves. Her fair hair looked freshly done, curling up at the tips, and she was wearing low-heeled pale tan slingbacks. She stopped and looked around and he approached her as you might a small deer.

'Can I help you?' he asked.

She smiled up at him. 'Yes, I'm looking for flowers.'

She could hardly have missed Penrose & Quinn's famously enormous floral display, the sole part of the shop where the natural produce had not been regimented. Only the hothouse roses in unnatural shades of red, yellow and orange conformed like soldiers standing to attention on their long thornless stems. The rest was a riot of stargazer and green-tinged lilies, delphiniums, plumes of gypsophila, tight buds held in green cups, blousy full-blown peonies and gladioli spears. They still specialised in wreaths and nosegays, and no one smart went anywhere else for their bridesmaids' headdresses and posies. He walked her across and said to Jacqueline, the resident florist, 'Can you help this young lady?'

Jacqueline smiled, and put aside the tight little bunch of pink rosebuds she was arranging. 'What did you have in mind?'

'I'd like one of your nosegays, white and yellow, that we can just put in water, please? It's for my mother,' Munty could hear her say as he strolled back to his post.

The girl's face stayed in his mind, and he glanced back at her as she watched the arrangement being made and then paid for it. As she walked out, she turned and thanked him. He knew that his friend Freddie would've asked for her telephone number or arranged a date. It was against company regulations, but the others were clever at diving under the radar. For the first time he wanted to. He took a step after her and opened his mouth, but nothing came out and he went back to his station feeling foolish.

The girl in yellow attracted him, she looked hesitant, there was a hint of anxiety. He regretted not approaching her for the rest of the day.

Queen Charlotte's Ball was the following week, and Lydia, a deb that year, had invited him to join her party. 'Daddy's thrown money at a table and someone's dropped out. Do come, Munty, Mummy's always asking about you.'

'Look, Lydia, I'm a bit old. Not debs' delight material anymore.'

'Don't be ridiculous, Munty. You look good in black tie, nice and tall. Harry Bowles is much older than you and he's still on the scene. And besides, you aren't married yet. You know, people are beginning to talk. I heard someone suggest you were VVSITPQ the other day, and we can't have that.'

'What on earth does that mean?'

'Oh, you know. Very very safe in taxis, probably queer,' and she left the floor in a hurry, laughing, to change out of her black dress and into something short, shiny and tight for the evening. It was true, Lydia's mother had sidled up to him on more than one occasion to ask him to keep an eye on her daughter. He blushed and muttered. He liked Lydia, but knew she had at least three boyfriends and wasn't looking for a husband.

He began his tour of inspection before leaving for the evening, and Freddie said as he walked by, 'Fancy a drink, Munty?'

He didn't have anything much else to do, so they changed together, setting out to stretch their legs with a walk down to the Star Tavern, tucked away in Belgrave Mews.

Restless in the May warmth, Munty knew he wanted something to happen but had no idea what it was. The angled evening sun bounced off the pavements and heated the air. A blackbird sang its piercing song in Green Park. They walked along talking about the day, customers and new lines coming in from abroad. In the Star there were always slightly sinister groups of men in corners, in very good Savile Row suits and brown suede shoes. Outside a couple of Jags gleamed on the cobbles, their drivers lounging against the bonnets gossiping, engines gently ticking over hazing the mews with blue exhaust. Inside, cigar smoke predominated over cigarettes, and a slight frisson of the upper end of the underworld spiced the atmosphere. Munty and Freddie ate steak and kidney pie and drank pints of beer and then, as it was Friday, decided to go on to the Keyhole in St James's.

Plunging down the steps into the smoky basement, they glanced around, seeing the usual mixed crowd of West End types, actors and low life. On the stage a plump naked lady graced a set built to resemble a raft. Flying from the stout mast, or rather flopping in the stale grey air, was a striped seaman's jumper. The lady spent some time elaborately wrapping her legs around the mast and attempting to hoist her considerable person upwards. It was as sexy as watching a seal shinning up a lamp post. To his surprise, she did begin to progress, panting, heaving and gasping and positively gleaming with sweat under the arc light that stood in for the sun. The ratty little man beside him whispered behind his hand, 'It's all very symbolic, you see.' Munty laughed. He was at that stage of boozing where everything and anything seems amusing.

Just as she had creaked and heaved far enough up to grasp the jumper, the lights went out and Munty would never know nor care why she so desperately wanted it, as it did not look ample enough to reclaim her modesty.

Turning back to the bar, he saw Lydia entwined around one of her more unsuitable boyfriends and greeted her with a wave. She disentangled herself and shimmied over on long white legs to talk to him.

'Munty, darling. I insist you come to Queen Charlotte's next week. You get the opportunity to see me wearing a long white dress and looking virginal as my mother wants me to for a change, and curtseying to a cake. Come on, it's surreal.'

'Just not sure it's me, but if you insist.'

'Look, I do insist. OK? I'll pout. I will.'

'OK, Lydia. I'll come. Are you organising dinners beforehand, or shall I just turn up at ten?'

'Daddy's bought dinner tickets for the ball itself of course, you know what he's like. It all starts at eight o'clock. I'll give you your ticket next week at work.'

Munty sighed. He tipped the last of his nightcap down his throat before setting off to walk home to bed. Behind him he heard the unmistakable sounds of a police raid. Those rolling thighs wrapped around that robust erection had probably been a bit more than the Lord Chamberlain's censors could tolerate.

Eight

Melissa
May 1966

Melissa was about five feet four inches tall, fair and slender with good legs and pale skin. She had a dreamy look as her blue eyes often seemed half closed, but this was deceptive, her mind was very busy. Her 'little hoof' had garnered her a great deal of attention from both parents, even though it was almost completely corrected by her treatment in America. The arrival of her twin brothers Julian and William when she was four had been a blow, but they vanished off to prep school quite soon, and she had Mummy and Daddy all to herself once again.

Besides, she could always get the attention she craved, even when the babies were crying, by going very quiet. This wasn't deliberate. Sometimes she didn't feel very well and only sitting on Mummy's knee and having a long hug, even when she was quite big, helped. These episodes were called 'Lissy's glooms' and, along with her giddy episodes – 'Over-excited and silly', her mother described them – were just part of family life. She loved the softness of her mother's large bust and the sweetness of Ma Griffe, brought back by Daddy from duty free whenever he went away. It didn't always work though. Sometimes she couldn't face going to school.

She picked her feet up and put them down precisely when she

walked, which made the nastier children look at her sideways. On bad days, she would creep home from school and up to her room without anyone noticing. She would lie on her bed to indulge in orgies of reading that left her dazed and blinking.

Now Melissa was going to be a debutante. She was eighteen and had left her day school with a couple of A levels that she had completed in one year. In the autumn, she was to start as a nurse probationer at St Saviour's Hospital in London, so she had the summer to fill. The Season proper kicked off in May with Queen Charlotte's Ball, where the girls dressed in white and curtseyed to whichever spare, usually exiled, royal had been recruited by the ball committee.

All the preparation for 'bringing her out' was fun for Mummy too, meeting up with old schoolfriends who were bringing out their own daughters, and reconnecting with her past. Sarah hadn't minded missing her own Season, as the war had broken out and she had been swept away into a new life. 'And I would never have met your father, darling, if I'd been a deb,' she would say. 'Which is no reason why you shouldn't be. Lots of new friends and fun, before you start your nursing training in September.'

Now it was a warm May evening, and Melissa got out of the bath and wrapped herself in a towel to climb the stairs to the attic bedroom in her Uncle Stephen and Aunt Melinda's house in Cheyne Place in Chelsea. She shivered with happiness as she looked at her slender white dress hanging on the back of the door. Her mother had made it using a designer pattern, with white damask fabric from Peter Jones. Melissa smoothed a new pair of American Tan stockings up her legs, and fixed them with suspenders hanging from her white cotton girdle. The square-toed, low-heeled satin pumps were on the floor by the bed. It was no good her trying to wear high heels – her ankle was not strong enough. Anyway the whole effect was Jane Austen to her eye.

She'd already glimpsed Daddy downstairs in the drawing room, looking unusually smart. He was wearing his father's white tie and tails, glad to play his part in his daughter's debut for one night only. He loved to see Mummy looking like a goddess crowned with light, in the silver and blue brocade dress she had made, with a full skirt and three-quarter length sleeves.

Sarah had visited her hairdresser earlier, with the family tiara lent by her brother Diggory – who was now Lord Elbourne – wrapped in a silk scarf in her handbag. Elbourne kept anything left of the family jewels in Lindell's Bank in London, so that his sister and sisters-in-law could borrow them. He lived with his Australian wife Lisa and their five children on a sheep station in Queensland.

'Lisa has no use for trinkets at home,' he said. 'In the unlikely event of a coronation they'll be here waiting for us when we come over.'

Sarah had taken Melissa and her brothers to see the house where she had been brought up, Abbots Bourne. It had been sold after the war and was now the headquarters of a pharmaceutical company, so they couldn't go inside.

'Always freezing cold as the enormous boiler cost a fortune to run. And hideous. Fun for hide and seek though. And of course I nursed there during the war.'

Melissa caught a wistful look on her mother's face as they walked in the grounds, where top-heavy trees were turning to gold, and great oblong brown cattle like chests of drawers grazed in the park beyond the ha ha. But it was fleeting, and soon they were eating cheese and home-made chutney rolls on a rug spread under the trees.

So far her first ball had been a bit of a let-down. The dinner started with stemmed glass dishes crammed with shredded lettuce, pink salad cream, and a few prawns like fat baby's legs dangling over the edge. This was followed by warm flat islands of meat in a sea of gravy, with tasteless potatoes carved into zeppelins and strangely sweet peas. The pudding was Poire Belle Hélène – tinned pears with vanilla ice cream and chocolate custard. School pudding. Such a contrast to her mother's wonderful tasting food.

The Reeves family, minus the younger brothers as they were still at boarding school, shared a table with other couples and their daughters. The other debs' mothers were just like hers, from outside London, taking part for the fun of it, to give their girls a bit of social life after boarding school and before they got on with the serious business of being grown up.

As court presentations had been abolished when the young Queen started to find it all too ridiculously uncomfortable in 1958, Queen Charlotte's Ball was the defining moment of the debutantes' launch. Before the war, her mother muttered, Queen Charlotte's was for those unfortunate girls whose parents had been divorced, to get some kind of a royal blessing, however obscure and European, as the poor things were banned from Court.

After dinner, Melissa had watched debs, trained in the art of the old-fashioned court curtsey by the dancing teacher Madame Vacani, processing four abreast down the sweeping staircase in Grosvenor House's main ballroom. Their object was a giant, two-tiered cake. This, which Melissa suspected was mostly made of cardboard, was presented on a wheeled table that had been towed by a different group of debs with silken ropes. She could see it was in fact being pushed from behind by two chefs. It looked like a giant wedding cake and Melissa was struck by the symbolism of all these girls clad in virgin white paying homage to a giant, fruit-crammed symbol of fertility. She kept her ideas to herself.

There was a visual same-but-different enjoyment to studying all the interpretations of the white dress. Some looked unfashionable, with wide skirts and tight bodices, others like hers were A-line with a high waist and straight skirt. The style suited the very slender only, on anyone plump it looked like a lampshade. Some dresses were very plain, others embroidered or beaded, even fringed. Hair was backcombed on top, and all the mothers had begged, borrowed or stolen a tiara. Everyone wore full-length white gloves. The luckier girls had cream kid, probably pre-war and inherited, while she and her mother both wore cotton. Little pearly buttons did up the placket over the blue veins of her inner wrist.

An ancient Romanov princess, leaning on a silver-topped cane and draped in yellowing lace and large, very dirty diamonds, was the true object of all the curtseys. Not the cake at all. But curtseying to the cake was an immemorial debs' joke. The princess was being a kind of substitute royal person, now the Queen had better things to do. A princess without a kingdom, whose close relations had been shot dead in a basement in Russia.

How odd the world was. Melissa wondered if the old princess was sad, if she had known the Tsar, his wife and all the doomed children. She certainly looked old enough. No sign of the communists here of course, the debs were trapped in an arcane ritual safe from revolution.

Outside the glittering ballroom crammed with lily-white virgins, the warming streets foamed with young girls in psychedelic short skirts, men with long hair and coloured clothes, sex and pop music. Her parents claimed not to be able to stand it, but she had seen her mother very slightly moving her hips to 'Love Me Do' on the radio while she did the ironing. Such a short time ago men had worn uniforms, or suits, nothing else, and their hair had been regulation short back and sides. There'd been no such thing as a teenager and nearly every man had killed someone. But not Daddy. One of the things that singled him out for her mother.

Melissa had not been chosen to curtsey – her mother had not applied. It was probably because, even now that her foot was so much restored, Mummy was worried that the effort of balancing on one leg in public might be too much for her. She didn't like having decisions like this made for her and resented it.

The men in her party were not debs' delights at all, but brothers, nephews and other dancing partners that the mothers had dug up from desperate corners of old address books. All very decorous and dull. Melissa could not help stealing glances at the table next to theirs, presided over by a plump and red-faced gentleman whose frequent roars of laughter drowned conversation on the Reeves table. There were three champagne buckets – Melissa counted them covertly. The girls were all dressed correctly in white, but just that bit more stylishly, with low-cut bodices. Their hair was professionally done, their jewellery not confined to a string of pearls like Melissa's. Their make-up was brighter too, with trendy pale lipstick and black eyeliner, and she detected false eyelashes as well. She was fascinated.

The men were quite obviously proper debs' delights. Older, good looking and smart in their dinner jackets. They had lit cigars, and the indefinably delicious smell wafted over to Melissa's table, speaking of tropical richness to her romantic mind. The conversation was lively and the girls kept swapping places to sit with the men they liked.

Melissa was having to bear the earnest conversation of her neighbour, a trainee accountant called Colin.

Colin explained to Melissa exactly what his training consisted of, and where he hoped his career would take him when he was qualified. Melissa was so bored it hurt, but had found her neighbour on the other side equally tedious and clumsy. She longed to flirt as the girls next door were doing, to wave a long cigarette holder around and flutter unnatural eyelashes. She toyed with the stem of her glass, wishing one of the fathers would buy some more wine. She noticed that there was no older woman at all on the exciting, racy table next door to keep the girls in check.

At one end of the ballroom the Lester Lanin orchestra, flown over from New York for the occasion, was just beginning to beguile the company with one of its long smooth medleys. No one was dancing yet, although people picked up their little cups of disgustingly bitter weak coffee and circulated into other parties. Melissa knew no one to circulate to and so was forced to continue listening to Colin, unable to help herself fixing her gaze on the angry mountain range sprouting from his forehead. Her eyes wandered once more to the other table. A red-headed girl was now sitting on the lap of one of the men, her arm round his neck, sipping from a shallow champagne glass and smoking through a long holder. Her dress looked like something out of Georgette Heyer, high-waisted and cut to show the tops of her bosoms. Colin turned at last to his neighbour on the other side, and she was free to drink in her surroundings.

At that moment, one of the men sitting on her side of the table next door turned outward and glanced around. His eyes appeared to skim over her and she had a moment of flinching invisibility, but then he glanced back, caught her eye and smiled. He was slim and fair, his blue eyes stuck out a bit and he didn't have a lot of chin, but his smile was warm.

'Hello,' he said.

Melissa said, 'Hello.'

'Isn't she a shocker?' he said, inclining his head in the direction of the girl on the man's lap.

'I didn't realise you were allowed to sit on men's laps at things like this,' she said, trying to sound sophisticated.

'You're not. But that's Lydia for you, she doesn't care. I'm just waiting to see if her father notices and says something.'

'Is that her father?' Now she had finished eating, Melissa untucked her gloves from the plackets and pulled them back over her fingers.

'Yes, that's Lord Dale. I think he's not quite sober enough to realise what Lydia is up to. I also fully expect one of the other girls to go over and perch on his knee any minute.'

'Oh, where is Lady Dale?'

'She's not well. She invited me and I only came because Lydia was so keen that her mother should see me here. And now it's all for nothing.'

He paused, looking at Melissa. 'What did you think of the cake?'

'The cake?' She was surprised by the question, but then said the first thing that came into her head: 'I expected a girl in a sparkly bathing suit and ostrich feathers to pop out of the top.'

She looked back at him, trying to gauge his reaction. He was smiling encouragingly. She tried again.

'I think it's so funny that all these girls in white are curtseying to an enormous fertility symbol. It's like something out of ancient Greece.'

She saw that he liked that too and added, 'What about those girls dragging it in on ropes?'

'Like in that Keats poem we all did for O level,' he said, '"Lead'st thou that heifer lowing at the skies, And all her silken flanks with garlands drest." Some kind of virgin sacrifice maybe? Who conjured all this crazy stuff up in the first place?'

'Perhaps Queen Charlotte liked birthday cake,' Melissa suggested. 'She was quite odd, not letting her own daughters or her ladies-in-waiting marry, and insisting everyone wore white dresses and wreaths of fresh flowers like a lot of superannuated bridesmaids. Must have been a bunch of Miss Havishams when they got older. She was a great fat Queen Bee, popping out endless little royal maggots and not letting anyone else have a go.' It was such a relief to say what she bloody well liked for a change, without being stared at.

He was laughing. 'I love history,' he said.

She smiled at him with a sudden sense of triumph.

He hesitated and then said, 'Would you like to dance?'

'But we haven't been properly introduced.'

'I don't think it matters. I'm Munty by the way, and you are?'

'I'm Melissa Reeves. I'd better introduce you to Mummy though.'

'Melissa, this is 1966, not 1866. You don't need to ask your chaperone if you can dance with me. Come on.'

She let him lead her to where Lanin and his orchestra were murdering the Rolling Stones via a medley of their hits.

'I was just going to slip away,' he continued. 'Lydia's taking everyone off to the Ad Lib for a bit of proper dancing. Lester Lanin doesn't cut it for this crowd.'

'Oh.' Melissa was disappointed but then he was holding her hand and walking away from his party. She allowed herself to be led towards the now crowded dance floor.

'I was going to go home,' he went on. 'I've got to go to work tomorrow.'

Everyone seemed to be dancing in the traditional manner, in a ballroom pose, which was a bit odd given the music. It was easier when Lanin stopped trying to be hip and played a waltz medley. Some people left the enormous dance floor, but Munty shifted his arm to take a firmer grip on her waist and start to swing her around. Before she knew what was happening, she was being waltzed right down one side of the dance floor, across the bottom and up the other side under the enormous crystal chandeliers. Munty's hold was firm, and she was breathless and light on her feet with the swinging pleasure of it. Smiling faces turned towards them and blurred as they went faster. Just at the point she had no breath left, and her foot was beginning to niggle, the waltz came to an end. Munty stood back from her and inclined his head. She bobbed him a little curtsey, and they both laughed.

'You're good at that,' she said.

'My mother made me take lessons when I was sixteen. It was awful at the time, so embarrassing. I must say I'm grateful now.'

'I must go and powder my nose,' she said.

'Don't disappear,' he said quickly.

When she came out of the Ladies, he was standing close to the top of the passage that led back into the ballroom. Delight welled up inside her.

He led her back to his party's table to sit down, although everyone else had gone. Sarah came over to her daughter when she saw her return, and told her that they were leaving, and it had been lovely. Munty stood up, and Melissa introduced him.

'Mummy, this is Munty. And Munty, this is my mother, Lady Sarah Reeves, and my father Dr Reeves.'

'How do you do?' they both said.

'How do you do?' replied Munty. 'My name's Mount-Hey, in fact, but everyone calls me Munty.'

Sarah smiled at him and turned to Melissa. 'Now darling, we must fly. Come back whenever you like, but make sure you don't get too tired.'

Melissa caught herself beginning to roll her eyes.

'Oh, Mummy. I'm fine. I've got a key. See you in the morning.'

She turned back to Munty as they walked away arm in arm. 'I have to confess something,' he was saying. 'This isn't the first time I've seen you.'

'You looked familiar, too, but I couldn't think from where.'

'I work in P&Q.'

'I came in to buy some flowers for Mummy, to thank her for organising all this for me.'

'I hope she liked them.'

'She did. Being a deb wasn't an obvious thing for me at all.'

She looked at him closely, trying to see whether it was the right thing to do, to tell him that she wasn't grand or rich. He was bending slightly to hear what she was saying over the orchestra. Knowing he worked at P&Q was reassuring as well. It was very smart, but in the end P&Q was just a grocer.

'Let's go up on the balcony,' he said. 'It's quieter, and I'll get us a bottle of champagne on the way.' He pulled out his wallet and went up to the bar as she trailed behind.

Then they were on the balcony, looking down on the dance floor packed with dancers: girls in white and men in black. Melissa narrowed her eyes to blur the swirling monochrome. It was a bit like watching television. Only the mothers were wearing colours, and they weren't dancing.

'Now,' he said. 'You were saying?' They sat with their elbows on the table, looking at each other. She liked his face. It helped that he wasn't handsome, which would have been frightening.

'Well, Daddy is a GP in Dorking, but Mummy is Lady Sarah, although she never mentions it except at things like this. Why are you called Munty?'

'It's a long story.' He was silent for a moment, and Melissa worried that she had annoyed him by asking about his name. Had she been rude? She seemed to be tuned up like a violin to his mood. Then he looked up at her, took her hand, kissed her fingertips and smiled. It was like the sun coming out, and Melissa melted.

'Completely unexpectedly, I inherited a title when I was thirteen. Lord Mount-Hey – everyone at school took to calling me Munty and it just stuck. It was a shock at the time and I don't talk about it much. Not since school in fact.'

Not since school? That must have been ages ago.

'I'm sorry your father died when you were so young.'

'Oh, no he didn't. I mean he didn't die then, he died when I was a baby, in the war. In an air raid. My poor mother had to cope with that, and then this strange business of me being a lord, and inheriting a tatty old house, all by herself. Well she had her parents, but they were more confused than her if that was possible.'

Melissa made encouraging noises.

'You see I don't come from a grand family at all,' he went on. 'That's why I work in P&Q. My grandparents are grocers in Eastbourne, although they're retired now. My mother runs the business with her second husband, who always worked for them too. My father was just an ordinary bloke but he was also a distant cousin of Lord Mount-Hey. So many people were killed in both world wars, or just died unmarried, that I ended up inheriting.'

A quietness pooled in her mind. She paused and then she said: 'You mentioned a house? Do you live there?'

'No, I've never lived there as it's almost a ruin. I've only seen it once. It's in Sussex. Rather lovely. Needs waking up like Sleeping Beauty.'

Again he stopped.

'What's it like? I love old houses.'

'It's so old that there was once a moat, although all that's left is a little lake.'

'A lake?' Melissa shivered.

'Goose walk over your grave?' he teased. He went on, 'It wasn't a castle back then just a moated farmhouse. At some point in the eighteenth century one of my ancestors became obsessed with Strawberry Hill Gothick and changed the name from Hey House to Castle Hey, altering the windows and adding castellations. The mount bit in Mount-Hey refers to a little mound nearby with a ruined tower on top – a bit grand to call it a mount.'

He hesitated.

'In fact if you like houses I'd value your opinion. You're probably busy but I was thinking of driving down to have a look round this weekend. It's properly mine now. The Ministry of Works let go.'

Melissa stared at him.

'Would you like to come and see it?'

Of course she would love to drive out of London with the first man who had ever shown any interest in her, and visit what might turn out to be a romantic ruin. She too hesitated.

'Sorry,' he said, looking rueful. 'Too bouncy, like Tigger. Of course you don't want to come and see some old house.'

'But I do, I think. How far is it?'

'Not far. I'm working for the rest of the week. I was thinking of going down for the day on Saturday. I don't think Castle Hey is habitable, otherwise I'd ask you to stay.'

She pulled herself up straighter and took a gulp of champagne, trembling with excitement. She told herself not to be so silly. Of course she could go off for a drive in the country with anyone she chose. She was meant to be nearly grown up now, wasn't she? He looked so nice and unthreatening, she was sure he wouldn't pounce or frighten her.

'I can put together a hamper at P&Q and we can have a picnic.'

Then he laughed and pulled her hand towards him, kissing her gloved fingers again. It was very late, and the dance floor below was punctuated with a last few couples leaning against each other and circling like hair in a drain.

When Lanin announced the last waltz, Munty raised his eyebrow at her, but she declined. Her foot had had enough. They went to the cloakroom to collect Melissa's long velvet cloak, clasped at the neck with the silver buckle from her mother's wartime VAD uniform.

Outside in Park Lane, the doorman hailed a taxi for them.

'Where to, sir?'

'Cheyne Place. Thank you.'

She expected to climb in alone, but Munty followed her. She had pulled the silk-lined hood up over her hair as there was a faint misty drizzle in the air. As he settled beside her, she peeped up at him from within her hood's creamy depths, registering as she did so a look of surprise. He leaned forward as if he couldn't help himself, his nose bumped hers and he muttered an apology. Then he put his hands on her shoulders and this time found her lips. She felt the softness of his mouth against hers and was uncertain what to do next. They sat for a moment lip to lip, looking into each other's eyes, then his lips parted and a sense of warm delight moved through her. After that, there didn't seem to be any need for deciding what to do.

She awoke the next day with her mother's lips on her uppermost cheek. Foggy threads of a dream evaporated as she swam up reluctantly from the bottom of sleep.

'Daddy and I are just going home. Wanted to leave you sleeping until the last possible minute. You were up very late. How's your foot after all that dancing?'

'Fine. Lovely,' she murmured, irritated as she always was by any mention of her foot, turning her head on the pillow away from her mother's warm, tea-scented breath.

'Was that young man nice?' Melissa could hear an interested note in her mother's voice. 'Munty? Was that his name? I suppose it comes from his title, Mount-Hey. I looked him up in your aunt's Burke's Peerage. Old title, rather fascinating. His ancestor helped to rescue Charles II.'

'Hmmm.' The irritation persisted. She wished her mother would go away.

'Most post-Restoration titles are descended from one of Old Rowley's by-blows, so it's interesting that this one is different.'

This was an annoying hobby of her mother's, perusing what she called 'the herd book' to see who was related to whom, and how they got their titles in the first place.

Melissa's returning consciousness brought the memory of Munty's invitation with it. She glowed and rolled her head back, consciously letting her hair flop across her face, all too aware that her lips were sore.

Pretending to be sleepier than she was, she stretched up her naked white arms to her mother and pulled her close for disarming kisses and farewells. She wanted to be alone to think. Sarah laughed and kissed her again, saying that they must be off for Daddy's afternoon surgery.

'Aunt Melinda's going to take us to the train. Do telephone to let us know what you're up to. Get plenty of sleep and take care of that foot of yours. Don't overdo it.'

'Yes, Mummy.'

Melissa was glad when her mother shut the attic bedroom door behind her. Hearing her tread recede down the uncarpeted stairs, Melissa let out a breath, opened her eyes properly and stared at the ceiling. When could she see him again? He knew where she was staying having brought her home, and she had responded to his request for her phone number by whispering it against his lips, 'Flaxman 3715,' over and over again. She was so close, so entwined and trusting, taking liberties with his mouth and breath as he did with hers.

He was smiling, and the tip of his tongue touched the inside of her upper lip, shutting her up. It was shockingly intimate, and she considered pulling away just for a second. That soft intrusion, sliding up over her teeth. She breathed into his mouth, 'Will you remember?'

'Oh yes, it's only four numbers,' he replied, before holding her all the closer until her insides were quite liquid with longing. Perhaps this is what the debs meant by Not Safe in Taxis, but at least he didn't try anything else, just this glorious kissing that went on and on as the taxi grumbled towards Chelsea. After a while, she noticed they had stopped and the driver was clearing his throat. She pulled back, embarrassed at having forgotten the third party behind the glass partition.

Munty had seen her to the door, after paying for and dismissing the taxi. The house was dark, the street quiet. He insisted on kissing her on the doorstep. He seemed already to be attached to her by invisible shining ropes which she was afraid to break in case they melted with the morning like goblin gold.

She knew she must remove herself, so she pushed her latchkey into the lock with one hand, and with the other gently eased him away down the steps. He clutched at her hand against his wilting shirt front, and she wriggled her fingers to release herself. Opening the door and holding her cloak around her, she gazed back at him, now standing at the bottom of the steps, looking up at her. She waved one gloved hand, mocking and imperious, and slipped inside.

'Keep something back,' she had told herself. 'Leave them wanting more.'

Thirsty now, she hopped out of bed to run across the passage to the lavatory, bending over the tap to drink from her cupped hand. While she drank she decided not to tell Mummy and Daddy what she was planning. She was quite old enough at eighteen to make up her own mind where she went and what she did – and with whom. No one need know, at least not until those gossamer ropes had woven her and Munty so firmly together that she could trust them with her weight. It was easy to be free these days and evade her parents' notice, as there were so many parties and weekend invitations, and they trusted her.

When she had had the curse for the first time at fourteen, her mother had sat her down for an excruciating chat about men and what they wanted from a girl, and how it was important not to give it to them until she was married. Her father had given her a book called *A Doctor Answers Young Girls' Questions*, asking her to read it all and come to him if she didn't understand anything. She would rather have died than ask him any questions. She was deeply grateful for the paper substitute, where she learned that she was in possession of a whole lot of things that sounded like Latin girls' names, Labia, Vulva, Vagina.

She giggled. There were deadly warnings about disgusting sounding venereal diseases. And a protracted and boring description of sexual intercourse that made you wonder why anyone bothered to overcome their embarrassment for long enough. This was followed by a detailed account of the journey that millions of battling sperm must make to meet the egg waiting, huge and passive like a sad planet invaded by tadpoles, somewhere up inside her.

She couldn't imagine herself doing anything of the kind, and contraception sounded so difficult and messy that she would prefer to remain a virgin until her dying day. But there must be something more to sex. Everyone seemed so excited by it these days. It was all about youthquake, she read in the *Daily Express*, and the dolly birds were on the Pill – a great improvement on all those gels and pessaries and rubber devices.

Melissa couldn't wait for Saturday morning to come, and the rest of the week's social life had lost its hopeful savour. On Friday she went to a drinks party and, spotting with the relief of the shy a girl she knew vaguely from debs' teas, she hurried over to catch up. She quickly noticed that the attention of the 'friend' was fixed on a search for the nearest man rather than on what she was saying.

'Nancy,' she said with uncharacteristic confidence, 'do stop looking over my shoulder, it makes you look as if you've got a squint.'

Nancy's eyes swivelled and locked on to Melissa's face. 'Darling,' she drawled, 'you must know by now, it isn't done to talk to other girls at parties. Not the point. Everyone will think you're a lesbian. Not a good look for you. These days it's men or nothing.'

'What if you can't get a man?'

'Well, then you have to hire one. You up your value considerably if you arrive at a party with someone looking adoring on your arm. You can get models and actors for eight pounds an evening. Good-looking hip ones, too.'

'Hire one? How?'

'There are agencies that hire them out. Bertie Shaw-Wiggins told me all about it. Bit short after dropping this year's allowance at roulette, he rang up something called Cockburn's Agency – he kept laughing at the name, couldn't work out why, isn't it some kind of port? Anyway, he said they measured him and photographed him and said he could go on their books for fifty per cent of the fee, and all the expenses he could keep for himself.'

Melissa had heard of men hiring women for unmentionable things, but not the other way around. Blushing wildly, she said, 'Do they have to do it?'

'Oh god, Melissa, you are such an innocent. Get with it, darling. Everyone's doing it. Bertie figured he might as well get paid for it, though with his gambling habit he'd have to do it an awful lot.'

Melissa knew she wasn't doing it, but that for the first time in her life she would like to and then blushed more. What would Mummy think?

Nancy was going on, and a little group had formed around them to listen: 'I think Bertie imagined he'd just be taken out to dinner by rich old bags. I believe he was rapidly disabused. Anyway, the idea of bumping into someone he knew and trying to explain – or even being hired by a friend of his mother's. Can you imagine? And they weren't all women if you know what I mean.'

Melissa didn't know what she meant, but everyone else was laughing, so she joined in and drank the champagne to help her keep up.

'Would you like another drink?'

Warm breath on her neck alerted her to a man she didn't know smiling down at her. She accepted, and drifted with him through the cigarette smoke to the bar at the back of the large Belgravia drawing room. Ceiling-high windows draped in gold damask looked out over a still-sunlit garden square, and the waiter with a napkin-wrapped bottle took her glass out of her hand. He picked up a clean coupe, filling it with champagne that never had a chance to foam up and waste itself.

'Would you like to have dinner afterwards?' her companion asked. Melissa, who would have been delighted just a few days beforehand, turned him down, and circled the room, nibbling canapés and unable to settle to anything or anyone.

She chattered and swigged champagne, noticing her hands were shaking with nerves. More men than usual invited her out to dinner that evening – as only one had done so previously this was miraculous. She was all lit up inside, and she couldn't wait for the days to peel away, exposing Saturday morning, raw with temptation.

Then there it was, Saturday, clothing her in hot light that streamed in through the curtainless window. She heard Aunt Melinda calling her from below, and trotted down the steep stairs into her aunt's chintzy bedroom, where she was holding up the telephone receiver.

'Melissa, it's Mummy,' she said, handing it over.

Melissa's stomach lurched with guilt. She glanced at her aunt's alarm clock and saw it was nine already. Panic joined the guilt in a nauseous cocktail of nerves.

'Hello Mummy,' she said, trying to conceal her quick breaths.

'Hello, just ringing up to find out where you're off to this weekend.'

Lies tripped across Melissa's lips like deceitful elves leaving smutty footprints.

'I'm going to some dance in Sussex, Mummy. Taking the train later. Having my hair done this morning first.'

'Anyone I know?'

'Don't think so. Some commuter-belt nouveaux riches. But all my friends are going.'

Melissa knew this would turn her mother right off the scent, no possibility of looking them up in the herd book.

'Who are you staying with?'

'Can't remember, but they sound perfectly nice. Some big house full of dog hair probably, where they'll give us a disgusting dinner. Why does no one cook like you, Mummy?'

Baby voice. She played on the knowledge that her mother was trying hard to adapt to this modern style of not having a clue where your daughter was from one day to the next.

To her relief, Munty had phoned to make plans the day after the ball, luckily when her aunt was out playing bridge. The conversation had been delicious and ridiculous, and she couldn't remember much of it, just that by the end of it she knew he fancied her. They were going to meet in the Chelsea Potter on the King's Road at lunchtime and drive down to Sussex. They had not discussed what would happen next and Melissa decided not to think about it.

Now she needed to get a move on if she was going to fit in her radical new haircut. She had to dress and pack for her supposed dance and weekend away, find the clipping she had cut out of *Modern Woman* showing the desired pixie cut, and get out of the house without arousing suspicion. Her aunt and uncle were going to the country too, and would not be back until Sunday night, so the weekend opened up in front of her, a vista of unaccustomed freedom – and temptation. But Aunt Melinda was ten years younger than Sarah, and not so easily bamboozled.

'What are you up to, Melissa?' she asked.

'Nothing at all. Just off to the country.'

'Sussex?'

'Yes, Sussex. But first I must get my hair done, and then I must catch the train from Victoria. I'm meeting the girls there and we're having lunch first. Carinda Seymour is wearing the York emeralds, and we've promised to sit close to her to protect her from thieves. She always wears them for the journey, with her neck wrapped in a silk scarf to cover them up. These nooves are frightfully well off, so well worth parading the family jewels for, if you've got them.' She chattered on, hoping to distract her aunt who was looking at her beadily, romance detectors on full alert.

'Well, just be careful, that's all.'

'Oh, don't worry. I'm sure I can detect a jewel thief a mile off.'

'Hmmm,' murmured Aunt Melinda.

Melissa clattered off back up the attic stairs to her little room, reached her overnight bag down from the top of the wardrobe – not that she would need it, she told herself. She had better take a party dress so she picked one at random and folded it round some sandals wrapped in a school shoe bag. It was so hot there might be sun-bathing opportunities, and she decided to see if she could find a two-piece bathing suit in the King's Road.

Her scent, make-up in a mini vanity case, toothbrush (wouldn't do to leave it in the bathroom), a cardigan for if it got chilly, and then – what the hell – a big jumper, pedal-pushers, socks and sneakers for a proper country weekend. She hesitated over nightie and clean pants. Would Aunt Melinda look under her pillow? She stuffed them in just in case.

She dressed herself in a sleeveless sky blue shift, and slipped flat pumps on to her feet. She put her confirmation string of pearls around her neck and looked in the mirror. Did she dare cut all her hair off? She flicked it around her shoulders, as if to say goodbye. It wasn't a very interesting colour, light brown, but in the sun it shone with fair highlights. She was tired of sitting under the dryer, curling and back combing. The pixie cut looked effortless in comparison.

Was Munty the kind of man who liked a girl to wear make-up? He didn't seem to object to Lydia, and she was caked in pan-stick, with false eyelashes, eyeliner and pale lips. Melissa fished in her vanity case and found her mascara. She licked the brush and scrubbed it on the black pigment, opening her eyes wide and pulling down her mouth. As she brushed the colour on to her pale lashes, it developed her eyes like a photograph in a chemical bath, gradually framing the grey irises. She stopped and chucked the little black box back into the case. A quick dab of her new scent Fidji and she was ready to leave.

Slinging her bags over her shoulder, she let herself out and walked away from the world she knew. A gulf had opened up, leaving the parents stranded on the other side, with their stuffy ideas about sex, clothes, hair and things being 'done' or 'not done' or just 'common'. 'Common' often looked like the best fun of all.

She trotted up Park Walk towards the King's Road. Chelsea mummies in Hermès headscarves, and Saturday morning husbands with regulation haircuts, were replaced by mini-skirted dolly birds and their long-haired guys in tight trousers and trendy boots. The very smell of the air changed, from Miss Dior and Virginia tobacco to sweet and strange exotic smells she didn't recognise. Her contemporaries seemed like the larvae of a different species. How could they possibly grow up to wear scarves and have children, Rovers, wisteria and Agas?

She nipped into a boutique called By Appointment and picked up a two-piece bathing suit, skimpy enough to be called a bikini, in navy blue with big white spots. Then it was time to lose her schoolgirl hair.

An hour later, washed and glossy with fashionably cut feathers all around her face, she dashed across the road to the Chelsea Potter. Her heart thumped. She didn't like going into pubs because men looked. Even a young pub like the Chelsea Potter, which was full of groovy chicks, could be daunting. She took a deep breath and plunged through the swing door, hoping desperately that Munty was already there.

'Melissa!'

It was him, thank goodness. Propelled on a wave of bravado, she had not quite taken into consideration the cost of deceiving her parents on her own nerves, and trembled.

'Hello, Munty,' she cried. 'How are you?'

'Fine. Like a drink before we set off?'

He already had a pint.

'Thanks, I'll have a Campari and soda,' she replied, thinking this would make her look sophisticated. She didn't know what to ask for in pubs, and had never tasted it, but it was a reassuring bright red in the advertisements, so was probably sweet and innocuous.

The drink arrived in a tall glass with a couple of cubes of ice and a slice of orange, looking delicious and refreshing. She took a good gulp as she was hot from rushing.

'Ugh,' she said, putting her hand over her mouth. 'It's so bitter.'

As soon as she said it, she wished she hadn't, and she looked in dismay up into Munty's face. He was smiling and then his lips were on hers and she melted.

'Disgusting stuff, I hate it,' he said. 'Let's get you something else. Would you like a Coke?'

It was all getting too much for her.

'Can we go?'

'Good idea, I'll just swallow this,' and Munty tipped his pint into his throat, snatched up her overnight bag and swung her out of the pub door into the sunshine.

'The car's parked in Flood Street. Come on.' He seized her hand in his and set off. The bright summer air warmed her bare legs, and her heart went hippety hop as she rushed along with him as if in a madcap film chase. Perhaps the Beatles would appear around the corner like in *Help!*

The car was an MG. She was popping with excitement, remembering in theory how to get into a low car in a short skirt without exposing her knickers, but not sure of the practice. Munty held the door open, having flung her bag in the back. Trusting to the strength of her thighs, she pressed her knees together and lowered her bottom into the leather bucket seat, arriving with only a very slight bump.

Then she swung her legs in sideways, still keeping her knees pressed together. Munty closed the door, and undid the catches on the canvas roof, folding it and strapping it down behind the vestigial back seat. He got in beside her and reached over, opening the glove compartment and pulling out a mauve chiffon square like a magician.

'You might need this,' he said. 'Your hair looks terrific, by the way.'

He folded the scarf into a triangle and tied it over her head, crossing the ends under her chin and taking them around the back of her neck. Then he pulled on the two ends to bring her face closer to his. The scarf tightened. Her eyes widened, but then he was kissing her again before pulling away and tying the scarf under her chin. She must have imagined the pressure as it loosened immediately.

The kiss made her bloom and blossom under his touch. Excited and pleased with where she was and what she was doing, she sat back. He started the engine and they were off, turning right on to the King's Road and roaring up towards Sloane Square.

'There are some dark glasses in there as well,' he said, and she reached into the glove compartment. She'd been worried that her eyes would start to stream and she'd end up looking like Chi-Chi the panda at the Zoo.

With a great gasp of pleasure, she felt she had arrived in the real London at last, spinning up the King's Road in a smart sports car, her hair short and chic, being admired and envied by the young crowd on the pavement. Not the stuffy old London of debs and their mums, ghastly Guards officers and frightful girls who looked over your shoulder for a rich husband. Munty took his hand off the wheel to hold hers, dotting the i in her happiness.

Nine

Munty
June 1966

Wondering what he had let himself in for, never having invited a girl anywhere further than a London restaurant, Munty had gone to Freddie for a briefing on how to deal with a day – or weekend should it develop into that – away with Melissa. Freddie had been quite specific, although he had snorted when Munty had said with a pained expression that he was looking for a wife not an easy lay.

'First of all, Munty, do her parents know where she's going?'

'I don't know.'

'You'd better find out. These over-protected girls can be the wildest. For goodness sake, Munty, you old stick. No need to get married to get into her knickers.'

'That's not what I want, Freddie. I know I can have that, but Melissa's not that kind of girl.'

'You'd be surprised. They're all that kind of girl these days.' Freddie rolled his eyes, a remembering smile spreading across his thin face as he seemed to lose focus. Munty let him have his moment.

'OK, Freddie. Listen.'

Munty hesitated. It was difficult to reveal the depths of his inexperience to the worldly Freddie Duggan. Freddie had the same skinny, ferrety quality as the young Frank Sinatra, and Munty was never sure if he liked him or not. They had been at school together, but Freddie was in the form below. Living off his P&Q earnings now and always in debt, Freddie was after a rich wife, but with no house to offer her, only the peculiar title of Lady Frederick Duggan. Munty shrugged. He knew more about all this titled stuff now, but it still surprised him that a woman might want to be called Lady Fred for the rest of her life and live with naughty Freddie, whose idea of a long-term relationship was about a week.

Munty remembered that at school Freddie wasn't averse to working off his sex drive on willing boys as well. It had offended him, this easy sex some of the fellows went in for. Surreptitious embraces in the woods, down by the lake. If you were caught, you were sacked, but the masters never went down there.

Boys did nothing for Munty. He had no interest in the groping and kissing that went on. The skinny white bodies in the communal showers aroused no physical response in him whatsoever. He once plucked up the courage to ask Freddie about this habit that had seemed so normal at school, but in the outside world was illegal and disgusting.

'Oh God, Munty, you're *so* middle class,' drawled Freddie.

What he heard made him heartily glad he had never been to prep school. Some of the prep schools sounded to him like vile dens of vice, where masters with an unsavoury interest in children introduced the boys to things they should have known nothing about. At one prep school, a feeder for Armishaw's, even the former headmaster was known to be a pederast. He was notorious for inviting his chosen victims to his study after lights out for 'strawberries and cream'.

The older boys did what they could to protect the younger ones of the type that he liked, white skinned and blond, but it was so bad that the governors believed the evidence and Mr Edgeburton was quietly retired. This seemed to be the origin of a lot of what went on at Armishaw's. Only a tiny minority stayed 'that way' once in the outside world. And they all said they hated 'queers', which they didn't seem to associate with the stuff they got up to at school. The floorwalkers he knew at P&Q who were 'that way' appeared to him to be brave, risking prison and public shame. It was well known that pretty policemen hung around in men's lavatories to trap the unwary, and even a fellow peer had gone to prison in the Fifties. If it was illegal and they still were uninterested in women, surely it was natural to them? Tough though. He felt sorry for them.

Was he a bit underpowered in comparison to his friends? Living in a small house under the eye of his mother, he had suppressed that side of himself out of shame. She seldom let him out of her sight, clinging to him as a reminder of the man and marriage that had gone. Escaping to Armishaw's had been an enormous relief. Being with boys and men day and night was alarming, the noise, the smell, the lack of privacy. Gradually he'd relaxed, the tense vigilance melting away.

From being quiet and retiring to begin with at Armishaw's, Munty began to imitate the rushing starts, loud bangs and impulsive plunges of his peers. It helped to conceal his uncertainty and shyness. When he came home, it was hard to rein his limbs back in. It didn't help that he had also grown to over six foot in the space of a year, so he was never quite sure where he ended. His mother had ornaments, small tables covered with lace cloths, fragile, tinkly things that were begging to be sent flying. At home he had to shrink himself down, and creep around leaving a lot of sea room in order not to break anything. When he forgot there was always a crash and tears. He associated women with tension, fragility and grief, but also a kind of businesslike independence. Outside the home, his mother was a very different person.

Her second marriage had undoubtedly made her happier and more relaxed at home. His stepfather was a very quiet presence, and Munty didn't have much to do with him, even after he moved in. He was relieved by the decrease in responsibility for his mother's emotions that Reg's presence brought. The clinging focus on every detail of his life dropped away and he had had some privacy at last. Leaving Eastbourne for good had been so much easier as his mother had Reg to keep her company.

Freddie had advised Munty to hire a soft top MG from a small garage that he knew, and to obtain a scarf and sunglasses for Melissa's comfort. And now there she was, sitting demurely beside him, the scarf tied around her head, keeping her new short hair under control, the sunglasses balanced on her small nose. He'd prepared with military precision. There were blankets on the back seat, a camping stove with a little tank of butane, a kettle to make tea and a large hamper of food and drinks to keep them going. He hadn't bought the French letters that Freddie had also recommended.

'It's not going to be a dirty weekend, Freddie. I told you. It may not be a weekend at all.'

Freddie had just smiled his own secret lascivious smile.

They stopped at a pub on the way for a late lunch, and arrived in the bright afternoon, entering the grounds between two dilapidated lodges with boarded-up windows at the bottom of the drive. As they swung around the curve, the long low pink brick façade, with its grey cornerstones and crenellations, confronted them, arched windows shining in the sun.

Melissa gasped.

Turning to him and taking his arm, she said, 'Do you come here often?' and then giggled. Munty laughed down at her.

'I've only been here once before. With my mother. We came to have a look long before the Army gave it back last year. They hadn't used the house since 1946 and it was all closed up. Since they left, the trustees have installed a caretaker who lives in the North Lodge, but there was no one there then, so we couldn't get inside. We just walked around the grounds a bit and peered through the windows. It's new to me too. It's nice, isn't it?'

'Is that true?'

'Is what true?' He replied, bewildered by her change of tone.

'That you've never been inside before.'

'I wouldn't have said it if it wasn't true.'

He was slightly hurt, but then realised she had a point. He looked down at her to reassure her, and saw she was anxious. He kissed her lightly on the lips and said, 'You've got quite an imagination.'

'It's just that some people might say that kind of thing to make some sort of impression.'

'Oh, I see what you mean,' Munty said. 'Oddly enough, it's completely true. I have never explored inside before. We just need to go to the North Lodge and pick up the key from Mr Stokes.'

They drove around the side of the house and up another drive overshadowed with birches and beeches coming into full leaf. The verges were bosky with grass and cow parsley, and Melissa took great breaths of the delicious air.

'I love it here,' she said. He just glanced at her and then seemed to concentrate on negotiating the car through the drive, narrowed with springing undergrowth.

'There it is,' he said.

The lodge was overgrown with ivy and hidden by saplings that grew right up to the walls between the older trees, next to a gate that looked jammed shut and overgrown. There was something dank and unappealing about the air just there.

'I'll stay in the car,' said Melissa.

Munty jumped out and went to the door, knocking. It was opened quickly, there was a brief conversation, and Munty came back holding a bunch of keys in his hand. Then he was forced to reverse the car all the way back to the house as there was nowhere to turn.

The last time Munty had seen Castle Hey was a dead November day, chilly and still. Rain had fallen, pitting the small lake. The trees shone black and dripping, seeming to close in on the house. Everything was overgrown and tired, the paint peeling off rotten window frames.

What a difference the sunshine made. Everything sparkled and the trees had burst into an electric firestorm of acid green leaves. The house itself glowed a soft pink – a Strawberry Hill Gothick pavilion. There were two floors of ogee-arched windows along the south front, the edge of its roof deckled with frivolous crenellations in pale grey limestone gilded with lichen. The silvery slate roof, planted with tall and twisting brick chimneys, rose steeply behind.

A well-grown buddleia sprang from the porch roof, and some of the windows were boarded up. But the house was tucked away enough to have avoided vandalism, and no one had broken in. Any remaining furniture and pictures were in storage, at least those that had not been sold to pay death duties. That was something else he needed to take seriously now. His mother's parents were prepared to give him his share of their eventual legacy whenever he wanted it, and this would provide seed capital for Castle Hey.

It wasn't a fortune, but it was enough to get things started. He knew his grandparents had made a good thing from supplying all the camps up on the South Downs in the run up to D-Day, and had no particular use for the money themselves. The house was definitely not self-supporting now all the land was sold off.

He'd asked Melissa to go away with him on a whim which was unlike him given his usual anxious planning. But then Melissa had stepped into his life by chance, halting and shy – he 'd had no suffocating sense of being pursued and trapped. Her reappearance at Queen Charlotte's so soon afterwards seemed like some kind of delightful fate. As they climbed out of the car her eyes seemed extra wide open as she looked about her. She'd told him she loved old houses and she appeared completely unlike the kind of society girl he was used to but didn't much care for. Those girls would have thought a great big dilapidated house one great big bore unless it came with a very large income.

The trustees had been patient but had written regularly asking if he'd managed to make a decision. As he watched her the girl and the house began to tangle themselves up in his heart. Both longed for, both feared. This was an unusual sensation, to want something so much that he was prepared to do anything in his power to get it. He was not quite sure what his power was. He just prayed this visit would be a success. He slipped an arm around Melissa's waist for reassurance, confident that she had not rejected a single advance so far but he was absolutely determined not to go too far. One of the things he liked about her was her innocence. She cuddled up to him, standing there on the muddy gravel in her little flat pumps, her head only just topping his shoulder.

'It's lovely, Munty,' she sighed. 'Absolutely beautiful. Yes, it's a bit tatty, but I'm sure you could do something with it.'

'It is lovely, isn't it? Shall we have a look inside?'

He opened the door with the big key, and they were in a small outer hall with a dusty beige velvet curtain hanging on brass rings right in front of them. Pushing it aside they found themselves in a large double-height hall that took up at least six of the windows in the façade. On one side, pushed against the wall, was an old sedan chair, but the rest was empty, the flagstone floor grubby and the walls rubbed and tired, painted a poisonous shade of green below the dado rail and cream above. It was still and silent, and the air was chilly and stale after the sunlit breeze outside. Munty held Melissa a little closer as they stepped together across the threshold, warily, like deer leaving the shelter of a forest.

'I think I need my cardigan,' said Melissa, pulling away from him and going back through the curtain and out of the front door. He stared around.

'My house,' he murmured.

The scale of the task ahead daunted him. But it was beautiful, the lovely height of the ceiling, the little Gothick arches around the top of the wall in place of a cornice, the pretty shape of the windows, all gave him pleasure. It didn't seem grand and frightening, but rather feminine. He wanted to rescue it. At either end of the hall were double doors pulled shut, and two doors also led from the back wall. He went to the front door to fetch the bunch of keys, thinking some of the doors within the house might be locked, just as Melissa returned, pulling on a white cardigan.

'Shall we explore?' He took her hand, and hesitated.

'Let's try in there first,' she said, leading him to the left.

They found a series of reception rooms, following one from the other, connected by double doors, and empty apart from some grey-painted metal desks and filing cabinets. Behind the reception rooms, with their antique wallpaper sadly damaged by pin holes, were the kitchen, pantry, sculleries, wine cellars, laundries and larders, reaching back into a courtyard, surrounded by repulsive-smelling sheds. Munty suspected they had been used as latrines, and was annoyed by the lack of care the Army had taken with his property.

To the right was a flat rectangle covered in brick rubble. 'What was that?' Melissa asked.

'There was another whole Victorian wing, destroyed by a German bomber discharging its load before it headed out to sea. Good thing too, the house is quite big enough as it is.'

Behind the rubble were the stables. Built of the same pink

brick as the main house, and surrounding a courtyard, they boasted a Gothick clock tower with what looked like a bullet hole pocking the enamel clock face. Melissa was quiet, and Munty wondered what she was thinking as they walked around holding hands. In one stall was a little governess cart which made her exclaim with pleasure, in another a rusting old Austin Seven which did not elicit the same joyful reaction.

They wandered back inside and up the main stairs to the first floor, which they found behind the right-hand door in the back wall of the hall. Munty hoped Melissa would enjoy the adventure of exploring the house. He wondered if they might stay the night as it was getting late and he remembered she had brought an overnight bag with her. He liked the idea of being there to protect her. Freddie's laughter echoed in his mind, but he dismissed it.

Most of the bedrooms were empty but for dust and sunlight, until they came to the main suite. The door was locked, and Munty had trouble getting the key to turn. Inside was an extraordinary room, rising into the roof above the porch and looking out over the lake. In the centre was the most enormous bed either of them had ever seen, with carved posts twisting like barley sugar. It was covered in dust sheets and Munty stepped forward to pull one away. There were no draperies, but the mattress was there, and they could see the canopy, carved with Gothick decoration like a church screen.

'What a strange bed.' Melissa walked towards it, running her hands over the writhing pillars. 'I'm not sure I like it. It looks like it belongs in a Hammer Horror film.'

'I think it's beautiful, and it does go with the house. Must

119

have been too big to take out of here. I wonder why they didn't dismantle it.' Munty crossed the room and opened one of the triptych of windows, letting in air and sunlight. On the other side of the room was an Army cot with a thin grey mattress covering its rusty mesh base.

Melissa was quiet, looking at the large room and the huge bed.

Ten

Melissa
June 1966

'Do you know?' Munty was saying. 'It's getting late, I think we may have to stay the night after all. Would you be OK with that?'

He hesitated.

'I promise I won't pounce.'

They would be arriving back in London in the middle of the night, even if they set off quite soon, and she hadn't ever planned in her own mind to do so. She'd burnt her boats when she had told her mother and her aunt that she was going to a dance outside London.

'I think you're right, Munty.' It made her nervous to say it. Did she trust him to save her from herself? She was confused by her own feelings.

She confined herself to saying: 'We can camp somewhere in the house, can't we? You've got blankets and stuff?'

Munty nodded uncertainly, so Melissa took charge.

'We can think about all that later. I'd like some tea now, please,' she said, backing out of the room. 'Only, Munty, what about washing and so on?'

'Damn, I should have turned on the stopcock when we arrived. I'll go and find it. No hot water, so no baths. Look, Melissa, it is a bit Spartan. We can go and stay in Rye if you like,

121

we don't have to stay here and rough it.'

It had been so daring of her to come all this way with a man. It was one thing to stay with him in seclusion and privacy, but quite another to go to a hotel in public. What if he wanted them to be Mr and Mrs Smith or something? Better to stay here, hidden away. Lying to Mummy was wrong, but so far there was nothing to be ashamed of and she meant to keep it that way. Looking out of the window, she noticed that evening had begun to creep towards the house, trailing chill across the grass. Mist lifted from the surface of the lake.

'What about finding a small room downstairs and lighting a fire?' she said brightly. 'We could boil a kettle on that little butane stove and have some tea. Did you bring cake or biscuits?'

Munty smiled at her hopeful face. 'Yes, chocolate cake. An American recipe called Devil's Food. The pastry chefs are always experimenting. I hope you'll like it.'

'Never heard of it, sounds gorgeous.' There was a lot to be said for going out with a grocer.

They went downstairs and found a small room they hadn't noticed before, tucked away off the hall. To their joy it even contained a sagging old sofa, and some packing cases they could use as tables.

'I'll go and find the stopcock, and bring the hamper in here. This can be our headquarters.'

Munty headed for the service areas.

Excited, Melissa went through to the kitchen to see if she could find any kind of cloth or duster. There was an old dish towel hanging from the range, and she picked it up. It was stiff, moulded to the shape of the rail, but it would do. She considered whether they could get the range itself going, but then decided an open fire and the butane stove would be more manageable. She tried the tap, and with a choking cough and whistling of pipes, a brown trickle emerged. She left it turned on, and went into the larders to explore further.

She couldn't help thinking they could pull all these little rooms out and make a nice big modern kitchen.

A sensation swept over her in a rush of coolness and heat. This beautiful house and a man who appeared to like her. She was only eighteen, but that wasn't all that young, was it? Could this be it? The thing that was meant to happen, where you fell in love and got married and lived happily-ever-after? The thing that was meant to solve your life? If that was what this was, then there was nothing to be ashamed of at all.

But what if Munty thought she was too easy, coming down to his house in the country and lying to her parents. She'd hardly struggled, gone over like a skittle in fact. Oh dear. But then this was all very different from what she knew of vile seducers. Wasn't it more plying you with Madeira and tipping you backwards on to a chesterfield sofa? Tea and cake seldom featured in the rapist's armoury in any book she had sneaked under the covers at night and read by torchlight.

Munty's arrangements seemed more calculated to be friendly and welcoming than seductive and scary. And he'd been so nice. Nice enough for her to trust him overnight?

Back in the kitchen, the water was now running clear, and she soaked the cloth, squeezing it out tightly. She heard Munty coming down the worn brick passage, and called out to him:

'Water's on. I'm just going to wipe up the worst of the dust in that room, so we don't sneeze.'

'Thank you. I've brought plates, cutlery, glasses but stupidly no teacups. Can you have a quick look in the cupboards and see if there's anything here? The Army might have left something. All the family china is in storage I think.'

Melissa had a look, and located some thick white pottery mugs in a cupboard. Having given them a wash, she also found a bucket under the sink. She'd better change out of her pretty blue frock if she wasn't to get into a mess.

She went out to the car to get her things. The lake shone pewter in the gloaming. Small clouds, grey on top, apricot underneath, floated in the duck-egg sky above a sinking sun which flung primrose light from the horizon. Cold air blew off the lake and wrapped itself around her ankles as she lifted her bag out of the car.

She located a large downstairs lavatory, and went and locked herself in, changing into a long-sleeved shirt, pedal pushers, socks, sneakers and the big floppy jumper with holes in the elbows that had belonged to Daddy. She immediately felt better, warm and safe. She caught a glimpse of her new bikini at the bottom of her bag. Perhaps she would have a swim in the lake if it was hot again tomorrow. In the sunlight it had looked so inviting, with the pontoon stretching out into the middle all ready to jump off.

Leaving the lavatory, she detected a delicious smell of wood smoke creeping towards her. Anxiously, she wondered when the chimneys had last been swept. She trotted towards their 'headquarters' and burst through the door, saying, 'Munty, what if the chimney catches fire?'

'Oh, don't worry, it's very unlikely to happen with just one fire. And I'm sure the chimneys were used during the war. Being the Army, they would have swept them.'

Reassured, she flopped on to the sofa, Munty's appreciative eyes upon her.

The kettle he had brought with him was just about to sing on the butane stove. The cake stood on the plate, darkly inviting.

'Mummy always says be prepared when you go out of town. English summers can be very tricky. Even when I'm going to a ball I always take a cloak and jumpers for the next day.'

'Sensible woman.'

He cut the dark squashy cake, and passed her a slice. He used little muslin sachets of P&Q tea in the pot. She had never seen them before – Mummy always used loose tea leaves – but it tasted fine. She bit heartily and appreciatively into her chocolate cake, which was quite unlike her mother's in taste, colour, texture and every other way.

'I love this,' she said. It was all so new and different, so happy, so daring, so exactly suited to her desire for a change. She was committed, she had to stay the night. He took nightlights out of the hamper and arranged them along the stone chimneypiece. Soon the room was glowing as it would have done in its heyday.

'The champagne isn't going to be all that cold,' Munty said. 'I think I'll go into the village to see if the pub can give us some ice. You'll be OK here by yourself, won't you? I don't think there are any ghosts.'

Melissa lay back luxuriously on the dusty old sofa, sipping her hot tea and nibbling her delicious cake. Even if there were ghosts, they would surely just be benign members of Munty's family.

'I'll be fine.'

He left and she could hear the engine of the MG starting up outside the window. It was odd to be in the big old dark house by herself. She wasn't quite sure what to do, so she tried relaxing on the sofa, but the desire to explore was very strong. She took a nightlight from the chimneypiece, put it on a plate and walked out through the door into the hall.

Her shadow appeared huge and stooped on the walls beside her. Now Munty wasn't there, she indulged in the idea that this glorious tatty space was hers to do with as she wished. Deep in her genes lay the sure commercial instincts of Big George Bourne. She knew from hearing her parents talking that lots of grand people were so broke that they had got rid of their big houses – pulled them down, handed them over to the National Trust or sold them to be schools or lunatic asylums. No one could afford to keep these old places going any more.

She had been to dances in houses that had been hired just for the night, both in London and in the country. Maybe smart people who had sold their 'big house' would like to hire Castle Hey for dances, weddings, parties, even family weekends? It was an exciting idea, and she walked through the big empty rooms thinking about how it would work. Munty owned it outright. It was just a question of getting it into show condition.

There were four reception rooms on the ground floor. Upstairs she counted eight bedrooms on the first floor – Castle Hey was not big enough for a school or other institution. There was only one bathroom. There needed to be more, and more modern plumbing. Her nerve failed her then and she couldn't face venturing further to see what was above. She was ashamed of letting her imagination run away with her too.

She heard the car coming back, and tripped down the stairs with her candle to greet him in the hall.

'Isn't this fun,' he said, clutching a big bag of ice. 'Let's get the champagne chilled.'

She followed him to the fire. He plunged two bottles of champagne into the bag of ice, then offered her olives and peanuts. She said she'd wait for the drinks, and they sat quietly watching the flames.

'So, Melissa, what do you think of the house?'

Not 'my house', she noticed.

'I think it's ravishing. I love it. I love how pink it is, and that it isn't too big. I can see it being beautiful when you've done it up.'

'Good,' he said, settling back with his arm around her shoulders. She turned her face towards him, knowing he would kiss her. They remained locked together for some time.

Does this mean I love him? she wondered. Was it wrong to let someone kiss you if you didn't love them? She liked him, and appreciated what he was doing for her. But she had no desire to die for him, for instance.

Munty pulled himself away from her and went over to the champagne, twisting the cork off with an expert flick and pouring the chilled wine into glasses he conjured from the hamper.

Sipping it, she decided she was in heaven. An ecstatic excitement boiled up inside her, but she knew from experience not to express it or let it overwhelm her. She had a lump in her throat, and her eyes filled with tears. He handed her a stuffed olive and settled himself back down beside her, not noticing her agitation.

'Melissa, I can't think of anywhere I would rather be, or anyone I would rather be with right now,' he said. 'You're the most lovely girl to come here and be with me in this old wreck. I don't think I could have faced up to it without you.'

Melissa took a big slug of her cold fizzing champagne, and turned her face into his shoulder to prevent him from seeing her flush. She breathed slowly to calm herself down. She didn't want to say anything, as excitement threatened to push her over the edge. What did he mean, he couldn't have faced it without her? If he was speaking the truth, and there was no reason to think he wasn't, she had made a difference to him. Shy Melissa, with her difficult foot and her unpredictable, overwhelming feelings. A real grown-up man was grateful to her. If he wasn't to be frightened off, she had to get a grip on herself.

Eleven

Munty
June 1966

Munty propped himself on one elbow and watched Melissa skipping away from him towards the glittering water. Her neck, revealed by the new short haircut, was slender, holding up her fair ruffled head. He was moved by her back view, its exposure to him and to the house behind with its rows of windows silvery and blanked out by the sunlight. She had pulled away, hot from his kisses and the noonday sun, and leapt up laughing, saying she wanted to cool herself in the lake. Jumping over rank tussocks, running down to the muddy edge, she squeaked when her bare feet hit hidden pebbles in the grass.

The sun shone into his eyes, blinding him. He pulled the brim of his Panama hat forward the better to appreciate her figure in the two-piece bathing suit. Freddie had dragged him off the year before to see a film called *How to Stuff a Wild Bikini*, where Buster Keaton, playing the world's most unlikely witch doctor, conjured a shapely girl out of pink smoke into just such a spotty skimpy bikini. He supposed that was what the two-piece was called these days. Whatever its name, he found he had to roll on to his belly on the blanket as he watched, ashamed of his reaction. He remembered the almost naked girls in the film dancing on the beach, and forced his feelings firmly down.

Melissa was a nice girl, and they'd only just met. Anything more than kissing was out of the question.

Those shift dresses concealed curves and, slender though she was, her waist was highly indented like a violin, only smooth and white. Her bottom stuck out, rounded and pert, encased in the tight-fitting blue knickers covered with big white spots. Her smooth white thighs, delicate knees and slender ankles were perfection in his eyes. He wanted her more than anything he had ever wanted in his life. In that moment he realised that he was in love with her.

She was a doctor's daughter, not an heiress at all, but the idea began to build that they could work out the conundrum of the house together. Before he hadn't had a clue where to start. She seemed so enthusiastic, describing all kinds of clever ideas she'd read about, in her breathless hurrying voice. He was touched by how careful she was to say 'you could' and 'your' house. They discussed the dashing Earl of Bankworth's water-skiing demonstrations on his lake, the wild animals roaming the park at Tillingham Hall, and Lord d'Ingham's giant dolls' house on display to tourists. All rather desperate measures to keep the property in the family – and the family in the property.

'Whatever works is worth doing though, isn't it?' she turned her questioning face up to his.

He'd do anything to make her happy. He found himself shrugging off the passivity that always led him to trickle into the path of least resistance. This sense that he could achieve anything if only she was near thrilled him. More honourable too to marry for love and passion, and not for money to mend the roof.

He glanced round at his house to take his mind off her

delicious body and the painful urgency he was feeling. Castle Hey stood behind them in the sunlight, glowing pink.

Like her lips, he thought.

The big arched oak front door stood slightly open. By half closing his eyes, he could transform the façade into something perfect. When he looked properly, he could see broken windows, sagging guttering, slates missing from the steeply pitched roof, one chimney snapped off halfway up. A near ruin and a big one.

They'd spent the night fully clothed and covered in blankets on the vast four-poster. Holding her warm body close to his, even hampered by fabric, had filled him with a visceral aching longing. In the end, unable to bear it, he'd slipped off the high bed, leaving her asleep, rolling himself in one of the picnic blankets to try and sleep on the Army cot. He'd surprised himself by waking up refreshed with the sun streaming through the dusty windows.

Calmed, he looked round again at Melissa, to see her tiptoeing along the old pontoon. Her hands were flexed as she kept her balance on the wooden slats.

'Melissa,' he called. 'I'm not sure it's safe. And the water'll be very cold.' She'd said she was just going to dip in a toe and maybe paddle.

He'd better swim himself to cool down. He took a deep breath and stood up, all evidence of his feelings for her firmly suppressed by thoughts of dry rot and leaking roofs, and walked across the grass on to the pontoon. He averted his eyes from Melissa's body.

There was a scream, a crack and a splash. He glanced up and she'd vanished. The rotten wood sagged under his feet, and he lowered himself to his knees, crawling towards the gaping hole where she had disappeared. He told himself he wasn't too worried, convinced she would simply pop up smiling having swum the five or so feet to the side of the pontoon. When she didn't instantly reappear, he stared down through the hole into the shadowed water, his heart hammering. As it became still in the breathless morning air, it revealed her green face looking up at him, eyes wide open, mouth clamped shut. The rest of her was invisible in the dark. He realised with a sense of dread that he had no idea how deep the lake was and quickly lowered himself full length on to the slats, plunging his arm into the water to grab at her, but she was out of his reach.

He shuffled to the edge of the pontoon, lowered himself into the freezing water and swimming under the slats tried to find her in the shadows. Then he saw an arm like a pale fish in the green light and grabbed at it throwing himself backwards. She shifted towards him but something appeared to be trapping her legs. He wrenched at her until she jerked free then kicked out dragging her by the arm. Daylight appeared and her head was above the surface. Air whooshed out of her. Eyes wide with shock she stared at him. It could only have been seconds but it felt like hours.

'Melissa! What happened? Are you OK?'

He cupped her chin in his hand and swam with her to where he could gain a foothold. Lifting her in his arms, oblivious of the broken mussel shells that slashed at his feet and the slimy mud, he carried her up the bank and over to the blanket. She lay quiet in his arms. Then she turned her head away and retched out the lake water in a thin stream. She began to cry.

'What happened, Melissa? Do you know?'

Hugging herself tightly and turning away, she ignored him.

'You're OK now, darling. It must have been a shock.' He trailed off looking at her white back goose-pimpled now. He tried to wrap the blanket over her and take her in his arms. She shrugged him off, wiping her face. He sat not knowing what to do or say. It had happened so fast. One minute bliss, the next disaster.

'Why didn't you tell me it was rotten?' she muttered.

'I didn't know. I did tell you to be careful. What exactly happened? Why didn't you swim out from under the pontoon?'

'It collapsed under me and I just went in,' she snuffled into the blanket. 'Something grabbed my legs, maybe plants or weeds. I tried kicking but I couldn't get out. I was so frightened.'

She opened her mouth and to his horror began to howl. Her face went red, her eyes were screwed up. He stopped himself from recoiling.

'You're OK now though. I got you out.'

'My arm hurts. You pulled the skin.'

She rolled herself further into the old tartan blanket and lay there saying nothing. He sat letting the sun warm him and his heart slow down. In the quiet he was sure all would be well, that they could reach back and grab what had been there before.

She spoke in a dull monotone.

'I shouldn't be here.'

'What?'

'I lied to my parents. I shouldn't be here and that was the punishment. I should have been more careful. It was a stupid idea sneaking away with some man I don't even know. Wrong, wrong, wrong. Dirty and wrong.'

Munty was crushed. Some man? She seemed to be talking to

herself. Five minutes beforehand he had been ready to throw his whole life into the air for her, now he was repelled.

'It's my punishment and I deserved it. For lying, and buying this stupid bathing suit, and not doing what I was meant to be doing. I want to go home. Now.'

'OK, look, let's go up to the house and get ourselves sorted out. There's some food left.'

'No, I want to go now.'

'You'll need to get dressed, and then I'll drive you.'

'They mustn't see you. They mustn't know.'

'OK, I'll drop you nearby and you can say you were on the train.'

She stood up, pulling the blanket around her, and stumbled away over the rough ground, wriggling white partings in her short wet hair. He watched her wincing progress across the overgrown gravel sweep, and then followed her, defeated. The one time he'd tried to do something different, that was just for him, the first time he'd tried to approach the house as an equal, it had caused damage. Frightened the only girl he had ever liked. Been so flawed and rotten that it had nearly killed her. Better just to do what she wanted now. He would drive her to Dorking, and take the hire car back to London. Then what? He was chilled and sad.

Twelve

Melissa
December 1966

From the first step she took in her regulation shoes, adapted to support her foot, Melissa knew she had made a mistake. The smell of the wards sickened her, she had no sympathy for the patients and she hated the supercilious doctors. So different from Daddy.

Her fellow nurses seemed to be from a much better, braver species than her own. She cringed at their forthright manner with the patients and their unflinching compassion in the face of gangrenous bed sores, dirty bedpans, obscene demented old men and all the rest of it. She was so terribly tired after only three months that she moved through a fog, haunted by a putrid odour that never left her nostrils.

She was on night duty yet again. She never seemed to be off it, and now it was Christmas at St Saviour's and everyone else was having fun.

She was dozing when she started awake to hear suppressed laughter in the corridor, and then exaggerated hushing. A little light came through the porthole in the ward door. It opened slightly, and a houseman she didn't know looked in at her. With him were two of her off-duty fellow probationers.

'Hello, Melissa? We just came up from the first-years' party to see if you wanted a drink.'

The houseman waved a hip flask at her. For a moment she was tempted to take a swig of brandy, to inject a bit of life into her weary carcass. But she was terrified of the night sister, who roamed the corridors like a ravening beast seeking out slacking nurses to devour.

'Go away!' she hissed. 'It's time I did my round.'

She was on geriatrics again, and heartily sick of the old and decrepit. Handling their false teeth and getting them on and off the commode made her retch. She still managed laboriously to summon up the necessary wall of numb indifference, but it was getting harder and harder. The stink and misery were breaking it down. Things within her were disintegrating. She was frightened that everyone would begin to notice the gaping hole where she used to be.

Her compromised vocation vanished as her foot swelled, and it became so painful by the end of every day that she never went out any more. She crept back to her cell-like room in the Nurses' Home and lay on her bed, often waking up hours later still dressed, sweating and headachy.

She heard the nurses and doctor retreating down the corridor, and switched on her torch to check the ward.

At the back of her mind, she knew her parents had been anxious about her taking up nursing. They had worried about her club foot. The unusual cure that her parents had organised in America had been a success. The deformity was not extreme, so a few months of splints and plaster had meant she was toddling before her second birthday. The day Sarah had brought her home was still celebrated in the family with a cake, as her new birthday.

But her left foot was not strong enough to sustain her chosen career. Was she too proud to confess her mistake?

Her parents had never found out exactly where she had been that disastrous weekend. They appeared to be worried about her when she could hardly be bothered to go back to London afterwards and continue with her Season. She spent a lot of time in bed sleeping until it was time to move to St Saviour's and start her training in September.

She mopped at her face with her crumpled apron but then realised with horror that she couldn't stop crying. The tears flowed down her face in a stream and she had to fight hard with herself to prevent her mouth dropping open. The next thing she knew she was on the floor and the night sister was shaking her.

'Nurse Reeves? What's going on? What's the matter?'

She sat up groggily, the chair she had been sitting on beside her on the floor. 'I don't know,' she said, 'I think I must have fainted.'

'Well, we can't have that.' Sister groped in her apron pocket and brought out a small bottle which she thrust under Melissa's nose.

'Come on, sit up on the chair, you should have your head between your knees. Now, I'm just going to check the ward. We don't know how long you've been out.'

Melissa realised in that moment that this had to stop. She could not be a nurse, she was not a nurse, she hated every moment of it and her body had rebelled. She wasn't strong enough mentally or physically to do what her mother had done before her, and she was ashamed.

Sister was coming back: 'There's only an hour to the end of

your shift. I'll take over here. Go and get some rest, and report to Matron tomorrow.'

Melissa hauled herself to her feet, and limped along the endless corridors, down in the lift and across the road to the Home. In her room she collapsed on to the bed, kicking off her shoes and pulling the sheet and blankets over herself, grateful for the non-regulation eiderdown that Mummy had insisted she take with her, falling into sleep as down a mine shaft.

The next day she woke up in a kind of dreary peace. It wasn't going to be easy extricating herself, she had no idea what she was going to do next, but she knew that when she went to see Matron she would be resigning. Glancing at her alarm clock, she saw it was already two in the afternoon. Matron saw the night shift nurses between twelve o'clock and two thirty. She had to hurry. She stripped off the crumpled dress she was still wearing from the day before, brushed her hair, washed her face in the little basin in the room, and changed quickly into a fresh uniform. She pinned her cap to her head with white Kirby grips, thinking with guilty joy that this might be the last time she ever had to wear it.

'Come in,' Matron called out.

Melissa opened the door and went in, filled with a sense of release instead of the usual dread. Matron had the ability to make her feel like a worm, but not today.

'Ah, Nurse Reeves, sit down. I hear you fainted on night duty. Everything all right now?'

'Well, no, Matron.'

'What's the trouble?'

Melissa looked down at her reddened hands.

'I'm sorry, Matron, but I've changed my mind about nursing.'

'You've changed your mind? How long have you been with us? Can't be much more than three months. It's always tough to begin with while you get used to the hard work and the discipline. Like the Army. But you'll soon get into the swing of it.'

'I don't think I will. You see my talipes is playing up and I think I'll have to withdraw for that reason.'

'Ah,' said Matron, her cap bobbing as she looked at Melissa's notes, which she had removed from a file. 'It says here you passed all the tests and the doctors made the decision that you were fit for nursing in spite of your limited talipes. Are both your feet sore?'

'Well, yes.'

Matron seized on this. 'All nurses have sore feet to begin with. You soon get used to it.'

Melissa wanted to cry, she had been so sure her talipes, which she had never used as an excuse before for anything, would be her ticket out of this hell.

'My left foot is worse than my right. In fact at the end of day shifts it's agony, and it still hurts when I start in the mornings as well.'

Matron looked grave. 'You realise that if you withdraw now you'll have wasted precious limited National Health resources that would have gone towards training another girl with more backbone, don't you?'

Melissa was ashamed, but stuck to her guns. She could not go back into the ward. She wasn't sure what would happen, whether she would be sick or faint if she smelt that sweetish rotting old-people smell again. If necessary she would go AWOL.

'Matron, I'm simply not fit to be a nurse. It was a mistake, I believed I could be like my mother, but I can't. I'm sorry, but I'll have to hand in my resignation as of today.'

'Well, Miss Reeves, this is poor behaviour in my opinion. You can give a month's notice if you like, but I am not going to allow you to leave immediately.'

Desperation flooding her, Melissa stopped looking at her hands, and stared into Matron's face. She saw red skin, a fuzz of fur on the cheeks and chin, round tortoiseshell glasses and a large starched cap. The small mouth puckered with disapproval like a cat's bottom. She hated what she saw, for what it represented to her. Pain and disgust and suffering. She had no vocation to be a nurse, needed to go home that afternoon if she wasn't to collapse. The desperation gave her courage.

'Matron, I'm sorry but I have to leave today. I can't take any more. I need to go home and rest.'

'Look, I know it's tough to begin with. And you have had a longer stint than usual on geriatrics, which can test anyone's vocation. But it will be surgical next, and I'm sure you'll find that more to your taste.'

Melissa remembered her experience so far of wounds and dressings, and her stomach heaved.

'I don't think so, Matron. I just don't think I have the right kind of character for nursing.'

'What will your parents think? They may have to pay a fine for you, I'm afraid. Your father is a doctor? They will be very shocked, Miss Reeves, as am I.'

She waited. Melissa said nothing.

Matron gave up abruptly.

'I can't waste any more time on this. If you are determined, you had better go now. Pack up your room, leave the key with the Porter. Please leave my office, I'll need to organise cover for your shifts. I'm very disappointed, Miss Reeves. You are dismissed. I'm afraid this will go on your permanent record.'

Melissa stood up slowly. Her 'permanent record' meant nothing as it occurred to her that she was free. At once the pain and gloom dropped from her. She stretched her hand across the desk to Matron, who ignored it.

'Goodbye then, Matron. As I say, I am sorry. It was my mistake.'

'All jobs are difficult, Miss Reeves. I don't know what you think is out there for you that will be better. Shopgirls stand up all day, and don't have the satisfaction of helping their fellow man.'

Melissa turned away and began to leave the office.

'You were a debutante, weren't you? Wrong class, no use at all, fit for nothing but marriage.'

Matron's barbs did not find their mark. Melissa went back down the long green-painted corridor, her heart lightening with every step. She knew she would come crashing down again soon, but enjoyed for that moment the delicious sensation of being free. Free to go home and allow her mother and father to look after her again as they always had before.

'No more bedpans,' she crowed, pulling her cap off her head and chucking it in a bin as she passed by.

Back in the Nurses' Home she looked round her cell with new eyes. Why had she forced herself to stay in this place for so long?

It seemed bizarre now that she had given herself permission to go home to her comfortable bedroom. The sweet soft protected cocoon of her childhood beckoned.

She swept through the room, now a whirlwind of effectiveness, stuffing all her clothes into a suitcase and putting her uniform into the communal laundry basket at the end of the corridor. Someone else could have it. She didn't want it any more. The only bits she kept were her watch, and the belt with her mother's silver VAD buckle that she'd snipped off her black velvet cloak to restore to its original use. One last glance round at the room that had contained so much pain, tears and exhaustion and she was free. The suitcase was heavy, and she wondered whether to leave it in the Porters' Lodge and get it sent on, but then decided instead to take a taxi to Waterloo. She stopped at the Lodge window and rang the little bell. All the porters in the Nurses' Home were women for the sake of some long lost propriety, and Melissa recognised Mrs Edge.

She put her keys on the sliding tray, saying, 'I'm leaving, Mrs Edge. Can you take my keys?'

'Leaving, Miss Reeves? Why?'

'Nursing doesn't suit me. It's too tiring and my talipes can't take the pressure.'

Once again the excuse slipped from her mouth. She was sure her mother wouldn't have ever excused herself in that way. But then her mother never let herself get away with anything at all. It was no use trying to be like Mummy. She was herself and had to find her own way of doing things. And right now that meant not being a nurse or anything like it ever again.

'Oh, I am sorry, Miss Reeves.'

'Do you think you could get me a taxi? My foot is very painful.'

Once she had started, she couldn't stop. The foot, which the whole family had viewed as something that should never stop her from doing what she liked, was now proving to be useful.

'Poor you, miss. Of course.' And Melissa heard her dial a number and speak briefly, coming back to say the taxi would be there in five minutes. Melissa prayed no one she knew would walk through the Lodge, but it was mid-afternoon and everyone would be over in the wards, doing all the ghastly things that she would never have to do again. She tried to summon up the boost of relief that had carried her thus far, but found her heart was beating in guilty thuds.

Just as the discomfort was getting unbearable, she heard the sound of a taxi and watched through the glass doors as it drew up. Mrs Edge came out of the Lodge and insisted on helping her with her suitcase. She gathered up the various bags and scrambled in.

'Thank you, Mrs Edge. You've been a great help.'

As the taxi pulled away, she waved at the back of Mrs Edge's head, which seemed to be shaking from side to side with pitying disapproval. She sank back into the seat and tried to calm down as they chugged towards Waterloo.

She'd considered whether to call her parents from the station and ask to be picked up, but something held her back and she took a taxi at the other end as well. The driver left her bags and suitcase on the step. Melissa knocked but there was no answer. She went around to the surgery door but found that locked as well. Then she remembered that her father went out on his rounds on

Thursday afternoons. She wondered if she had a key and groped around in the bottom of her bag looking for one. She had been so sure someone would be there to let her in, to welcome her home. She'd imagined warmth, tea, sympathy, not locked doors. She went around via the garden to see if the back door was open and that too was locked.

At a loss she sat down on the porch bench to think. It was getting cold and dark, houses on the other side of the road were lit up and she saw people drawing curtains. Some had Christmas trees covered in fairy lights. Nobody came home. Melissa realised she had been foolish not calling her parents and making sure they were there. She began to cry as the chill seeped into her bones and a vicious little wind whipped around her ankles. She pulled her luggage and herself deeper into the porch and curled her legs up beside her on the bench leaning on a bag. So exhausted was she that in spite of the cold her head began to nod.

'Melissa? What are you doing here?' It was her mother, shaking her shoulder. 'You weren't meant to be coming home until after Christmas.'

She awoke, numb with cold, to see her parents standing over her, looking worried. She unwound herself and stood up, stumbling slightly, and saying, 'I'm sorry, but I couldn't stand it. I've resigned.'

Her parents didn't look as pleased and welcoming as she'd hoped.

'Well,' said her mother. 'We'd better get you into the warm. How long have you been here?'

'I took the three o'clock. What's the time now?'

'It's seven o'clock. Why didn't you call and let us know you were coming?'

'It was a bit spur of the moment.'

They had the front door open, and her father, looking grim, picked up her luggage and ushered her inside.

'Don't go to your room, it isn't ready for you. I've been giving it a good turnout with Mrs Lewis, so it's all upside down. You'd better go along to the spare room. There should be enough hot water for you to have a bath to warm yourself up.'

Melissa knew what she had been expecting – the kind of unconditional loving welcome that she had always had before. That her parents would instantly make everything all right again. Not this, being treated like an unexpected and not very welcome guest. Her mother bobbed forward with a kiss on the cheek, but Daddy didn't hug her as he usually did. She could see that they were not pleased with her and this was the very first time in her life she had ever experienced anything like it.

She moved towards the stairs looking back to see her unsmiling father carrying her suitcase and her mother gathering the scattered bags.

'You get warmed up and we can talk later,' she said. Melissa turned away and went along the upstairs passage to the spare room.

Thirteen

Melissa
April 1967

Dreaming the afternoon away, Melissa slouched on a chair behind the counter, her face resting on her cupped hands. There were few customers mid-afternoon, mid-week, to her relief. Anyone conceivably interested in Lord Groove's array of purple tie-dyed T-shirts, love beads, granny glasses, loon pants and fringed waistcoats was either stuck behind another counter, a typewriter or a desk. It had been a struggle for her, to begin with, to attract the customers' attention and sell them things. They all seemed so sophisticated and knowing, and she quite invisible and shy. She quailed at the thought of suggesting items that might suit them.

She was alone with her dreams and the slow passing of under-occupied time. Her boss, whom she delighted in her mind in calling 'your lordship', although his real name was Alan Smalls, expected her to spend the hours ripping open the outer seam of second-hand jeans he bought in bulk, and inserting colourful corduroy triangles to convert them into bell bottoms. The sewing machine was silent, a fly buzzed against the shop window and her eyelids drooped.

She wished she had something concrete to think about, some future in view. At least she was sitting down and the smell of joss sticks was better than bedpans.

Returning to live at home had not turned out as expected at all. There was no drifting back into the irresponsibility of her childhood. After the first chill, her parents had been kinder but a new brisk note had crept into their conversations. They asked her all the time what she was planning to do. Did she want to go to secretarial college or even retake her A Levels and go to university? They didn't mention nursing again and accepted that her foot had made it difficult for her. She was considering it but she wasn't drawn to any one subject. The idea of being a teacher or a secretary in some dull office afterwards filled her with horror.

She was also expected to take a full part in the family's domestic arrangements and not just the fun bits like cooking. Her mother had breezily told her that she wouldn't expect rent – this hadn't occurred to Melissa – but would require a good deal of cleaning and tidying in exchange for room and keep.

She found herself scrubbing the kitchen floor as an unpaid skivvy for her parents. Relations became strained quite quickly. She also had a queer suspicion she was in the way. She was amazed at the amount they went out, even for whole weekends, leaving her alone at home. They never invited her to join them.

The present seemed formless and uninteresting. All work, high tea, evenings in with the television or books or Scrabble, and hoovering, dusting, mopping and folding. Her brothers were still away at school. Even when they did come home they ignored her just as they always had. It was mutual though so didn't cause any further dismay.

She had always taken it for granted that her parents loved each other, but now she noticed how united they were, that her mother was essential to the smooth running of her husband's practice, as his office manager and receptionist.

Having shied away from it to begin with – her terror of the lake blocking her dreams – she found herself straying in her mind back to lovely sleeping Castle Hey. When she remembered how she had treated Munty she blushed with remorse. It was unlikely she would ever see the house or him again. Then she relived his kisses. She couldn't forget that with Munty she had been the cool envied girl, driving up the King's Road in a sports car.

She'd been horrid to him, blaming him, frightened and embarrassed by her accident, and guilty about lying to her parents. The gloom had come upon her with terrifying speed and she wasn't able to shake it off. She realised now she had taken it all out on that gentle man who had treated her with such kindness and admiration. She regretted it bitterly and Munty began more and more to occupy the echoing wastes in her mind.

She liked to lull herself to sleep by picturing herself in something gorgeous from Quorum, floating through magical candle-lit rooms at Castle Hey, Munty adoring at her side, directing teams of people to perform various unspecified tasks.

She designed her wedding dress over and over again in her mind – should it be a white mini, lace headscarf and go-go boots or something more traditional? Whatever she was wearing, it was always Munty's fair head and slender back encased in the same black tailcoat that she had seen him wearing at P&Q, waiting for her at the top of the aisle. Turning to smile at her. When she woke up from her fantasies to the dreary day-to-day of housework and Lord Groove, she sometimes fell into a gloom and, much to his lordship's irritation, had to take days off sick.

She was lucky to keep her job.

In the absence of Munty, no other man she knew invited her out on dates, and it was difficult to meet anyone interesting in Dorking. She regretted bucketing out of her Season where at least there were men to meet. What on earth had possessed her to waste such an opportunity? There was no going back now. She was stuck.

Half dozing when the bell in the shop doorway tinkled, she snapped awake and looked up to see someone tall standing against the light. Her well-primed heart leapt with recognition.

'Munty!' she cried out, louder than she meant, so delighted that her ridiculous dreams had conjured him up at last. It was clear to her from his worried expression that he was expecting to be rebuffed.

'Melissa, hello. I was just passing.'

'Passing? You were just passing Dorking?'

'Well, yes. Driving down to Castle Hey.'

Then she laughed, thrilled that he had come to find her.

'I called at your father's surgery and the nurse told me where you were.'

'Ah!'

Melissa lifted the hinged section of the counter and stepped through. She was wearing a long-sleeved short shift in bright peacock blue, with strings of beads and flat sandals on her feet. Lord Groove insisted she look the part. She looked up at him smiling, raising her arms, and the anxious expression left him as he bent to kiss her as if he couldn't help himself.

He came back the following Saturday to take her to Castle Hey. As she stepped once again across the threshold of her dream house Melissa let go of last year's fear. Her parents knew where she was and approved. She decided to remember only the fun, the kisses, the promise that Munty and his house would be her busy exciting future.

Work had started in earnest, windows were flung open, sunlight streaming in while workmen scrubbed the scarred walls and slapped on whitewash. Munty told her that he'd been spending every weekend here himself for months working alongside the men.

'I wanted to show you something much better than when you came before,' he said. 'At least half the problem must have been what a mess it was. I didn't blame you for wanting to run away.'

Melissa knew that that hadn't been it. She'd been excited by the possibilities of the house as soon as she had seen it, about being with Munty and making it a special place where people would want to stay. About behaving like a grown-up. It had been the lake that had ruined the weekend. Nothing else. She looked at Munty with new eyes so grateful that he'd tried again.

'Oh no, not at all,' she replied gazing around at the transformation.

That evening they sat again in the little room where they had had their first picnic, drinking P&Q's house champagne.

'We could see each other a bit, don't you think?' he said.

'I'd like that very much.'

She hugged to herself the secret sense that she had needed rescuing from the dragon of boredom. She glanced sideways at her prince on the shabby old sofa. Fair and pale he looked just right to her. She leant over and kissed him.

Fourteen

Melissa
October 1968

Melissa had poached the small purple plums she'd found in the old orchard. She was pressing them through a sieve when the first dull twinge invaded her. She stopped and looked out of the window as the sensation swelled inside her before dying away. Bit like the curse. The huge old kitchen, warm with heat from the Aga, had become her preferred sanctuary as the year rolled away from the sun's warmth. There she cooked and stored, day after day, against an unimaginable future: jam, whole meals for the freezer, chutney and pickles.

Munty always knew where to find her when he came home from London, rushing in to sit at the table, drink tea and talk to her. He was always so pleased to see what she was making. His mother had never made jam or cakes for him. She'd been too busy working.

Pearl and Reg had sold the family business. Having read the trade papers like runes to see the future, they had cannily decided that the new supermarket in the High Street was a severe threat to the traditional grocer. The average age of their customers rose sharply. The younger ones had deserted them completely, preferring to snatch TV dinners from huge chest freezers and ready-bagged sugar from open shelves, chucking it all into those wire trolleys imported from America. They had no desire to allow their customers to help themselves as if they were in some of kind of uncouth cash and carry. It seemed so perfunctory and unhelpful. Retirement to the warmth of Malta beckoned, as Reg had service family there, so off they went for a new life.

Munty kept in touch by letter but there was still an awkwardness between mother and son. His mother had been fine with Bert but Munty was another matter, growing away from her, particularly after her new marriage and the deaths of his grandparents. Add Melissa and the house and it was just all too difficult. The invitation to visit was always there of course but they could barely afford to mend the Castle Hey roof let alone fly to Malta.

The unexpected pregnancy following so quickly after their quiet wedding had delayed their plans for the house. Munty told Melissa that she must rest, they could have exciting business ideas after the baby was born. To begin with she was disappointed and frustrated. She'd hoped to get going, like her mother did with her father, with all the loving and helping she had dreamt about. Even those ideas began to shimmer like mirages.

The pregnancy had changed her. She was finding it more and more difficult to remember what had been so lovely about the idea of marriage and Munty. She was so tired sometimes she just wanted to cry and the dreaded glooms came over her more frequently and refused to shift. It was this ridiculous bump swelling her apron like a sail before the wind. When her waist had returned she was sure she would be better. She just had to grit her teeth and bear it.

As the pregnancy had advanced she was plagued once again by

a fear of failure and foreboding. Failing as a deb, a nurse and now failing as a wife. Would she fail as a mother too?

She hadn't wanted to be pregnant within months of the wedding but after a bit of fumbling around with French letters it had seemed less embarrassing to do it without. That was when everything stopped being pleasant and started being frightening. Strangeness crept up on her with the developing pregnancy. She woke often in the night and stared into the dark worrying and worrying about the huge house that loomed and boiled up all around her.

It was so big and shabby and there seemed to be no end to the money it would suck up before anyone would want to pay to be there. She put the sieve down and straightened herself, leaning a hand against the base of her spine in an ancient, unconscious gesture.

Real married life would begin, she told herself, and she would surely be a proper, grown-up Lady Munty once the baby was born. Not the sad creature dragging itself about when no one was looking. She heard her own voice aggressive inside her head.

'Pull yourself together,' it said. 'You're a lucky girl. Stop being so hopeless and useless and feeble.'

She would cry. Then she would make sure she had washed her face and powdered it thoroughly and plastered on some kind of a smile-shaped expression for Munty when he came home.

She could picture herself as a tiny ant-like creature scuttling about preparing meals and vegetables for the chest freezer they had been given as a wedding present by Pearl. It sat, half empty, demanding offerings like some malevolent icy god. It should be such fun to have so much space and her own home, but when she was alone the space closed in on her. In her dreams she attempted to shore up this toppling pile with something small and useless like a teaspoon or a flower. Maybe the dreams would leave her when she was free of the baby. Maybe she would be able to love Munty again.

She was upset that she didn't want him to touch her, but she felt so fragile, like tissue paper that would tear in his hands. Her skin crawled at the memory of his fingers on her body. She was rapidly forgetting why she had liked it before.

One night a few weeks into the pregnancy he had pushed up her nightie and put his hand on her belly, wandering a little lower and delving gently between her soft folds. Previously a delicious sensation would begin to creep over her like a warm breeze and her thighs would fall apart as she sighed and smiled in the dark. This time she sat up, slapping at his hand and sobbing as if in pain.

'What's the matter?'

She could see how much she had upset him. They were both virgins when they married and he was quite shy and reserved about sex. She knew Munty had bought a book and read it carefully in order not to let her down. Why was she frigid all of a sudden?

'I don't know. I just don't want you to do that.' She twisted her legs together and put her hands over her face. 'I don't think we should. Not while I'm pregnant.'

He dropped back on to the pillows beside her.

Soon afterwards she'd moved out of the master bedroom and into a smaller room down the passage with a dressing room off to one side. She felt frantic with guilt, leaving him marooned alone in the great Gothick bed where they had spent their first chaste night more than two years ago. It was so high you had to run up to it and jump and she'd used this as an excuse. She could quite easily have asked him to bring the library steps upstairs.

She was less panicky in the new room. She didn't have to be close to Munty at night, and feel his disappointment like a cold draft as their warmth crumbled to ashes. Sarah came over to stay, and helped her make curtains for the windows and dressing table of her new room. Her mother didn't say anything, but she could tell that she disapproved of her leaving the marriage bed. So she had twittered on about making it nice for guests after she had recovered from the baby. She was ashamed in front of her mother just as she had been when she had left nursing.

She scooped the thick damson puree into the jam pan and wearily stirred in the sugar she had warmed in the Aga, stopping each time the waves of sensation poured through her body. Half an hour later, she potted up the damson cheese, added waxed discs and secured the cellophane lids with elastic bands before licking and sticking on the labels she had written earlier. The warm jars gleamed like garnets on the shelves.

It was time to give in to the pains, to accept what was coming and allow her pregnancy to end. Beyond that, there was a landscape hard to imagine. There must be a baby in the picture somewhere, but it eluded her. The wriggling mound that had disturbed her sleep for the last few months seemed to have no human form. When she lay awake in the dark, heart pounding, she was frightened by the separate life that dwelt inside her like a parasite – a cuckoo or a worm.

She left the kitchen and walked up the brick passage, relieved that her mother had chosen and paid for Miss Smith, a combined midwife and maternity nurse, to look after her at home. She'd dreaded the idea of going to a hospital.

'Miss Smith?' she called. 'I think it may have started.' As she stood there, she felt a warm, wet gush between her legs and something splashed on to the stone flags of the hall. She looked down terrified and ashamed at her loss of control to see water gleaming on the floor.

'Miss Smith? Something's happened.' She was frozen to the spot. The liquid dripped uncomfortably down the insides of her legs, making her shiver as it cooled in the draught. Maybe the baby would just fall out. She began to cry as the waves of sensation built to crests that she had not experienced before.

Miss Smith came down the stairs in dignified haste.

'Don't worry, your ladyship, it's just your waters have broken, we'll soon get you cleaned up and into bed. With any luck it won't take too long, that's a very good sign. Now don't cry, it'll soon be over.'

She took Melissa's arm and helped her to step over the puddle, supporting her up the stairs. Melissa was vaguely comforted, but then was gripped by another pain coming much more quickly after the one before. She stopped, and grabbed the banister, squeezing her eyes and gasping for breath.

'Just try to breathe steadily, dear. Come on, we're nearly there. You can have some gas and air for the pain as soon as we've got you into bed.'

Melissa, with the idea of pain relief ahead, sped up a bit, but had to stop every time a pain started welling up. Quite soon Miss Smith had installed her in a clean, fresh bed, with a waterproof pad underneath her bottom. She was examined which was always a bit embarrassing but her mother had warned her, 'You have to throw yourself open to the public when you have a baby.'

The reward was a red rubber mask through which she could suck blessed dizzying relief until she nearly blacked out. Miss Smith hurried out of the room to telephone the doctor and report progress. First she told Munty what was happening. While she was gone, he sidled into the room.

'Are you all right, darling?' His anxious face made her want to laugh, but it might have been the gas and air.

'No.' She turned her head away from him. 'Go away.' She heard him leave.

Dr Murphy called a couple of times to check her progress during the ten-hour labour, asking to be summoned for the birth itself as it only took him a few minutes to get there. He listened to the baby's strong and steady heartbeat and said he was perfectly satisfied that all was as it should be, and he could leave the management of the labour to Miss Smith. The birth itself surprised Melissa very much by reminding her intensely of going to the lavatory. An overwhelming sensation that she could not deny, as her body took over from her anxious mind and everything else, determined as it was to expel the presence inside.

She bellowed like a bull, an animal noise that was as disconcerting as the sensation. Her baby emerged very quickly after that, Miss Smith gently steadying its progress into the world. As soon as the baby was out, Melissa lay still, deafened with the absence of her own sounds.

'It's a little girl,' said Miss Smith, wrapping the baby quickly to keep her warm, and dealing efficiently with the cord. Melissa didn't sit up to look. She just lay back flat on the pillowless bed. Then she noticed dimly that Miss Smith had moved to stand beside her, offering her something, and she craned round weakly to look. A ridiculously small face, roughly the same colour as the damson puree and clenched into folds, lay within a white cotton blanket.

Meanwhile, Dr Murphy, who'd come back for the birth, was delivering and checking the afterbirth. He examined her thoroughly before saying, 'I'll be off then, Lady Mount-Hey. Call me if you need anything else, Miss Smith, but I think she'll do. Good, easy birth for a first timer, well done.'

Melissa nodded and tried to smile.

Within a few minutes, Munty was in there too and Melissa heard Miss Smith say, 'A little girl. Eight pounds, my lord. You must be so proud.'

'Eight pounds of what?' she heard him answer. A flash of irritation made her shudder.

Miss Smith was clearly disconcerted. 'The baby weighed eight pounds, sir.'

'Oh, I see.'

Melissa focused on her husband and she could see he looked uncomfortable. He crept up to the crib and looked down at the tiny roseate face with mole-like paws up near its chin.

'What do you want to call her?' he asked his wife.

Melissa groped around in her mind. What do you call a baby? Did it matter? She remembered the satisfying garnet pots she had labelled in the kitchen. 'Damson,' she said, her eyes closed.

'That's fine,' he answered. 'We can give her my mother's

name Pearl as a second one. If it had been a boy we would have called him Baillie. Never mind, next time!'

The false cheerfulness of his voice grated across her mind. Next time? What did he think she was? A brood mare? She supposed he wanted a male heir and a baby girl wasn't good enough for him. She hated him.

She vowed silently that no child of hers would be called an awful common name like Pearl and planned to summon up the strength to register the baby herself. Her mother-in-law was a distant figure to her, appearing at the wedding in a globular hat made of pale blue nylon and then vanishing off abroad. What did she matter to any of them? But then there did seem to be a lot of liquid still seeping out into the pad that Miss Smith had pressed to her bottom. Would she ever want to stand again let alone walk?

Miss Smith moved around the room and told Munty that he must leave Mummy and Baby to rest now. Melissa could see from his face that he was only too delighted to go back to his safe male world. She was so tired.

Fifteen

Melissa
November 1968

Melissa snapped awake. Instantly her heart began to hop in her chest. Voices in the passage. Miss Smith and Munty. She crept out of bed to lean against the door and listen.

'I understand you must leave us soon, Miss Smith – month pretty much up, eh? Lady Mount-Hey doing well?'

More of that forced jollity in his voice. She despised him for it.

'I've hired a girl from the village to help out and Lady Mount-Hey's mother is due to be here any day too.'

Her husband's voice made her feel panicky guilt, an agitation in a mind which was mostly just blank and woolly.

Oh God. Please don't go. Please don't go. Please don't go. The words repeated over and over in her head making her dizzy again as she slumped to her knees by the door.

It was just under a month since Damson's birth and the little girl was settled into a routine by Miss Smith's firm but kindly management. This included four-hourly feeds, with the baby brought to Melissa in the daytime and bottles at night 'so Mummy can get her beauty sleep'. There was nothing much for her to do apart from 'Rest, your ladyship.' Miss Smith did suggest from time to time that she tried dressing and going downstairs, but she always managed somehow to avoid it.

She lived in a hazy sad little dream when no one was near. Even reading was beyond her although she kept books by the bed and pretended to. She looked out of the window at the trees but spent a lot of time with her eyes shut trying to blot things out. Something gnawed inside her. She feared what was waiting for her out there. The only time she needed to do anything much was when anyone came to see her. Even then she could get away with a certain amount of wilting. Munty was the worst. He made her feel guilty. She was finding it hard to remember meeting him and what that had been like. There seemed to be a grey curtain between her and the recent past. A couple of days after the baby was born her parents had driven the thirty miles to visit their first grandchild. Melissa knew she must be cunning about this visit. The grey fog wasn't quite so dense and persistent in those early days. It was possible to act as people expected her to for short periods. They would accept that she was very tired. Her parents mustn't notice that she didn't love or even like Damson, didn't care about her at all. That Munty was not someone she wanted anything to do with any more. Bitter, stomach-churning guilt and shame engulfed her once everyone had left the room, but it made no difference.

She rolled her head and bit the pillow, groaning and sighing. Her whole life was an appalling mistake. Letting everyone down was the worst of it. She glanced over at the delicate ogee arch at the top of her bedroom window. After Damson came she couldn't get out into the miniature park, with its little reed-choked lake, so she couldn't use the charms of the woods coming down to the water, from which deer would emerge to drink, to cheer herself. It was just bed and meals on trays, and hushed voices, then that demanding mouth wrapped round her nipple, sucking and sucking at her.

Miss Smith knocked, and then came in with her lunch on a tray. Nice white napkin, dahlia in a glass, nasty-looking brown slop on a plate, carrots floating, floury potatoes with black marks on them. There was also a big glass of water.

'Thank you, Miss Smith,' she said, hauling herself up on the pillows and trying a smile.

Miss Smith seemed to be hovering, so Melissa put a carrot on the fork and carried it up towards her mouth. Miss Smith turned away to fold something – she was always irritating Melissa by folding things – and Melissa dropped the carrot back on the plate, but ostentatiously chewed and swallowed.

'That's fine, your ladyship. You make sure you eat it up, and drink all the water. I am a little worried about Baby's weight, and we may need to use the bottle more, not just at night. I'll make sure there's plenty of Cow and Gate before I go, and we'll have a little lesson about hygiene. It's all very simple, but it's very important that you use the Milton sterilising solution every single time.'

Melissa wasn't listening. She couldn't fit the information into her mind. She tried a little bit. Yes, Milton (what was Milton? The poet? *Paradise Lost*? A level English?). She tuned back into Miss Smith, who was saying, 'And you must be very careful indeed about how much Cow and Gate you put in each bottle. If you put too much powder in, Baby will be very thirsty. Won't you, poppet?' She had walked into the other room and picked up Damson, cuddling the misbegotten scrap in her cobweb shawl.

When the midwife had gone, Melissa slipped out of bed and fetched one of the brown paper bags from the maternity pack sent down from John, Bell & Croyden, the smart London chemist, to put her disgusting pads in, and quickly scooped all the food off the plate. She slid it under the chintz valance of the bed, with the others, awaiting a moment when everyone was asleep or out and she could get down to the dustbins. Some of it went out when the sanitary bin was emptied but she didn't dare put all of it in there, in case someone noticed.

Then she went to run herself another bath. No wonder she wasn't hungry with that ghastly whiff in her pants. She took baths to try and get rid of it. She called it the birthy smell and it made her sick.

Dirty, dirty, dirty, she sang in her head.

If the sun shone through the window in the afternoons, it seemed so ridiculous to be sad and crushed and trapped and ill when there was nothing wrong at all, and she had a lovely baby, as people kept calling that ridiculous sucking purple thing. Melissa knew she had nothing to complain about, but she also felt nothing. Not for the baby, or for herself. She just wanted to sleep. So far, asking Miss Smith to look after Damson while she had a little doze was working very well for her. What would she do when there was no one to take Damson away?

There had been plenty of signs the safety couldn't last. Munty made her feel guilty, he looked confused and unhappy. But she couldn't help him. She couldn't remember why she was here in the big cold house in the country. The voices outside the door continued to sound a knell.

'I was booked for the month, my lord,' Miss Smith was saying quietly. 'To attend the birth with the GP, and then supervise the lying in and settle little Damson into her routine. I need to move on to my next mummy now.'

'Yes, of course,' she heard Munty saying slowly.

'My lord.' Miss Smith was hesitating. 'A month is the usual lying-in period. It was just that Baby was late. And anyway, I think we need to have a little word about her ladyship.'

Behind the door, Melissa tensed.

'What is it?'

'She doesn't seem very well, tired and sad, unenthusiastic about Baby. I'd like to call Dr Murphy in to see her.'

'Really? The doctor said it was an easy birth and she should recover very quickly. She is young after all. There's nothing wrong with her that getting up and about won't cure. It's all this lying in bed that's the problem. She was always so active before the birth.'

'That's what I mean,' said Miss Smith. 'I think her ladyship may have a very rare illness that happens to a handful of mothers after birth.'

'What do you mean?' Melissa could hear the anxiety in his voice.

'It's when the new mother is sad and confused for no reason. It can be quite serious.'

Then she heard her husband say, quite distinctly, 'Some trick cyclist nonsense, I suppose? Read about this kind of thing. They invent diseases, so you have to spend a fortune lying on a couch and talking about yourself. She's just feeling sorry for herself. As I say, if she got up and out into the fresh air, she'd be fine. She's probably missing her walks in the park. Don't worry, Miss

Smith. If there's nothing physically wrong with Lady Mount-Hey, there's no reason to make a fuss. She's probably looking forward to having the baby to herself.'

'Oh, is there no nanny booked?'

'No. But Melissa's mother will make sure she gets used to it all when she comes.'

Melissa had known for months that there would be no nanny, and she'd been relieved then. She knew Munty was looking for more ways to earn a bit of cash. It wasn't his fault, but Munty clearly felt that Castle Hey wasn't his, that he didn't deserve it. That the house punished him for his undeserved occupation by sucking up every penny and refusing to be done up. Every time some part of the roof was repaired, another would spring a leak. Dry rot had broken out in disgusting brown pancakes all over the attic. There had been a time when she had tried to help him come to terms with his accidental inheritance, spinning dreams of opening the house up to the public, making it pay its way. That just seemed too much trouble now.

'I understand,' Munty was saying. 'I'm grateful for all your help with Lady Mount-Hay and the baby. I'll run you to the station this afternoon. Is that OK?'

'My lord?'

'Yes?' Melissa could hear him beginning to walk away, then hesitating.

'My lord, I would be easier in my mind if you would call Dr Murphy in before I go.'

'I'll talk to him, I promise.'

'Thank you, my lord.'

Melissa pulled herself up using the doorknob, and ran shakily back to bed on her bare feet, just pulling the covers over herself as she heard a knock on the door. What could Dr Murphy do? There was nothing wrong with her, was there? Just this sickening feeling of failure. And doctors couldn't cure that.

'Your ladyship? May I come in?'

'Yes, do.'

'I'll need to bring Damson in for her feed in a minute. How are you feeling?'

'A bit weak, but I'm on the mend.' Melissa managed a bright smile. 'Ready to get up and dressed.'

Miss Smith stood hesitating and Melissa tried smiling at her again.

'As you know, I need to move on to my next family. The baby is due in a couple of weeks, and I've had a letter from the Duchess today. It's her fourth. I do like to have a week's rest between each confinement.'

'Of course you must. I've taken up far too much of your time. Those nights in the first week can't have been easy.'

'Oh no, not at all. Damson's such a good little girl, aren't you, darling?'

It never ceased to amaze Melissa that Miss Smith could summon up so much affection and enthusiasm for all the babies she delivered and then nursed in the first weeks of life. Didn't they all blur into one? She told endless stories about little Viscount Storrington, who'd been so early that they'd despaired of him, 'The size of a bag of sugar!'

And Lady Amelia Wilcox, who'd had to be rushed to hospital in the middle of a ball in her father's Rolls. Miss Smith had arrived at the Manor the next morning to get things ready for when she came back, disappointed not to have attended Lady Amelia's delivery. Melissa had giggled at all the titles trotted out like show ponies – but that was before she forgot how to laugh or why she had ever wanted to.

'How she adored her little boy,' she went on as she offered Damson up to Melissa's breast. 'Couldn't keep her eyes or hands off him. I always believed she'd be one of those mummies who left it to the nannies while she got on with parties and fun, but no. I heard they'd never had a nanny, but she had them all mounted in little basket saddles by two, and following her out hunting. I even heard she took them to Glyndebourne, and left them in the keeper's cottage so she could feed them in the interval.'

Melissa's womb contracted sharply with a pang of guilt and grief that she could not understand such mothering at all. Couldn't imagine taking the baby anywhere, even downstairs. Tomorrow was entirely a darkness to her. She stared down at the baby's little sucking cheek and longed for it to stop.

She had frightened herself one day, when Miss Smith had left the room, by yanking the baby off the nipple and rolling her over and over in her shawl right down to the end of the bed, kicking at her with her feet.

The baby had shrieked her indignation, which had brought Miss Smith running. Melissa had hastily snatched her back into her arms before the midwife entered the room. She held the baby's face into her shoulder to try to stop the cries.

'What happened?'

'Oh, I wasn't concentrating and she fell off the breast.'

She'd been aware that Miss Smith was eyeing her, but she

made no response and merely took the baby, saying, 'I'll just go and change her.'

While the midwife was taking her afternoon rest, Melissa crept through into the nursery to look at the baby. The room had not been redecorated in any way, and was just a little dressing room off her bedroom. A pile of snowy nappies was geometrically arranged on top of an old-fashioned mahogany chest of drawers which contained the baby's little clothes. There was a wide, large basin in one corner, with chrome legs, and a glass shelf which had been removed so Damson could be bathed while she was still so small.

The bassinet had wheels, and Miss Smith was always pushing it through and placing it beside her bed in the daytime. Melissa wished she wouldn't.

Sixteen

Melissa
November 1968

Miss Smith had said goodbye to Melissa in her room, bringing in Damson for the last time and kissing her before placing her tenderly in Melissa's arms. Then she'd leant over, kissed Melissa's face, and said, 'Good luck, my dear. Your husband is going to telephone Dr Murphy, and when he comes to visit, you must tell him exactly how you feel now. Won't you?'

Melissa had noticed she wasn't 'my ladying' her now. She shrank away from the sympathy, then tried to make her lips smile again, but sobbed instead, 'I don't want you to go.'

She stretched out a hand to the midwife, clutching at her sleeve.

'I know, my dear. Your mother will be here soon and your husband has employed someone from the village who's coming in a couple of days to take care of domestic matters while you rest. I don't think you're quite over the birth and I want to make sure you get extra care.'

For a moment, there was a tiny flicker of hope. Perhaps it was just the birth that had stopped her in her tracks. Her heart seemed to flutter. All the things she used to do to keep calm had deserted her. She couldn't read, she couldn't cook, she couldn't walk in the park. As soon as Miss Smith had left the room, glancing back at her and smiling, she put the baby down on the pink candlewick counterpane.

She had no idea what to do next, how to live, even how to look after the baby now that Miss Smith was whisking her calm competence away.

She hadn't been listening as she had stood in her slippers and quilted nylon dressing gown while Miss Smith tried to teach her about bathing, nappies, feeding and all the rest of it. She'd been blocking out the sound of her voice and anything to do with the future, living in tiny chunks of time.

After a while, the baby woke up and began to whimper. This bit was sort of automatic, although she missed Miss Smith's calm positioning of the head, with chin tucked in, against her breast. She was able to slip the cup of the nursing bra down and allow Damson to suck. After a couple of minutes, the little girl came off the nipple and cried. Melissa searched her mind. Ah, yes, winding. She lifted the small limp body on to her shoulder and patted it tentatively. A small burp rewarded her efforts.

She put the baby back on the nipple and she sucked away. It was very quiet in the room. The electric fire glowed orange in the corner. Outside, the autumn afternoon was utterly still. There wasn't a wind moving the trees, or any clouds to look at. Just sky, grey like the inside of Melissa's head.

The baby drowsed off the nipple, and Melissa went on holding her without bothering to do up her bra again. She heard footsteps in the passage outside, and hastily pulled the cup up over her breast.

Munty knocked and looked around the door.

'Hello, Melissa. How are you?'

'I'm fine, thanks. How are you?'

'OK. Now Miss Smith said I must get Dr Murphy to you. Would you like me to do that?'

'Oh no, I'm absolutely fine. Just getting used to not having Miss Smith. I'm seeing him soon anyway for my six-week check.'

'It's up to you,' he smiled at her. 'Nice to have you to myself again. And by the way, a girl called Pauline Hadaway from the village starts on Thursday. She'll do the cleaning and cooking and so on. It would be best for you to have the time to rest and be with the baby. Meanwhile we can still manage with all that lovely food you made for the freezer.'

It had not occurred to Melissa that she would be required to do anything but she tried to smile and say thank you as it seemed to be expected. Dimly she remembered that Munty was a nice man.

'And there's a letter for you.' He held it out and she recognised her father's handwriting. 'I'm not going to put the heating on but you can have the electric bar heater in here as much as you like,' he said.

She looked at him. He seemed ghostly now, not there, his outline wavering. She was quite clear that he would never be allowed to come near her body again. That there was never going to be a 'next time'. Not that he would want to, with the smell and awful leakiness never mind the ridiculous cartoon breasts.

'Melissa? Are you sure you don't want me to call Dr Murphy?'

'No. Thank you.' She hated Dr Murphy, his patronising laugh and habit of patting the top of her thigh. His attitude seemed to be that now it was all NHS there was no need for a bedside manner, although she had heard him sucking up to

Munty with a 'my lord' this and that. No need to suck up to her, just a stupid girl, all disgusting and empty.

Putting the baby down, she opened the letter.

Dearest Melissa,

We have had a letter from Miss Smith this morning telling us that you are not completely recovered from the birth. After a month you should be feeling more yourself. As I always say to young mums, get up and about and you'll soon feel better. I'm not at all keen on all this bed rest.

Also, I am so sorry but Mummy is still not well enough to come and help so soon after her flu. I am making sure she takes care of herself this time, and stays at home. Also, I would not want you to catch it. I don't know if you remember, but she ignored the flu last time and took far too long to get completely better. Anyway, as soon as she is stronger, she says she will come and stay with you. She can't wait to get to know your little Damson! Meanwhile, we both send you all our best love.

In haste,
Daddy

Oh dear, now she wanted to howl. Munty was still hovering, and he simply couldn't be allowed to see the black vomitty stuff that was inside her head. She didn't know where it had come from, but she was ashamed to have allowed it in. She couldn't let it out or show it to anyone. It was nothing to do with her and she wished it would go away. At the same time she liked it. She wanted to be alone with it, lapping and lapping at her, pushing her down and down. Why didn't Munty leave?

'Thanks, Munty. I'm going to have a go at getting up. You go back to your study and I'll try bringing the baby downstairs. OK?'

Munty looked relieved and backed out of the room.

Seventeen

Damson
October 1977

Girls flooded through the passage that led from the cobbled yard out on to packed earth denuded of all grass by generations of small running feet. Damson trailed along behind, thumb marking the place in her book as she went.

'Damson? Is that a book you've got there? You know the rules.' Mrs Collins was kind, but could be strict. Damson was fascinated by her drawn-on orange eyebrows that sat at least half an inch above what must have been their natural position.

She turned back reluctantly. Then she returned to the door and, peeping out, could see that Mrs Collins had moved away to watch some girls skipping. So she scampered back quickly to go into the outdoor lav for a quick read.

Skittering across slimy cobbles, she let herself into the dark little lavatory under the arch that went through to the old stables. There was no lid on the wide wooden seat, so she perched on the edge, angling her book to the tiny, high-up window that let in a little dull autumn light. Then she settled back into sunlit ancient Byzantium with a sigh, oblivious to the suspicious puddle on the stone floor, the clammy smell and the cold.

Someone was trying to open the door. 'Damn.'

'Hurry up, I'm popping.'

Damson once again put her thumb in the book, then stood up and pulled the rattling chain to flush for authenticity before leaving. She would have to go outside and play now, there was nowhere else to sit and read in private.

Hilary Denning pushed past, her thumbs already hooked in her green woven knickers, shoving her out of the way. Damson went back into the cloakroom, pausing to fling her book up on to the top of the water tank in one corner out of sight.

There was a splash. Damn, the top had been removed since she last hid a book up there. Damson scrambled on to a bench in a vain attempt to save *The Road to Miklagard*, but it was sinking to the bottom of the tank, swinging and swaying in the dim light. She was miserable as she watched it disappear, taking with it her current world of Vikings. She wanted to be there, in that tiny wooden world, crossing seas. Not here, at Hartwood Grange, with bare knees and tight green nylon long socks, shrunken mauve jersey, two pairs of pants – white liners and green woven outers – and a green duffle coat so stiff it stood up by itself. Unable to escape except into books.

There were things she liked. Mainly the library, and Mr Sewell, the headmistress's ancient husband who had taught chemistry at a boys' public school in a former life. White coated, he'd gathered her class together, as he did every year's Remove B, to see if they were worth his while teaching – as he could clearly be heard grumbling. He'd filled a glass bowl with water. With a penknife he scraped off a tiny piece from a white lump of what looked like putty. This he flipped neatly into the water where it startled everyone by whizzing fiercely around, fizzing and bursting into white flames. Some of the girls shrank back. Others giggled or didn't seem to notice that anything interesting had happened. Damson's hand was in the air before she realised what she was doing.

'Anyone who has put her hand up come over to this end of the classroom,' he said. 'The rest of you can go.'

The other girls shuffled out. When they had gone, he said:

'OK, do any of you know what that was?'

Damson shook her head. She was interested in most things, particularly practical ones like marauding Vikings, Roman legionaries and how your body worked, volcanoes and dinosaurs and archaeology. Bored of copying from textbooks, she was sure that Mr Sewell's classes would provide something different that she would like. She didn't know what it was that did that when it hit water, but she was desperate to find out. She wanted to do it herself, preferably with a large piece of whatever it was, so it would go on for longer.

Damson knew that Hartwood Grange had been Mrs Sewell's family home until the war. Her brother had been killed, and she had set up a boarding prep school for girls to fill the financial gap. The food was all vegetarian. Mrs Sewell was a big fan of Bernard Shaw. Every year the girls would put on a Shaw play, directed by herself. She wasn't motherly at all, and she and Mr Sewell had never had children of their own, but she was kind in her own way. Damson loved Saturday evenings when Mrs Sewell read out loud to the school in three groups according to age. Also there were slightly stale ginger biscuits. For the permanently hungry little girls this was a treat, even though they had long since lost their snap.

She found it a bit difficult when the other girls were talking about their parents. Telling people that her mummy had died appeared to embarrass them. They didn't know what to say, or how to treat her. Explaining exactly what Munty did, and why she didn't call him Daddy, was also excruciating. When she had asked him once, he'd said with a laugh that he was a 'Lord on the Board', but he seemed to spend a lot of time in his study with his feet up on the fender, reading history books.

When the other girls were homesick, and cried in their beds at night, she was dry eyed. She missed Crumpet, Grandpa's little old nondescript terrier, and Granny's pug Toast, more than she missed Munty and her home.

On Saturday her grandmother came to take her out for a day's exeat. As usual she was parked on the carriage sweep waiting for Damson at the earliest possible moment that she could be picked up, bang on nine o'clock. Damson had run down from dorm inspection knowing with joyful certainty that she would not be late – unlike Munty who always was. She jumped into the leathery front bench seat of the old Rover, leaning to kiss her grandmother's cheek and receiving the characteristic squeeze around her waist that went with it.

'Now darling, we're going to be at home this morning. We can walk the dogs and have lunch. Then Grandpa wants to take us to a film he likes the look of in the afternoon. Not sure if I fancy it, *Star Wars* it's called. But you know how much he loves his science fiction. This Disney film about mice looked better, but he says you're a bit old for mice. You and I will make something nice for tea, and then I'll pop you back to school for seven o'clock.'

Only the last sentence was not so much to Damson's taste,

but she resolved not to think about it, to savour her grandparents' uninterrupted loving attention for a whole day.

They drove through the sunken lanes that led down the hill from the school, and out on to the main road that led to Dorking, chatting all the time about the comforting minutiae of family life – the sewing, the patients, the garden and the dogs.

'How is Munty?' Granny asked.

'He's fine. Just the same.'

Damson heard her grandmother make the characteristic sound that she always made about her son-in-law. Something between a sucked-in sigh and a grunt. It didn't bother Damson.

With her grandparents she could relax and the days flowed freely. It was different at home. Munty had set times when he saw her: for supper off trays in front of the television in the evenings, for breakfast in the kitchen every morning. At other times, she suspected that she was intruding if she went into his study to find him. He would look impatient, ask her what she wanted and tell her to 'run along' as he was 'busy'. He never looked busy like Grandpa was busy with his patients.

Her grandparents never asked her what she wanted or made her feel unwelcome. She would sit on a footstool in Granny's sewing room, with the dogs in a basket beside them, listening to Radio Three, Granny looking through her half-moon glasses as she stitched. Damson knew not to disturb Grandpa in his surgery during the day. After the last patient had gone home, she could go in and sit with him while he finished his notes and Nurse Thomas tidied up.

She had been quite clear from an early age that she wanted to do what Grandpa did when she was grown up. Better than sitting in the study as Munty did at home, reading *Flashman* books and writing letters. She didn't know much about his London life, although she knew he went to church and had friends there. They didn't come and stay at Castle Hey. Munty said it was because there wasn't any shooting, and once let slip that he was ashamed of how tatty the house was.

Grandpa and Granny had also lost Damson's mother of course, but they never seemed sad in the same way although she knew that Melissa was still very much in their hearts. But then Munty was alone and her grandparents had each other. For her father, she, Damson, didn't seem to make up for Melissa's absence. When she was small she used to hope he would marry Pauline. Pauline always laughed when she mentioned it.

'Me? Not posh, dear. And you've forgotten about my Fred. Anyway he needs someone with enough money to mend the roof.'

Damson's regular expeditions with Pauline up to the top floor to empty buckets that caught the drips were tedious. The roof clearly did need mending. She wondered what it would be like to have a stepmother. Apart from not having to empty the buckets, she couldn't think of any other benefits.

Eighteen

Munty
September 1982

Munty watched the Reverend Harold Griffin coming towards him accompanied by a small, good-looking blonde woman with two young girls in tow. Startled, he noticed that the girls were identical, dressed alike in long flowered cotton dresses with white lace collars, one blue and the other brown. They were slightly taller than their mother, slender as wands: both together would make up her substance. The sun shone through the windows, and he was struck by a sense of wonder at the light bouncing off all three golden heads so that they seemed to be haloed.

It was post-church coffee time at the Wednesday Evensong at St Anthony the Great, Belgrave Square, always a very sociable occasion but not at all alarming. Munty found parties difficult, but church was different. The vicar knew his circumstances, and had been the first person that Munty had ever talked to properly about Melissa. Apart from the police of course, and the coroner. And he had not revealed the depths of his despair and sense of failure to either of them. The vicar had not said much, but had listened, sighed and said, 'Well, she's gone to a better place.' Where that was Munty didn't know, but it was comforting if he didn't think about it too much.

At St Anthony's, everyone was kind and helpful, and Munty

was made to feel completely at home. The vicar was an Honourable as well as a Reverend, and Munty's wasn't the only or even the grandest title in the pews.

'Ah! Munty. You must meet Mrs Mullins. Her daughters are about the same age as yours, I think? Mrs Mullins? This is Lord Mount-Hey.'

In the warm post-service glow, Munty found himself looking down at a pretty round face with a small retroussé nose. Her lips were painted a soft glossy pink, which was appealing. She had thick golden hair pushed back with a padded velvet Alice band and was wearing a navy blue pleated skirt, navy shoes with a gold bit across the front, navy tights and a white blouse with a bow at the neck.

'How do you do?' He held out his hand.

'Very well thank you,' she smiled, taking it, and then hesitated before saying: 'This is Clarice and this is Eunice,' waving a hand at her daughters.

'Mrs Mullins has joined us from St Peter in Chains, in Nottingham,' said Harold. 'One of our outreach churches, so she knows the form.'

'Ah,' said Munty, a bit lost. Then he tried a safe topic. 'Have you moved to London, Mrs Mullins?'

She was smiling at him, and said, 'Oh yes. Lock, stock and barrel. After my husband died, there was nothing for us up there. No family you see, and it would be more fun for the girls to come to London.'

'How sad for you,' he said, but she looked surprised, and he wondered whether the death of Mr Mullins was not quite such a terrible loss as his widowing had been.

The girls nodded. Munty could see they were around the same age as Damson, although they looked very different from his daughter. He wished she was with him, but she was away at school and never came to church on Wednesdays in London with her father. He had slipped into the habit, while she was boarding at prep school, of coming up to London from Monday until Friday during term time. Getting away from Castle Hey was a relief. He stayed in a bed and breakfast in Pimlico, from which he could walk both to Westminster and to church as well as to P&Q where he was still a director. If he was required to sit in on board meetings of the various companies of which he was chairman, then that was convenient too.

A fellow peer he had met in the Bishop's Bar at the House of Lords had introduced him to St Anthony's and his social life such as it was revolved entirely around the kind, impersonal people he had met there. Otherwise he would have been entirely bereft in the long sad years since Melissa had abandoned him. Castle Hey was much the same as it had been when she died. He hadn't had the heart or energy to go on with the restoration, let alone fulfil their plans for turning it into a moneyspinner. He had the great Gothick bed dismantled and sent to auction. The room was locked up and he never intended to use it again.

He had to suppress his memories of the last time he had seen Melissa or he would weep even now. He had bent over the coffin in the undertaker's chapel of rest and kissed her smooth white forehead. To his lips it was rock hard and freezing cold.

Nineteen

Damson
August 1983

Damson was lonelier once Clarice and Eunice had moved into Castle Hey after their parents' wedding. They briskly instructed her to call them Clarrie and Noonie 'as all our friends do' but that didn't help. Already very pretty and vivacious at fourteen, they didn't mean to make her feel so dumpy and dull. They were sort of kind in a detached way, but turned inward towards each other in a flurry of private jokes, shared giggles and seamless communication. She told herself that they were twins, they couldn't help it.

She longed for fun and parties, and their presence only highlighted how tedious home life was in the holidays. She was worried that they might be bored, and she tried hard to make friends with them and start up conversations. That just seemed to make them curl around each other like two little cats leaving Damson out in the cold. Her skin itched and prickled with embarrassment.

When Margaret was sharp with her, which she quite frequently was once the first novelty of the marriage wore off, Damson sensed Munty's discomfort. He didn't intervene, although she had seen him retreat from the scene when Margaret was telling her off for being lazy in the house. This felt so

183

grotesquely wrong, but she didn't know how to complain, or to whom. Granny looked disapproving when she tried to raise the subject.

Damson knew that she could be rude and difficult if she didn't get her own way. She was uncomfortable about this and felt that Munty was only too happy to let someone else deal with her. Pauline had never made Damson lift a finger or told her off. Damson knew when Pauline was cross because she looked disappointed and refused to talk to her. Hugs and kisses and pleadings saw Pauline eventually forgive her.

Damson was lying on her bed reading the latest *Angelique* from the library after lunch one Sunday when someone knocked on the door. She didn't answer. There was no one in the house she wanted to talk to.

'Damson, I know you're in there. What are you doing?'

It was her stepmother's voice.

'I'm reading.'

'But we all need to clear up lunch, don't we? Come on, Damson, please unlock this door and come and help.'

Damson unlocked the door and stood sulkily in her room, staring at the wooden floor. The room where she had been born, unchanged since.

'Thank you, Damson. Now, I think we need to have a little talk about manners and helping around the house.'

The girl cringed, as her stepmother let her know exactly what she thought of her behaviour. She realised it was fair, but it was excruciating to have it spelt out. Particularly as the twins in their odd twinny way often cheeked their mother and ran off without helping, and got away with it. Perhaps Margaret worried that they wouldn't love her if she told them off. She clearly had no such worries about Damson.

'I know you've never known a mother, but I've been here for six months now and you've never even looked at me. Please look at me, Damson. Look into my face.'

Damson slowly raised her eyes and looked at her stepmother. She saw a woman not much taller than herself at fourteen. She was wearing pink lipstick. Damson scanned her stepmother's face, hating the colour of her foundation, an orange shade that came to a halt at her chin.

When she was cross her voice changed. Damson didn't know anyone else who spoke like that.

'I said look, don't stare.'

Damson lowered her eyes.

Twenty

Damson
December 1984

Damson had been invited to the party as a job lot with the twins. The hostess, whose sixteenth birthday it was, was at Farningham with her stepsisters. Damson was not at the same school as the twins. She went to a more academic girls' school nearer to her grandparents. Her school looked down on Farningham, where the girls were told not to bother too much with exams and so on, as it was implied that they would all make 'good marriages'. Damson, determined to follow her grandfather into medicine, found this odd and old-fashioned.

She was nervous at the idea of meeting some boys. Bubbles popped in her tummy at the thought of kissing. It sounded disgusting, tongues and so on, but she was determined to do something about still being 'sweet sixteen and never been kissed'.

They'd all gone by train, clutching their sleeping bags, jewel-coloured taffeta party frocks stuffed into one suitcase between them. The only parties she'd been to so far had been schoolfriends' girly sleepovers. There had been the odd brother lurking around, covered in spots and embarrassment, sneering at his sister yet hovering close to the hormonal soup.

She hadn't been to any that included boys before the twins came, as Munty seemed to have no idea how to make friends with neighbours who had children the same age as his daughter. At least the twins had shaken things up a bit.

All the teenage girls were changing together on the attic floor of the big farmhouse occupied by their hosts. Noonie did Damson up when she found her clutching her dress helplessly and roaming the corridors. It had thin straps that you needed to cross over and tie at the back. It wasn't a dress you could manage by yourself.

'Would you like some help with your make-up?' she asked. Damson shook her head, and put on a little mascara and lip gloss. Then they all huddled into their Huskies and Barbours, and climbed into a blanket-lined trailer behind a tractor to be towed across the freezing fields towards the barn where the party was to be held. The huge door was open and golden light flooded out on to the frosty grass. As they bumped closer, wood smoke met their eager senses. For ever afterwards, Damson associated the scent with anticipation.

The two-storey barn had a beaten earth floor which had been partly covered with drugget. In front of the fireplace was the traditional Snog Pit, where cushions and rugs were piled up for people to sit on. As the evening wore on, the space became full. It was a badge of honour to snog someone at any party, and Damson longed to join in.

She had been hovering upstairs, talking to some schoolfriends, but not having a very nice time at all as they were picked off by the circling males. She stood by the buffet and nibbled bits of the huge chunk of cheese that had been served with French bread and pickle.

She was tired of trying to look pleased and happy despite the crawling embarrassment of not being a chosen one. As they were in the farm buildings, there was nowhere she could go and hide from the merciless exposure. She had not danced even once.

She saw someone detach themselves from a group on the other side of the dance floor and walk through the prancing throng towards her. She stopped picking the cheese and stood waiting to see what would happen next.

The music changed tempo, always the worst moment for the abandoned, when everyone was paired off and slow dancing. 'Turned a whiter shade of pale,' wailed Procol Harum. Then a boy was standing in front of her, smiling down at her. He took her right hand in his left and led her gently on to the dance floor. There he put his arms around her, encouraging her to put hers around his neck, and began to sway to the music, the length of his body pressed against hers. It had happened so quickly she hadn't had time to see what he looked like, although she knew he was very tall. She rested her head against his chest, which smelt of Eau Sauvage, and gave herself up to the music and the swaying sense of unreality.

After a while, she peeped up at the underside of his chin. He sensed that she had moved and looked down at her and smiled. He had a sweet smile, his skin looked very white with dark freckles showing up in the ultraviolet disco lights. His hair stood out like an aureole of dark gold frizz. He had very full pink lips, a shapeless wodge of a nose and pale eyes with dark lashes. He dipped his head and kissed her upturned mouth.

This is it, I'm being kissed. And then, at last. His lips parted and she felt his tongue against her teeth. What to do now? Oh well. She opened her mouth a bit and let it happen. A bit yuk, but not sweet sixteen any more, thank goodness.

The music stopped, and the couples left the dance floor dreamily hand in hand, some to the bar for more cider, others downstairs to the Snog Pit to carry on horizontally what they had been doing vertically.

'What's your name?' asked her rescuer.

'Damson. What's yours?'

'Tamsin?' He had an American accent.

'No, Damson. Like the fruit.'

'That's kind of unusual. I'm Daniel.'

She smiled and let him lead her downstairs to the Snog Pit. But he didn't take her there, he led her through the door and out into the chilly starlit night.

'Where do you come from?' she asked.

'Canada. I'm here studying for a term on an exchange programme.'

She was a little sad that it wasn't likely she would see him again, but so taken up in the moment of being chosen that it didn't register. They walked a little way from the building and the noise, and he just stood, holding her hand and staring upwards at the sky. As they were out in the country the stars showed piercingly bright against deepest blue.

He sighed.

'Damson,' he said. 'My host family gave me something called damson jam. I had no idea what it was, but it was a kind of confiture. I like this peculiar English damson.'

Then he asked her if she was warm enough.

Damson had no experience of boys, let alone of one being kind, and she fell into bliss as if down a well. She was desperate to kiss him again, and she wanted to look at him properly.

She pulled away from his encircling arm and turned towards him, looking at his face. He wasn't handsome exactly, his light eyes were small and creased up as he smiled at her so sweetly.

He flung his arms around her and kissed her upturned mouth, out there, under the reeling stars, the vast and endless chill of space above their warm teenage heads.

Twenty-one

Damson
August 1986

The sun streamed through the ogee-arched hall windows as Damson crept towards the front door. Beside it was a little mahogany and glass box into which the letters cascaded every morning. She had spent about seven slow minutes sitting at the top of the stairs before venturing down to meet her fate in the letter box. No one else was about, the house was very quiet. Only the tock of the grandfather clock, with its engraved brass face, disturbed the peace.

Frightened that someone would come down and witness her triumph or disaster, she took a rush at it, lifting the little glass door and snatching the post inside. Brown, white and blue envelopes addressed to Lord Mount-Hey, Lady Mount-Hey, The Hon. Clarice Hayes (which she isn't, she's just plain Miss Clarice Mullins). All delaying tactics exhausted, Damson dropped the other letters on to the hall table and held in her hand an official white envelope from the examinations board.

Her heart banged in her chest as she folded down the edges and tore with exaggerated care along the dotted line. She shut her eyes as she unfolded the piece of blue paper and held it up to her face.

She turned her head away, trying to catch a glimpse of her A chance to follow him to St Bennet's, if they'll have me.'

She was seized by a sudden doubt. She hadn't expected As. She glanced at the paper again, and there they were. Lovely as a row of teepees. She would always love the letter A.

There was a hot light burning in her chest as she went over to the old sedan chair beside the front door. Inside lived the black Bakelite telephone with its chrome dial and its cohort of phone books, address books and doodled notepads, with a biro attached to a shelf with a piece of string and a drawing pin – Munty's vain attempt to stop people wandering off with it.

'I'll go and make some tea for Margaret,' said Munty, pottering in his old sheepskin slippers down the passage to the kitchen. She looked after him with affection – with results like that she could love anybody. And she liked the way his hair was fluffy and silvery in the mornings.

Her grandmother answered the phone quickly. A lifetime of calls from patients, before all these things became automated, had accustomed her to grasping the point very fast.

'Oh darling, that's simply marvellous news. I must go and tell Grandpa.'

It had always been to Granny that Damson fled whenever she could, and to her kind, faintly antiseptic grandfather. While she knew she was no replacement for their beloved lost Melissa, she was at least female and physically there, in arms and on laps, in cots and on sofas.

Everywhere that her mother wasn't.

Her grandmother – and indeed anyone who'd lived through the war – would not burden others with her grief, particularly not her own granddaughter. The warm thrum of love in her clear that the death had been a complete shock to everyone. Damson had been just five weeks old. She was so used to the story that she didn't think to ask for more.

Her response to her grandmother's going uncharacteristically quiet was to climb up on to Sarah's knee and nestle into her warm, comforting and sweetly scented bosom. As she grew older she would carefully move the reading glasses on their string out of the way first.

'Darling Damson,' her grandmother would murmur, resting her chin on the little girl's head and holding her tight.

Twenty-two

Margaret
April 1987

'Iris, I need to look at the guest list. Can you bring it here?' Margaret was in her boudoir, as she liked to call it, a lovely room with a high ceiling overlooking the lake at the front of Castle Hey. Her Biedermeier desk was positioned in front of the triptych of arched windows framed in chintz scattered with creamy, golden-hearted lilies, and she gazed out across the sparkling water at bright trees in new leaf. What had been rank grass and mud when she had arrived as a bride, was now turfed to an Englishman's dream of a lawn, running down beyond the carriage sweep to the neat and tidy gravelled lake shore beyond.

Margaret had had a very clear idea of her marketable assets from her earliest teenage years. She was born after the end of the war, conceived during her father's last leave, but he didn't come home – his fate was an enduring mystery – and Helen, her mother, never mentioned him and didn't remarry. There was nothing unusual about fatherless children in the Nottingham street where she had been born, or in her school.

Helen took in piece work, and her hands flew at the industrial Singer day and night to support herself and her one child. It hadn't been deprived, but it was very ordinary. Yet Margaret never felt ordinary. Her friends had all left school at fifteen and worked in shops and factories, the additional income welcomed by their families. But Margaret insisted on stretching the family budget by completing a secretarial and business college course. If she could get into an office, she would meet a better class of potential husband.

She planned her progress through the best available offices, gaining experience. At twenty-one her certificate of excellence landed her a job in the secretarial pool at Mullins Industrial. The day Mr Mullins' personal assistant Miss Atkins developed shingles and ceased to perform her Cerberus to Mr Mullins' Hades, fate took Margaret in hand and threw her high.

The wedding followed on as night does day. Mullins had been a childless widower for many years. It was all perfectly respectable. Miss Atkins sat in the front right pew of St Peter in Chains, glowering and glaring from under her purple velour hat.

Margaret, very much a Christian – the Church Youth Club had been much more her style than the secular one – and a virgin whatever the mutterings, wore a long, blindingly white dress with bell sleeves. She didn't take the trouble to worry about romantic love, 'Soppy stuff, so impractical,' she would tell herself, shaking her head. Love, for her, was what she felt for her mother and later for her twins. Gratitude was what she felt for Mr Mullins.

After eleven years of peaceful marriage, Joe Mullins had died suddenly. They'd been in the Bahamas. She was lounging by the pool flicking through *Modern Woman*, while the girls, who were ten at the time, played tennis.

She had glanced up and seen that Joe was face down in the pool. Screaming for help, she'd jumped in and tried to turn him over. But he weighed seventeen stone and she wasn't strong enough. The pathologist said he'd died of a heart attack, not drowned, so she was reassured that she could have done no more.

He'd been a good husband, and had loved his identical girls, delighting in their prettiness and unable to get over how he, 'an ugly old walrus' as he called himself, could be father to two fairy children with golden hair.

After two years, there was nothing for her in Nottingham any more, especially as her mother, who'd moved in with them after Joe's death, had also died. She dealt with her grief at that terrible loss, her faith sustaining her, and then in her usual efficient way moved on. Relying on the best professional advice, she sold their home and all her shares in Mullins Industrial, appointing a financial adviser to handle the resulting capital, and started a new life in London. She was richer than even she had expected, she'd had no idea of the depth and breadth of Mullins' business activities, but everything came to her, enough to lead a very interesting life after his death. She would never have met Munty if it hadn't been for Joe, and she remained grateful to his memory.

As soon as she had seen Castle Hey, she grasped its – and Munty's – potential, and focused on moving him briskly to a proposal. She was very charming and she arranged all kinds of entertainment for this sad widower and his unresponsive daughter.

As soon as they were married, Margaret began to transform Castle Hey. When she arrived, her boudoir had been curiously empty. She wondered briefly why such a large light room at the front of the house had been shut up and neglected. But then a lot of the house remained very much as it had been when the Army handed it back in the Sixties. Munty hadn't had the capital or the will, after Melissa died, to do anything apart from prevent it leaking as much as possible. That meant living in a handful of rooms, and locking any that could not be heated or decorated.

She had not been able to persuade the twins to make proper friends with Damson, but threatened to cut off their allowances unless they were as nice to her as they could manage. She explained to them that the house, although it looked to them like a dump, could be restored and would be a lovely place for parties and dances. She took them into her confidence on the subject of titles, and how desirable they were for people who wanted to get on in the world. The twins got it at once and, while not overwhelming in their friendliness, set out to convince Damson that it wouldn't be an absolute nightmare to have them as stepsisters.

Her social secretary Iris bustled on her trotters over to the desk where Margaret sat surrounded by fabric samples, menus, invitations and all the other paraphernalia required to arrange a deb's coming-out ball. An advertisement in *The Lady* had brought Iris Long to Castle Hey. She was a small rotund creature whose feet bulged out of her neat size-three navy courts. Her several chins were only partially concealed by the frilly ruff that decorated the neck of her blouse. Blonde highlights and a blow dry, pussy bow and a navy pleated skirt completed the look, which was Miss Piggy as Princess Diana.

Margaret appreciated Iris's tactful social coaching, The first girl she'd employed for the joint role had been not only sneering but also wrong about lots of things – such as serviettes and pastry forks. She'd left in a huff when confronted. Margaret was eager to get it right and had no pride when it came to adjusting her behaviour in order to move up and fit in. Iris's wages reflected this extra duty. Some of the advice was surprising, such as answering, 'How do you do?' when someone said, 'How do you do?' to you. She'd blushed when she remembered replying, 'Very well, thank you'. The twins' dance was, barring any future weddings, the apotheosis of Margaret's dreams. She was so determined to get it right that she would pay any price to do so.

Iris was also good with Damson, whenever Margaret became exasperated with her stepdaughter's ingratitude and rudeness. Damson seemed indifferent to all the trouble and expense that were being lavished on the party. She'd even turned down Margaret's offer to have something made to go with the twins' dresses, preferring what her grandmother could run up from a *Modern Woman* pattern.

The new Lady Munty had been thrilled to receive one of Peter Townend's letters, in turquoise ink, suggesting that she should bring out her girls with the Hon. Damson Hayes, who must now be the right age. Townend, Margaret's research had told her, was on a personal crusade to keep the whole debutante boat afloat after the end of court presentation in 1958. He had an encyclopaedic knowledge of genealogy and Margaret was only too pleased for him to be aware of where the money for the big Castle Hey dance came from. Money rapidly gained lustre when attached to a genuine hereditary title, particularly an old one.

The twins responded to the whole deb scene just as she'd hoped. They went out of their way to be nice to Peter, linking both his arms, one on each side, and whispering gossip into his ears to make him laugh. They knew exactly which side their bread was buttered, and could see that everyone thinking they were Hons meant a lot in that world. They relished the effect of their good looks and liveliness on the debs' delights after years of single-sex boarding school.

The Season was no longer the preserve of gentry and aristocracy. The Royal Household didn't police who could or couldn't take part as it had in the strict old days of Drawing Rooms and presentation to the monarch. The last trace of snooty exclusion left, like the whale's hind leg, was applying for the Royal Enclosure at Ascot. It was money that counted for everything these days and the Season had been revivified by a healthy injection of cash and new blood after the nadir of the Seventies. Everyone complained that corporate entertaining was taking over the riverbanks at Henley and even Chelsea Flower Show. But for anyone who chose to be a deb, things went on much as they had before. The twins told their mother that they loved the debs' tea parties, the inaugural events of any girl's Season, and made lots of friends who were like themselves both in appearance and background. First generation private school so no need for elocution lessons. Margaret was not frightened of anything or anyone, but when she'd found out that Munty's mother had worked in a shop and Melissa had been a doctor's daughter, it certainly helped her social confidence.

Even so, after Munty had asked her to marry him one night in the Poule au Pot, Margaret had visited a discreet address in South Kensington to brush up on her vowel sounds. She still had refreshers regularly to make sure she kept control of a whole herd of brown cows.

She was exasperated to hear from the twins that Damson, who had tried one tea party, said it was boring and went back to her part-time job as a medical orderly at St Saviour's Hospital.

Noonie and Clarrie were turning into the sensation of the Season. The newspapers loved them. They starred in the Berkeley Dress Show, dressed in the same styles in different colours. Damson was rejected as a model. She'd turned up to the audition late, looking a mess, and knew she was at least a size too big. Noonie and Clarrie had been 'finished' for a bit of polish after school, and had learned all kinds of useful stuff at Jilly Dupree's establishment in Knightsbridge, from secretarial and modelling skills to deportment and grooming, even – using the frame of an old MG in the garden – how to get into and out of a sports car without showing their knickers. Damson had been studying for her Cambridge entrance exams down the road.

As for the Season itself, Margaret took her usual approach: educate herself thoroughly and get the best help and advice money could buy. She'd loved the preliminary mothers' lunches. She'd been a little worried that she wouldn't be accepted by the others, but discovered quickly that more than half were not grand at all. There were younger second wives of rich men who'd discarded an ageing spouse in favour of their pretty secretary, ex-models married to bankers, well-off nobodies in particular – all impressed by her title and in-depth knowledge of the Season.

Marrying Munty had been well worth it, even if he was still in love with his perfect dead Melissa. She couldn't help being irritated by her predecessor's gravestone. Why wasn't there something suitable from the Bible on it instead of that mawkish poetry? But she comforted her husband by talking about them all meeting up again in Heaven. Secretly she wondered to herself how she would deal with that situation socially but, ever practical, the second Lady Munty thought she'd cross that celestial bridge when she came to it. She could never quite envisage her Mullins among the company of angels but tried hard to think of him there in her prayers every night.

Her guidebook to bringing out the girls was an old copy of the Fifties classic, Petronella Portobello's *How to Be a Deb's Mum*, which she kept in her capacious Hermès handbag and referred to at all times. She was better informed than many of the other mothers as a result, able to assume pole position and advise on everything from what to wear at Henley (skirts on the knee, certainly not above), to announcing dates for your dance well in advance to avoid clashes.

She knew that marriage was not the debutante's goal in the Eighties, but if her twins had not befriended their way into valuable connections by August, she would eat her mink toque. The other girls had brothers after all, and wide social networks to which she herself didn't have access. As for Damson, she despaired. She did her Christian duty by her stepdaughter, but Damson had always been cool towards her, appearing to grudge everything she did for her. She plainly believed herself to be above it all, superior because she was going to Cambridge. It annoyed her that Damson went to the parties at all. In fact, Damson and her scruffy room, that she hadn't allowed Margaret to touch, were the only dark spots in all the brightness, warmth and luxury of the renovated Castle Hey. The girl disconcerted her and sometimes made her furious. How dare Damson, with her mousy hair and untidy appearance, think she was better than

Margaret's own golden twins?

She didn't want her own girls to have any particular career. They were not academic and she could see they would make good wives for rich men. With any luck they wouldn't have to work after marriage. But that was all later, maybe in their mid-twenties. She was looking forward already to planning their weddings, getting that nice man from *Society* magazine in to do the photography, with lovely Castle Hey in the background. She dreamed on, dismissing uncomfortable thoughts of Damson in her practical way.

The twins had chosen to have their dresses designed and made by Landy Lane, a new British couturier famous both for his sexy curvaceous evening dresses and his close ties with the more stylish bands. Margaret shook her head. It was a bit late now to start trying to control the twins' choices, and everything was working out very well, so it didn't seem necessary. But Landy Lane? He seemed a bit sophisticated for teenagers, and debutantes at that. She was hoping they would choose society designer Arabella Pollen for their coming-out dance, but no, it had to be Landy Lane and his artful wisps of fabric.

Margaret insisted on going with the twins to Lane's Notting Hill studio. The designer was rumoured to be fitting a rock star's muse in the inner sanctum, and was running very late. They flicked through *Modern Woman* and *Society* magazines, and chatted about what they would like to wear and whether it should be the same style in two different colours or the other way round.

Then Lane appeared, his yellow-white hair sticking up like a cockatoo's crest, his measuring tape behind his neck. He was tall and extremely thin, wearing blue linen peg-top trousers tight around the calves and ending in pointed silver shoes, with a baggy white linen shirt only half tucked in. His loosened tie was also blue, and decorated with a picture of Donald Duck with a machine gun and cigar.

Margaret exclaimed: 'Ah, Mr Lane. I wasn't sure about using you, as the girls are only eighteen, but they adore your dresses and it is their special party.' She tailed off as Lane ignored her and appraised the girls' bodies. After all, the model on the latest cover of *Modern Woman* was wearing Lane, and perhaps the normal rules about manners did not apply.

'Hello, lovelies,' he said, grinning.

Their mother watched with pride as her twins blossomed from lanky limbs sprawled on the gilt chairs under the warmth of his smile.

'Stand up, will you?'

They bounced to their feet and stood in front of him, both wearing tight pedal-pusher jeans, with braces and big men's shirts, their blonde hair curling over their shoulders. Lane walked round them, while Clarrie said, 'We really liked that album cover you did. With the angels, all in gold and silver. We'd like to look like that.'

'Oh you would, would you? Not at all what I have in mind. Do I just measure one of you? Are you identical? Ha! Joke.'

And he set to work measuring every inch of them. Margaret knew his dresses were constructed with an artful internal geometry so that, externally, they appeared to be barely clinging to flesh, but in reality were fiercely structured and engineered. When he'd finished measuring, and his assistant had written everything down on quick sketches, he said: 'Now, twins are a bit freaky.' Margaret suppressed her reaction. 'And I think dressing them identically is naff.'

Both twins winced this time.

'We are going to do something completely different for each girl so they don't look identical at all. Can one of you dye your hair silver?' They glanced at each other as he went into the back room to fetch silk swatches of the kind of embossed, embroidered and painted fabrics that gave his dresses a three-dimensional quality.

Before they arrived, he had asked to see colour photographs of the house where the dance was being held. Margaret sent over a recent copy of *Historic Décor* magazine that featured the restoration of 'forgotten Gothick jewel' Castle Hey.

There were colour photographs of the south front, the linked drawing rooms, the single-colour garden borders in blue, pink, coral and green, and the reclaimed eighteenth-century fountain Margaret had had positioned in the shallows of the lake.

'You, on the left. You're gonna wear grey. And you, the other one, you're gonna wear pink.'

They both began to protest.

Margaret hushed them and looked at the couturier. 'It's to do with your house. And not any old pink, the pink of those old bricks and the grey of the stone. I'm going to get the fabrics painted and embroidered to look like they have moss and lichen and stuff on them. The grey dress will be modelled on the statue in the fountain, classical drapery, and slit to the thigh. I'll commission flat Greek sandals in silver for you. And the brick pink will be a strapless mermaid dress with a net fish tail embroidered with tiny crystal beads, like the mist coming off the lake.'

The girls looked dumbfounded. Margaret had taken them foraging in Aladdin's Cave in Berwick Street and come back with gold and silver crystal organza samples, which were now destined to stay forever in their Fiorucci handbags.

He was sketching briskly as he talked, *Historic Décor* open on the desk beside his pad. Then he picked up the pieces of paper and handed one to each girl. He had captured them, and when they saw themselves in what he had designed, the little family realised his mastery and succumbed to it.

'The toiles will be ready this time next week. You'll need to come then for one hour-long fitting. Then the dresses will be made up, and you come in again for a final fitting. They'll be finished and the embroidery done exactly one week before the party, so don't put on any weight. You won't need bras. I'll also need to talk about your hair and make-up, as we don't want you spoiling the designs with anything crap. I have people I can send to you.'

Margaret knew then they would outshine any other deb at their dance, including Damson, who appeared to show little or no real interest in what she wore or how she looked. No need to make allowances for her either. She couldn't possibly remember or mourn her mother as Margaret did hers.

Twenty-three

Damson
June 1987

Miranda grabbed her arm. Damson welcomed the attention as she didn't have anything much else to do apart from stand around in her blue taffeta waiting to be asked to dance. She had wanted so much to fit in to the Season as the twins did so effortlessly and at least to meet boys and have fun but sometimes it felt more like hard work.

The Season was decidedly separate from her ambitions to be a doctor. Secretly she wanted to reconnect with her ancestors, cut off from her by the random way in which her father had come into his inheritance. So she stubbornly persisted with the parties, however uncomfortable, as it felt important to do what vanished generations of Hayes women had done before her, even if she knew nothing whatever about them. She loved to please her grandmother too, who thoroughly approved, and enjoyed making her dresses and hearing about the people she met. She had a vague idea that her mother hadn't taken to being a deb, and had disappointed Granny, although of course she had met Munty.

She let Margaret arrange everything – her Season was only a by-product of the twins' anyway. Their confidence and superior networking abilities meant Clarrie and Noonie were invited to more, better and different parties. They had proper allowances from their mother too, which made everything easier for them. Margaret had rented a little flat in South Kensington for all three of them to stay in for the duration too. Munty was always strapped for cash, and gave her 'handouts' rather than a regular allowance.

She had made a few acquaintances and danced a bit, even kissed some boys. But none of it had stuck, and she was grateful that she was off to India, and then there was Cambridge at the end of it, so she didn't have to be a 'success'.

Miranda was beautiful and frightened Damson a little bit. She appeared to be living by a different set of rules and didn't care what anyone thought. She had waving reddish hair and long slender freckled arms and legs.

'Come with me,' Miranda said, a gleam in her green eyes.

Damson let herself be led into the Ladies.

'Here.'

A small pungent brown bottle was thrust under her nose.

'Go on. Sniff hard.'

Damson sniffed obediently. Instantly her head began to lift off her neck, and her face seemed to boil. Her mouth dropped open, her body inside the tight taffeta dress pulsed with heat and her heart raced. Miranda tittered. Damson staggered over to the wall where there were some chairs and slumped down, her skirt billowing around her. Miranda wandered off to the basins and stared at herself in the mirror, licking a finger and stroking her eyebrows into place.

After a minute, Damson said, 'What was that?'

'Poppers. Do you want some more?'

Damson said, 'And people do that for fun?'

'Yup.'

'Oh.'

When she had recovered, she went over to the basins herself and looked in the mirror. The bright red face she had dreaded wasn't there. She took a compact out of her little gold bag and patted it over her face, adding a slick of strawberry-flavoured lip-gloss.

She knew what it was. As a future doctor she bloody well ought to. Amyl nitrite, or heart starter, great for angina. Also used as an antidote to cyanide. What was Miranda doing with it? Well, she'd done it now. She would never have to do it again.

'Shall we go back in?'

'Nah,' said Miranda, heading for the cubicles, rummaging in her bag as she went.

Damson rejoined the dance, uncomfortably aware of the poppers smell lingering in her nostrils. The pink walls of the huge hotel's largest ballroom were decorated with real branches dotted all over with flowers flown from South Africa. It was the coming-out ball for Bellissima Connaught, the cosseted only child of South African diamond magnate Biggins Connaught and his wife, former Miss South Africa Tristesse. If any deb looked as if she felt more out of place than Damson it was Bellissima. She was a blank shapeless girl who projected an air of panic. Her dress was a cruelly frilled confection of mauve crystal organza, her hair bubble permed and teased, her make up professionally laid on with a trowel. She looked like a sad child playing dressing up and never had a girl been more unfortunately christened. She sat with a large dull young deb's delight beside her, talking to no one, while her glamorous mother danced and danced with all the most handsome and eligible men in the room.

Damson returned to her table and sat down, as usual hoping someone would ask her to dance. The damask tablecloth was heavy against her knees. There was an arrangement of pink roses in the centre of the table. She might try to filch one at the end and take it home to her grandmother on Friday evening.

Twenty-four

Damson
June 1987

Damson sat in front of the glass-topped, kidney-shaped dressing table. She was always irritated by its fussy ruffled skirt that Granny had made to match the curtains before she was born. Her legs tangled in its folds, but she'd long ago discovered that you could pull the skirt aside and there were drawers underneath. In the drawers she had found a set of Carmen rollers that still worked, and a cache of her mother's make-up. It had been the first time she had ever found anything that belonged to Melissa.

It was the evening of the Castle Hey dance, and her sash window, with its Gothick arched top, was opened as far down as it could go on to the warm June air. She'd had her bath, and was rubbing faintly sparkly golden body cream into her shoulders and over her breasts, when there was a knock on the door. Her hands snatched at her towel and she huddled in it, calling out, 'Come in?'

It was Margaret, dressed and ready, her hair done. Damson was startled to notice that she was wearing a tiara. She didn't dare ask where it came from, just as she had skirted around any mention of the bounty that appeared on all sides, glowing from room to room, transforming her tatty childhood home into something out of, and indeed in, *World of Interiors*. All the gorgeousness felt wrong and as if she needed to deserve it, which she was failing to do. Margaret's dress was bright sapphire satin, tight-waisted with black chiffon half sleeves and an organza fichu around the shoulders, pinned at the front with a large diamond brooch. A strong whiff of Estée Lauder Private Collection accompanied her.

'Hello, Damson. I just came to see how you were getting on.'

'I'm fine, thank you, Margaret.'

'Do you need anything? Some help with your hair? Lionel will be finished with Noonie soon.'

'It's OK, I've got Carmens. I'll just curl it a bit.'

Damson's hair fell way down her back. It was quite fair, bleached by many summers of sun, but it was what she called 'hair-coloured hair', mousy pale brown when left to its own devices. It could look quite pretty when tamed by the heated rollers. She picked up her dryer and began to run the warm air over its length, lifting it with her fingers.

Margaret said something else, but she couldn't hear her over the whirr of the little motor.

'Sorry?'

Margaret left the room, closing the door with a decisive sound, and Damson realised she had been rude and wondered to herself whether it was on purpose. She just couldn't embrace the Margaret thing, where her stepmother barged into her room – and her life – and tried to do things for her and then snapped at her when she didn't accept.

She knew the deb business was for the benefit of the twins, and not for her. She had Cambridge in her future. They had futures mapped out that depended far more on making a success of hair and make-up and dresses. None of those thoughts stopped her being happy now though, in this moment.

She glanced at the bed where her golden taffeta dress was lying on top of the duvet, underwear arranged in the appropriate places. Maybe she would meet someone nice tonight. So far she hadn't met anyone who seemed to like her as much as Daniel. They had written to each other for a bit but, with the Atlantic between them, the romance had fizzled out. All she'd had of male company recently had been a few dances, the odd kiss in the rhododendrons, but not a sniff of a proper boyfriend.

Boys danced with her because they wanted to meet the twins. She tried not to let the feeling gain entrance, but she couldn't kill the green tendrils that proliferated when she saw their effortless ability to attract suitable men. She didn't care much what she wore, unless she was going to a party, and Granny made most of the decisions for her. The twins on the other hand bought everything in Beauchamp Place or down the King's Road, they wore bright silk dresses and huge hats for Ascot, and suits with big shoulders, and immaculate white Levis with pastel-coloured cashmere jerseys.

They were invited to model for *Society* magazine, taken to Stayle Hall and styled by the fashion editor for a decadent country house weekend story called *Come Out at Night*. This included lingerie shots embracing each other in the grand bedrooms, which Damson could see that Margaret was being brave about. It wasn't the kind of exposure she had envisaged. Damson laughed when she thought of the remarks that *wouldn't* be made at St Anthony the Great during coffee.

Damson was baffled by their fixation on Princess Diana, what she wore, what she said. As far as she was concerned Diana was a silly girl who'd failed all her O levels twice. The twins had no interest in the princess's academic record but avidly copied her every reported outfit. They had Calvin Klein and Gloria Vanderbilt jeans, Gucci scarves tied around their necks, cocktail dresses by Thierry Mugler, hats by Stephen Jones for society weddings, and everything they needed to attract the attention of exceedingly rich 'suitable' husband material. As the beautiful – and rich – Hayes Twins were seen and photographed everywhere, designers fell over themselves to dress them. No mention of Mullins now.

She began to roll the hot Carmens into her wispy fair hair. The rollers, stained tea brown by time, stood in two rows in an oblong black plastic box. Damson sat assiduously rolling and pinning them up until all her hair was dangling around her cheeks, heavy with curlers. Then she paid attention to her face, peering into the mirror and assessing herself through half-closed eyes. She wished her cheeks were not so round, craning and twisting her neck to try and locate some cheekbones under the plump smooth surface.

Failing this, she flipped open a copy of *Look Now* and tried to work out how to copy the information about shading and defining, using a Rimmel palette she had bought for the purpose. She had a go at painting on *trompe-l'œil* cheekbones by brushing the darker brown halfway up her cheeks, frowning with concentration. When she had finished she had another look and burst out laughing. She looked like nothing so much as Adam Ant, with dark ridiculous stripes slanting from her nose up to her ears. She read the instructions again, tried toning it down and then gave up. She rubbed it all off furiously with cotton wool and Anne French cleansing milk, leaving her skin red and shiny.

It was getting late. She quickly dusted her face all over with pale loose powder she'd found in the dressing table. It said Coty on the box and smelt faintly of roses. There was a white velvet pad inside, stained flesh-colour on one surface. She held it to her lips for a moment, closing her eyes. Her bare shoulders tingled with desire for loving hands. She knew she was indulging herself, trying to conjure a concerned presence that was missing from the empty room like a cold anomaly in the warmth. She put a hand behind her back, scrabbling at the air, trying to tear away the pernicious membrane between her and the past that had contained her mother in this very room. Why was time so different from space? She wrapped her own arms around her upper body and squeezed, shuddering, breathing out.

Also in the dressing-table drawer was a little black Rimmel box with a sliding lid and a tiny toothbrush-type brush. She opened it now and looked. There wasn't much of the hard black cake left, it was worn down to the silver metal in the middle. It must be some old-fashioned sort of mascara that you needed to spit on. The warm stink of spitting into the electric bar heater came back to her from bored nursery evenings huddled in her towel in this room. Her mother should have been there, then as well as now, rubbing her hair dry, cuddling her in her towel, warming her nightie in front of the fire, reading her a story. Not Pauline, who'd never read to her. Her grandmother had, but not in here, in her bedroom at the house in Dorking.

She poked out her tongue and touched the little black cake with its tip. No taste, not a ghost of Melissa's spit. She glanced in the mirror. Her tongue had a black smudge on the end. She rubbed the brush across and tried it on her lashes. Nothing much happened. She spat into the box and rubbed more vigorously, thinking you definitely could not cry when wearing this kind of mascara. At least now her spit was mingled with her mother's.

She pulled open the drawer and chucked the little box back. Then she groped around for her mother's scent: Fidji, just a brown stain in the bottom of a square glass bottle. She pulled out the stopper and sniffed at a faint whiff of carnation, trying to conjure up some memory but without the slightest stirring. She preferred her Yves St Laurent Rive Gauche, and sprayed herself with it.

She picked up a black kohl pencil and ran it all around the inside of her eyelids, which tickled. She brushed greeny-gold eye shadow on to her lids hoping it would enhance her indeterminate eye colour, grey with yellow streaks. Unpinning the curlers one by one, she slid them back on to their spindles. She pulled some of the curls into a half ponytail on the back of her head with a slide. She put dangly earrings made of sequins in her ears. They matched her golden yellow taffeta ball dress and high-heeled strappy sandals.

Wandering over to the bed, she dropped her towel to the floor and wriggled into her sensible cotton knickers. She wished she had lacy ones but it couldn't be helped. She discarded the straps from the new firm and complicated bra that Granny had bought for her when she realised the boned strapless bodice was squashing Damson's bosoms flat. There was another knock on the door while she was stepping into the dress.

'Thank goodness, Granny, I was just wondering what to do. I

thought you were downstairs with the parents, and I couldn't come running down with my dress flapping off. That's the trouble with strapless, there's nothing to hang the bodice on while you do up the back.'

Come here then,' said Granny, taking a tight grip on the back of the dress's waist, pulling up the zip and fastening the hook at the top. 'There you are.'

Her warm hands on Damson's shoulders, she turned her round and stepped back to look at her. The dress had a little gather in the centre of the bodice giving it a sweetheart neckline and a full skirt with a tulle petticoat sewn inside to make it stand out. Damson slipped her feet into the sandals, admiring the gold nail polish on her toes and doing up the slender ankle straps that crossed at the back over her Achilles tendons.

'What do you think?'

Her grandmother's eyes were suspiciously shiny. 'I think you look beautiful,' she said. Damson swirled her skirt around her ankles, dancing at Sarah, flinging her arms round her and laughing and kissing the older woman.

'You look lovely too.' Her grandmother was wearing the Elbourne tiara in her silvery curls and a V-necked black lace dress with long sleeves and a scarlet satin sash.

'I first met you in this room. Tiny thing in a crib. Your mother.' Sarah stopped. Damson went quiet and still. 'Yes?'

'Your mother would have been so proud of you,' Sarah said, pulling Damson against her bosom. They stood together for a minute before Sarah let her go and backed away. 'Mustn't let our mascara run.'

'Darling Gran, was she anything like me?'

'She wasn't shapely like you, darling. She was very slender, which was just as well given the Sixties fashion for boyish figures. You're more like me.'

'No, I mean like me in character.'

Her grandmother sat down on the bed. 'I have to say, no, again. She wasn't like you. I've never worried about you. And I did worry about her.'

'In what way?' Damson sat down beside her.

'Well, you worked hard at school and you knew what you wanted to do. She took a couple of A levels, but the grades weren't good. I know you aren't taking all this deb stuff seriously but that doesn't bother me. We went to a lot of trouble for her but she refused to carry on after a while.'

Damson thought it would be nice to be worried about for a change. Everyone just expected her to get on with it. She didn't always feel wonderful, sometimes she was sad and lonely. She would love to find a boyfriend but hadn't a clue how to go about it.

'She never knew what she wanted to do,' Granny continued. She looked down at her strong-looking hands and twisted her wedding ring.

'Wasn't she a nurse?'

'Yes, but not for long, she dropped out and came home. I think you know she had a mild case of talipes and all the standing was too much for her. Our mistake, but she seemed so determined to begin with.'

'Yes, I remember you telling me. Then she met Munty, didn't she?'

'Well, you know the story about her meeting your father at

Queen Charlotte's Ball the summer before. When she was at home, we were very worried about her. These days I suppose people would think it was normal for teenagers, but she used to stay up late and sleep late in the morning. She did go back to work, but it was just part time at a ridiculous shop in Dorking called Lord Groove. Anyway, Munty turned up at the shop one day when she was there. Said he was passing which we doubt. He was always a conventional young man and Lord Groove's tie-dyed T-shirts weren't his style. Anyway, he seemed to cheer her up and they were married that autumn.'

It was a familiar tale. 'Not for long though,' said Damson.

'No, not for long, but then there was you.'

'I'm sorry, Granny, but it's always so difficult to know what it would have been like to have a mother all of my own.'

'I know, darling. But you've had me and I hope I've been able to do some mothering. Remember, I wasn't mothered either. My mother was hopeless. Sat about all day being grand.'

Damson had heard all about her great-grandmother and her unwanted advice about what 'ladies' did and didn't do. She held her grandmother's hand up to her lips and kissed it. 'We ought to think about going downstairs now. Have you seen the twins yet?'

'I think the hairdresser's still with them. He's done your stepmother. Alexei did mine in London this morning.'

'Yes, I saw. She's wearing a tiara too. Where did that come from? Munty doesn't have one.'

'I think she hired it,' said Granny. 'Not the sort of thing you go out and buy anyway.'

Not even Margaret.

Granny could be quite disapproving if she was openly

disrespectful of her stepmother. Damson went back to the dressing table and sprayed on a bit more scent.

'I think I'm ready. You?' Picking up a little gold, purse-shaped evening bag that she had also found in the dressing table, she popped in her lip gloss and powder compact while her grandmother left the room, following her along the corridor and down the stairs.

Only family and the catering staff were present, there was time for a quiet celebration before the guests arrived. There would be a dinner for thirty, and then about three hundred guests coming on afterwards, having been entertained to dinner at their house parties in the district.

Having known no one when Damson was little, the Mount-Heys now had masses of friends within a twenty-mile radius, all of whom were only too delighted to entertain house parties. Particularly as it meant an invitation to what sounded like the most exclusive private dance of the Season. Sarah was rustling off in the direction of the drawing room when Damson spotted Greg Owen from *Society* magazine waiting at the bottom of the stairs. She slowed down.

Greg glanced up and took several pictures in quick succession as she processed towards him. She raised her chin and dropped her lids, pulling her spine up and her shoulders back, flinging him a smile. He shot again, but then made a gesture with his hand, looking past her. She turned and there were the twins above her on the stairs. Her heart sank. They were dressed for a change completely differently from each other. Noonie wore smoky draped silk spattered with dark green embroidery, one white shoulder bare. Her hair was silvery blonde and caught up with a diamanté crescent. Clarrie's strapless mermaid dress was dusky pink, embroidered with a grey, geometric pattern, a mist of tulle springing out below her knees, tiny crystals trembling in the folds.

They looked like embodiments of Castle Hey, the bricks and mortar and Margaret's new fountain in the lake.

This party was nothing to do with her.

She moved to one side, dipping her head, so Greg could get good pictures of them. Then she heard him say, 'The three sisters together, please. Damson in the middle. Arms around each other. That's great.' She was pulled forward and wrapped in her stepsisters' sweetly scented arms, their soft curls tickling her shoulders. She glanced at each in turn to see their identical faces smiling back at her.

'You look like the sun and the moon and a pink sky at sunset,' said Munty, coming out of the drawing room carrying glasses of champagne. Margaret's care had undoubtedly cheered him up. He was so much more noticing and loving now than he used to be. Damson should be grateful, she supposed.

Twenty-five

Damson
October 1987

With her fellow first-year medics Damson trampled through golden leaves to the gross anatomy labs, only half listening while they spooked each other with stories about the guy who hid under a sheet on an empty table, and sat up when the other students came in. Another prankster had put some prunes in his cadaver's abdominal cavity, extracting them with tweezers and eating them. They repeated the perennial medics' myth about the student's ghastly discovery, at the very end of the course when he finally reached his cadaver's head and face. Damson couldn't go on listening.

The students entered the building and their nervous chatter died away as they shared a sense of dread and awe in the face of imminent contact with mortality. Damson's super-sensitive sense of smell could detect formaldehyde seeping through the lab door, and salty liquid erupted in her mouth causing her to swallow hard. The overwhelming scents of India – jasmine and lavatories, joss-sticks and rot – had made it a relief when she had had to come home early. She must develop a method of not-smelling if she was ever to be a successful doctor.

A boy close to her whispered, 'I think I'm going to be sick.'

Damson walked briskly away from him and stood beside a

223

sensible looking Chinese girl, who turned and smiled at her.

'I'm Mary Wong,' she said.

'I'm Damson Hayes.'

'Tamsin?'

'No, it's like the fruit. D-A-M-S-O-N.'

She often wished she was called Annabel or Catherine. What was her mother thinking of?

'Oh, I see.'

They were directed to the female changing room, and told to bring only notebooks and biros with them. Damson slipped on the green scrubs she found in her locker, tied a face mask loosely around her neck and grabbed a pair of rubber gloves from the box marked non-allergenic. Then she shuffled with the others through into the anteroom for the preparation lecture.

Charles Godwin, professor of anatomy, was beginning to speak as he moved through the group to stand by the door.

'Hands up who's already seen a dead body?'

About a third of the students raised their hands. Damson wasn't sure if she qualified, so kept hers down.

Years before, an Army friend of her father's had brought back a head from Borneo in a woven basket. Aged ten, she'd taken a long time to pluck up the courage to go into the billiard room and look. She'd imagined a skull, shining like an ivory billiard ball, grinning with perfect teeth, comfortably ensconced in something like Pauline's wicker shopping basket.

'It's probably a Jap,' Sidney Faulkes had said. 'The Dayak headhunters were given tacit licence to go after Japs during the war. A relief after we'd forcibly got them out of the habit of beheading the neighbours to decorate their homes.'

She'd waited until the house was quiet, and peeped round the door. A grey thing sat on the window seat and she crept towards it. In a kind of woven ball of what looked like creepers, sat a dusty-looking rounded object punctuated with black holes where its eyes had been. She'd shuddered as she saw that there were bits of black and kippered skin and hair still stuck on in patches. It had no lower jaw so could not grin. To her relief and Pauline's, Faulkes took the head with him when he left the next day.

'Now, it is important that you understand why you need to work with cadavers before we enter the dissection room,' said the professor. 'It has been said that we need to learn to heal the living by first dismantling the dead.' And he was off on his well-honed speech to first-year medical students, designed to stop as many of them as possible from fainting and cluttering up the floor.

'It is impossible for you to imagine the normal variations and three-dimensional qualities of human anatomy from diagrams and models alone. It helps if you have seen a cadaver before, but this is not essential. If you are fulfilling a vocation to become a doctor, you must have prepared yourselves mentally for this moment.

'It is vitally important that you rapidly develop a coping mechanism that allows you to depersonalise the cadaver in your care. It is also vital that you treat it with the utmost respect.'

Damson had felt sick with nerves ever since she'd arrived in Cambridge. Could she keep up with her fiercely intelligent and hardworking fellow medics? Already some of them were boasting of all-nighters, and the jump from sailing through science A levels to absorbing several chapters of her medical textbooks each day was beginning to tell on her.

The prospect of what she had to do now was not going to help keep her cornflakes down. She had assumed a strict, self-imposed diet of macaroni cheese, baked beans and peas, the only items in the buttery she could stomach, and it was having a bad effect on her digestion.

'Please understand that all the individuals whose cadavers you will be dissecting,' went on Professor Godwin, 'have donated their mortal remains to medical science for your benefit. This is a great gift to society and to you as future doctors, and I don't need to tell you to treat these fine, public-spirited people with the respect they deserve. In Thailand, the first person voluntarily to donate his body to science was a professor of literature. Teachers are held in very high esteem over there' – he paused for polite laughter – 'and it seems he wished to maintain his teacher status after death. So, think of these people as your teachers. You may believe they cannot speak, but every tiny nerve and sinew will be telling you something vital. So listen.

'When you enter the room, you will be shown to your table. Starting with the arm, you will work on your cadaver, with your dissection partners and under the direction of your tutors. When the year of learning is over, the remains will be returned to relatives for a funeral and burial.

'Now, let us proceed.'

Damson held back a bit, trying to keep her nausea under control. But she had to go in eventually. The room was brightly lit, and each workstation was in the form of a steel bed with a drain at one end, sitting on a thick steel pillar. There were two stools at the head end of each one. The bodies lay under coverings, with just the left arm exposed, palm up. Each student had been assigned a partner, and Damson's, a spindly boy called George, leaned forward to touch the fingers of their person as if in greeting.

She liked George for doing that. In fact she clung to the idea of liking George altogether. He seemed less driven and efficient than some of the others, which appealed to the quailing inner Damson that she hoped to conceal.

Before she had any more time to think, the coverings were removed by the professor's assistants and she could see the whole cadaver. A man lay before her on his back. Not old, his hair was still brown, smoothed back from his forehead. The colour of the skin was greyish, and the nose stood out sharply, the nostrils looking very dark and cavernous.

'Pork,' she thought desperately. 'It's like pork at the butcher.'

But pork was not grey like this. Like a fungus in the shape of a man.

The professor was speaking again. They would start by reviewing the bony landmarks and osteology. Then they would abduct the arm, and remove fat and lymph nodes from the axilla. If they could come over here he would show them all where to place the first incision. Damson reached into her pocket for her glasses, and walked across to the cadaver of a very old and thin woman.

The professor took his scalpel and made a first incision down the full length of her forearm. There was no blood of course, but the violation of the skin was too much for Damson.

When she woke up she was sitting back in the anteroom with her head between her knees. Two of the lab assistants were with her.

'I think I'm going to be sick,' she muttered.

One of them helped her up by the elbow and into the Ladies, where she just got into the cubicle before throwing up.

The underlying beat of panic that seemed to infect everything she did now grew more insistent. When she emerged from the cubicle, Mary was waiting and offered to take her back to St Bennet's but she refused, muttering about food poisoning, only dimly aware of the kindness. She didn't want to disrupt anyone else's first day.

When she felt steadier, she walked back from the labs pushing her bicycle. There was a chemist on Silver Street, and she stopped, looking in at the coloured glass jars and stacked arrangement of laxatives, trying to get her breathing under control. Then she propped her bike against the railing, locking it up. Inside the shop, she was relieved to find no one beside herself. The pharmacist came out from behind a glass partition and asked her what she wanted.

'I would like a pregnancy test, please.'

The pharmacist said nothing, just turned and took a long package off the shelves behind her, putting it on the counter.

'That's five ninety-nine, please,' she said.

Damson was resentful for a moment. Money that would have kept her fed for at least three days. She put the money on the counter and tucked the test into her bag.

The jaunty pink packaging had given her an intense jolt of anger as she had to face up to what was happening inside her, the sickness, the tender breasts, the intense exhaustion. Why had he done this thing to her? Whose fault was it anyway? What the hell did she think she had been doing? She was furious with herself all over again.

In some closed-off place in her mind she'd known for weeks but, as denying the rape had swiftly become a mental habit, denying its consequences followed. She didn't pay much attention to her periods, but had become aware that she had not had one since she got back to England six weeks before. She had vaguely imagined that the mild dysentery that is the fate of all backpackers had temporarily put paid to her cycle. Denial with a big dose of false logic, she realised now.

Maybe if she stopped looking like a woman, she would somehow avoid the immemorial fate of raped women. Her wardrobe now consisted of stuff picked up in the men's sections of charity shops: big old collarless shirts, army surplus trousers held up with a leather belt, corduroys, tweed jackets and baseball boots. As a concession to going to university, she'd visited a barber and had her chewed mess of hair tidied up. She had to wear a bra, particularly as her breasts seemed to be getting bigger, and so chose a very plain sports bra like a tight vest that squashed her flat. Luckily other students were dressed in all kinds of extreme ways, so no one said anything – except for one guy, cheerful at a King's Freshers' Week party, who'd insisted on calling her Mellors.

When Munty and Margaret had come to fetch her from Heathrow on her return from India, Margaret did not comment on the way home, but Damson knew that it would only be a matter of time. Margaret's often expressed approval for the way the twins presented themselves told Damson all she needed to know. But it was already September and she was busy getting ready for Cambridge, so she didn't need to put up with Margaret's 'helpful' comments for long.

In her bedroom at Castle Hey, which she had insisted was not touched by the ever-present decorators, her wardrobe was still exuberant with ball gowns in bright colours, whispering the ghost of Rive Gauche. The fact that Granny had made all her dresses caused her to hesitate for a moment. But the desire to reject colour and prettiness and femininity was very strong. She also did not, for the first time in her life, want to see or be seen by her grandparents. She feared her grandmother's sharp eye might seek out her shame. She knew her grandparents never worried about her. She didn't want them to start worrying now.

She left the dresses where they were, deciding not to think about the dancing and flirting, the high heels and glamour. She drove herself into Canterbury and scoured the charity shops for a replacement wardrobe, and that was when the comments started.

'I understood when you got back from India that you might be looking a bit scruffy, but you don't need to dress like that now, do you? There's no need these days to look like a man to do a man's job, dear,' said Margaret one morning over breakfast. Munty hid behind his *Daily Telegraph*.

Damson was defensive but determined. 'It's comfortable and practical if I'm going to be in the labs all day. Don't want to wear heels and stuff. Anyway, I like dressing like this. Like Annie Hall,' she had trailed off. Margaret said nothing more to her relief.

When she got back to St Bennet's she made straight for the women's lavatories and peeled the wrapper from the wand. She read the instructions, her hands shaking so much she could hardly focus, let alone hold the stick still enough to pee in the right place. When she had managed it she wrapped the fateful stick in loo paper and crept back to her room to wait ten minutes for the result.

She sat on her narrow college bed in her sunny little room, so hopefully furnished with posters from Athena. Bending right over, she clutched her upper arms with her hands and squeezed herself tightly. The sobs that would not be suppressed geysered up to the surface. It was a relief just to let the hot painful tears come and she grabbed at her box of tissues, blowing her nose and mopping her eyes and beginning to plan what she would do if it were positive. Which she knew it would be.

The future that had seemed so exciting and defiant, that would mark her out from the tide of obedient helpless women, was in danger of being ripped away, leaving a jagged edge that she could not confront. Her mind veered and tacked wildly across a grey and stormy sea of blame, regret and visceral pain, trying to find any kind of safe harbour. What would she do if she couldn't be a doctor, if she had to be a single mother instead? She couldn't keep a baby conceived in that stupid way. Flirting, kissing, going too far, giving him the wrong idea. All her fault. No one would force her to keep it, would they? Her mind shied away from the shameful scene in the Indian stable. It wasn't her choice to be a mother. It wasn't even carelessness that had led to this conception. She was raped, wasn't she? What would people think? She couldn't see a way back to the person she had been before. The person her grandparents never worried about.

After ten minutes she went over to the loo paper bundle on the window sill and unwrapped it. There it was, the big purple positive splodge.

What to do? Who on earth could she talk to who wouldn't

either judge her or be unbearably upset? How could she tell
Granny, the person she loved the most in the world, that she was
pregnant? And in such a compromising way? There might be fear
that Damson would die as well of whatever it was that had killed
Melissa. After all, Melissa hadn't been much older. Damson
knew with piercing certainty that her grandmother would want
her to keep the baby. But she could not imagine herself wanting
to hold on to a reminder of the worst thing that had ever
happened to her. She had never disagreed with Granny about
anything. How could she now? At all costs, she must never know.

She began to search her mind, conjuring pictures she'd seen of
Melissa. Standing with Granny, both dressed for a ball. They
were holding hands. Another one, a white-bordered snap of
Melissa, in the garden of her grandparents' house, wearing a stiff
yellow mini-dress and displaying pretty legs. Melissa, as a little
girl in the Fifties in a party frock, skirt sticking out, strap shoes
and knee socks, holding her mother's hand. Always holding *her*
mother's hand.

'Can I hold your hand?' Then: 'Mummy?' Her tongue was
clumsy saying the word. Conscious that she had never said it
before out loud.

She sat down again and shut her eyes, reaching out with her
right hand. What? What? She had no physical memory of her
mother at all. Her eyes snapped open. She looked down at her
bitten nails and long strong fingers. Any hand Melissa knew had
been something else. Something tiny and soft. She shied away
from the idea of a soft new-born hand. Into her mind flew a
poster she had seen in the women's toilets downstairs.

Pregnant? Worried? Call Gate Advisory for confidential 24-hour service. Don't delay.

OK, abortion. And quickly, before she could think any more about hands. She jumped to her feet, reaching for pen, paper and some change. A few minutes later she was in one of the row of scribbled fibreboard phone boxes by the Porters' Lodge, armed with the number. It was horribly exposed and public, but she knew the walls were soundproofed, which immured whiffs of spit, sweat, breath and desperation.

The receiver was warm when she put it to her ear. She dialled the number, the line rang and a woman's voice answered.

'Hello?' she whispered.

'Hello, Gate Advisory here, how can I help you?'

Damson paused. She was nauseous and hungry at the same time, and tearful. Then she said quietly, 'I think I'm pregnant.'

'OK, have you done a test?'

'Yes, and it's positive.'

'Right, how are you feeling about that?' The voice was impersonally gentle, annoyingly so.

'Terrible.' Damson couldn't say it out loud. She'd never said it out loud and she wasn't even sure if it was true. Saying she'd been raped might just be a comforting excuse for stupidity. She paused.

'Do you want to talk about it?'

Using that word was weak and wrong. Carelessness seemed like a better word for what had happened.

'I want an abortion.' Abhor. Abhorrent. Abortion. Horrible words. It came out like vomit.

'Right, you have three options and abortion is one of them. I can give you some information now, but it would be better if you could come into the Centre tomorrow to talk to one of the nurses in person. Are you in Cambridge?'

'Yes. But can you tell me what would happen if I did have an abortion?'

'How many weeks along do you think you are?'

'About eight.'

'You'll need to get consent from two doctors, but we can help you with that. Do you have any children already?'

'No, I'm not married. You see, I've only just started my course. I'm a medical student, and I can't have a baby. Not now.' She was trying so hard not to cry.

'Right, you'll need to explain to the doctors that having a baby would upset your mental or physical health more than having an abortion. That means you need to tell them how the pregnancy would affect you. I think from the sound of it, they would be sympathetic.'

'So I can just tell them I don't want a baby as I want to be a doctor?'

'Yes, you'll need to tell them that it will upset your mental health if you can't study to be a doctor.'

I want to be a doctor, so I'm going to try and convince two doctors that I'll go mad if I have a baby and I'm prevented from becoming a doctor. Like them, she thought desperately.

Her forehead creased into painful folds as she tried not to cry. It gave her a headache. She shuddered.

'As it's very early on in the pregnancy, the procedure is very straightforward, nothing to worry about. You're in and out as a day case. And there's plenty of counselling available before and afterwards. Our clinic is a little way outside Cambridge but we don't advise cycling. There's a bus, and we recommend a taxi home and rest for a day or two. But most of our patients are up the next day and absolutely fine.'

'Fine?'

'Yes, fine. As I say, it's a simple, straightforward, safe procedure. The clinic is on Lawrence Road, Gate House, at number 135. Can you get there easily? We open at ten o'clock. If you like, I can take your name and you can make an appointment, but you can also just drop in for advice and support. In the end, it's your decision, but we can give you all the information you need to make an informed one.'

Damson paused again. The nurse stayed on the line.

'I want to know what they do.'

'You want to know how the abortion is carried out?'

'Yes, but what do they do? How do they get the baby out?'

'Well, it isn't a baby at this stage. Just a cluster of cells. There's very little bleeding and usually you can go home after about an hour. But it would be much better to see you in person, Miss?'

Damson rang off. She sat in the box, breathing the spitty air in and out slowly to calm herself. Then she got up but had to sit down again because silver swirls appeared in her vision. She just had time to bend over, putting her head between her knees, grateful as full consciousness returned.

Back in her room, she made herself a cup of tea, wanting sugar in it which was not her usual taste at all. Damson had always been instinctively against abortion. She held the lofty view that people should do all they could to avoid an unwanted pregnancy, but if they did fall pregnant then to take the consequences of their actions. Why punish the innocent? But that was before she had any real experience. She was ashamed now to have been so judgmental.

Try as she might, she could not get her head around the idea that what was growing in her belly was just a random mass of cells. The trouble with the way she had conceived was that she had been unable to choose to use any contraception. So she couldn't make a decision to be sensible, could she?

The memory of that night was crystal clear now. All denial was ripped away by the consequences. She knew with shame that she had been excited by Ronny's attentions. She also realised that she had ridden into the milky Indian moonlight completely conscious of the sexiness of the situation. The horse's body had been hot and vigorous between her thighs. Ronny's frequent glances sent shivers down her spine – never mind his kisses, which made her burn with longing more than any of the soft boys who had kissed her before. What if it had been just a shade different, that episode in the stable? What if she had given in to what was happening instead of struggling against it, enjoyed it even? She might have been eager for more. But, as it was, she went out that night one kind of girl, and came back to her room in the morning a completely different person.

She tried to remember her last period. It must have been just after she arrived in India, because she remembered being glad to have packed so many tampons and the tiresome business of disposing of them properly. She had arrived in New Delhi around the twentieth of July? It was now the fifteenth of October.

The scientist in her kicking in, she took down her Obstetrics and Gynaecology textbook and looked up 'gestational age eight weeks'.

'Zygote, morula, blastocyst, embryo,' she muttered to herself. 'All clumps of cells, nothing very human there. Sounds like a spell.'

There was nothing magic about it though, just the rapid march of a biological process. She started to sob as she read, hardly able to see the words through her tears: *It is at the end of the 'embryonic' stage and moving to the 'foetal' stage.* 'You bet,' she hiccupped, examining the medical drawing of a tiny human with bird-like ribs and an enormous, serious forehead. *In the normal foetus, everything needed for human development is already present. Ears continue to form, facial features take shape.*

It has a bloody face, how can a bunch of cells have a face?

The embryo is one inch long.

She flicked to a pregnancy calculator and worked out when the baby was due. June. By then she was completely lost and trying to suppress her yelps of grief and rage at this stupid thing she'd done.

The easy way would be to slip off to Lawrence Road tomorrow just after ten o'clock and get on the roller coaster to finishing the thing before it had started. Then she wouldn't have to tell anyone at all. Ever. Simple, quick, virtually painless. Get-out-of-jail-free card. Lying to the doctor about going mad if she couldn't be a doctor. The whole idea made her want to scream. Because it had started, however mistakenly, there was no denying its humanity, however tiny.

The other option was filled with terror, confusion and confrontation, but came without the guilt. What would

Margaret's reaction be? She'd spent a whole lot of money 'bringing Damson out' with the twins, and Damson knew she'd never expressed proper gratitude for that, or even for making Munty so much happier and more comfortable. In fact she resented it all, another source of guilt. The transformation of her scruffy old childhood home was not to her taste, but she could at least recognise that Castle Hey had woken up from its long sad sleep. Munty didn't look defeated any more. Margaret took him to Trumpers to have his hair cut properly, bought him hand-made suits in Savile Row and stocked the cellar with excellent claret. She realised she was glad he had someone to look after him. Damson couldn't look after him. She had wanted him to look after her

Margaret would be so furious when she found out Damson had 'got herself knocked up' as she would call it. If she carried it to term, what would happen to the baby? Should she just go home to Castle Hey and bring it up, forgetting about Cambridge and a career? She couldn't imagine Margaret allowing that. A child messing up her lovely pristine rooms, full of chintz, swags, tails and draped tables, good china ornaments to break, fringes, tassels and cream-coloured carpets. One bright spot – if she decided to dodge the slippery temptation of abortion, she would at least attract Margaret's approval as a Christian.

Easy way out. A little visit to the clinic, the rapid application of a vacuum to her cervix and all would be over. Damson lay back on her bed, squirming with discomfort. The rape would be compounded and she would be violated all over again, with a plastic tube this time. Sickened with herself and what she had done. Baby bird thing inside her didn't have to suffer too, she was folded around it, layers of blood and water, fat and skin, padding it against the wicked world. If she went through with the abortion, there would be something like those smashed pink naked nestlings she used to find in the garden, but in a kidney dish.

Then there was adoption which meant her shame would be exposed, particularly to her shy, prudish father. As far as Munty was concerned, women married and had babies rather strictly in that order. Abortion, sex before marriage, the Pill and all the rest of Sixties sexual liberation seemed to have passed him by. Perhaps the Sixties was optional, you could stay in the Fifties if you didn't like it and hop straight on to the boring Seventies. By the time she was conscious, he was living a monkish life.

She shuddered at the idea of her father thinking poorly of her, but if she let it grow until it was big enough to be free of her body safely, then it could go to a family who could love it. You didn't love a baby conceived like that, did you, so it wouldn't hurt to give it up. And she would be free to defer, go back to Cambridge and grow into a doctor like Grandpa when it was all over.

Instinctively she knew that the last person on earth in whom she would confide might hold the answers. She grasped at Margaret's efficiency and organisational skills. Damson didn't know much about her background, except that her father had been a sailor and her mother a seamstress and that she came from somewhere very different from Castle Hey. Margaret didn't love her so she wouldn't be hurt. Her grandmother did not deserve the pain of this knowledge. She had suffered enough.

Then Damson would come back to Cambridge, rewind her

life, crunch through another autumn's worth of golden leaves on her way to the labs. There would be different Georges and Maries to make friends with, and it would all be as if it had never happened. And no one at Cambridge would be any the wiser.

Munty hadn't had much time or space in his life for his small daughter. He was as good a father as he could manage to be and loved her in his own way. It would be frightening to expose her shameful pregnancy to him. He couldn't love her any more after that, could he?

She knew Pauline would be fine whatever decision she made. Pauline was earthy and realistic, brought up on a farm. She let her mind rest on Pauline. She would be a refuge, she would not judge.

Coming home from Cambridge two weeks after going up was excruciating, but there was also relief when Margaret took charge. After a pause in the usual rush of words, her stepmother was briskly kind and made no attempt to ask probing questions or scold once she understood that Damson had turned down an abortion. Margaret would sort it all out.

In her usual way, Margaret had hired a proper old-fashioned trained nanny when the twins were born. Nanny had been a wise choice, sensible and kind. She was now retired to Balham, living in a little house belonging to Margaret which she shared with her sister. Damson was to go and stay there out of sight until the baby was born, after which it was to be handed over to a suitable adoption agency. She went along with this sensible plan without arguing. Her father never said a word. As soon as she had told them both, he'd quietly left the room.

Pauline, when Damson visited her in her house in the village, said simply, 'Is this what you want?'

Damson nodded. If she said anything she knew she would start howling, so she kept quiet.

Twenty-six

Damson
June 1988

Damson did not visit her grandparents. They had written to her as usual, the letters forwarded from St Bennet's or home, but between the cheerful words about 'being so pleased that you are so independent now' she could detect that they missed her. Trying to reassure them, hating to deceive them and wanting nothing more than a proper cuddle with her grandmother, she'd sent upbeat letters saying that she was so busy with her studies she couldn't get away. That she'd taken an extension course (unspecified) which meant her studies went on for longer.

It was only a few months. Infinitely better for them never to know they had a great-grandchild.

Pregnancy in Balham was dull. Nanny and her sister were not sure how to treat her so they led very separate lives in the tall thin house. Damson had an attic bedroom to herself with a fridge, a gas ring and a microwave. There was a small bathroom on the landing. She had nothing to do but read her textbooks, go for lonely walks on Clapham Common and devour detective stories that she found in the library. Sherlock Holmes was perfect, as were early Dorothy Sayers and some of the drier Agatha Christies. Anything with a hint of romance was taken straight back. She cried much too easily over wars and disasters in the papers. The birth came as a relief.

The midwives' attitude had been peculiar and daunting as if they didn't approve of her choice to have her baby adopted. She slowly paced the wards for hours and hours until she was exhausted and lay gasping at the Entonox.

The pain became so agonising that she requested an epidural. The sensation of pain disappearing out of her body was one she thought she would never forget but of course she did immediately.

Every now and then a midwife would come and examine her.

'How's it going?' They knew she was a medical student by this time. One shift of midwives told the next. They didn't bother even to speak quietly around her.

Just outside her cubicle: 'She wants to go back to her medical studies. The baby'll be adopted.'

'Oh,' accompanied by sideways glances. Her social worker Eva Williams had looked in to see how she was getting on. She wouldn't normally have done this as Damson presented no challenges at all but she had a problem case in the maternity ward at the same time.

'All right there, Damson? I'm just down the corridor this evening,' she'd said in her cheerful Australian way, the 'ning' swinging upwards in an eternal antipodean question that could never be answered. Damson nodded, too tired to speak and Eva went away to deal with the heroin-addicted mother of eight all in care who was having number nine tonight and sadly could not be allowed to keep it.

Her stepmother had dealt with the private adoption charity Elgin Robbins which specialised in baby adoptions. It had been quite difficult to find the right people to help as they didn't advertise. There were so few babies up for adoption in England that if Elgin Robbins had put themselves in the Yellow Pages they would have been swamped by desperate prospective parents. In the end Margaret had confided in the priest at St Anthony's about Damson's predicament. He had been very kind and helpful about the whole thing and suggested a number of small private agencies that he knew about through his own counselling.

Damson had had a series of interviews and also some counselling herself. This didn't make her feel any better as she never told anyone anything, just that the father was from India and they had had a brief affair. No she didn't want to disclose his name. No he knew nothing about the baby and never would.

Margaret reminded Damson repeatedly that she must not damage her chance to be a doctor, as if she was afraid her stepdaughter might backslide. Damson didn't have the space to be surprised by her stepmother's sudden interest in her career prospects.

They chose Elgin Robbins because on enquiry it turned out that they had some Indian couples on their books, which was unusual. This was because a childless Maharaja and his wife had adopted a son in England through their agency and this had become known in the Indian community. Elgin Robbins were sensitive to the cultural and spiritual status of children within traditional Hindu beliefs. In England babies born out of wedlock to Indian girls were rare so the options for Indian couples were few.

The social workers would abide as exactly as possible by strict rules about cultural matching. A mixed-race couple would be perfect but Indian parents would also 'advantage' the child enormously. Damson suspected she was a most unusual sort of person in the non-judgmental Eighties to be giving up her baby.

The midwife came in and looked at the readout from the monitor strapped to her belly, then she hit the red buzzer on the machine and it was all go.

The doctor came hurrying in, glanced at the readout and said to the midwife: 'Prep her. We can get to her immediately.'

Damson was bewildered. 'What's happening?' she asked.

'Oh, sorry. Baby's a bit tired so we're going to have to perform a caesarean. Nothing to worry about. Lucky you chose to have an epidural, we can just get it topped up and whip baby out in no time.'

So she wasn't going to give birth after all. First they were going to take the baby out of her, then they were going to take it away. She was overwhelmed by helplessness and began to cry. The midwife, coming back in, misunderstood. 'Don't worry, dear. There's nothing to be frightened of. A caesarean is very straightforward these days. You'll be fine.'

Damson wiped her eyes on her indecent hospital gown. She signed the consent form, then the porter came in and she was wheeled rapidly down to the operating theatre. There she was prepped and a green curtain erected between her and the scene of the action. She didn't like this at all but the surgeon was adamant.

She was completely numb as they'd topped up her epidural. There was a sensation of someone rummaging. Then there was a pulling and release, a pause while they cut the cord, and a mewling cry that receded away from her.

'At least it's alive,' she thought.

No one popped a friendly face around her curtain to tell her the happy news. Clearly the staff didn't think it was appropriate.

She lay like a chest of drawers that a burglar had tipped on its back and ransacked. Tears prickled her closed eyes. Then she was aware that someone was pulling her back together, stuffing things in any old how and locking her up tight. After a while, she ventured, 'Is the baby all right?'

The theatre nurse bustled round to her side of the curtain and said briskly, 'It's perfectly all right, the midwife's taken it into the recovery room. Now let's get you cleaned up. Mr Wells is just finishing off your incision and then we can get you through as well. How do you feel?'

'Sad.'

'Now, now, none of that. Baby's fine and so are you. You'll soon be back to normal.'

Normal? How could anything ever be normal again? The tears slid down her temples and into her hair. She couldn't find the energy to lift her hand and wipe them away.

'What is it?' she sobbed.

'What's what?' said the nurse, whose name Damson did not want to know.

'The baby. What is it?'

'Oh. OK, it's a little girl.'

'What are they doing with her?'

'Just warming her up a bit and sucking out some mucus and stuff from her little tummy. You were in labour for a very long time and she got a bit distressed. But she's going to be fine.'

'Can I see her?'

The nurse looked worried for a moment and went and consulted with the obstetric surgeon. She heard him say, 'I don't see why not. She's the medical student, isn't she? She'll be sensible.'

He poked his head over the green curtain and said, 'That's you all stitched up, Miss Hayes. Nice clean scar. We can get you back into the ward and resting in a minute.' The curtain was removed and Damson looked down at herself. Lying on her back, she wasn't breathless or dizzy as she had been in the last couple of months with the immense weight of the baby pressing down on her vena cava and causing supine hypotensive syndrome – naturally she'd looked it up. Not caring that Mr Wells was still there, she hauled up her surgical gown and examined herself. All was flaccid flabby flatness now. A great pool of flesh veined with purple stretch marks, the scar neat and pink with staples shining in the light and her pubes shaved off. The life that had made beautiful the fidgeting mound was gone. She was heaved on to the trolley and wheeled away.

In the recovery room Damson shifted herself up on to her elbows to see the midwife standing in front of something that looked like an infrared grill, attending to whatever was under it. All she could see was one tiny pale arm.

'Do I dare call her Melissa?' she whispered to herself. 'My own honey?'

After a few more minutes the midwife leant forward and lifted the baby with both hands, settling it into her left elbow and turning to Damson. She wasn't smiling. It was probably quite difficult and embarrassing to know what to do with a baby that was to be adopted. Particularly when this was not at all like the usual care situations where social services hovered like so many ladies-in-waiting around a queen.

She couldn't help smiling down at the baby and then turned the smile on Damson.

'She's a beautiful little girl. Aren't you, precious?'

In an instant Damson was very angry. Why wasn't she the first person to look at her baby and tell her she was beautiful?

'Give her to me,' she said.

'I'm not sure that's wise in the circumstances you might bond with her,' said the midwife, holding her against her uniform. 'Anyway, you need to lie flat for a bit. You can have a hold when we get back to the ward. We've arranged for you to have a side ward for a bit of peace,' she added.

'Give her to me, I need to see her now,' Damson repeated, trying to keep her voice level. The midwife could see that she was about to lose control so she leant down towards Damson's teary face holding the baby closer to her.

Damson saw a rumpled rosebud with a tuft of black hair peeping out of the hospital-issue cotton blanket. She reached out a finger and touched the petal cheek. The little creature's eyes snapped open gazing with deep purple irises at her mother. Anguish shot through her from groin to heart. She opened her mouth and the wail tore through all her careful constraint.

'Now, now, no need for that. Stop making that noise, you'll upset your baby. Come on.'

Damson tried to shut her mouth but she was wracked by waves of love and pain that threatened to overwhelm the frail barque of her sanity.

'Move her out of here quickly and get her into a side ward,' the midwife instructed her assistant. The assistant kicked off the brake and they went in a tearful hurried procession out of the recovery room.

Over the next few days she recovered physically. She wasn't allowed to feed and bathe her daughter although she hovered and watched. A few times she'd held her, particularly towards the end, but there was no doubt that the midwives had been told to minimise contact. She realised that she must not call her child Melissa, so she chose something that sounded similar and Mellita went on the birth certificate. Both names meant honey after all. The adoptive parents would no doubt change it but at least she had named her on purpose first. She stayed as long as she could by complaining of pain. She was in pain but not from her scar.

When the time came to part she was driven to the social services contact centre by Eva Williams with Mellita in a borrowed car seat beside her in the back. She leant over her daughter trying to imprint the infant face upon her mind's eye.

She insisted on carrying Mellita into a room painted yellow with a frieze of ducks. Eva Williams was brisk, showing her the Moses basket in which the baby was to be placed and hustling her gently to get it over with. Her heart was beating too fast as Eva stretched out her hands to take Mellita away.

'Can you leave me alone with her for a minute?'

Eva looked doubtful. 'Are you sure you're OK?'

'Yes, I'm fine. I just want a moment.'

Eva hesitated. 'OK then, Damson, just pop her into the basket and let yourself out of the other door. I'll be by the car.

The family will be here in ten minutes and you need to be gone by then.'

Damson sank down on one of the armchairs. What do you do when you have to fit a lifetime of mothering into ten minutes? She knew she must not cry, so she sang wordless lullabies instead and examined her baby's hands and feet. After what seemed like seconds, she heard movement outside the door and a soft knock. She stood up, holding her little honey close to her pounding heart. Wrapping the shawl about her baby's tiny body, she kissed her and settled her in the basket, bending over to touch Mellita's cheek with her own. The baby never made a sound. Then she left.

How could she have done that? Only by slamming an enormous door that reached right up to the stratosphere, across to every horizon and down into the great iron ball at the centre of the Earth.

Someone else would see her baby fill out like a rose coming from the bud. A butterfly packed into a chrysalis emerging into the light. Someone else would worship her and watch her grow.

Twenty-seven

Damson
February 2005

Damson cycled slowly up the hill towards her cottage. She was tired and unfit at the end of a long cold winter. Her basket sagged on to the front wheel, which made a faint and ominous squealing noise that she could not be bothered to do anything about. She had put a couple of cans of beans, Heinz tomato soup, salad, sliced brown bread and cottage cheese in the basket. Also a pint of milk.

It had been five years since she had bought Swine Cottage and moved to Fenning in Derbyshire, and she still wasn't quite sure why. Originally it had been about indulging a passion for hill walking and cycling in the wind-scoured landscape, where granite burst through turf like bones in a compound fracture. Its wildness had appealed to her, so different from the safe leafiness of her Home Counties childhood. The colours were muted, the air had a bracing chill much of the time. When she was up on the hills alone, wearing warm weatherproof clothes, the cold wind against her face would almost empty her mind.

She had made no close friends, only acquaintances whose Christmas parties she would attend. Her fellow doctors in the practice were all immersed in their own family lives, and a single woman, particularly one who did not go out of her way to please, was not easily assimilated into the local social scene.

Going home to Castle Hey was always difficult because Margaret followed her around with Boden catalogues, saying, 'They do awfully nice trousers,' and offering to 'get her colours done'.

'Damson, darling, while I realise you want to blend in up in Derbyshire, I don't think everyone expects their doctor to wear sludge green and those awful old jumpers. Where do they come from?'

'Marks and Spencer men's department,' Damson muttered. 'Or these days, Primark. They're nice and roomy and they keep me warm. It's cold in Derbyshire.'

'Why do you live there at all? I don't understand it. I'm sure your father would like it if you came to live nearer home.'

Margaret's words cooked up the usual simmering resentment.

Pricking her in her tender places, Margaret would then say, 'And you'd be closer to your grandparents. They must be getting on.' Sarah and Arthur had been phased out of the Castle Hey social scene over the last few years. Damson's visits to them were warm and regular but not so frequent now.

Damson had learned not to blaze up like tinder and Margaret was more restrained now as well. She had decided there was nothing much she could do about Damson, so she made her point by giving her ludicrously inappropriate Christmas presents like a pink mohair shawl or expensive scent. The war between them was colder these days, their shared secret long buried.

The twins took their lead from their mother. They invited her to major family occasions but otherwise did not seek her out. They knew nothing of the baby Mellita. Damson told herself she didn't mind and could ignore them most of the time. That was until Damson's mobile had rung at ten o'clock one Saturday night waking her from a doze in front of the television.

'Damson?' Is that you?'

She didn't even recognise Noonie's voice at first.

'Damson, it's Noonie. Are you at home?'

'Yes, why?'

'I'm not far from you.'

'Where?' Damson was sleepy and confused, and could not work out why her ultra-cool stepsister sounded so agitated.

'It's Ottie, I think she's ill. Can you come over?'

Damson's only contact with Ottilie dated from her christening, an adorable baby in a long silk and lace dress that Noonie had purchased from Harrods. No doubt the Victorian cotton and lace Hayes christening robe would be embarrassing in front of all the smart City godparents. Damson realised that Noonie was crying and woke up properly.

'Where are you exactly?'

'Hugo and I are staying with the Stapeleys at Cross Court, do you know it? We brought Ottie with us because Nanny was ill and couldn't have her this weekend. We were down at dinner and when I went to check her, she was very hot. She's got some kind of rash on her tummy. I can't seem to wake her properly.'

Damson snapped into action. It didn't occur to her to wonder why Noonie hadn't been in touch before the emergency. Their relationship didn't include that kind of thing. Besides, it could be meningitis but there was no way of telling until she got there. Calling an ambulance to make its way through the winding roads up to the Court would be slower than if she took her beat-up

Freelander along the familiar lanes.

She grabbed her medical bag, thanking God she hadn't had a drink that night, and ran for the car, still talking into her mobile.

'OK, take all her clothes off and sponge her gently with a warm flannel until I get there. It's about fifteen minutes. Call 999 now for an ambulance, but I'll get to you before it does.'

She clicked off the phone, jumped into the car, opened the window and popped her magnetic Kojak light on the roof. She flipped on the siren, set the satnav and pulled out of the gate.

As the Stapeleys' family doctor, she'd been to Christmas parties at the Court every year, but the reassurance of the satnav was always useful. Headlights on full beam, she put her foot down and just drove, swinging the sturdy car around the twists in the road with skill undiminished by fear. Ottilie was what, three? four? She hadn't dared ask Noonie to do the glass test.

The great artichoke-topped gate posts swung into view on her right. Someone was there with a powerful torch. Damson opened her window and recognised Basil Stapeley with his teenage son, looking worried.

'Thank you so much for coming so quickly, Damson. I'll wait here for the ambulance, Benjie will take you straight into the house. Go round into the stable yard, it's quicker to get to the nursery up the back stairs.'

Benjie jumped into the passenger seat, and then they were there. Damson grabbed her bag and followed him through the back door, down the stone-flagged passage and up the back stairs two floors, to the day and night nurseries. Noonie came to the door, dressed in a red cocktail frock with bare feet and looking terrified.

'Damson, thank God. She's in here.'

'Hello Noonie. I'm sure she's fine, but the ambulance can take her into hospital if necessary.'

Ottilie lay on her back, naked, rolling her head with its blonde curls, and Damson could see three or four of the purplish pinpricks she was dreading on the soft rounded tummy. She took out her stethoscope and electronic thermometer.

'Ottie, darling, here's Aunt Damson to look after you.'

'Get me a glass, please.'

Noonie didn't argue for a change, just brought her stepsister the tooth glass from the basin in the corner of the big old-fashioned night nursery. Damson pressed it very gently on to the spots. If it was a meningitis rash they would not fade and, as she had suspected, they remained visible through the glass. She went to the basin and washed her hands with the yellow coal tar soap that was there.

'She's not allergic to penicillin, is she?'

Noonie shook her head.

Damson took a pre-filled syringe from her bag, tapped it down and with a practised hand moved the child to one side, injecting her in one dimpled buttock. The girl didn't seem to notice.

'What did you give her?' Noonie asked in a small, frightened voice. She was crying. Damson stopped for a moment to put an arm around her stepsister and kiss her wet cheek.

'Benzylpenicillin as a precaution.' Damson quickly wrapped the child in the cotton waffle blanket that was on the bed to carry her down the stairs.

'I gave her some Calpol, but she sicked it up,' said Noonie.

'Try not to worry.' Damson knew how useless it was to say that to a terrified mother. 'I'll come in the ambulance with you both, and get it sorted at the hospital. Bring my bag, will you?'

Noonie snatched up the bag and came down the front stairs with Damson to find the paramedics in the hall. Ottie was taken straight out to the ambulance, its blue light revolving in the darkness of the gravel sweep.

The two women climbed into the back and sat watching the paramedic working over the unconscious child. Strapped in they could do nothing for Ottie, so Damson took Noonie's hand in hers and held it.

In the very worst of the achingly lonely nights, Damson had told herself that Noonie and Clarrie didn't love their children as she would if they were hers. They both had full-time nannies to allow them to continue the complex international social lives afforded by their husbands' City bonuses. When she saw Noonie's face that night, she was desperately ashamed of herself.

At the hospital Ottie went straight into intensive care, was intubated and put on fluids and an antibiotic drip. A lumbar puncture was taken. Damson was glad she was there to remove Noonie from the room – even amid the fear for Ottie, Damson was happy to be wanted by her stepsister, able to comfort her and tell her that it wasn't her fault. They both agreed it was lucky Ottie happened to be with her mother that weekend and not with the nanny, Noonie thanking God that Damson was close by too. The night was dreadful but as dawn came the little girl woke up and said, 'Mummy'. After that, with the resilience of small children, she recovered very fast and without any permanent damage.

Noonie didn't forget what she thought of as Damson's role in this miracle, and made more of an effort, even inviting her to stay in their Oxfordshire country house once or twice. It wasn't an enormous success. She couldn't join in the women's talk of schools, nannies, kitchens, property prices and skiing, with a sprinkling of the Bahamas, Burberry and other subjects she considered complete bollocks. The men annoyed her by saying in surprised tones, 'Goodness, that's a difficult job!' when they heard she was a GP. She knew they would never have dreamt of saying such a thing to a male doctor.

So Damson asked, if she was going to be invited, could it be when there were no other guests? That was not very often but she did like being with Clarrie and Noonie's children, just as she liked looking after the babies and children on her list. A post-natal visit was always a treat for Damson.

There was a stone wall in her mind behind which lurked the idea of a relationship with a man. When she went to stay with her grandparents for her annual week in August, she knew they avoided the subject. She would listen to them bickering fondly and grieve sometimes that she would never grow old with someone beloved. Instead they talked about medicine, patients and memories, or sat in companionable silence, just as they had when she was a child.

She never met anyone in Derbyshire who remotely fitted the bill, and lacked the confidence and determination to put herself in the way of meeting men elsewhere. Nor was she sure what she would do if she was expected to have sex with someone. It seemed so inconceivable to her that any man would want her now. But her subconscious nursery door was wide open and phantom babies streamed into her dreams. When she lay in bed at night waiting for sleep to come she would indulge herself in 'what if' fantasies.

She had begun to want another baby of her own with a longing that penetrated her limbs and made her cry. She had considered getting herself pregnant somehow, but her body baulked at the idea of having sex with anyone. Artificial insemination and IVF seemed invasive. She hated having cervical smears, and it would be like that, only repeatedly and worse. Plus, those injections of hormones to prepare her body she was convinced would send her round the bend. She'd seen too many women in her consulting room broken by the pressure of repeated fruitless cycles and the hormones they were forced to endure.

She looked into adoption and fostering and applied to go through the process of being examined by social services for her suitability. A lot of information arrived, but she soon found that she was beyond unlikely to get an actual baby to replace that little bud of a face topped by a tuft of dark hair. She should be able to get one back as she had put one in. It was only fair. Then she laughed at her craziness and completed the process, but without any intention of accepting an actual child.

She told herself that she was much better off without a baby. She was free to take off by herself on adventure holidays and swimming treks across the Hellespont without any worries about what to do with an inconvenient child.

With no one else to consider in her personal life, she could enjoy being selfish. Her professional life was a different matter of course. And yet in the hushed dark just before dawn, she knew she lied to herself. As she lay in bed too restless after a late call-out to sleep, she would think of the just-delivered women, saggy and soft, leaky and exhausted though they were, as they gazed delightedly at their new-borns. She would remember her voice rising to a baby-friendly squeak and her own besotted smile.

Thank God for the internet, at least she had the illusion of friends in the online medical community, where everyone forgave and offered support and love anonymously. Where you could moan about or mourn your patients, or share triumphs and failures. For a shy, lonely, reticent Englishwoman, it took a bit of getting used to, but she persisted.

Now she had close friends among women physicians all over the world, who were thousands of miles away and whose faces she had never seen. There was no danger of meeting and it was all anonymous. Some even shared similar experiences of date rape and having a child adopted, of mothers dying young and difficult stepmothers. It was a relief not to be unique. All shared the simultaneously humdrum and dramatic daily life of a doctor.

With the online community's support, she now knew without any doubt at all that she had been raped, and that it was not 'her fault'. She also knew that women could love their babies, however they were conceived.

It was a comfort and an outlet for her. As time went on the online community soothed her and allowed her to heal and to forgive everyone concerned. Even Margaret.

Twenty-eight

Damson
October 2008

Damson jolted her bike into the rack behind the surgery and locked it. Pulling off the cycling helmet that channelled rain so efficiently on to her scalp, she pushed open the glass door of the Sixties low-rise housing the Hillside practice. Patients stared down at a carpet stained beyond steam-cleaning by years of their predecessors ignoring the notice not to eat in the waiting room. She didn't look at them, but hurried through to her consulting room, waving at Tina on reception as she went.

'Can I have five, Tina?' indicating her sopping hair and hoping to dash through into the loo to dry herself under the hand blower.

'First patient here for you, Dr Hayes.' Tina's monotone could penetrate anything.

'OK, right there.' She knew her bright tone didn't deceive Tina. Were all doctors slightly scared of their receptionists?

Knowing full well that damp did not give you pneumonia, she took off her yellow cycling cape and hung it on the back of the door. Her sludge-coloured men's corduroy trousers were soaking. She ignored the squelch as she sat down on the plastic chair, and turned on the computer. Her appointments flashed up in front of her, and she blinked. A new patient, inherited from the recently retired Dr Bentley.

A faint knock, and Damson called, 'Come in'.

The door opened and a very stout woman sidled in. Probably younger than she looked. As her bodily profile was about the same width as most people's facing forwards, this required the door to be fully opened. Damson let herself for a moment rest in peaceful contemplation of her patient's sweet smile and pleasing, round and fuzzy face.

Then she snapped back to professional mode, and opened the patient record for Ada Lindley. BMI 34.5, well into the obesity range, poor duck. She swung her chair around to face her patient, and leaned forward resting her hands on her knees, prepared to give Ada the attention she needed if she was ever to stop comfort eating.

'Good morning, Miss Lindley. Now Dr Bentley has retired, I'll be looking after you. Is that OK?'

'Yes, Doctor. Thank you. I've just come for my tablets.'

Damson could see from the screen that Dr Bentley had some time ago prescribed antidepressants and some mild appetite suppressants, but these had long since been replaced with the next best thing to placebos. Not particularly ethical, she knew, but widely practised.

'I have something much better for you than tablets, Miss Lindley.'

Ada looked crestfallen. So Damson hastily added, 'Something new and exciting that's much more effective and specially designed for cases like yours. Now, your test results show you may be at risk of a metabolic disorder, and that means I can help you in a different way.'

'Dr Bentley gave me tablets for my glands.'

'Did they work?'

'I think so. I'm not sure.'

Damson could see that Ada had been gradually gaining weight and that she was a perfect candidate for the new scheme. She took her blood pressure to check that it was still high. She fitted all the criteria, and at last the NHS had approved something properly preventative that might just work.

'Perhaps if you gave me different ones?' Ada added.

'I think your tablets may have stopped working. So I have something else to prescribe for you. You'll need to commit to a programme that's run in the church hall every week. It's called Fast Friends, and it's all about helping you speed up your metabolism and get your glands really working hard.'

Did that sound patronising? Damson wanted to kick herself when things like that fell out of her mouth. Ada was unperturbed.

'OK, what do I have to do?'

'Well, you turn up and there will be a whole group of you with the same metabolic issues. You can gain points and win prizes every week. It sounds like great fun. There's a health coach there, and she'll explain the programme. You'll need to eat special foods to help your glands, but it isn't expensive and there's some easy exercise to do as well. And the meetings are completely free. You'll all be working together to be healthier. And it's a way to make new friends as well. There's a website and you can chat to the others online between sessions,' Damson finished with a smile.

'OK,' Ada replied uncertainly, taking the printout from

Damson's hand and clutching it with both of hers.

'I'll be there myself, I could do with some advice about healthier living as well.' Damson knew her diet was appalling. Her body was slim and fit from cycling up hill and down dale, but she never cooked, just ate the easiest thing, usually standing up. That's what being alone did to you. Why bother to cook for one?

Ada perked up at the idea of a slim doctor also needing the same kind of help. Damson knew from her own bitter experience what it was like to be told you were fat. She remembered a plain dull man, during her first of two Freshers' Weeks at Cambridge, who'd told her she would be quite pretty if only she were thin. She'd been pregnant at the time but hadn't yet realised.

Damson could easily understand that Ada couldn't bear to be told she was too fat, it just sent her home defeated to the fridge and the biscuit tin. And her colossal mother.

'The health coach comes to your house as well,' Damson added. 'To teach you about food and help you get your cupboards and fridge ready for the new way of eating.'

'What will Mum say? She doesn't like strangers indoors.'

'I'll call on your mother and explain before we start.'

Ada nodded.

Damson had called on Mrs Lindley before and found her sitting, monumental and unmoving, as she did all day and all night, in an armchair in the front room. That was when she wasn't in hospital having gangrenous toes removed and her ulcers treated. She had full-blown diabetes, and was managed by the specialist nurse.

'Haven't been upstairs since my Ada was born,' she would say proudly. Her small, sad postman husband had retired at sixty-five, dwindling away and dying shortly afterwards. Being stuck indoors with his wife, at her beck and call all day long, had been too much for his heart, according to the retired Dr Bentley, who had old-fashioned views about what was what.

Ada heaved herself on to her spread feet clutching her prescription.

'Thank you, Doctor. Mum's in all the time, you can call when you want.'

The intercom squeaked, and Tina said: 'Next patient has signed in as a visitor. Leeta Delapi.'

She pressed the buzzer on her desk. Seconds later, there was a knock on her door.

'Come in.'

Fumbling for her glasses and peering at her computer screen, she tried to gauge her day's workload as her patient sat down in the chair beside her desk and sighed. She glanced round and saw a slim Indian girl, clearly pregnant. Unusually coloured eyes looked at her from a pale rather blotchy face. The girl's nose had an elegant curve, her mouth was small and well-shaped and she had a neat, determined chin from which had erupted a large angry spot.

'Hello. What can I do to help?' Damson looked back at her computer screen.

The girl looked down at her Ugg boots. Her slender legs were clad in skinny jeans. On top she wore a large soft grey jumper that failed to conceal a neat bump.

'I filled in a form to be a visitor,' the girl began. Her accent was much more private London girls' school than Mumbai or

Derbyshire. She seemed to be having trouble meeting Damson's eye, although she looked confident and held herself well. Her head tilted forward on a long, delicate neck, glossy dark brown hair falling across her face. Her fingers came up to fidget with the spot.

'Date of birth? I have your name.' Damson had opened the relevant page on her computer, and started to fill in the form.

'The twenty-fifth of April 1988.'

'Occupation?'

'Medical student.'

Damson's eyebrows rose involuntarily. 'What stage are you at?'

'I'm pre-registration, but I've deferred the hospital internship because of this.' She gestured at her belly.

'Up here on holiday?'

'Not exactly.' She hesitated, opened her mouth to say something else and then stopped.

Damson paused to give her space, but then carried on as nothing seemed to be forthcoming.

'OK, what can I do for you?'

'As you can probably see, there's this.' She gestured at her belly with her long slender fingers. The nails were particularly beautiful, almond shaped, curved over and around the top of the finger with only a tiny edge of ivory but they weren't very clean. Damson was aware of her own red and bitten fingertips. There was no wedding ring, but Indian brides didn't always wear them, did they?

'Where do you usually go for antenatal care?'

'I haven't had any. This is the first time I've been to a doctor

265

for this.' She nodded down at her tummy, unsmiling.

This was obviously a nicely brought-up Indian girl and a medical student. In trouble, as they used to say?

'I see. Where do you usually live?'

'In London.' There was a touch of defiance, as the girl tossed her long hair over her shoulders and looked Damson in the eye. 'But I don't live there at the moment. I don't live anywhere right now.'

Damson wanted to ask what she was doing so far from home, and what she meant, but it seemed intrusive. She wondered about mental health issues but continued with all the usual questions.

'Date of the first day of your last period?'

'I don't remember.'

'OK, approximately.'

'I don't remember, but I only had sex once. On Valentine's day.'

'Well that narrows it down, doesn't it? We should be able to do a calculation. And I'll be able to tell more by examining you.'

Damson was very used to her patients lying to her – particularly about sex, drugs and alcohol – but she wasn't used to calculating due dates these days. All the young mums went online, working out exactly when the baby was due at the first secret hint of a suspicion. She sighed at the extremely detailed knowledge they had at their fingertips. Pre-internet it had been easier to allay their fears. Now most mothers could probably breeze through midwifery exams. Those that didn't find their way into the more extreme US forums for free-birthing and other dangerous nonsense.

Damson got her tape measure out of the drawer in her desk.

'We'd better have a quick look. Can you hop up on the table? Do you want a nurse to attend?'

The girl looked at her from almost lilac eyes. They had a darker ring around the iris.

'No, I don't need a nurse. You are a woman after all.' There was something chilly and defensive in her tone, which Damson put down to embarrassment at her condition.

The girl hoisted herself on to the examining table and lay down, lifting her jumper and the T-shirt underneath. She was thin, and the bump stood out, round and proud, seamed with a brown stripe up the centre. Something did not compute. Even her clothes, very low-cut Seven for All Mankind jeans that conveniently fitted under the bump with a button undone. Damson's fingers detected cashmere as she moved the jumper out of the way. Noonie-type clothes. Hardly what a medical student usually wore either.

She stretched the tape measure over the bump, which looked as if there was a beach ball stitched in under the creamy skin.

'OK, about thirty-seven weeks. We'd better work it out on the computer. As you probably know, the centimetre measurement from the pubic bone to the top of the fundus is the same as the number of weeks. Converted me to metric.'

'I do know,' said Leeta. 'I just didn't want to do it myself. I was trying to ignore it I suppose.'

Damson hesitated. Then she said: 'Would you like to hear the baby's heartbeat?' She took out her foetal Doppler.

'No.'

Damson herself did, so she pressed the monitor gently against the bump and the sound of a healthy heartbeat of 130 bpm filled the consulting room. Damson saw the girl's hand come up as if to push the instrument off her belly, but then drop back.

They sat down again.

'Are your periods regular?'

'Yes, about thirty days, and I never usually miss one.'

Damson did a quick calculation online. 'If you ovulate about fourteen days after your period, and not everyone does, then your last period should have been in early February, so you're due around mid-November,' she said. 'Ninth of November is a likely due date, but it can be as much as two weeks on either side and still be a completely normal pregnancy. Due dates aren't an exact science. Not much time to prepare then.'

'I know,' the girl said again.

Damson couldn't help being irritated, but she swung into the usual routine, took blood pressure and handed Leeta a little wand to pee on when she had left the consulting room. But nothing felt right. Unease had crept into the room with Leeta, and curled up in the corner like a pitiful little dog.

'I know you said you haven't had any antenatal care, but are you booked in somewhere for the birth?'

'No.'

'When are you going home? This close to the birth beds are limited, and you may not have a choice. Luckily there are plenty of maternity units in London.'

'I'm not going back to London just yet. After the pregnancy ends, maybe.'

The girl looked intently at Damson as she said this, and the doctor detected something in her look that was out of place. It was questioning, defiant.

'Booking you in somewhere is the most important thing right now. The pregnancy and you both look healthy, and your age is in your favour. It seems a bit pointless to get you scanned now, but we can if you like.'

'I don't think any of that is necessary.'

'As you know, we can detect many conditions in the foetus early, which gives the parents time to prepare or make decisions. There are other conditions that affect pregnant women exclusively that can be quite dangerous, but have no symptoms until it's too late.'

'I know. Pre-eclampsia. More common if the couple haven't been having sex very long, or in first pregnancies. And diabetes, but I'm so skinny I figured I could ignore that one.'

Damson sat and let all this wash over her.

'You said my blood pressure is fine. And I've been taking it myself, just in case, as I don't want to die of this. As I only had unprotected sex once and I read about that new partner risk in the *New Scientist*, I bought a blood pressure monitor at the chemist. I figured the odds were pretty low for any other problems. If the baby's disabled, well so be it. I won't be keeping it anyway.'

Damson absorbed this information. 'Are you in touch with social services about adoption?' she enquired gently.

Really, the consultation was going on far too long.

'Not yet.'

So, late pregnancy, no antenatal care, medical student giving up baby for adoption, social services not aware (at least she herself had done things properly). Had answered no to drug and drink questions. But also possibly homeless while wearing cashmere. Damson examined these anomalies, unable to make sense of them.

Damson was quite used to the peculiarities of pregnant girls. It was just that the more problematic ones were never Indian, and seldom educated. And often in their mid-teens, not grown women in their twenties. Damson, particularly when she was tired and had PMT, had to suppress a desire to point out that some of the problems she was presented with could have been avoided with the application of common sense. Her grandfather Dr Reeves had been famous for scolding his patients. They'd found it comforting. If he didn't scold them, they knew something was seriously wrong.

'Where do you think you'll be living until the baby is born?'

'I don't know. It all depends.'

'On what?'

Then the girl said: 'Well, on you actually.'

'On me? Why?' Mental health issues after all. Here it comes. Not the first time a patient fixated on their GP, but unusual during a first consultation.

'You are Damson Hayes, aren't you?' The girl's voice had dropped to a whisper.

'Yes?' Damson was bewildered by the question. The unease in the room uncurled itself from the corner and came cringing towards her, tail clamped between its meagre buttocks, tip wagging, ears close to its head. Damson's skin crawled.

'I lied about my date of birth,' the girl was saying, hurriedly, as if trying to get the words out of her mouth fast before she changed her mind.

'Why?' Damson continued to stare straight ahead at her screen, blinking.

'Because I wanted to talk to you first. To see what you were like.'

'Why?' Damson repeated. The situation was sliding from her control but she tried to summon all her professionalism to take what was coming.

'Because my birthday is the twenty-fifth of June?'

'Oh,' said Damson.

Her hands reached for the keyboard, to correct the date in the form.

'Also, I was originally called Mellita.'

'You said your name was Leeta,' she heard herself say.

'I am called Leeta by my parents. I think Mellita is what you called me.'

Damson buzzed through to reception with a trembling hand.

'Tina? I'll need a double appointment for this patient. Can you push my others forward. Oh, and apologise for the delay? Thanks.' She didn't wait for Tina to acknowledge.

She swung her office chair round and looked at the girl.

'Mellita?' she repeated.

The girl looked back at her. Damson smiled to see what would happen. Her heart pounded in her chest. She realised the girl was still talking:

'I came to find you. I'm sorry I didn't warn you. I need your help. I didn't realise you were a GP actually, until I googled you. I didn't know anything else about you before, I didn't even know you existed. I only recently found out I was adopted.'

Damson was finding it hard to breathe, and her mind flashed back to the only practical things she had been able to do for her child in the lonely years since she had given her away. 'I registered with various things such as NORCAP contact register. And then I waited and registered with the Adoption Contact Register to be ready in case my child wanted to get in touch when she turned eighteen. But I heard nothing then.' She realised she sounded as confused as she felt.

'I didn't know when I was eighteen,' Leeta said. 'It was only in January this year. I was listening outside the door when my parents were talking to my Dadima – my father's mother – about finding a good husband for me. To tell you the truth, I liked the idea. I have cousins in the USA who've had a great time, they've got excellent bridegrooms. I had no idea how to go about finding a husband for myself and my parents are fairly traditional, although they had a love marriage.'

There was a pause.

'Do you want to hear all this? I realise this is a very odd situation.'

'Tell me. But I have to warn you that we don't have more than a few minutes.'

'I overheard Dadima, who's even more traditional and bossy and grumpy, saying something about how difficult it was going to be to find a good groom, and whether anyone would want me as I wasn't their child and, "I told you no good would come of it when you went against me and adopted her", and no one knew who I was. And hoping my parents had an extra big dowry organised to make up for it all.'

The last time Damson had seen Mellita – if this woman was her Mellita – she had kissed a tiny version of that face, placed her gently in a basket and walked out of the social services contact centre into an empty future.

Damson's arms jerked forwards. Reaching for that long-ago baby, her small girl with eyes of purple-grey who'd stared at her with primeval calm. Whose nose was dappled with tiny yellow dots. Whose skin didn't fit very well. Wrinkly knees, non-existent bottom, tiny neck like a ridiculous stalk on the top of which bobbed a flower of infinite beauty.

The only thing oddly that hadn't altered much was the colour of her eyes. They had lightened but not changed colour. Babies' eyes nearly always change colour. Leeta's grey eyes still had the slightly purple look that a new-born baby's eyes have. And she didn't smile. New-born babies don't smile either.

Damson glanced down at her hands which she found were grasping the girl's upper arms. Leeta didn't move at all. She just looked into Damson's face, closer now. The desire to pull Leeta into her arms and kiss her pale cheeks was so strong that she had to let her go and turn back to the computer. Her face caught fire. With shaking fingers she typed her own address into the online form.

'Dr Hayes?'

'You'd better call me Damson.'

'Damson? What shall I do now, do you think?' She sounded young and uncertain for the first time.

'Well, I'm sorry but I have to work the rest of today. One of the other doctors is off sick and I have a double caseload.'

Damson didn't want to leave Leeta, whoever she was, wandering around all afternoon in Fenning in her condition. She made up her mind. There was nothing valuable at the cottage and little harm she could do even in the most troubling interpretation.

'I'll give you my key and you can go to my home and rest. You can stay tonight and we can talk this evening about how best to help you.'

'OK. Thank you.'

Damson found her door key with the silver Tiffany key ring (a present from Noonie) in her bag and gave it to Leeta, hurriedly drawing a little map on a piece of paper to show her the way to Swine Cottage.

'There's a spare room at the top of the stairs on the left. You'll have to make up the bed, the linen cupboard is on the landing. This is my mobile number and you can call at any time. Do help yourself to food and tea and so on. Make yourself at home. And, Leeta?'

The girl turned towards her, and Damson looked at that face again, trying to find her baby there. 'You do sincerely believe that you are Mellita?'

'Oh yes, I applied to see my birth and adoption certificates. Your name was there, and mine, Mellita. But no father's name?'

Damson left the question of Mellita's father.

'Do you have them with you?' was all she said.

'No, but I can get them for you. I understand, Damson, this must have been a shock. I am sorry. I am me though, I promise.'

Damson watched her as she left the room, then pushed the buzzer on her desk for the next patient, her heart thumping in her chest as hope mixed with doubt.

Twenty-nine

Leeta
October 2008

Leeta let herself into Damson's cottage, putting her small bag down on the stone floor and looking around at the plain, pleasing room. She was eager to pick up clues about herself from her birth mother's tastes and habits. The bare uneven walls were whitewashed and Afghan rugs were scattered about. There was a computer on a table in the corner. It wasn't a feminine room, but then her birth mother was clearly not a feminine woman. Leeta was incredulous when she compared Damson, with her cropped mousy hair and baggy sexless clothes, with her mother Mira's long plait, soft curves and gorgeous saris.

Thirsty, she found the kitchen through an arch to one side of the inglenook, and made herself a cup of sweet tea. Taking a biscuit she went back to settle herself ponderously into a deep red linen-covered armchair. She slipped off her boots to curl her legs up beside her, and found that the stone flags were warm underfoot. Damson had a comfortable home at any rate. She sighed and drifted, tired after all the courage it had taken to meet Damson. Hoping this might be a refuge at last, even if it did come at a heavy emotional price, at least until the end of the pregnancy.

She had been so desperately frightened that her parents would reject her if they found out about the baby. It had been such a struggle being away from them, staying in a scruffy bedsit in Bournemouth, lying about working in a medical mission in Uganda 'to gain a bit more experience'. Luckily a Ugandan Indian friend was there doing exactly that, and she used details from Parvati's blog to lend colour to her emails to her parents. Mira's responses expressed so much concern for her safety and their careful, irrelevant medical advice made her feel guilty and sad.

She remembered the year before sitting in a booth at the back of an Ealing café comforting Padme Patel, both of them in the West London girls' uniform of skinny jeans, Ugg boots and huge cashmere jumpers. Padme's mother had found her pink bubble packs of the Pill in her bathroom and the row had been horrendous and terrifying.

'I suppose they expected me to go through life in a restrained way, but not my bloody brothers,' her friend had whimpered.

'How did she find them? Weren't you careful?'

'I was. They were in my sponge bag. She must have gone in there for something. Or maybe she suspected. Anyway, I got home yesterday and they were both in the sitting room. Neither of them is usually home that early. I knew something was wrong immediately as they looked so grim.'

Leeta reached a hand across the table and squeezed her friend's forearm.

'I had to see you, Leeta, I knew you'd understand.'

At that time, Leeta's parents correctly had no reason to suspect she was anything but a virgin, so there had been none of those scenes in the Delapi household.

'Papa shouted at me. He's never shouted at me before. He told me I was bringing shame on the family and called me dumb for being stupid enough to have sex with some randy English boy. He threatened to throw me out of the house and stop my allowance.'

'Oh, poor you, was it as bad as that?'

'Worse. He's had email approaches about marriage from "nice" boys' parents. He told me he was so ashamed he'd deleted them all because I was "soiled goods". They're going to throw me out. I know they are. Oh, what am I going to do?'

'What do you want to do? What did you say?'

'I was so scared. But I managed to stay calm and just told them that the Pill had been prescribed for PMT as it was disrupting my ability to work hard at my studies every month. I reminded my mother about how moody I always am just before my periods. I said I would have hidden them much more carefully if they'd been for anything else. They seemed to calm down a bit after that. But it's been awful in the house.'

Leeta remembered the lovely Patel home on Mountbar Hill, a palace of polished floors and professional interior decor, with a rambling garden. Padme had a whole floor to herself, with her own kitchen, bedroom, bathroom and sitting room now her brothers had set up homes of their own.

'I don't want to have to move out and get any old job now. Just when I'm getting qualified.'

Padme had finished her first dentistry degree, and was now studying at King's for an MSc while working in her father's thriving West End cosmetic practice. That little pink packet of pills might just scupper such a safe, successful future for her in the bosom of the family home and business.

'Have you told Jake?'

'No, and I never want to see him or talk to him again. I can't risk my future for that silly disgusting nonsense, can I? How stupid could I be?'

Jake was the elder brother of their mutual schoolfriend Annabel. He was studying the metaphysical poets for his MA at Goldsmiths and had wooed Padme for years, sighing that 'Thou by the Indian Ganges' side/Shouldst rubies find: I by the tide/Of Humber would complain.'

He had floppy hair and Leeta had always thought he was pretentious and annoying and that his great love for Padme was a pose. A year ago Padme had told a worried Leeta that she was so in love with him she'd risk anything. She was even contemplating running away from home to be with him. She'd only gone on the Pill a couple of months before, giving in as he had seemed so desperate. Leeta already had the impression that love in a bedsit with a mouldy shared student shower had been a bit of a wake-up call.

Now the cold water of her family's disapproval seemed to have sluiced away all that idealistic romantic nonsense, leaving icy facts in its place. If Padme wanted a nice, comfortable, safe life, she needed to toe the family's party line. And that meant 'virginity', a good, probably arranged, marriage and a successful and very lucrative career as a cosmetic dentist. There could be no other options – certainly not sexual ones – and it was not down to Padme to plan her own future.

Leeta was at a loss. Then, before she knew she was adopted and half-English, she had had no intention of spoiling her future for the sake of sex with some scruffy English boy. Now of course she wanted to kick herself for her smugness in thinking Padme had been a fool.

'Do you think they believed you?' Leeta had asked.

'I think they would like to. I think they do love me and sweeping the whole thing under the carpet would be the best possible outcome. Can you go and see Jake and explain for me?'

'Are you mad? Of course not. Look, let's call Annabel and tell her what's going on. She can tell Jake,' Leeta suggested.

Padme shuddered. She said she never wanted to see Annabel again either. She didn't want to be reminded of her dangerous folly. She wailed that she knew she was being horrible but Jake and all his silly poetry could go to hell.

'He'll probably love moping around and write a poem about his broken heart or something.'

Leeta saw her friend was defaulting to traditional Indian daughter mode, and judging Jake's emotions by her own, which had turned out to be puddle shallow. She leaned towards Leeta and whispered in her ear: 'Sex is dull and disgusting. He asked me to do things that were sick. I tried to like it, but it wasn't worth giving my life up for – so embarrassing. Don't understand all the fuss. I didn't like looking at him naked either. It looks silly, all red and flabby. And his room was so cold and messy.' She'd giggled, close to tears. Leeta had given her a hug.

Both Padme's mother and her father had arrived as children with their parents from Uganda in 1972 when Idi Amin had done what was not called ethnic cleansing in those days, but amounted to the same thing. The families had been housed in an ex-RAF barracks while they recovered from the shock of having their smart, sophisticated lives in Africa stolen. Like other Ugandan Indian families, the parents had settled down and rapidly set up shops and small businesses, working hard to raise their own children back to where they had been before their expulsion. Padme's mother Manisha was an accountant, and her father studied dentistry. Manisha now worked as business manager for the family's thriving Busy Smiles Dental Clinic in New Cavendish Street.

Both Padme and Leeta had been shocked when they met girls brought up in Chennai or Mumbai where, among the well-off, traditional values were being eroded left, right and centre. Hedonistic drinking and partying sounded wilder than in London. Ugandan Indians on the other hand, living in the UK or America, were known to be particularly keen to hang on to respectable Fifties Gujarati values.

Both Padme's parents were protecting something infinitely precious, something that had been hard won against bitter odds. There was no safety net that allowed for sloppy Western values to spoil what their parents had created for them out of their smashed lives, and what they had made for themselves. Leeta's parents had been born in India, were both doctors and were not so insular, but she knew they still valued the traditions, and condoning a pregnancy outside marriage would have been unthinkable.

Padme did not have a rebellious streak. She was too soft, too loved and spoiled, to risk it all for love. She liked all her berries far too much: Mulberry, Burberry and Blackberry.

Padme and Leeta had often discussed the emotional mess in which many of their British schoolfriends lived, with bitterly divorced parents, all 'Mum's boyfriends', dismal weekends with Dad, and microwaved ready-meals.

'It's just not worth it,' wailed Padme. 'It's OK for my brothers. They had lots of English girlfriends before they married, and the parents never said a thing.'

Leeta sat curled up in Damson's chair remembering Padme's look of naked fear. She was quite sure that the same terrible rejection, or worse, would have happened to her if she had confessed to this shameful pregnancy and thrown herself on her parents' mercy. How could she have been so stupid as to get drunk and go upstairs with that boy? Afterwards she had huddled her clothes on and run from the house.

Damson would be home soon to find her there. Presumably giving her up as a baby had been painful. She remembered how Damson had clutched her arms in the consulting room and the wild look on her face before she visibly controlled herself and let go.

Was she going to hurt her birth mother by flitting into her life, using her as a solution to a problem, and then leaving? She wasn't sure she cared, as she herself had been abandoned. Fenning was just a refuge while she sorted out the consequences of her mistake. Damson was someone who would potentially help. It was as simple as that. She would have to stay with this strange woman who was her real mother, who looked like a lesbian. Perhaps she was a lesbian, and that was why she had given her up. But that would be an odd reason.

As for Padme, presumably her parents had decided to overlook the Pill incident and carry on as normal. She had heard that Padme was engaged now, to a dentist. She wondered if a discreet visit to Harley Street to restore certain torn membranes had been arranged as well.

Leeta wasn't even wholly Indian. She panicked as she imagined Papa, who was always so kind, proud and encouraging, flinging cruel words at her, as Padme's father had, about 'your slut of an English mother' and 'bad blood showing up as soon as it could'. She couldn't trust them to understand. Padme was at least the real child of her parents, and taking the Pill had prevented her foolish lapse from ending in pregnancy.

Damson had shown herself trustful and willing at least in the short term when she gave Leeta the key. With any luck there would be no trace of this stupid pregnancy on her perfect body. Her thick creamy skin was resilient and there were no stretch marks. Youth and the gym had seen to that. She shied away from the word 'baby' in her own mind.

She remembered with crystal clarity what had happened earlier in the year. Hearing Dadima's cold words, first she'd flung open the sitting room door and stared at them all. Then she'd run up to her room, turning the key in the door and flinging herself on the bed, too stunned to do anything but stare at the ceiling.

'Leeta, let me in.'

It was her mother at the bedroom door. But not her 'mother'. No, some stranger now. Great sobs shook her.

'Leeta, *meri jaan.* Mummy is here. I am so sorry that you should have heard like that. Please let me in. Your Dadima was very wrong to blurt it out where you were likely to hear.'

Leeta was so lonely in that moment. All that was sure and certain had splintered and crashed away from her, leaving her standing on the brink of a void. 'Who am I?' she said, out loud. But she loved Mira, her soft, sweet-smelling, practical mother, so she got up and unlocked the door, going back to lie down without looking at her. The bed dipped as Mira sat down. They were silent for a bit. Leeta wanted to do something dramatic, like sob loudly or kick her mother off the bed. Treat her as she had never treated her before. Because she had never had any reason to do anything but love her mother. Her mother? Stunned, she continued to look at the ceiling.

'I wanted to tell you years ago.'

'Why didn't you then?' Leeta didn't care that she sounded rude.

'Papa said not. And he had been so good about having you in our family when his mother didn't want us to adopt. I didn't want to go against him again.'

Leeta knew how chilly her Dadima could be.

'You should have told me. I had a right to know.'

'I know you did. But you don't understand. We just don't adopt like people do in the West. Or if we do, we keep very quiet about it. Living in England it's easier, because you can just go to India, adopt there and then come back with a baby. We would have gone to India ourselves if you hadn't become available so quickly after we were approved.'

Leeta digested the idea of 'becoming available' after a lifetime of believing she had 'been born'.

'What do you know about my birth mother?'

'We know she was clever like you. She was studying to be a doctor, again like you – and us.'

'Oh, I suppose her family wanted a cover-up, and made her

have me adopted so she could get married respectably. Is she here or in India?'

'I think she's here but I don't know.' Mira stopped, looking confused. Leeta, who was trying to get used to this new idea, was so desperate for comfort that she snuggled into her mother's armpit where she was safe, breathing in the warm familiar scent of her skin.

She didn't say anything else, just wrapped her arms around her daughter. Leeta pulled away slightly and looked at her, sensing her hesitation. Mira looked down.

'What happened to her? Is she dead?'

'As far as I know she's fine, nothing out of the ordinary. The thing is that she is not Indian, she's English.'

Leeta fell back on to the bed. Mira bent over her anxiously.

'It's OK, *meri jaan*. She was clever, from a good family, not just anybody.'

Leeta stared at the ceiling, still dotted with plastic luminous stars from when she was little and would watch them dim until she slept. Safe with Papa and Mummy downstairs, and smells of cooking wafting under the door.

Leeta rolled slowly on to her side with her back to Mira, drawing her knees to her chest to take up as little space as possible in this house which was no longer home.

She examined her long, shapely hands, her bony wrists. Then she sat up again, taking Mira's hands in hers: small hands with soft palms and wrists rounded like smooth pipes, no bones or tendons visible. Had she ever wondered why she was so much taller and lankier, and – she had to accept this – paler than her parents?

'As soon as I saw you, I fell in love with you, my darling little Leeta. Let Mummy hug you, come on.'

Leeta could not resist, and crept, tall though she was, back into her mother's embrace. Making herself small to fit. They sat quietly, each absorbing comfort from the other's breath going in and out, in and out, as if nothing had happened.

'Your Dadima's always been a bitch,' said Mira, unexpectedly. Mira, whom Leeta had seen touching her mother-in-law's feet, always so respectful.

'It was such a relief when we came to practise in London, and I didn't have to live with her in Jaipur and be submissive. I never liked her, and she was so jealous of me. So spiteful and critical all the time. Who can blame her? I had studied medicine at university, she had just been a housewife. Papa is her only son. As you know, ours was a love marriage, and she was a widow, and had had no say. Perfectly suitable, but not arranged by her. She didn't like that at all.'

'How did she work out that you'd adopted me?'

'I think she wondered repeatedly out loud why you were so pale and had grey eyes, and in the end Papa told her. But he also told her to keep it a secret. As if that would work, but men always have a rose-tinted view of their mothers. She's come storming over to interfere and talk about arranging a marriage for you. I think she was afraid you might meet and marry an English doctor. Of course it would have been different if you had been a boy. She simply could not understand why we had adopted a little girl who wasn't even properly Indian.'

'Why did you?'

'Because it turned out to be quite easy. Few Indians were

adopting in the Eighties, and the whole idea was for mixed-race babies' – Leeta winced – 'to go to Indian parents. I couldn't conceive, you see.'

Leeta was listening hard, though her face was hidden from Mira's.

'We went through the business of having a social worker round to ask all sorts of awkward questions. Papa played his part, although he was so embarrassed by the intrusion. Then they told us they had a baby on the way we might be interested in. It all happened much more quickly than I expected.'

'You had me from birth?'

'Pretty well. You were a week old. We picked you up from the social services contact centre. Your mother had brought you there from the hospital.'

'You mean you met her?'

'Oh no, that wasn't allowed. But she had said goodbye to you in the room from which we collected you.'

Leeta uncurled herself. She'd put an arm around her mother. 'What else do you know about the birth parents?'

'We know that she needed to return to her studies. That's all. We know nothing about your father, except that he was Hindu.

'If your Papa had been conservative, he would never have consented to any kind of adoption. In the old days I would have been put aside as a barren wife, useless.' Mira looked stricken. 'And your Dadima would have been right behind that, I can tell you! She always wanted an obedient daughter-in-law she had chosen, whom she could boss around.'

'Do you know what my birth parents looked like?'

'We were shown a photograph of her, but we have no idea

what your father looked like. He must have been tall I think. She didn't look very tall and had fair, short hair.'

'Was she pretty?'

'It was difficult to tell. Just a snap, and she wasn't smiling. Her face looked pleasant, I think.'

'OK.'

Mira had dried up and Leeta was frustrated as an insatiable need to know more opened like a wound inside her. Remembering her manners, and the shocked look on Dadima's face when she had burst into the sitting room, she said: 'Do I have to come back downstairs and face Dadima again?'

'I don't think so. I'll tell her it's all been a bit of a shock and that you've gone to bed. I'm sure Papa will have been furious with her. It was a mean thing to say.'

Leeta hugged her mother close, nuzzling into her neck. Mira smiled, pushing her gently away. 'You always did that, you little pussy cat.'

She sighed.

'Now let me go to bed, Mummy, I'm so tired.'

Mira went back downstairs. Leeta threw off her clothes and climbed into bed naked, rebelliously. Who the hell was she, if she wasn't Leeta Delapi? An English mother? Why had she given her baby away? What would she herself have done if she had found herself pregnant at university? An abortion probably – anything to get rid of the shame. Well, her unknown mother hadn't got rid of her at least, she'd allowed her to grow in her reluctant body, and then given her to Papa and Mummy, who'd loved her. She tried telling herself it wasn't all bad.

She had drifted off to sleep that night not sure she would ever want to meet the oddity of an English birth mother. She'd worried that Mira would feel hurt and rejected if she did. But this unknown woman would hold the key to the pale skin, the bony wrists, the grey eyes, the very size of her in comparison to Mira. She used to think there was something wrong with her, but Mira reassured her and just said that a lot of second-generation Indian babies in the UK were much bigger than their parents had been, it must be something to do with the food. Many of her Indian immigrant patients had had to have caesareans because the babies were too big to be born naturally.

'Did you have a caesarean, Mummy?' she now remembered asking.

'No, darling. I didn't.'

Thirty

Damson
October 2008

A young mother picked up her toddler and made for the door clutching a prescription for Amoxicillin for his swollen tonsils, and Damson pushed the buzzer on her desk.

'Is that it, Tina?'

'Yup.'

'OK, you can go. I'll lock up. Thanks.'

All the other doctors in the practice had gone home an hour ago, as usual pleading family responsibilities. Damson was late due to the double shift, and anyway she was always last, not having any family to take responsibility for. But what now? She wondered if she should have pleaded illness earlier and gone home with Leeta, but with Dr Symes off sick it would have been impossible. And she had needed a little time to think, away from the overwhelming physical presence of Leeta.

She had been distracted all day by the knowledge that Leeta was waiting at Swine Cottage, while patient after patient filed through her consulting room. She had tried to concentrate, refer, prescribe, diagnose, sympathise, while her mind flitted back and back to the tall, slender, pregnant girl who had burst into her well-ordered life that morning.

A very small part of her considered it was some kind of

psychotic episode brought on by her recent mid-life broodiness, and that she'd hallucinated the whole encounter. She had rung her own home number mid-afternoon, and there had been no answer. Now she dialled again, shaking with anxiety. She realised she had seldom or never rung her own landline in all the years she had lived at Fenning. There had been nobody there to answer it before.

'Hello?' It was that voice, somehow familiar.

'Leeta? Damson here. How are you?'

'I had a rest, and I went out to the shop to get some food as there didn't seem to be much here. I'm making some supper. What time will you be home?'

It all sounded so normal and practical that Damson was invaded by a sudden onrush of joy. She paused to let it sink in, that her Mellita had grown into a complete woman without any help from her. Now, as Leeta, she did need her help. Damson was ready and willing. But she was frightened of what the immense gap in time, space and natural expectation had done to any potential mother-daughter relationship. They probably could not have one, but even being in the same house would be beyond anything she had expected.

'Sounds lovely. I'd like to do a bit more here, can dinner wait about forty minutes? Do we need anything else?'

'There isn't much milk.'

'OK, I'll pick some up on the way home.' The conversation was as if Mellita had been in the habit of dropping in on her mother regularly ever since she went away to university.

When she had registered for contact, for weeks afterwards she had checked repeatedly to see if her child wanted to know her. It hadn't occurred to her that the child didn't know she was adopted. It had been a blow when no message arrived. It didn't matter in the slightest that Leeta had now been driven to her by desperate need, rather than a desire to meet her birth mother. Any crumb was good enough for Damson.

She also knew perfectly well she must find out for sure that Leeta was Mellita, and not some imposter preying upon a lonely woman, however unlikely that seemed. She had considered just trusting Leeta, whoever she was. Using the stored-up love that had never had a channel along which to flow to carry her to whatever safe place seemed right for her. The idea of checking up on her baby seemed so intrusive.

She knew in principle what DNA testing entailed, but it too seemed intrusive. In a small town in the depths of Derbyshire, DNA testing was a closed book. No one had consulted her on whether she thought their babies had been swapped in hospital or their embryos in an IVF clinic, and no father had ever wanted her confirmation that the child he was supporting was his blood and bone. It seemed the stuff of tabloid nightmares.

Leeta had, with great daring no doubt, tracked her down – easy enough with a unique name like Damson. She knew she wanted very much to believe she was who she said she was, but Damson wasn't stupid or gullible either.

DNA testing was easily accessible these days. If she had needed to find out about Leeta even ten years ago, it wouldn't have been nearly so simple. She typed 'dna testing maternity' into Google, and what confronted her came straight from the worst bits of *CSI Miami*. She read about the need to freeze faecal matter, about the benefits of Juicy Fruit chewing gum over other flavours for DNA collection, about making sure the person whose used handkerchiefs you were filching did not have an infection.

It was like some twenty-first century witch's recipe: dried umbilical cords, teeth and bone, refrigerated condoms, ear wax on cotton buds, exhumed tissue from deep within the thigh, 'properly collected blood stains'. The site seemed to expect everyone to be wading in the murky waters of disputed inheritance, child support and infidelity, even murder. And the home page was decorated with five jaunty three-dimensional stars – the right-hand points very slightly clipped – to demonstrate very nearly five-star customer satisfaction with this sinister service.

Damson shook her head and applied herself to finding a UK service. There were several advertised, each claiming to be the best in the country. The difference in the tone was stark. The UK sites went into none of the details of what samples were most useful and in what form. On the 'maternity testing' page there was a nice picture of a (potential) mother hugging her pretty little (potential) daughter and only three conceivable reasons why anyone might want such a test: adopted children reunited with their mothers (Leeta and her), IVF mix-ups and swapped babies. For the 'peace of mind' option it was only £140, as opposed to the legal one which was more like £500.

The tone was far less alarming too. It discreetly talked about 'in-home testing characterised by the self-collection process' – no midnight grave-robbing horrors here. She noticed there was a 'free testing kit' which, it was promised, would arrive in twenty-four hours, by which time she should be ready to use it. Then she clicked around the site a bit more. Even if she wanted to, the UK sites did not allow for the sneaky stealing of a hair complete with follicle that the US sites advocated. You had to get permission from both parties, and anyway she was not at all sure how she would finesse the taking of swabs from inside Leeta's cheeks without an explanation. Leeta was a medical student, she would know exactly what Damson was up to.

What would her reaction be if she was in Leeta's position? Leeta was a clever girl. She would understand that, if Damson was going to commit herself to a mother's role, financially and emotionally, she would need physical proof that she was a blood relation. She decided to risk it, and clicked 'send' to get the kit. The results would arrive within a few days of posting off the samples.

When she got home, it was strange to knock on her own front door as she stood in the damp October dusk. It swung open, and there was Leeta, wearing soft grey jogging bottoms and a T-shirt. She had managed to light a fire, and Damson's home was warm and suffused with a delicious scent of frying onions that made her mouth water. The very first time she had ever been welcomed into Swine Cottage.

'Hello,' Leeta said, holding the door open for her. 'I hope you don't mind me making myself at home?'

'No, not at all,' Damson replied. 'That's exactly what I meant you to do.'

She looked around as she stripped off the yellow poncho and cycling helmet. Then she looked at the girl who said she was her Mellita. Again she had a strong desire to touch her, hug and kiss her, even though she was still a stranger, or a bare acquaintance at best.

'Would you like some tea? I've made a pot.'

'Yes. Thank you.'

They walked through the arch together, and Damson found her kitchen full of unfamiliar smells of cooking.

'I couldn't find a tea cosy,' Leeta was saying, indicating what looked like a pile of drying-up cloths. She poured the tea from the pot hidden underneath into a couple of mugs.

'Do you like sugar?'

'No, thank you.' Damson was quite bemused. This was so completely unlike her usual way of living, as if an ultra-polite alien had crash-landed its spaceship through her roof.

'I don't like sugar,' said Leeta. 'But since this,' she indicated her belly, 'it seems to make sense for some reason.'

They went back into the sitting room to sit down on either side of the fire.

'How was your day?' Leeta ventured.

Damson looked at her in amazement. Chatting seemed a bit strange at a time like this, and they did need to communicate properly.

'Well, it was quite something in fact. Leeta, we do need to talk.'

'I know. I'm sorry.'

The girl looked down, her curtain of dark brown straight hair falling forward and hiding her face.

'Look, Dr Hayes.'

'Please call me Damson.' She wondered for a moment what it would be like if Leeta called her Mummy or Mum.

'Damson, I realise this is an awkward situation, and I am truly sorry for bursting into your life like this. You must think it was a mean trick that I planned to play on you deliberately, pretending to be a patient. I'm sorry.'

'No, it's fine.' Damson would forgive Mellita anything just for the sake of spending any time with her at all.

'Well, the thing is, I wasn't thinking of deceiving you, I just wanted to be alone with you for a few minutes. You understand? I couldn't think of any other way to do it without you suspecting something. In case you didn't seem like the kind of person I would want to spend any time with or even like. If you'd been cold and disapproving or something. I don't know. If I had hated you, I would have simply left without telling you who I was. But in fact Mummy and Papa are both GPs so it seemed so easy and familiar that you are too.'

'I remember now, I was told they were doctors. Made it easier somehow. My grandfather was a GP too. You said you were on your way to residency?'

Leeta sat up. 'Well, I've done my first three years at Cambridge, and I need to move on to the next stage. I took my A levels early and didn't have a gap year.'

'Do your parents know where you are?' Damson realised too late that this was a stupid question.

'No, of course not.' Leeta spoke as if it should be obvious to Damson. 'Why would I be here if they did? If my parents found out, they would reject me, and I couldn't bear it. I love them, you see. I've always loved them so much. It was the three of us, always. It's been so ghastly finding out they weren't my parents. I couldn't bear to disappoint them and let them down when they took me in and looked after me and paid for my education and everything.'

'So what happened? How did you get pregnant?'

'Oh God. I was so miserable, it was as if my world had come to an end. I went to a friend's Valentine's party and drank a lot of gin. Stupidly, I let myself be taken upstairs by some guy I knew and quite fancied. We were kissing and before I knew where we were he was inside me. It got out of hand. I pushed him away because it hurt. I didn't think it was enough to get pregnant.'

'Didn't you think of the morning-after pill?'

'I suppose I was in denial. And for weeks and even months, it didn't show. But then it did, and baggy jumpers weren't enough, so I pretended to my parents that I wasn't sure I wanted to complete my medical training. That I was thinking of being a banker. I lied to them, told them my tutor had recommended I did a year of voluntary work so I could think about where my life was going. I told them I was going to work in a clinic in Uganda. I went and got a job as a waitress in Bournemouth. But then I was so pregnant and I just didn't know what to do.'

'OK, Leeta. What do you want from me?'

'Shelter.'

The word dropped between them.

'For how long?'

'Until the birth.'

'What if I say no?'

'Would you?'

'No, not if you are who you say you are.'

'Right, otherwise I could find a hostel and then go into hospital at the last minute as an emergency.'

'What about the baby?'

'I could give a false name, leave it there and go. I read about a woman doing that. It seems simplest.'

Damson couldn't breathe properly. That her own child should be so desperate that she would plan to abandon her baby. She remembered how she had been when she found herself on the slippery slope, greased for her by efficient Margaret, to the adoption of her baby. Numb. Until the actual birth. But before that just numb, looking ahead to going back to how things had been before, because there was no room in her life for a baby.

'Sorry to be so blunt,' Leeta continued. 'There is an alternative.'

Damson didn't say anything, but she could sense what was coming. She controlled herself to appear and sound neutral, as she did with her patients, whatever Leeta should propose.

'I could live with you until the birth. Then you could have the baby.'

In one day Damson had gone from single, childless woman, to mother, to future grandmother, to potential foster or adoptive mother. It was too wild a journey for less than twelve hours. She took a deep breath, as quietly as she could. Emotion had no place in this exchange.

'OK, let's get real here, Leeta. I work full time in a demanding job, and you're expecting me to drop everything and just take on your baby? For one thing, I'm not sure what social services would say. We've had no relationship since you were adopted.'

'Why do you have to tell them?'

'Well, there are several reasons. I know they prefer to place babies and children with family members. I could take the baby for a bit maybe, until you knew what you wanted to do, but I think you need to consider including your baby in your future plans.

'For instance, what about me looking after it until you qualify?' Damson went on. 'You could study somewhere up here. Then you could see your baby whenever you like.'

Leeta just looked blankly at her as if she was mad.

'Study here? But I was planning to go to America to finish my training. Perhaps find a husband out there, like my cousins. Why would I want to stay here?'

'Because of the baby?'

'No. Oh no. Nothing I do can be "because of the baby". You can't make me. I have to go on being Leeta Delapi, not some flaky girl who sacrifices everything because she got herself knocked up during a drunken fuck. That's not me at all. That's you.'

Damson stared at her. 'What do you mean?'

'Did you get yourself pregnant in India? What was it, too much country wine and a big fat spliff in Goa?'

'No, not Goa.'

Leeta's voice was rising, her eyes wide.

'So I'm right? You don't have a leg to stand on. You gave me up because you wanted to go on studying, why shouldn't I do the same?' She was shouting now.

This strange angry creature jolted Damson profoundly. She stood up and walked towards the kitchen, stopping to lean on the wall in the passage to get her breath. She must not cry or shout. She had to remain calm, to be the adult in this situation.

Leeta hurried after her. 'You gave me up, you abandoned me.

Why? You had plenty of money didn't you?'

She was yelling right into her mother's face. Tiny spit drops spattered Damson's cheeks and nose. Damson had to say something. But it was all true. She remembered her powerlessness. Her father standing in the background, wispily disappearing into the hand-painted wallpaper, as Margaret set out the programme for Damson's 'rescue from her moment of madness', as she called it.

'The agency will take care of everything,' Margaret had kept saying. 'You don't need to worry about a thing. Just go and stay with Nanny until it's born and then you can return to university as if nothing had happened. Your father and I are right behind your decision, aren't we, Munty? Isn't Damson being brave?'

Damson could see her father in her mind's eye, looking sad and bewildered while his wife managed away his first grandchild and disposed of it like an unwanted puppy.

Munty was getting older now. He had four nicely-brought-up step-grandchildren via Clarrie and Noonie. How would he react to being introduced to his one true grandchild? Damson didn't care what Margaret thought now. Family was all that mattered.

Leeta had calmed down. She moved to stand beside her mother and lean against the wall. They were quiet for a bit. Leeta was looking at her Ugg-clad feet. They were breathing in sync when Damson started speaking again. To explain.

'If you knew how much it hurt, Leeta, giving you up. I'd made the decision to carry you to term as soon as I knew I was pregnant, so I went home to brave my stepmother and father. She took it all in her stride and simply organised me and organised me until I was back at Cambridge, a year behind, without you and miserable.'

'Do you want me to be sorry for you?' Leeta's voice was low and expressionless.

'No, of course not.' She made the decision never to tell Leeta that she was the result of rape.

Silence fell, to be broken by Damson.

'Shall we have something to eat?'

Over the days that followed, they did talk, but it was stilted and forced. Damson would try to convince her daughter that it would be so much better for everyone if she, Leeta, let Damson take the strain, Leeta should stay with her baby. Damson was ready to make any sacrifice.

Leeta was adamant, the baby would ruin her carefully constructed life plan, and must not be allowed to do so. Damson owed it to her to make it go away, to make it right for her. It was all Damson's fault for abandoning her in the first place. Damson would hesitate, and plough on.

When Leeta learnt one evening that Damson had been brought up in what sounded like a stately home, she became sad and even angrier.

'Surely there was a room somewhere there, where you could have kept a baby?' she kept saying. Then the sunny, carefree London girl would reappear and admit that she had been very happy with her adoptive parents, and the idea of being tucked away in some attic like a shameful secret would have been intolerable.

One day, Damson got tired of saying the same comforting words over and over again, and said instead: 'You do understand, because now you want to do the same thing.'

Leeta stared at her. 'What do you mean?'

Damson bit her lip so hard it hurt.

'I just want to be sure this is what you want. After all I gave up my baby to complete strangers, albeit professionally vetted ones. At least you're giving up yours to your own flesh and blood.'

Thirty-one

Damson always awoke when Leeta got up in the night, but she didn't make a sound, just listened for her daughter's safe return to her bed. She found it hard to get back to sleep, puzzled as she was about what to do. For the first time in many years, she was not in control of her life. Looking back, that control had been pretty sterile. It involved keeping as far away as possible from anything that tweaked her nerves, like her stepmother. What had she got to show for it? A cottage, a career and lots of patients, but no one just for her. None of the joyful, messy stuff that comes with a family.

Mother and daughter lived parallel lives in Damson's cottage, suspended in a time of waiting. The birth was the horizon, representing the curved edge of their known world. They would both sail over it together, and Damson had no idea what lay on the other side.

Leeta had been an easy guest in all practical ways, keen to cook and keep house for Damson, which surprised her. Damson wasn't domestic, the despair of her grandmother with her larder full of jam and her freezer full of home-grown vegetables. Damson had shut down that side of herself so young. Unsexing herself, wearing men's clothes. Eating any old thing. Making herself appear shapeless. Getting super-fit and hard-bodied by hiking, swimming and cycling. Hiding anything soft about herself. Losing a mother. Losing a daughter. Losing her own femininity. It seemed easier to remove all evidence of womanhood, as then it couldn't be taken away ever again. She hid herself behind a strong handshake, firm voice and baggy cords and jumpers.

Damson encouraged Leeta to study, but Leeta bought magazines like *Modern Woman* and *Gossip*, and read those instead. She claimed to be resting her mind and, even in matters as unimportant as this, she resisted absolutely Damson's attempts to influence her.

Damson also tried to talk to her about what would happen after the baby was born, but her daughter jibbed every time. She noticed that Leeta never used the word 'baby', never speculated about the sex, never wanted to go and buy things like car seats and clothes. Worried, and manoeuvred into taking responsibility, Damson went out one Saturday to Derby and stocked up on a basic layette, a car seat that clipped on to a pushchair, and a Moses basket and nappies. Hesitating, she also bought organic new-born formula, bottles and an electric steriliser just in case. If Leeta was behaving as if the moment of birth was somehow the end of something, there was no point in forcing her to think about breastfeeding.

Rebuffed by Leeta's passive resistance, she wasn't quite sure what else to do, and concealed her purchases in the deep cupboard in her room that went a long way back beside the chimney breast.

It was such an unprecedented situation. She must hold out

her arms with total generosity to receive anything that dropped into them when the time came. And she recognised something in Leeta that was completely familiar. They had both been solitary inhabitants of their particular nests. Leeta's had been feathered with love, Damson's not so much. But they shared that essential independence and – Damson had to admit this – stubborn bloody-mindedness. Now Leeta was in flight and had barely alighted like a bird on a wire. Gone soon.

Much was unsaid, particularly about any kind of future meeting beyond the birth. Anguished conversations had petered out into politeness. Leeta liked best to sit and eat her supper in front of television dramas and chat. Damson slipped into the role of quiet cherishing. She had a rushing sensation, as if the skin of her face was being blown backwards against her skull by the speed of time passing.

For years Damson had been mired deep in a life she'd chosen in response to her past. It bored her and she hadn't been able to work out how to force a change. Now her past had erupted into her present and she lay in bed at night aware of her heart beating in little quick hops, as if trying to catch up with the tiny window of motherhood. It was only two or at the most three weeks until the end of Leeta's pregnancy. Longer than the ten minutes she'd had in the yellow-painted room.

She would get on her bicycle and pedal furiously over the hills, coming back to herself twenty miles away, hot but not exhilarated. The now of Leeta – she didn't dare think about the unknown baby – crashing in on her consciousness as she stood, resting for a moment by the side of a track, one foot on the ground, one on a pedal.

Watching her daughter folding sheets, ironing or standing at the stove stir-frying strips of chicken, Leeta reminded Damson of Sarah.

'The domestic gene seems to have skipped a generation or two,' she remarked, seeing Leeta reduce a pile of vegetables to matchsticks in moments. She'd been a frozen veg person for years. Sarah was the cook, and Damson had never had any inclination to join in.

'Oh, yes, my mother taught me,' Leeta would say.

Damson became adept at dodging the darts of pain that these remarks inflicted. Every day she saw more of herself in Leeta. Independence, a career that made a difference, and her own home, had been Damson's ambitions. Leeta's choices were different in detail, but she could recognise the same drive, the desire to have the life she had visualised and worked hard for. In addition to a career, Leeta hungered for a traditional marriage and the glow of approval that would be hers when she fulfilled all parental and religious expectations in one go. Damson could see that Leeta believed marriage would restore her to her adoptive family once more, and how important that Indian identity was to her. As far as she knew, the adoptive parents believed Leeta to be in Uganda and had no current intention of rejecting her at all. The fear was all in Leeta's mind.

There had been no such marital pressure on Damson, even though Munty had no male heir. Once again the title would go to a distant cousin, although the law of entail had changed and the estate was no longer attached to it. As Margaret's money had saved Castle Hey from being sold or simply crumbling to dust, it probably belonged to her stepmother by now anyway, or had been left to her in Munty's will. The subject had never been discussed.

The DNA test results had come back rapidly, irrefutably confirming their relationship. Damson offered to put her life aside, to move anywhere in the country or even the world that Leeta fancied, to share the care of the baby while Leeta trained in the hospital of her choice. Leeta made no attempt to interrupt. She deadened the air between them with her concrete silence. Or she would stand up and leave the room.

So Damson loved helplessly, the buried pain of the yellow-painted room resurrecting like a zombie, shocking her with its gnawing intensity. She must bear it as she had borne everything else and try to live in the present.

Leeta behaved unknowingly like the princess that she probably was. Damson well remembered Ronny's autocratic rule over his tiny kingdom, and longed to tell Leeta about him – the more interesting bits of course – but the risk was too great. She didn't seem curious.

If Leeta wanted something, she was well able to ignore the emotional damage she or anyone else might sustain in order to get it. During one of their conversations – the baby was a small elephant in the room – Leeta had enthused about the glossy NRI lifestyle she had experienced in New York and Connecticut when she'd stayed with her cousins during her summer holidays.

Damson had had to ask what NRI meant. Leeta gave her a look: 'Non-resident Indian', she spelt out. So different from boring old London and, Damson suspected, boring old Damson.

Perhaps if Leeta had had a different, more westernised attitude to sex, she could have accepted her baby as a fact of life, and rearranged her future to accommodate it. But Damson could see that her conditioning was wrapped around the baby like a tumour around an optic nerve, blinding her to the beauty of a child as an entity in itself and associating it only with shame, a drunken fumble in the dark and banishment from the heart of her family. Damson slid slowly into sleep as she puzzled once again over her daughter.

'Damson, please wake up?'

She opened her eyes from a dream of baby elephants covered in red mud crashing through her garden wall, to see Leeta standing by the bed, leaning back slightly with her hand on the base of her spine. She was wearing a T-shirt with baggy cotton jersey trousers and her smooth bump showed between one and the other.

'What is it?' she said, stupid with sleep. 'What time is it?'

'It's about five o'clock, and I think it's starting.'

Damson sat up and rubbed her eyes, swinging her legs clad in men's striped pyjamas off the bed and taking Leeta's hand. For once her daughter let her.

'Are you timing the contractions?'

'It started as soon as we went to bed, but I didn't want to bother you when they were ten minutes apart. I thought it might be Braxton Hicks still, as they weren't painful just a bit surprising. But then they started being longer and more purposeful.

'They're about five minutes apart at the moment.'

The girl broke off, let go of Damson and reached gropingly for the edge of the chest of drawers with both hands. Her eyes closed, and she began to breathe through her nose, while executing what looked to Damson, from long-ago prep school dancing lessons, like a deep plié.

Damson began to count in her head, reaching sixty seconds as Leeta straightened up and let out a long breath.

'Hmmm. Think you may be getting to the end of early labour. Would you like to go to hospital?'

Another contraction started to build, and Leeta was quiet for a while, doing her slow incongruous plié against the chest of drawers. Damson went to get the bag she'd packed for Leeta and the baby, as well as her own medical bag, and helped her daughter downstairs and into the car. The Royal Derby Hospital was nearly forty minutes away and Damson did not want to deliver the baby at the roadside.

The birth went smoothly, but the baby spent not a single moment with Leeta once he was free of her body. Even as the midwife guided him into the world, she rejected him utterly, flinging her arms over her eyes. Damson didn't say anything. The pain was replaced by joy at her grandson's appearance. He made little sound and she witnessed the healthy pink flush across his skin like a sunset as he emerged.

Even before the cord was cut, the new mother rolled abruptly on to her side, lifting her leg over her infant, leaving him behind her on the bed. She drew up her knees, foetal herself and covered her face with her hands. Damson, seeing what was happening, quickly moved round to the other side of the bed. The midwife dealt with the situation by clamping and cutting the cord. Damson found herself rapidly undoing her shirt buttons with one hand, before holding out her arms, and the midwife simply handed the naked baby to her. She took him in both hands and nestled him against the skin of her breasts, covering him with her shirt and cardigan, caring nothing for the vernix and amniotic fluid – there was very little blood – enfolding him close to her heart. The buttery coating of his just-born skin transferred itself to hers.

'Now, Leeta,' she heard the midwife say. 'I need you to roll on to your back so we can deliver the placenta.'

Leeta groaned but complied, her hands still covering her face. The midwife deftly injected her thigh with syntocin and held on to the cord to guide the placenta from her body, reminding Leeta to push, which she did half-heartedly. Damson was only half aware of this in her wonder at what was inside her shirt. Once she had made sure the baby was warm and close, she tipped him away from her with her hand behind his head so she could look at his face.

'Hello, little man,' she said, detecting as she did so an impatient movement from the bed behind her. But she wasn't going to be constrained by Leeta in this sublime moment.

'How beautiful you are,' she crooned, bending to kiss his sticky little head. Her breasts tingled as she snuffled his new-born scent.

He was a rich pink colour all over now, drying rapidly and giving off waves of balsamic new-born perfume, funky and strange, tropical in its intensity. As he was moved, his pink paws made a startled gesture, and he opened his eyes. If she had been drifting down the tide before, she was utterly lost now, sailing on an open sea of love. She seized him back against herself and held him with her own eyes closed. Then the midwife wanted him back, so she handed him over, rejoicing in his perfect APGAR score and his seven-pound heft.

He had had the consideration to be born at lunchtime with the paediatrician available for checks, so there was nothing to keep them. They went home just as soon as Leeta had showered in the adjoining bathroom, dressed and declared herself ready. Damson had brought maternity pads, which she handed to Leeta, and a bag of things to dress the baby in, which she did herself. Placing a tiny disposable nappy around his frog-like hips, she admired his splendid tripartite manhood, out of proportion as always in a new-born awash with hormones. Anxiously, she covered his chest with a crossover vest and eased his still folded arms along the sleeves of the old-fashioned soft cotton nightie she had bought for him, and then folded him into a cobweb shawl. It was only when she got to the car and realised she would have somehow to strap him into a car seat, with a strap between the legs, that she regretted her impulse to dress him like that.

Leeta climbed into the back seat, making no attempt to help Damson as she fumbled with buckles and belts. When Damson was satisfied that her charge was firmly strapped and comfortable, she got in and sat quietly for a minute. She needed to calm down before driving.

'Well, are we going?'

'Hang on, Leeta, I'm just getting my breath. Are you OK?'

'I'm fine, don't know what all the fuss is about.'

'Well, I think you should rest. The more you rest now the sooner you'll be back to normal.' And she turned the key in the ignition and pulled slowly away from the parking space to set off home.

When they arrived at Swine Cottage, Leeta eased herself out and disappeared through the front door, again doing nothing to help. Damson had thought giving birth might switch on Leeta's awareness of herself as a mother but clearly it hadn't, at least not yet.

She undid the belt and removed the car seat, carrying it by its handle and putting it down in the hall. The little boy was asleep, lulled by the motion of the car. Upstairs, she heard Leeta's door shut.

He was in the big bedroom with Damson from birth, bonding against her breasts and staring into her eyes while he sucked from the bottle of formula. When the extraordinary intimacy became too much, she would put him down in his basket and creep away to stand outside under the sky, riding waves of emotion such as she had never experienced before. Even more intense than anything she had allowed herself during her scrimped and scraped minutes with baby Mellita.

To be so completely involved with his physical presence that she might as well be his mother was overwhelming. But she must give Leeta every opportunity to be his mother herself. If she showed the slightest softening towards the baby, Damson would step aside willingly.

Thirty-two

Damson
November 2008

The baby was on the small side and Leeta very slim and young. Damson's English, fair and fragile skin was seamed even now with silvery stretch marks like the Nile Delta, but Leeta's belly had snapped back into shape with no lasting damage at all. Damson had to be quite bossy and insist she stayed in bed for a few days, as Leeta wanted to behave as if she had never had a baby from the moment she had come home from the hospital.

They went to the register office together, and Damson held the baby while Leeta filled out the forms. Leeta was surprisingly practical when it came to shedding responsibility. It was vital that there should be no immediate questions, so she suggested that she give him Damson's surname as well as her own to avoid confusion. But Damson made sure that Leeta chose a first name for him. It was the one moment when the girl seemed to allow herself to think of the baby as a person rather than an inconvenience. She chose Hari, after her adoptive maternal grandfather who had died when she was five, and whom she remembered as being kind.

Hari Hayes Delapi, it was a good name. No father's name went on the birth certificate of course, as there was no father present. They paid for the full version of the certificate, Damson insisted. And then she made sure they had the baby professionally photographed, and ordered a passport for him as well. Just in case, Damson said.

As soon as she was well enough, Leeta explained that she needed a new wardrobe in preparation for leaving Derbyshire. She'd gone into Bakewell on the bus and used her credit card to buy clothes at Franca. Damson had given in and prescribed her Parlodel to stop the milk, as she knew that Leeta would simply order it on the internet, and it could be fake and harmful. Although she knew with her mind, Damson's heart had not realised she would lose Mellita again so soon.

Damson was careful to put Hari down before she went to Leeta in the tiny room, offering to help her pack and sort out her possessions. Hari's presence appeared almost unbearably irritating to Leeta and Damson did not dare to guess at her daughter's feelings. Leeta stuffed anything that might remind her of being pregnant into a black sack for the charity shop.

'Can you take it into Derby for me? No one must ever know about this.'

Damson's unaccustomed mother's heart bled for her daughter.

'See how you are. I'm always here if you need me,' she said timidly, while knowing that her utility for Leeta was now over.

'I think it would be much better if we didn't see each other for some time. I don't want anyone to know anything about this or connect me with you. If my parents or a prospective husband found out, it would be the end of everything. And please don't say you're my mother and you'll look after me. I can't bear it if you do. I'm Indian, and my family is Indian, and that is how I'll live my life. I'm not like you at all. When I look at you, I don't see a mother.'

'What do you see?' said Damson.

'I see a person.'

'What do you mean?'

'I see a person wearing corduroy trousers and an old jumper with holes in the elbows. A shapeless person in dull-coloured clothes with no hair.'

Damson glanced down at herself and could only agree. She knew that Leeta was building up a head of negativity to power her exit from the cottage.

'I don't want a link between us at all. So I'm looking at you and seeing something that isn't feminine enough to be a mother.

'I love my parents and I can't let that love go. So I can't love you. Do you understand? There isn't any room for you.'

Damson had never had a mother so she wasn't at all sure what loving one might be like. She had no expectations in her heart. But there was a little boy asleep in the other bedroom. It was a reminder of her love for her own tiny Mellita. Attaching that love to this bold defiant girl was strange but it was there.

She knew she was on dodgy ground accepting this private fostering arrangement in the twenty-first century, but she couldn't make Leeta understand her point of view. Any mention of social services sent Leeta into point-blank refusal to discuss it. There was a niggling worry about her professional status, but she thought she could explain things to any authority that bothered to ask. Hari was her grandchild. She had some experience of a certain laissez-faire attitude when it came to middle-class cases.

Damson was also old enough to know that you can never rely

on other people to act as you would in almost any circumstance. It would've required Leeta to override her lifelong conditioning as a dutiful Indian daughter. The whole regrettable business, from pregnancy to leaving the baby behind, appeared to be a violent sustained reaction to discovering not just that she was adopted, but that she was half-English too.

'So there's nothing I can say? And you will take care of your health? You should take it very easy for at least six weeks – get yourself checked by a doctor.'

'What would I say? I've had a baby and abandoned it?'

'Well, no. I don't know. It's up to you. What time's your train? Would you like me to drive you to the station?'

'I've ordered a taxi. The train's just after seven.'

'Where are you going?' she ventured, thinking it was unlikely she would be told the truth.

'I'm taking Eurostar, going to St Tropez to stay with a friend. I've told her I've had glandular fever and need to rest somewhere warmer than England. You've got my email address, but don't use it unless you have to.'

After all, Leeta was an adult. She could do what she liked. Even Indian parents didn't need to know where their adult children were every day.

'Do you need money?'

Leeta glanced up at her.

'No, I don't. But thanks.'

The doorbell rang.

'That'll be my taxi.'

Damson's arms lifted, reaching towards her daughter.

'No. Don't touch me. We can't risk stimulating the milk.'

315

Damson's hands dropped to her sides. 'Have you got all the medication you need?'

'Yup. There doesn't seem to be much going on in there now, those pills work.'

Leeta pulled up the handle of her smart new wheelie suitcase, packed with fresh clothes. She was wearing high-cut jeans that looked like they had a little blue corset to hold in her tummy, and a sky blue jersey. She carried a soft black leather jacket over her arm. She looked young, free, slender, fresh and beautiful. No one would ever think she'd recently had a baby.

Leeta hesitated. The taxi driver hooted his horn outside.

'He'll be worried about blocking the lane. I'm sorry the gate is shut, or he could have pulled in.'

'It doesn't matter, I'm going now.'

She started for the door, and then turned back. She looked uncertain for the first time since the baby's birth.

'Damson, I've asked so much of you.'

'Yes, you have.'

'I've been a bit muddled, I'm sorry.'

'That's OK. You've just had a baby.'

'I'll be OK, remember I'm nearly a doctor too. I can be my own doctor. I know what the danger signs are and if anything starts I'll go to the nearest A&E for help. So don't worry.'

'How will you explain your condition?'

'I'll say the baby is with its grandmother in England. They'll understand, I'm sure.'

Leeta paused. She turned round to face Damson, and stood quite close to her, looking into her eyes.

'You should know that I wanted to pay you back for

abandoning me, by disrupting your life and forcing you to have a baby after all. But that isn't what I feel now. You've the space for a baby in your life now, haven't you?'

'Yes, I have. Thank you for trusting me.'

She left quickly after that. She hadn't touched Damson, and Damson made no further move towards her.

She listened to the minicab disappearing down the hill. A baby's cry sounded through the cottage. She turned to go up the stairs.

Thirty-three

Damson
February 2009

The baby was heavy as he slept against her sweaty breast. Damson bent her head to kiss the top of his damp head and plodded onwards leaning on a stick she'd found beside the path. Baby on the front rucksack on the back balanced her but she was sinking into the ground with every step after a mile or so. Acclimatising herself to India by travelling around in the cooler hilly parts of Gujarat was all very well but a pushchair would have helped. Hiking with a baby was not one of her better ideas. When she could finally take both baby and rucksack off she seemed to float above the ground. It was almost worth it for the sensation.

The idea of travelling had begun to grow as soon as it became clear that Hari was an easy baby. Damson had become determined to cut loose from almost every aspect of the barren life she had built for herself at Fenning almost as soon as Leeta had erupted into her life.

She resigned from the practice and put Swine Cottage on the market. With plenty of savings and a young and portable baby to look after, travelling seemed obvious while she decided what to do next. Leeta's physical presence had brought back memories of India and what had happened there. Why not return, carrying the triumphant end-product of that long-ago disaster, and consign the whole sorry business to the past where it belonged? She examined herself closely to make sure this was a reasonable thing to do. Without anyone she trusted with her secrets to advise her, she had to give herself permission.

If she was to go travelling with Hari, it was important to do so before he got mobile but after he had had his immunisations. She brushed up on how to keep him and herself safe, and gave him his antimalarial medication crushed up in his mashed banana. She would keep away from wet, mosquito-infested areas, and make for the airy hills as fast as she could. She bought a pop-up cradle with an integral mosquito net that had been impregnated with an effective insect repellent.

She arrived in the relatively cool month of February, travelling between places she hadn't visited before in easy stages while she built up her courage for the main event. She always booked herself into the Ladies' Carriage on any train. With the rise in what was innocuously called 'Eve teasing' – known in the West as sexual assault – she'd read in the *Times of India* that Ladies' Carriages, which should have been phased out years before, were more in demand than ever. There was a long official notice nailed to the inside of the carriage door detailing what constituted harassment and promising that Indian Railways exercised zero tolerance. Even singing could be an assault.

When she'd gone back to Cambridge after Mellita was born, she'd taken the free self-defence classes for women undergraduates, determined never to be so vulnerable again. Tucked into the side pockets of her rucksack were two powerful chilli pepper sprays to deter both human and animal attacks. She imagined that she was too old to attract much attention as a woman this time but thought that being prepared did no harm.

Hari had been a great hit everywhere, creating an instant and healthy bond with both women and men. Toothless grandfathers in enormous red *puggaris* had stretched out lean hands to touch the top of his head. Young men smiled and women melted at the sight of his large grey eyes fringed with thick dark lashes. She fished him out of his carrying pouch and dandled him on her knee so he could wave and gurgle at other babies.

Damson noticed that many babies had large black spots painted on their faces like eighteenth-century court beauties and asked a friendly mother why. Instead of answering, she rummaged in her bag, bringing out a little pot of kohl. Dabbing her finger into it, she gestured for Damson to bring Hari closer to her. She made a nice round black mark on his golden cheek, saying: 'He is very beautiful. You don't want him to attract jealousy and the evil eye. I have made him ugly for you as a precaution.'

It was clear when she first arrived that while the women approved of Hari they thought she looked awful. The less polite sniggered and pointed, covering their mouths with the ends of their saris. It was beginning to make her self-conscious and she questioned why she should still dress in such an ugly way.

One incident in particular encouraged her to shed the sexless camouflage that had become a thoughtless habit. Two women climbed into the same compartment, empty except for her and Hari, asleep on her lap. The older one appeared to be the younger woman's chaperone, addressed as Auntie. They greeted Damson politely and peered with interest at Hari, asking how old he was and what was his good name?

Damson said, 'Hari. He's nearly five months old.'

Everyone smiled at his sweet sleeping face. The women got out the usual steel cups and tipped water straight down their throats without stopping to swallow. Damson had a large thermos of chilled boiled water for herself to which she'd added a pinch of salt and the juice of a *nimbu* or little green lemon. This enabled her to refuse their kind offers to share without appearing rude.

When Hari awoke, she sat him on her knee, and he looked about with a great deal of interest, crowing his pleasure and smiling at his audience. Damson pointed out of the window.

'Look, Hari, in the trees. Can you see the monkey?'

Hari was perfectly capable of responding to her suggestion, and he swivelled round to look as she held him under the arms and bounced him gently.

She glanced at the girl, wearing for an everyday journey a fuchsia pink and silver sari. Damson had heard somewhere that bright pink was the 'navy blue of India' – it was simply normal to look so glorious. The train had no corridor, so the two women were her companions until they reached the next station an hour away. The girl's cap-sleeved blouse or *choli*, also pink, had silver rosebuds embroidered all over it. Her firm tummy showed above where her sari was meticulously pleated into the petticoat and the rest of the vivid fabric was thrown over one shoulder.

The girl's auntie was dressed in dark green cotton with a geometric pattern in subtly glossy red silk woven into the selvedge. The older woman's brown midriff emerged in two folds. Given the prevalence of 'Eve teasing' a chaperone was a vital necessity, just as this kind of protection had been needed in Europe in wilder, earlier times.

Damson glanced down at herself. On her feet were ugly greying trainers. Her legs were hairy as she never bothered to shave them. She wore men's army surplus shorts that were much too big for her and had to be held up with a belt. Over the top she was wearing a baggy T-shirt. Nowhere on her person was the slightest expression of herself as a woman. No colour, no shape, no fold in any fabric, no suggestion of female softness or style. For the first time since she had dumped her femininity in her room at the Vhilaki Guest House, she desired something different. How ridiculous she was, thinking she could make the whole thing go away by dressing like a man.

She leaned towards the girl and said, 'I love the colour of your sari. At what age do girls in India usually start wearing one?'

'It varies,' and the girl smiled and confided: 'When I was fifteen, my mother was away, so I decided to try on one of her saris. I was so proud of myself when I had dressed up in it that I walked out into the town.' She giggled, hiding her mouth behind her hand. 'I thought people were staring at me because I looked so lovely and grown up. But the whole lot was trailing all down the street behind me. Now I always get Auntie to wrap my sari for me. She pulls the waistband really tight.'

The girl went on, 'Sorry if you think I am rude, but I always wanted to know. Why do European women dress like men? Or like bad women?'

'Do you think I look like a man?' Damson asked.

'No, you don't look like a man,' she hastened to add. 'But it is not pretty what you are wearing, and your hair does not look nice. Doesn't your husband mind?'

'Hmmm,' Damson glossed over the idea of a husband.

'It's practical, I suppose,' she added, feeling ashamed as she remembered that even the women breaking stones to make roads wore saris, tucked up neatly out of their way, but still beautifully folded and often coloured. And other women wore *salwar kameez* – trousers with a tunic – with a *dupatta* or scarf thrown effortlessly over the shoulder, controlled with fluid gestures of their hands.

The conversation with the two women had resulted in the younger playing peek-a-boo with Hari, while Auntie wrapped a sari from their luggage around Damson, telling her how nice she looked in apricot. That was the beginning of a change which had been creeping towards her ever since Hari had been put into her arms. She began to experiment after that, buying some embroidered cotton *salwar kameez*.

Her hair started to grow out which looked awful. Instead of going to a barber as she usually did and getting it neatly shorn, she gritted her teeth and let it grow. She squeezed lemon juice on to it, and gradually it grew fairer in the sunshine. Holding a baby on her hip made her sway from side to side in a rocking motion that soothed him.

After a couple of weeks, she moved north, booking herself into the Vasa Hotel in Rikipur. Then it was just a matter of taking the little rack train up into the hills to Hunters' Halt. When she booked her ticket, she'd found out that there was only the one day train these days, and you had to request a stop at Hunters' Halt, otherwise the train just went straight on up to the old hill station of Girigarh. This chimed with the mysterious absence of the Vhilaki Guest House from the latest edition of the backpackers' bible. She could find no trace of it anywhere on the web either, and when she had asked about it down in the town no one seemed to know what she was talking about.

Damson wasn't planning to stay up there anyway. She'd left her big rucksack firmly padlocked to a staple in the wall of her room at the Vasa Hotel. She carried a light rucksack, big enough to hold her chilli spray, changes of clothes, nappies, food, ready-to-feed formula and her thermos, plus Hari's little pop-up cradle strapped to the top. She had an emergency medical kit with her as well at all times, containing medication as well as disposable latex gloves and sterile syringes. In the peace and privacy of the empty carriage, on the final leg of her journey back into the past, she could feel herself tensing again. She examined herself for pain and scars from her last visit to the Vhilaki Guest House, and then glanced at Hari. Because she had him, it should be possible to close the loop whatever she found there. She realised she didn't have any expectations. The demands of looking after a baby anywhere, let alone in India, were all-consuming and elbowed out other emotions.

Although it was already quite hot on the plain, even early in the morning, it grew cooler as they clanked slowly through the forest ever upwards, the sun dappling through the trees into the carriage. She'd popped up Hari's little travel cradle and settled it on a plastic bag on the carriage floor, lifting him from his carrying pouch and laying him on the sheepskin inside that she used as a mattress.

After her visit to the Vhilaki Guest House, she planned to settle into a villa she had rented near the beach in Goa for a proper holiday. There she would see if she could experiment with getting some new Western-style women's clothes made up from sari fabrics. She craved colour. Maybe she would have her eyebrows and legs threaded. She sighed when she thought of the prettiness of sheer youth that she'd wasted with her stubborn concealment. Drifting and dreaming in this novel world of womanhood, she was brought back to the present by Hari protesting.

She rubbed antibacterial gel onto her hands and took out and opened a bottle of ready-made formula. She screwed a sterile disposable teat to the neck and then unzipped the mosquito net to lift Hari out, settling him into the crook of her left elbow to feed. Mothering Hari never failed to give her intense pleasure – a joy she'd believed would never be hers as she moved into her forties – even when he woke her several times every night as a new-born.

He was not at all what she'd assumed babies were like. But then she was so completely his that he had nothing to complain about and enjoyed an excellent digestion. The trouble with being a GP is that she had experienced far too many sick, miserable babies, rather than healthy, happy ones.

She reminded herself regularly that her daughter could change her mind months or even years down the track. Damson was already irretrievably bound with hoops of steel to her grandchild so it made no difference when this happened. She told herself that this was Leeta's absolute right although she trembled at the prospect.

When she woke at four in the morning and couldn't get back to sleep, she conjured all kinds of possibilities to test her own ability to bear them. She imagined that Leeta never had another child. That her glamorous arranged marriage didn't work out or the ideal husband found out about her past. There was so much that could go wrong. You couldn't just leave a living chunk of your life behind and move on all fresh and washed clean, could you? Not without damage.

By giving her own infant away, Damson had hoped to eliminate that dark and dirty tumble in the straw from her mind and life. But it didn't work like that. It clung about you like a smell and affected all that you did and were.

She hoped Leeta was stronger than her. That leaving her baby with someone so closely related, even if relatively unknown, would work a magical charm on her psyche. That she might grieve without knowing it, but that the comfort would be there so that the existence of Hari did not distort her life. Damson had set up a password-protected image account online where she uploaded pictures of Hari that Leeta could access if she wanted. A small part of her didn't want to share him, but the better Damson knew that she must and she sent the login details to Leeta's private email address.

Even if Leeta did change her mind, Damson knew that her own life was transformed. There was the faintest tinge of guilt that she and not his real mother should be having this joy, but there was nothing to be done about that. When he had finished his bottle, she lifted him up and sniffed his nappy. Nothing, just a little damp.

Thirty-four

Damson
March 2009

The rickety rack train with its angled wooden carriages slowed down. They must be approaching Hunters' Halt by now. She strapped Hari back on to her chest and unpopped his cradle, attaching it to her rucksack and putting everything away. She stood up and pulled the window down, reaching for the door handle standing sideways to avoid squashing Hari.

Hunters' Halt was deserted, the ticket office shut up with a rusty padlock. It looked as if no one had used the station for years. She stepped down, trying to remember what it had been like last time. Caroline had been there of course, complaining as usual.

She got her bearings and set off down the forest track that was the only visible path away from the station and led solely to the Vhilaki Guest House. Vegetation had narrowed it and she didn't think a Jeep could get through easily now, there was certainly no trace of tyre tracks. She set off, swinging along the path over a thick carpet of fallen leaves with Hari lying against her breast. She could hear birds but little else, and stopped from time to time to rest, propping Hari on convenient perches like tree trunks and rocks to ease the weight. She was glad she was still fit.

At the bottom of the path was the gate with the guardhouse

beside it. When she had last been here, a guard armed with a *lathi* sat on the little verandah, drinking *chai* and smoking a *bidi*. But there was no one there now. She went on up the drive, seeing the Guest House off to one side looking dilapidated. It hadn't been pristine when she was last there, but it now looked like an abandoned farm building with at least one broken window. It was quiet, and she began to feel uneasy, wondering what she had brought herself and her little boy into.

Everything was very overgrown, and she realised that she had no sense there were any horses. She glanced over to the stable block. The big door was half open and she went over and pushed against it.

Even the smell of the horses was gone. Sunlight fought its way through dirty, cobwebbed windows. She couldn't remember exactly which stall Ronny had led her into. She wandered slowly between them. Nothing was left, not even straw on the floor or traces of the meagre feed rations which was all the skinny horses were ever given. She didn't want to be there and walked rapidly out through the door, leaving it open behind her.

She turned left and went up the main drive towards the Hunting Lodge itself, an incongruous red brick Tudorbethan pile in the middle of the jungle. Ronny had told her that it was built by one of his great-grandfathers to entertain British and Indian grandees for a spot of *shikar* up in the hills, and maybe a few *nautch* girls, champagne and revelry, well away from the *memsahibs*. She remembered laughing at the time. An enormous peepal tree had heaved the bricks apart and one corner of the house was becoming detached.

The front door was closed. Maybe it was less painful to find it deserted. What else had she expected, after all? It meant she would have to hang around for a few hours until the rack train slowly creaked down and stopped at her request around four o'clock. She and Hari could while away the time wandering in the woods, bird watching, eating a picnic and resting in the shade.

Had everyone gone? There was no way of finding out what had happened up here, but she assumed it was too remote now to be viable. That no one like Ronny had emerged who wanted to live in shabby semi-feudal splendour in the middle of nowhere in the twenty-first century.

She tried the door, turning the cast-iron ring with both hands and pushing. To her surprise it gave and she found herself in the baronial hall with chequerboard tiled floor across which drifted dried leaves.

As she stood looking around in the dimness, she heard a very faint sound and tensed. Where had it come from?

She ventured across the hall floor her arms wrapped around Hari's warm little body and pushed open the door to one of the reception rooms. The sound became louder and she identified it as gasping breaths. She could also smell vomit.

'Is anybody there?'

She moved over to the window where heavy velvet curtains were open a crack, and pulled them back, looking round the room to see where the sounds came from. Whoever the sufferer was, they didn't sound in a fit state to mount an attack.

Beached on a chaise longue in one corner was a mountainous man. His hand waved feebly at her and dropped back, his eyes were half shut and his mouth slightly open. She hurried over, dodging the pool of vomit on the floor beside him, her doctor's instincts kicking in. She noted that the man was elderly and a dreadful cheesy colour under the natural tan of his skin, his body a great collapsed heap against the worn cushions.

She backed away from him, popped up Hari's cradle and laid him inside, zipping it up to keep him safe. Reassuring him, she went straight back to the man.

'What's happened here? Do you know what's wrong with you?'

He muttered and groaned but could not articulate. 'I'm a doctor,' she said. 'I can examine you and perform some first aid, and then we must get you to hospital. Is the telephone connected? If not I might be able to get a signal on my mobile.'

He didn't answer. She opened her medical emergency bag and took out the stethoscope, noting that his heartbeat was very rapid. His face, although pale, looked symmetrical.

There were several possibilities for this kind of collapse, but a faint memory stirred and she asked, 'Are you diabetic?'

The man's head rolled but he seemed to be nodding. Could it be? There really was only one person it could be. All power and prosperity, that had fuelled Ronny's disregard for the rules of post-Independence India, were gone. The house was grubbier than ever and much more neglected. It was pitiful to see the devastation that time had wrought on Ronny's once fine and muscular body, the flesh sagging off in great folds. He was dreadfully dehydrated. When she pressed her thumb into his arm it left a thumb-shaped pit. She thanked providence that she'd brought so much disinfectant gel with her to protect Hari, and she moved the baby's cradle further away.

She didn't have time to sterilise water from the taps, so she gave him *nimbu paani* from her thermos which he tried to gulp down. She had to ration it to stop him choking. Hari gurgled and she marvelled at his patience. She could see him through the netting reaching for his bare toes.

The man managed to drink two cups over about fifteen minutes before she was able to stop. She stepped back and looked down at him.

She'd no idea what Ronny had been thinking more than twenty years ago when she'd arrived with Caroline – probably nothing very coherent. Perhaps he'd spotted the cracks in her confidence and separated her from Caroline like a leopard cutting out an antelope from the herd. Maybe it had just been a whim to woo her because he liked well-educated English girls, and they were thin on the ground at the Vhilaki Guest House – but then things had got out of hand. One thing she was sure of, she'd said no and meant it. Now he was helpless. She could just walk away and leave him lying there – the perfect revenge for a ruined life. Except that she couldn't and wouldn't. She was a doctor and her life wasn't ruined at all.

She turned away, her eyes filling with tears. It might not be a ruined life, but what would it have been like if she'd left with Caroline and dodged her fate? A husband and family of her own? Self-pity darkened her thoughts.

Like the sun coming up, the reality of Leeta and Hari pushed aside the darkness in her mind. She remembered Ronny carrying her through the warm night and into this house. Not locking her into a room, just leaving. She even remembered him saying 'Sorry'. Sorry didn't really cover it.

Whatever had happened then, right now Ronny was in need of her skills.

She bent down close to him and asked: 'Do you have a proper insulin kit, and if so where is it?' His sunken eyes opened slightly and rolled towards the door. 'Upstairs?' she asked. He nodded.

She took Hari out of his cradle and tucked him under her arm, running out of the room and up the staircase. She'd never been into his bedroom of course, but imagined it would be at the front of the house. She tried various doors off the well-remembered corridor lined with trophies and found many of them locked. Then she saw one slightly ajar and made for it. Inside the room smelt badgery and looked neglected. The mahogany four-poster had a grubby-looking mosquito net draped over it and the sheets were grey and half off the mattress. This must be it. She glanced around the room, spotting what she needed on the bedside table. A red nylon zip-up case lay open, alcohol swab sachets and testing strips scattered on the floor and the bed. She was relieved to see he had a digital blood glucose monitor, as well as pen-style syringes full of insulin.

He must've been struck with weakness while downstairs. Risky to live alone in a remote place but perhaps he was so used to his diabetes that he thought he could handle it. It can't have been more than twenty-four hours since it'd started or he'd very likely be dead. He was lucky she'd arrived in time to reverse what was probably diabetic ketoacidosis or something similar. The symptoms were all there including the faint whiff of pear drops on his breath. She knew that confusion often led patients to misread the signals of onrushing disaster.

The presence of his kit could only help her diagnosis, and she gathered it all together with one hand and ran back down the stairs.

With Hari back in his cradle, she put on gloves and wiped Ronny's hands with a swab before pricking his fingertip to add drop of blood to a test strip and read the results on his metre. As she had suspected, his blood glucose reading was high. She injected him with insulin. After a few minutes, while she monitored his return to full consciousness, she found herself cradling his grizzled head in her arm and encouraging him to take more sips of *nimbu paani*. First aid to begin with, then she'd telephone the hospital and get him cleaned up. A little colour was coming back into his face. She waited until his breathing was settled and he appeared more comfortable, and then she said:

'You're Ronny Viphur, aren't you?'

'Yes indeed and who are you?'

'I'm a doctor. I was passing and decided to come and visit the old place. Oh, you wouldn't remember me. I was just some girl who stayed here years ago.' She sighed and then said. 'Do you think the telephone is working?'

'I don't know.'

His eyes began to close again. He was not acting particularly rationally and she worried that there was some other underlying issue. She picked up Hari again and hurried in search of a phone. She had her Indian mobile phone but in such a remote place a signal would be a lucky chance. She found an old black telephone with a corkscrew cord and lifted the receiver. No tone.

She switched on the mobile and began to walk about. She was relieved to find a single bar of signal in the hall which increased to four bars as she went up the stairs.

She went back to him.

'We need to get you to a hospital. I've found a signal, who should I call?'

He was drifting again. She shook his shoulder and he looked at her bewildered, then seemed to come to and said. 'Try 108 or 112. Same as English 999.'

'I am sorry,' he said. Just for one mad second she thought he had recognised her and remembered.

'For the mess.'

'Oh, don't worry about that. I'll clean that up while we wait for the paramedics.'

She was connected with remarkable speed to the emergency doctor at the hospital in Rikipur. She told her that she was with Ronny Viphur at the Vhilaki Hunting Lodge and described his condition. The doctor explained there was no road for an ambulance to get to isolated dwellings in the forest. Only an all-terrain motorbike could manage it, with two paramedics to carry Ronny to the rack train that set off back down the mountain at four o'clock.

Before describing the history as far as she knew it and probable diagnosis to the doctor, she mentioned that Ronny was very large and heavy, and to carry him on a stretcher all the way to the station would take two strong men.

The doctor said she would send such men, and agreed that she didn't think Ronny was now in any immediate danger, although he would probably need intravenous rehydration. Damson explained that she would make him as comfortable as she could, and the other doctor told her to ring back at any time, and that the bike would be on its way soon.

Now it was time to clean up. Hari had gone to sleep. Hesitating only for an instant, she slipped out of the room, this time looking for a bucket, cloths and disinfectant. She ran around the house gathering what she needed, going back to the sitting room to check on Hari and, she realised, his grandfather, to whom she gave further sips of fluid.

In the kitchen, she managed to light the stove, filling the kettle and putting it on to boil.

When she returned, Hari was beginning to grumble in his cradle. He didn't like being confined, or lying on his back for too long with nothing to play with but his toes. Clearly feeling better, Ronny had rolled slightly on to his side and was peering in Hari's direction.

'What have you got there? A baby? Why did you bring a baby up here? Who are you?'

'Right, my name is Damson Hayes. I stayed here in 1987.' She hesitated, watching him. He registered no recognition.

'Why are you here now? I closed the Guest House twenty years ago.'

'I'm not sure really. Various things happened in England that made it seem like a good idea. Now just relax and I'll make you more comfortable.'

She pulled on silicon examination gloves and cleaned up the vomit with disinfectant. Then she turned her attention to Ronny, washing his face and hands. He submitted, murmuring, 'Something is wrong with my legs. I was very ill and came to lie down in here.'

Damson let him carry on talking about himself for a bit. He seemed to have forgotten why he was interested in her presence at all.

Hari was beginning to cry intermittently which added to the stress of the situation. She found a narrow necked jug in the kitchen and offered it to Ronny as a urine bottle. She threw everything that smelt out of the front door and opened the windows to let in the clean sunny air.

Once more she went out to the kitchen to boil yet another kettle and wash and disinfect her own hands before picking up Hari and a jar of pureed vegetables for his lunch. In the now Dettol-scented room, she pulled up a chair beside Ronny and prepared to explain her presence while she fed Hari.

'Now,' she said. 'If you're feeling better, we need to talk. First, as I mentioned before, I am Damson Hayes. When I was staying here in 1987, we spent some time together, riding and so on, and there was an incident. After which I ran away.'

He turned towards her.

'You. You're Damson?' He looked shocked. 'I remember. Oh God, I am so sorry.'

Tears started to course down his drooping cheeks. Nothing was left of the virile man she had fallen for so catastrophically.

'Yes, I am Damson.'

They were silent for a bit. Then he said, 'I will go to the police as soon as I am better. Turn myself in.'

She shook her head.

He explained he'd been bitterly ashamed and upset when he found her gone the next morning and had tried to trace her. He hadn't had the heart to continue with the Guest House after that and it had dwindled to nothing quite soon. He told her that he felt as if a monster had been unleashed, and he didn't trust himself ever again to have young European women staying in his compound. She looked at the broken heap of a man on the sofa and an old anger stirred inside her.

'But you always had a choice. You could've stopped yourself.'

She might have done all she could to help him medically but she wasn't going to let him off the hook. She knew it was wrong to stir up strong emotions in a sick and ageing man, someone whose relationship to her was that of patient to doctor, but there might not be another opportunity.

After a while he asked her who she'd married and where was her husband.

'I never did marry,' she replied, explaining that the baby wasn't hers. That he was in fact her grandson. Then she said: 'He's your grandson too.'

The look on his face was one of the purest astonishment and then to her surprise a smile moved his sore lips.

'Grandson?'

'Yes. What passed between us produced a daughter and this is her child.'

He rolled stiffly on to his back and put his hands over his face.

'There are no descendants. The family dies out after my brother and myself. And now this.' He sighed, wiped his eyes with the back of his hand and began to explain.

'None of this is any excuse, but you must know that I had a wife long ago. It was a suitable arranged marriage and we were very young. At that time, my mother was still alive and we all lived in the *haveli* down in Rikipur. They couldn't get my brother to marry, so the idea was that Tara and I would produce lots of heirs to the whole bang shoot. She had a good dowry and we were happy for a while. I'd been educated in England and I realised my brother was homosexual. But of course nothing was said to our mother. She went on presenting suitable girls, and the story was that he was just very fussy.'

'Is he still alive, your brother?'

'Oh yes, he still lives in a small part of the *haveli*. I don't see him very often. He never did marry and our mother was very sad, but then she died. And Tara never got pregnant, and after a very short while she wouldn't let me into her bedroom. Then she began to stay up later and later, and finally all night, sleeping during the day. It was impossible to lead any kind of normal life. She would blunder all around the *haveli* or disappear and turn up in the Bombay Hilton days later, having spent so much money.

'So we were divorced, and her family, which was old, rich and powerful, began to spread rumours about me. I was threatened with public disgrace. They pretended to believe her stories which were fantasies from her diseased brain. Certainly no other family would accept me as a bridegroom.'

To Damson it was obvious that the poor girl had been very ill indeed but Ronny appeared to have no empathy for his former wife's suffering. He thought only of himself. It was entirely consistent with what he had done to Damson.

He stopped then and looked at her sadly, saying, 'Given what I did to you, you may not believe me.'

Damson nodded. Hari had finished his lunch so she gave him a cup to drink from.

Ronny went on: 'I had to come up here to get away from it. The family had always known she was sick but had managed to conceal it for long enough to marry her off. They took everything

I had in the divorce settlement – hush money really.'

He lay back again exhausted. She hadn't known anything about him she realised, just the rumour that he was educated in England and related to a local *thakur*. It had seemed rude to ask somehow.

'I remember enjoying your company,' he said.

Damson looked at him, startled. She felt it was much too late for anything like that. She didn't answer, so he went on.

'You had a daughter? Mine?'

'Yes, yours,' she said briskly, irritated by his questioning tone.

'What did you do?'

'I had to have her adopted.'

'I'm sorry.' He didn't ask why, he could probably imagine. She cuddled Hari close. He twiddled her growing hair and sucked his fingers while she talked.

'She was fine,' she reassured him. 'An Indian family took her. Doctors. She was very happy. But then she found she was going to have a baby she didn't want, so she came to find me for help. She left Hari with me to look after and I decided to come back here. I'm not sure why, something to do with closing the loop.'

'Lucky for me you did as you're a doctor,' he said.

'Your daughter is a doctor too or at least studying to be one.'

'What's her name?'

'Leeta Delapi. I called her Mellita and her parents gave her a name that sounded like her birth name.'

Ronny said nothing. Damson wondered what he was thinking but then decided she didn't really care. This had all been for her not for him. His rescue had been incidental. She broke the silence:

'It was a long time ago, nobody died and I have Hari now. You'll probably recover. But I don't think we can meet again.'

'I don't know,' he said. He seemed sad and resigned, too ill for extreme emotions. He'd stepped so close to death. Then he summoned up some strength: 'But the baby,' he said. 'Please write to me about the baby and his mother.' She nodded.

'No one left. No descendants. The family was dying out until now. It's important.' He reached out and touched Hari's head. 'Thank you for coming back and bringing him to me.'

Damson was startled to realise she hadn't factored in the blood relationship between Hari and Ronny, let alone Leeta, and that it might be important to them all in terms of family. She'd known nothing about the Viphurs and their *haveli* in Rikipur. Another complication. Nothing could happen without consequences. She would think about that later. So this wasn't – this couldn't be – a closed loop.

They heard the sound of the bike arriving at the front door. Damson went to greet the paramedics, having put Hari back down in his cradle. She left them to prepare Ronny and move him on to a stretcher, packing a few things for his stay in hospital while they did so. He said little, just confirmed his name. Thankfully, the men didn't think to question what she was doing there. She'd simply introduced herself as Dr Hayes.

She got herself and Hari organised, changing his nappy and giving him a wash, and then followed the carrying party up to Hunters' Halt for the four o'clock train. The two men positioned the stretcher in one of the carriages, and one paramedic stayed with Ronny for the journey, while the other went back through the trees to follow them on the bike down to Rikipur. Having said a brief goodbye to Ronny, and promising to write care of Viphur Haveli, she went to a carriage at the other end of the train.

Thirty-five

Damson
April 2009

The villa was surrounded by palm trees about five minutes' walk from a beach strewn with coconut husks, and half a mile from the village. It belonged to a schoolfriend of Noonie's called Susannah Hall, a trustafarian and latterday hippie, who had bought it for fun but then found the attitude of the local police to cannabis a bit restricting. Now they rented it out when they were organised enough to get a tenant.

Damson had told Noonie that she was off to India for a sabbatical, although not who was with her, and Noonie had mentioned the villa in passing. It was ideal. Painted a soft blue-green, with white window frames and a wide balcony, it harked back to the Portuguese style even though it had been built in the last ten years.

Susannah had had children by various fathers, so the house was full of cots and changing trolleys, everything Damson needed to look after Hari, and there was a sweeper who came in daily, and an ayah on call, plus a guard. Damson was ready to let go completely under the palm trees and accept some help with Hari. She had been immersed in him for months, attending to his every need and keeping him safe. Now she had some work to do on herself, sorting herself out before she went back to England to face up to the turn her life had taken. A profound sense of peace was hers as if more than two decades had passed in a dream.

She lay in a broad canvas hammock on the veranda looking out over the sea with Hari tucked into her left armpit. They both dozed. A breeze frolicked across her skin, waking her up. She looked down at what she was wearing and laughed.

When she had put on the white cotton sundress for the first time, her uncovered legs pressed themselves together with embarrassment. But the warm sea breeze had tickled her unaccustomed skin and she found herself spinning in the sunshine, spinning and spinning until she was dizzy and tears ran down her face. Now those legs, so long hidden in trousers, had been threaded to a pearly smoothness and tanned to a pleasing gold by the Indian sun. She didn't have to prove anything to anyone any more. Not that she ever did.

Damson remembered Munty, during one of their London lunches long ago, looking a bit bewildered, asking, 'Are you, what do they call it these days, gay?'

'No, Munty. Not gay. Just not feeling very womanly these days.'

He'd accepted that, and never mentioned what she was wearing again. Nor did he mention the baby that Margaret had so neatly managed away, although he must have wanted his only child to marry and have more children. Her strange appearance had clearly caused him to abandon hope that she ever would.

Thirty-six

Margaret
March 2009

Her laptop stood open on the Biedermeier desk. As she went over to it, Margaret glanced at her softened reflection in the old Venetian mirror. Not bad for sixty-four, although a subtle touch of Botox helped. It was March, and the daffodils that her landscape designer had succession-planted on both sides of the lawn edged her vision with trembling gold. She sat and focused on the screen and noticed she had two new emails.

The first was a long newsy one from Noonie, who was having a late skiing holiday with her husband in Verbier. Ottie and her younger brother Hector were both boarding at Brantham Prep now, so no need to come and spend time with Granny these days when their parents were abroad.

The second was a rare one from Damson, writing to Margaret because Munty didn't do email. In his late sixties now, Munty still preferred paper and asked Margaret to print out anything interesting. Damson knew this, and was aware that Margaret had always preferred to put her excellent shorthand and typing to good use for his correspondence rather than employ a secretary.

The subject line read 'Please print for Munty'. Damson was singularly uncommunicative as a rule, but a month ago, she had emailed to say she was going to be in India on holiday for a few weeks. Margaret had been surprised that her stepdaughter wanted to go back to India after the unfortunate consequences of her last visit.

Dear Munty and Margaret, I need to ask you a favour, and hope this is going to be OK. I would very much like to come and stay to discuss my plans with you both. I am still in India, but will be back in a week.

How odd, she's never asked for anything before.

My news is I have decided to take a sabbatical and maybe retrain.

Maybe she's lightening up a bit at last.

I want to make some serious changes to my life.

About time.

As you know I never found anyone to marry.

Not surprised.

So I have been exploring other ways of becoming a parent, including fostering.

Margaret's shoulders sagged. As the years went by she had walled up the memory of whisking away what turned out to be Damson's one chance at motherhood. It had been Damson's decision though, hadn't it? An acceptable alternative to abortion. The trouble was, she comforted herself, Damson had never made an effort to be normal and attractive to men. An unwelcome thought began to intrude. How old would the little girl be now? In her twenties. She wondered what had happened to her.

She read on:

> *Last year Dr Grimsby, who is near retirement, offered me a partnership, and I was considering buying into the practice. I am very glad I didn't, because I have decided not to live in Fenning any longer.*

All her usual jauntiness deserted Margaret. What was coming?

> *And the good news is that a little boy became available for fostering more rapidly than I had anticipated.*

Ah.

> *So we will need somewhere to live temporarily while I decide what to do next, and I wondered if the North Lodge was habitable. I know no one has lived there for years, but thought it might be OK to do it up a bit and stay there while we sort ourselves out?*

Margaret took refuge in immediately renovating the North Lodge in her mind. Why hadn't she thought of it before? Probably because it was a dull Victorian building, and anyway it was all a bit overgrown up there as the North Drive had not been used in living memory. The two South Lodges, both delightful thatched Gothick beehives, had been done up years ago, with Smallbone kitchens and Farrow & Ball colours everywhere. Both brought in an income as picturesque holiday lets, and were useful as extensions when the Castle itself was rented out. If the Castle was full at the weekend, she and Munty would stay in one of them themselves.

Not so the North Lodge. It wasn't a pretty building. The roof was regularly checked, but the windows were boarded up.

Perhaps something should be done about it. She brought her reluctant attention back to Damson's email.

> *If that is OK, I would like to come down to discuss our options. Can you let me know if you will be at the Castle in ten days' time, and if I can come and stay? I will have the baby with me, but can bring all the equipment I need in the car. The contents of Swine Cottage will be packed up and stored by Pickfords until I have somewhere to put it. The cottage is on the market, but no buyer yet. I want to move fast now, so would like a response as quickly as possible, please. Otherwise I will need to make different plans. Hope to see you soon. Love from Damson.*

Well, thought Margaret, sitting back in her chair. What to do? She reviewed her relationship with Damson over the years, from sulky teenager to reluctant deb. And then the awful shock of the baby, and the danger to her twins' reputation. She shuddered when she imagined what Nigel Dempster would have made of 'the Hon Damson's mystery love child' had the *Daily Mail* got hold of the story.

Luckily Damson had made no impression on the society columns while she was a deb. What on earth had the girl been up to in India? She'd never dared ask.

She had done her best, hadn't she? Made sure that Damson was properly looked after. Organised the adoption. She desperately hadn't wanted Munty to see his only child obviously pregnant. It would have upset and embarrassed him she was sure. Unmarried Damson with a huge belly? So common as well – a teenage pregnancy. She'd been his little girl such a short time before. It was a pity those homes for unmarried mothers had been shut down.

Margaret had made sure her husband didn't have to worry about the poor little bastard. Neither of them had ever seen it, of course. Thank God she had been there to rescue him. Poor man, what would he have done without her? What with Melissa dying like that he hadn't had much luck with the women in his family until she arrived.

She was pleased at least that Damson had included her in the email. After all she could have written a private letter to her father. Not that she and Munty had any secrets between them.

She clicked Print. When the sheet of paper had spooled out, she went downstairs to share it with Munty. His study was to one side of the hall, a comfortable room unchanged by Margaret. She'd wanted to add a club fender and other leathery paraphernalia, but he had resisted and she soon gave up. After all, the rest of the estate was her playground.

Her heels clicked more and more slowly on the polished York stone floor of the hall until she hesitated outside the mahogany door with its egg-and-dart edged panels. In all their years of marriage, she'd never been at a loss for words, and he'd always gone along with whatever she organised. To begin with she'd been very careful to make sure he agreed with her decisions, but it became a habit just to get on with all her excellent ideas. He hardly ever objected or questioned anything. Melissa's death must have knocked all the stuffing out of him.

She paused, thinking. Munty's will left Margaret a life interest in Castle Hey, and then everything to Damson after she'd gone. The twins' husbands were in receipt of multi-million pound bonuses and they got her residual Mullins estate. Margaret could have made sure Munty left her Castle Hey given what she had invested. But she hadn't, had she. She was not a wicked stepmother.

Did she want Damson back here now with some baby nobody knew anything about? Surely what she had done all those years ago was to stop this kind of awkward situation?

Her debutante daughters had had such a wonderful social success – they hadn't put a foot wrong. Then Damson had come back from her ill-advised trip to India, clearly having had some sort of breakdown, looking bizarre and being very difficult. Margaret had been so relieved when she'd gone off to Cambridge. Then there she was on the doorstep a few weeks later, pregnant.

The guilt, always tugging at her sleeve as Damson grew older and showed no signs of marrying or having any more babies, unveiled its white weeping face. Her eyes widened. She could no longer look away. Standing in the hall, surrounded by evidence of her revivifying powers – the well-dusted console table, the Persian rugs, the Hayes ancestors in oils tracked down and borne home triumphantly from auctions – she was confronted by what she'd done. She gasped. What business had she depriving Munty of his one true grandchild?

The breathless cheek of it and her just a girl from a Nottingham back-to-back. All these years she'd kept that thought in its place, filed under E for 'Expedient'. And now this. Damson, back on the doorstep – or very nearly – clutching a baby. Whose baby? Perhaps it was her baby – she was only, what? Forty-one? Perfectly feasible. That would make it all right, wouldn't it?

I must talk to him, I must explain why we had the baby adopted – it was what Damson wanted, wasn't it? Oh, but I made it happen. I must apologise for what I did. I meant well, didn't I?

She knocked on the door. Usually she would just walk in.

'Come in?' He wasn't used to her knocking.

She pushed open the door to see him sitting by the fire.

'Darling, I've just had an email from Damson.'

His face lit up. 'Damson? Let me see.' He felt for his half-moon glasses around his neck on a cord.

She handed it to him. As he began to read, she stood before him.

He said: 'She wants to come and stay for a while? She hasn't done that for years. How lovely. Have you replied yet?'

Then he went quiet, reading the rest of it. She watched him until he glanced up, saying, 'Do sit down, Margaret.' A log softened by fire collapsed with a soft sound into the grate.

Her legs gave way and she found herself kneeling before him. 'I'm so sorry, Munty.'

He continued to look at her. Then he spoke. 'We'll do our best for her this time, won't we.'

'Yes, we will.'

She knelt there for a few moments. He stood up and took her hand, raising her to her feet and kissing her cheek.

'Don't worry, Margaret, I am equally to blame.'

She sighed, and he turned away and went to his desk, picking up the telephone and dialling. She heard him say, 'Sarah? How are you? Oh, Damson's been in touch with you? Yes, she's definitely coming here to stay. Looking forward to seeing you here soon.'

Thirty-seven

Damson
April 2009

Hurrying through the green customs channel at Heathrow, with Hari strapped to her front and pulling her big rucksack on wheels, Damson was nervous. To her relief, she had had an email from Munty, warmly inviting her to live in the North Lodge for as long as she liked. No mention of Margaret. So she had felt able to ask her grandmother to come and stay with her there and help her settle in.

Then, on impulse, she had emailed her grandmother from New Delhi just before she got on the plane to ask her to meet her at Heathrow, saying there was someone she wanted her to meet. Sarah was well into her eighties and Arthur, a few years older, was no longer alive. No more time to waste on keeping secrets.

Arthur had died one June morning two years before. He'd gone upstairs after breakfast and, according to her grandmother, 'just kept on going' – all the way up to heaven no doubt. The practice long since closed, she had moved from Dorking into the granny flat of her son Julian's house in Clapham. Damson would visit her in London a couple of times a year and they would go to the theatre or for walks. They would talk about all kinds of things, but never the main thing. Sarah mourned Arthur deeply but with her son and his wife for company she had been able to take pleasure in life once again. She never said anything to Damson that revealed any kind of uneasiness at the way her granddaughter chose to live, without love and without a man. She did not judge.

There was Granny, upright in her brown brogues, face pink and hair quite silver in its bun at the back of her head, smiling and waving beyond the barrier. Damson sighed with relief and hastened towards her, faster and faster. Layers of concealment streamed away from her peeling like sodden bandages from a hidden wound.

'Darling, there you are.'

Her grandmother looked startled for a moment.

'You look wonderful.' She smiled. 'And who is this?' Her large and capable hand, roped now with veins visible beneath transparent skin, reached out towards the baby at the same time as kissing Damson.

Damson lifted him slightly away from her body revealing his face.

'This is Hari, the person I wanted you to meet,' she said. 'Let's go and find somewhere to sit down. Thanks so much for coming out to Heathrow.'

'Not at all, I couldn't wait to meet the new person. And you look so different, Damson. What's happened?'

'Let's sit down somewhere, and I'll explain.'

Soon they were sitting with cups of coffee, Hari released from his baby carrier and seized by Sarah to be perched on her knee.

'Now, darling, tell me all. He can't be yours? Or have you adopted him in India? Isn't he gorgeous? I thought you were

353

going to introduce me to a boyfriend!'

'Oh no, not that. I need to tell you something complicated. I'm not sure where to start.'

Sarah kissed Hari's curls and reached out a hand to press Damson's.

'Take it slowly. I'm listening.'

'Well, do you remember when I went to India in my year off?'

'Yes, of course.'

'What else do you remember?'

'You cut off all your lovely hair. Then you went up to Cambridge. I remember not seeing nearly as much of you as I would have liked. Arthur and I thought it was as well to let you go. We always had a policy like that with our own children, in their late teens they must have their freedom. Not good to have them hanging around at home, stunts the growth. We pushed them if they didn't jump by themselves. Your mother went to do her nursing. Julian and William were sent to opposite ends of the earth to get away from each other in their year off. No contact for months. It just seemed a bit abrupt with you. One minute we virtually shared your care with your father. The next we didn't see you at all.'

'I'm not sure how to say this.' She looked at her grandmother who was gazing at her with pale blue eyes.

'Well, I came back from India that time pregnant.'

'Was that it? Oh, my darling, why didn't you tell me? We could have helped. Did you have the baby?'

'I had a little girl, I called her Mellita.'

Damson caught the look in her grandmother's eyes. Her jaw seemed to tighten. 'Go on.'

'She was adopted by an Indian family over here. This is her

child, my grandson.'

The words had tumbled out. Sarah gave a small gasp and, having been holding Hari casually, she pulled him close and wrapped her arms around him. Her eyes closed. He wriggled and then settled, tucked beneath her chin, reaching up for her silvery hair and sucking his fingers.

'I'm so sorry. I didn't want to hurt you. I had to give Mellita away. It seemed like the best thing at the time. But she came back last year to find me and ask me to look after her baby.'

Her grandmother's eyes were pressed shut.

'Thank God,' she whispered into the top of Hari's head. 'Damson, what you must have been through. Who looked after you? What happened?'

'Oddly, Margaret.'

'What about Munty?'

'I don't know, we never discussed it. I just wanted you to know before you come to Castle Hey. I must get everything wrapped up in Derbyshire now, but we'll be together there. I'm so sorry I didn't tell you. I thought you'd had enough grief with my mother, you didn't need to know about Mellita as well.'

'Darling, we would have looked after you and done whatever you wanted. Although we may have been a bit old to offer to take her on. I assume Margaret didn't offer that option?'

'No, she was too busy.'

'I see. And you would have wanted to get back to Cambridge as well.'

Sarah gazed into the past. Then she said:

'When you're my age, twenty years seems a very little time. And I'm holding a baby of the family right now in this place and he wouldn't be here if it hadn't been for Mellita. And Melissa.'

Sarah handed Hari back to Damson and they both stood up. She slipped her arm around her granddaughter's waist and kissed her proffered cheek.

'My goodness,' she said. 'A new baby at last. We can talk properly in Sussex when I come down to help you settle in. I feel so sad for you that you had to go through that alone. I don't really understand.'

Damson saw then that her grandmother was getting old.

'I'm fine. The main thing is Hari.'

They walked towards the station together and parted.

Damson reached Swine Cottage in the late afternoon, Hari tired and fractious after his long journey. Both of them slept well that night, and then she was up, filled with the energy of change. The removal men arrived very early to pack, load everything on to the lorry and take it down to Castle Hey.

Damson and Hari camped that night in the empty cottage, and the next morning Damson called Munty to let him know she was setting off from Fenning for the last time. She could see him in her mind's eye answering the red plastic Trimphone in his study, so very modern when her mother Melissa had chosen it for him in the Sixties.

'Hello?'

'Hello, Munty? Damson here, just letting you know we're leaving in a minute.'

'So pleased. Take care, won't you.'

She hadn't noticed before that his voice sounded older.

'Oh, and Damson. I'm glad you're coming, and I'm looking

forward to meeting the baby. What's it called?'

'He is called Hari.'

'Harry? That's nice. When do you think you'll get here?' Munty asked.

'Well, the route finder says nearly four hours, but I think you should allow five as we'll need stops on the way. It's eleven o'clock now, I'm hoping to be with you by teatime.'

'Well, I won't start worrying until drinks time,' said Munty. 'We got the North Lodge ready in record time, 'We got the North Lodge ready in record time. Pickfords unloaded and unpacked everything late yesterday. It's a bit of a muddle but we'll soon get it straight.'

'Thank you, I didn't expect you to do that. I thought I would do it myself.'

'Well, what with the baby and so on, we thought we would make it nice for you before you came,' said her father. 'It all looks very comfortable down there, the Raeburn's been on all week and the beds are made up. We even did a bit of decorating. It's a very nice little house.'

Damson couldn't remember much about it.

'There's a big corporate cocktail party and dinner in the main house, and I thought you and Hari would prefer to move straight in to your own place. Otherwise there would be the bother of all that baby equipment moving around. I remember what it was like with Noonie and Clarrie's children. Margaret and I are in one of the South Lodges, keeping out of everyone's way.'

'I see. No, that's fine. Very good idea. But no one had lived there for a long time?'

'Well, we went and had a look as soon as we got your email,

and it was in remarkably good nick. Just needed a jolly good spring clean and the garden cleared. So we commissioned an industrial clean from top to bottom. But it's people who make things dirty, isn't it? And there have been no people there for many years.'

'Yes,' said Damson, bemused. 'People do make things messy.'

'Anyway, I think you'll find it very comfortable.'

He sounded uncertain.

Damson's mouth, which seemed a lot more mobile these days, broke into a delighted laugh.

'I can't wait, Munty. It sounds absolutely lovely.'

'Well, you take care now on the road. Come to the left-hand lodge, and I'll have the pleasure of escorting you to your new abode.'

She could hear that he was smiling.

And she kissed the baby on her hip, as he reached up to twiddle her growing hair while sucking the two middle fingers on his left hand.

'Damson?'

Pause.

'Yes, Munty?'

'It will be different this time. You'll see when you get here.'

'Different?'

'Yes, darling, different. I can't tell you how welcome you are and how much I'm looking forward to seeing you both. You should have been here so much more. Wasn't right. I am sorry, Damson. The whole thing. Not all right at all.'

'Munty, are you OK?'

'Yes, I'm fine. We can talk when you get here.'

Damson's eyes filled with tears as the love that had been dammed up behind walls of secrecy and loss now flowed freely. She must pull herself together.

She had last seen her father in London the year before, when they had had one of their regular lunches. His relieved and loving phone call, after she had been able to help Noonie with Ottie's meningitis in Derbyshire, had melted some of the discomfort between them. But there was an unspoken rule that they meet away from Castle Hey – and Margaret.

The last time she had actually stayed at Castle Hey – she realised to her horror it must have been for the Millennium – had been different.

The celebrations had been magnificent. All the local grandees were there. There had been an extraordinary *son et lumière* display on the lake, with interweaving water jets lit up to resemble fireworks, and dancing in time to a live orchestra that played both Handel's Water and Fireworks Music, as well as the Hallelujah Chorus. Damson had tried to find her father among the guests, but couldn't and gave up, going indoors. She'd tracked him down to his study and found him sitting in front of the fire.

'Can I come in?'

He nodded.

'Not watching the display, Munty?'

'No, not my thing. I was a bit cold.'

He seemed to hesitate as if he was going to say something else.

'What's the matter, Munty? Are you OK? Health OK?'

'Oh, yes, my health is fine. Had my annual check-up, Margaret insists on it. Lots of walks and an excellent diet.

Nothing to complain about.'

Damson sat down opposite him and the silence grew and spread between them, impossible to puncture. She shifted in her seat. He didn't seem to want to look at her. This didn't surprise her, she wasn't decorative. He stared into the fire. In the end, with an inarticulate word or two, she had kissed the top of his head and left him to it, going up to her old bedroom to lie awake. She'd left very early the next day before anyone was up.

They drew up outside the left-hand South Lodge at five o'clock. Damson hopped out of the car and rang the bell. She wanted to get Hari straight into the North Lodge so she could give him his tea and bath, plus a bottle and story before bedtime. Munty came to the door wearing his Barbour and pulling a flat cap over his bald patch. He was smiling, and held her shoulders, kissing her cheeks.

'You're here,' he said. 'You look wonderful. Darling, I'm so pleased.'

A great warmth spread through Damson. She had made an effort and was wearing trousers, but very different from the shapeless old cords she had affected before. Her shapely hips were revealed in a pair of tapered jeans tucked into high-heeled brown boots, and she wore a fitted white shirt.

'Where's the baby?'

Damson led him round to the other side of the car, and there was Hari, strapped into the car seat and fast asleep.

'I have to ask,' said Munty. 'Is he yours?'

'No, he isn't, not exactly. I can explain. Hop into the passenger seat and let's get to the Lodge. He'll wake soon and need his tea.'

Damson was playing for time. She wanted to be sitting calmly when she told her father what had happened.

He seemed to accept that and climbed up into her Freelander. It only took a couple of minutes, driving very slowly in case of deer, to get to her new home. They drove into the woods and curved round to the back of the lake, and there was the little house. Munty handed her the key and told her to have a look round, he would unload and keep an eye on Hari.

She turned the old-fashioned mortice key in the lock and stepped over the raised threshold. There was a very slight whiff of closed-up house, but there was also lavender, beeswax and wood smoke. The windows were open still, airing the rooms. Hard to tell it hadn't been lived in for years.

She rushed around upstairs to look at the bedrooms, where her bed was already made up with her sheets, and then down to see the old-fashioned but spotlessly clean kitchen and bathroom beyond.

There was her kettle, full of water, so she clicked the on switch and popped a couple of teabags from the red and gold P&Q tin tea caddy into the teapot. She got out a little pot of organic carrot and rice puree and put it to warm in a pan of hot water on the stove, pouring some more boiled water into Hari's cup to cool down. Munty came in, carrying a suitcase in one hand and Hari's car seat in the other.

'I've brought your little boy, he was beginning to ask for you,' he said.

'And I've made some tea. Let's just get everything in here while it brews, and then we can sit down and talk. I'll need to give Hari his tea as well.'

She went back into the kitchen and put milk from the well-stocked fridge, and cups, on the tray with the pot, amused to see a red and gold P&Q tea cosy in the shape of a crown waiting for her. Then she carried the tray back into the sitting room. Munty had just lit the fire made up on the hearth, and Hari was beginning to ask for his tea.

'It's nice and warm in here, but a fire's always cheerful,' he said, getting up stiffly. 'We had the chimney swept. Generations of starlings' nests up there.'

When the fire was going, he went and sat on one of her red armchairs drawn up to the hearth. He leant forward, looking into her face, his elbows on his knees. 'Forgive me, I don't want to intrude, but who is this charming little fellow exactly?'

'You have every right to know.'

She took a breath. 'I wasn't telling the complete truth when I said Hari was a foster child. He is, but only in the loosest sense. It's what you might call a private, informal arrangement. The correct term I suppose is kinship fostering. Hari is my grandchild.'

Munty's face lit up, and he jumped from the chair, his hands stretched out. 'This little boy is ours?'

'Yes, he is. Yours and mine. And his mother's. Although she has stepped aside from motherhood just at the moment. I'm hoping that will change. Let me give him something to eat, he's hungry. And then you can get to know him.'

Her father was overcome. His eyes glittered and the end of his nose was pink.

'Please pour the tea,' she said, thinking he needed something to do.

Seating Hari on her knee and tying a muslin around his neck, Damson spooned warm puree into his willing mouth. Then she turned her attention back to her father who was quietly beaming and wiping his eyes on a large cotton handkerchief.

'I can't believe it,' he was saying. 'This is the most splendid thing. Thank you so much, Damson, for coming back and bringing my grandchild, no, great-grandchild, with you. You've made me so happy.' He blew his nose loudly.

By this time, Damson was crying too.

'Do you have a clean hankie, Daddy?'

'Daddy? I like that. Yes, I've another one here.' He stood up and walked across to her. 'How did it happen that you always called me Munty?'

'I don't know. Do you mind if I call you Daddy? Look at us,' she said shakily. 'Crying like a couple of babies.'

After a bit of snuffling and blowing, he went on:

'So, what happened? How did you end up with the baby?'

Damson told her father everything that had happened, up to and including Leeta leaving Hari with her in spite of all her frantic attempts to get her to stay.

'I wanted her to so much. It was desperately upsetting when she left. But she was in such a state I couldn't force her to do anything. Maybe she'll come back later. If so we'll be waiting for her, won't we, Hari?'

'It is quite a tricky situation,' he was saying. 'But I think under the circumstances we can probably sort it out. I would so love to see her as well.'

'Me too. Having her for a short while and then losing her

again was sad. I have her parents' contact details but I've promised not to get in touch until she feels comfortable, if ever'.

'Right. And by the way, I'll tell Margaret all about it. You don't have to worry about repeating yourself.'

'I wondered where she was.'

'I decided I wanted to see you on my own first.'

'Has something happened?' Damson was intrigued in spite of herself, she didn't remember being alone with her father for any length of time, apart from their London lunches, for years. And they had never talked about anything important. He shied away from emotional stuff. She had always excused him by thinking of him as a typical stunted English public-school-educated man. He was still talking. 'Not exactly, but I must tell you that she very much regrets what she did when you were pregnant. She feels she did the wrong thing and should have left you with more choice.'

'Does she? She was kind in her way and I hadn't a clue what to do.'

'Do you think so? She didn't force you to give the baby away? She'll feel so much better.'

'Oh, no, Daddy. It was what I'd already chosen to do before I came home. Margaret just made the whole thing much easier. I hadn't a clue what to do about adoption or anything really. She rescued me I realise now.'

'That makes an enormous difference. I have felt very much to blame too all these years for being a coward at the time and letting you both get on with it. Women's business I thought. So relieved when you just got on with your life afterwards. Realise now of course that it was family business and I should have been involved properly.'

He looked sad. Damson reached over and patted his hand.

'It's OK, you know.'

He interrupted, 'I know she can sometimes seem a bit demanding, but if you knew what she had done for me,' he paused and then continued.

'She rescued me too.'

Hari spat a large globule of puree out indicating he had had enough. Damson gave him a sip of water.

'Sorry, I interrupted, wanted to tell you how I had felt and you were going to say something else? We aren't very used to this modern kind of talking about feelings, are we?' He wiped his eyes again.

'I never told you what happened. Why I was pregnant.'

He tensed and gazed at her, waiting. She groped with her right hand for the handkerchief that was on the arm of the chair. 'It isn't very nice what I have to tell you. I'm sorry. The thing is, I suppose, that the sex was non-consensual.'

'What?'

'I was raped.'

Her father looked horrified. She hastened on, 'Oh, it wasn't some stranger in a dark alley, I knew him a bit and he didn't hurt me. He just didn't stop when I said no. I was frightened but I was also mortified at getting myself into that position, that's why I didn't tell anyone. These days, they call it date rape.'

'Is this something to do with why you went back to India?'

'Yes, I went to see if I could find him. I wanted an explanation or some kind of closure. I found him dying alone in his isolated house. You couldn't make it up,' she smiled ruefully.

'I helped him and called for aid, probably saved his life. He offered to give himself up to the police, said it was the only time he'd ever done anything like it and that he tried to find me afterwards. I ran away from his house you see. I don't know if I believe anything he said but at least he said it. Perhaps people don't lie when they are close to death. They do lie to survive though. I don't know.' She'd thought about it all so much and there were no real answers.

Munty didn't ask who the man was but his fists clenched and then relaxed. They sat quietly, then Damson got up to change Hari's nappy. When he was clean and happy, she placed him on his great-grandfather's lap with a muslin to catch any overflow. Munty grasped Hari firmly by his middle and lifted him to stand on his knee so their faces were at the same level. They examined each other with interest. Then Hari carefully removed Munty's half-moon glasses.

Thirty-eight

Damson
April 2009

Hari slept right through the first night of their new life. The next morning, Damson got up, excited at the idea of arranging a home for them both. She dressed and fed Hari, and left him on the floor, the safest place for the very young and not yet mobile. But Hari didn't like lying on his back unless he was sleepy. He had taken to rolling on to his front and then raising himself on his arms.

He was lying in front of the unlit fire, on the hearth rug, with the old nursery fire guard hooked on to the chimney breast on both sides, while she nipped upstairs. She came back down a minute later into her new sitting room to find him gone. She felt herself go into shock. She had a momentary sensation as if she had dreamt it all, that he was a phantasm called up by her intense longing to be allowed to have a baby. Or that Leeta had changed her mind, crept in and stolen him away.

She took herself firmly in hand and searched, finding him in the kitchen doorway on his front, having wriggled off like a baby seal to find her. He looked at her over his shoulder. She laughed out loud and seized him in her arms, covering his pleased golden face with kisses, blowing raspberries in his soft little tummy. Her nerves were shot.

Damson would never get anything done if he was roaming free. She remembered there might be some old-fashioned, solid equipment up at the Castle dating from when she was a baby, so she called her stepmother's mobile.

Margaret answered, and said, yes, she could meet her up at the Castle. Damson put Hari's coat on and strapped him into the three-wheeler pushchair, jogging up to the Castle, pleased to get some exercise and spring air into her lungs. Margaret opened the door, smiling at her shyly. Damson kissed her stepmother, and thanked her for the trouble she had gone to in getting the Lodge ready. Margaret bent over Hari and took his hands in hers, saying, 'Welcome, little man,' and kissed him on the head. She seemed unusually quiet, only remarking on how nice Damson looked. Damson examined herself for her usual irritable reaction but found it was quite gone.

Leaving Hari safely strapped into the pushchair, they went up and searched the attics above what had been the old nurseries. In the dusty space under the roof they found an old-fashioned playpen in the form of a folding wooden cage that collapsed inwards if you lifted the solid wooden floor. It was heavy, so Margaret brought it up to the Lodge in her car. She commented that she'd used something similar for the twins, because they were complete monkeys, plotting together to wreak havoc.

Once it was delivered, Damson invited Margaret to stay for coffee, but she declined, just saying that she was always there if Damson needed anything and it would be lovely to catch up.

Damson took her hand, 'Margaret, there is nothing to regret. You helped me to do what I had already decided to do. Honestly.'

Her stepmother looked surprised, and squeezed Damson's hand. 'Thank you for that,' she said. 'I'll leave you to it, but let's talk soon.'

She bent to kiss Hari again and then left.

Now Damson could move freely around their new home without worrying about him. He would peer out through the bars at her and make meeping noises to attract her attention, and she scattered a selection of rattles for his amusement. After an hour of unpacking Damson heard a car draw up outside and, looking out of the window, she saw Munty with Sarah in the passenger seat. They were both smiling, which gave Damson joy. Previously, she had always noticed a reserve in her grandmother's manner with Munty.

There was a knock on the door, and Damson went to answer it.

'Granny.'

Munty waved from the car and drove off.

They hugged each other, Damson losing herself in the sweet-scented softness of her grandmother's bosom.

'Now then,' said Sarah. 'Where's Hari?'

'He's over there.' They turned to see Hari lying on his back in the playpen strumming his toes.

Sarah went over to the playpen to pick Hari up. She held his face against her cheek and kissed him. Then she put him back.

Damson went to put the kettle on, saying over her shoulder, 'I'll give Hari a bottle and then put him down for his rest.'

Sarah poured the tea. Damson picked up Hari, and settled him comfortably on her knee for his bottle.

'There are a few more things I want to talk about.'

369

Sarah nodded.

'Do you mind if we talk about my mother?'

Sarah turned her face away, and was quiet for a minute.

'Don't worry if it's too painful. But I know you were ill around the time I was born or just after, so you weren't with her when she died?'

'No, I wasn't well enough to come over and help. And everything went wrong very quickly after the monthly nurse left.'

'Went wrong?' Damson was alert to her grandmother's tone.

'Yes. I felt terrible that I hadn't been there.'

'So did they get her to hospital? Is that where she died?'

Sarah took a deep breath.

'No, she died here. Pauline found her.'

'Pauline found her? It must have been very sudden. Septicaemia? Or was it her heart?'

Sarah's pale downcast face alarmed Damson but now she had to know the details. She dreaded digging up painful memories, and her grandmother was looking so sad and agitated. Hari continued to drink his milk peacefully.

'Munty and Arthur decided that no one should know what happened. Most of all they didn't want you to know. I'm so sorry, Damson.'

Thirty-nine

Pauline
November 1968

Pauline sloshed up the drive in cut-down wellingtons, unable to see much under her tightly clutched umbrella as the wind threatened to turn it inside out. It was her first day helping out up at the Castle, and she assumed she should cross the scruffy yard and go in through the kitchen door. Something made her glance to the right, towards the lake at the bottom of the sloping lawn.

She thought she could see through the driving rain what looked like a pram in the lake, and beside it something very pale, floating. A noise escaped from her mouth, and she began to stumble across the grass, calling 'Help, help' – screaming now, the words whipped from her mouth by the wind, the umbrella dropped, forgotten and bouncing across the ground behind her.

As she drew closer she could hear a baby crying. Thank God. Crashing and splashing into the water, her attention was on that white and blue thing. She could see something rounded and something else washing gently around it. Then her mind, reluctant, made sense of the shapes. Long white legs, heels and buttocks, pale blue material floating like ectoplasm. She reached out but her boot gave way in the mud and she sat down hard, up to her waist in the freezing water, all the while screaming and screaming for help.

'Oh God, oh God, oh God.' She recognised Lord Mount-Hey splashing past her, pushing his arms under the woman's stomach and trying to lift her sodden weight. She floated away from him, now face upwards but under the water. He tried again, clutching at her, half pulling half lifting her out of the lake. On the bank he fell to his knees, and his wife's body rolled from his arms. Her eyes stared up at the weeping sky. Her hair, dark with water, streamed across her face. White arms, palms upwards, flopped on to the grass. Lord Mount-Hey immediately started artificial respiration.

Pauline struggled to her feet, kicking off her boots and wading across to move the pram out of the water, glancing at the screaming baby and hastily covering it up in the blankets that lay inside. Then she went to the woman and with both hands pulled the wet blue nylon gently down over her thighs to restore her dignity.

It stuck and was completely transparent. She was wearing nothing else at all, and Pauline shied away from seeing through the clinging fabric the blue veins marbling her breasts, the dark nipples. She turned, feeling vomit rising in her throat and, lifting the baby out of the pram, started to trot on her stockinged feet up to the house, gasping over her shoulder: 'Going to call ambulance and police. Where's the phone?'

He looked up at her.

'In the sedan chair. Like a little hut, by the front door on the right.' Then he bent again to try and blow air into his wife's lungs.

She knew Lady Mount-Hey was dead. Still as stone, white and cold. How long had she been in the water?

In the hall, she opened the door of the antique chair and grabbed at the receiver, dialling 999 with a numb, wet forefinger and dripping water all over the floor. The baby wailed in her ear and she couldn't hear the response. She was worried by how cold the baby must be but could do nothing but put her down on a sofa and go back to the phone.

'What service do you need?'

'Ambulance. And police. A woman has drowned. I think she must have died. She's very pale and her eyes are open.'

'Are you OK?'

'Yes, it's Lady Mount-Hey. She was in the lake.'

'Where are you?'

'At Castle Hey. Just outside the village of Hey, up the hill. The police will know it. Army had it during the war.'

'On their way. Now, can anyone there do first aid?'

'Her husband's trying.'

She dropped the receiver, checked the baby, who was crying but seemed unharmed and relatively dry, and ran back out of the house, down the lawn to try and help Lord Mount-Hey.

When she got there, she saw he was kneeling by the body, staring at it. He stood up heavily when he saw her coming and went over to the pram. He took one of the blankets and carefully laid it over his wife's face.

'She's gone.'

She could see he didn't know what else to say, but the ambulance arrived at that moment, its bell ringing and the blue lights flashing.

Lord Mount-Hey turned his stricken face towards Pauline: 'Can you look after the baby?'

She nodded and ran back to the house. She looked back once to see the ambulance men race to the body, check for a pulse and heartbeat. The police arrived.

She peeled off her soaking coat before picking up the baby. Unwrapping her, she noticed that she was not wearing a nappy. Then she remembered seeing the missing nappy, still inside its rubber pants, lying on the hall floor. It had better stay there for the police. She couldn't imagine what had happened to Lady Mount-Hey, or why she was in the lake, but she must do all she could now to make sure her baby was warm and fed.

The baby was scarlet in the face from screaming, her tiny hands and feet purple with cold, and Pauline hurried her upstairs as fast as she could. Lord Mount-Hey had pointed out his wife's room the day before, without introducing her, so she knew where to go. She hastily switched on the electric heater and shut the top of the window. In the little room next to the bedroom, she found chaos. There were nappies and baby clothes all over the floor. The enamel buckets were so full that the lids had fallen off, and the room smelt awful.

She took the screaming baby's nightie off, and noticed she was not wearing a vest or any other clothes. There were a couple of clean, dry nappies on top of the chest of drawers. She quickly folded one, looking round for a pin. There they were, sticking out of a large bar of Wright's Coal Tar soap. She pulled the nappy as tight as she could and pinned it round the baby's tiny behind. A rubber nappy cover lay discarded on the floor. She smelt it gingerly, but the priority was warmth rather than cleanliness so on it went. Then she found a clean nightie in a drawer, and a cardigan, booties and a shawl, and tried to dress the little girl who was red and rigid with furious protest.

She laid her in a Moses basket. She realised she was sopping wet and cold herself. She pulled off all her clothes, leaving them in a heap on the floor. There was no one to mind. Lady Mount-Hey's stained blue quilted dressing gown hung on the back of the door. It smelt stale, but Pauline slipped it on, looking round for slippers. She couldn't allow herself to think about the person who had last worn these garments. She shuddered as she did up the buttons.

The next pressing need was to feed the baby. She remembered seeing bottles and Cow and Gate in the scullery, when she had looked around the day before. She thought about the poor lady in the lake, and began to cry as she carried the Moses basket with the screaming baby inside down the stairs. In the kitchen, which was at least warm from the Aga, she pushed two Windsor chairs together and put the basket down on them. She hurried into the scullery to find the means of making up a bottle. The angry sounds of hunger and distress pierced her ears and made her fumble with the kettle, powdered milk and measuring spoon.

While the kettle boiled, she peeped inside a huge chest freezer, thinking to pop the bottle in there when made up to cool it down quickly. It was full of plastic bags of vegetables, prepared and labelled, presumably by Lady Mount-Hey. There were plastic tubs of stews and other meals she must have made before the baby came. The shelves above were full of jam in neat rows of pots, also labelled – the most recent said *Damson Cheese, October 1968*. When she remembered the mess upstairs, the crumpled sheets, overflowing nappy buckets and the terrible smell, it didn't seem like the same person.

Forty

Early, and the chill mist that crept from the lake had muffled the trees from view. Melissa got up and padded barefoot into the dressing room. Once there she couldn't remember why. Something moved in the shadows. There was nothing she could do for it now.

She pulled off her knickers and the tangle of elastic that held her maternity pad in place. Yanking them down her legs she kicked the whole lot under the cot. It was time she got away from this ridiculous pathetic fake nonsense. The sodden smeared nappies. The stinking buckets. Her weeping body.

She went over to the cot and rolled what was in there from back to front, picking it up and holding it under her arm. Opening her bedroom door she stepped out, carrying it along the passage and down the stairs, shawl dropping away. Small mottled legs bicycled in the chilly air as Melissa's hands had rucked up the Chilprufe nightie. The heavy wet terry nappy with its rubber cover followed the shawl, slipping from minimal hips and landing with a damp soft sound on the cold stone flags.

The big carriage-built pram stood in the hall. She pushed a tangle of blankets out of the way and put what she was carrying inside. Best to take it with her. Who would look after it in the big empty house, with its dusty deserted rooms? There was a man there at night, but Melissa couldn't remember what he was for. The warm repulsiveness began to seep between her legs again, reminding her to hurry. She felt a dull delight that she was going to wash it all away.

Twisting the iron ring, she found the front door wouldn't open. The big key was in the lock. Her need to get outside lending her strength, she managed to turn it with both hands. She bumped the pram down the steps. The thing inside began to make the noises that were so irritating, but then it stopped as she pushed the pram over weedy gravel towards the grass.

As Melissa felt the sloping remains of the lawn begin to take the weight of the pram, she considered simply letting go. Then she noticed the thing had shifted until its head was at a funny angle against the end. She leant over and pulled it with one hand by its small purple feet to straighten it out. As her fingers touched the cold toes, she hesitated. The grass was wet and chilling under her own feet, but she didn't mind. It felt refreshing after the stinking hot sheets of her bed. She was burning up in there. She walked on, letting the pram's weight pull her towards the lake.

At the bottom of the slope the land began to flatten out again and she needed to push the pram once more as she came closer to the water. In front of the house the reeds had been cleared and there was a muddy shore. A rotting boathouse stood to one side, with a half-sunk punt tied to the pontoon. She had a vague memory of the pontoon, of being frightened. She wouldn't walk on it this time.

She stopped. The mist had thickened into drizzle. Glancing down she could see that the little thing was getting wet, so she pulled up the navy blue waterproof pram hood and fastened the mackintosh cover with big poppers on either side. As the motion ceased, it began to grumble again. Melissa remembered vaguely what this meant. She'd managed to feed it at some point in the night, but that had to be the last time.

It was so terribly painful, her nipples angry with the contact. They itched and looked strange to her, crusty and rough. One of her breasts was agonisingly hot and hard. When it had been sick, there were streaks of red in the posset. She wasn't able to give it pure milk, even that was adulterated with her dirty blood. Between her legs and from her breasts. She was a filthy creature. But it was OK, the lake would wash it all away. That man had rescued her before, hadn't he? Images fled through her mind, not stopping – sunlight, then a splintering as wood gave way beneath her. A horrible cold shock and something holding her down under the water. But that was long ago.

She kept pushing. The rank grass had given way to wet clay and stones. The lake had not yet filled to its full winter depth, but she shoved the pram through the shallows until the water was up to the axles. She looked down and could make out the shapes of huge freshwater mussel shells, broken and just visible through the swirling mud.

The dawn wind strengthened and blew rain into her face. The pram didn't want to go any further so she left it where it was and waded past it, looking down at the cold water around her knees. She glanced up as movement caught the edge of her vision. Trees jostled on the other side, their trunks black and slick. A deer stepped out from between them and looked around before bending its neck to drink.

Melissa felt a dart of enchantment shoot through her. There was a jerk as if she woke up from a dream of falling. Her heart raced. She looked back to see the pram in the water behind her. She could hear her baby mewing inside. Sobs choked her as fear and love swelled and broke through her body. Crows cawed and flapped through the wet wild air.

The rain fell properly now in cold fat drops on her parting as she turned and tried to get back to the pram. The lake bottom was slimy, sucking at her feet. She was in too deep, moving too fast. Clumsy and stricken like some poor heifer sliding in a bloody shambles, trying to reach her calf. A broken mussel shell stabbed deep into her foot and she slipped, her legs shooting out from under her. She felt herself falling and gasped to scream as her face hit the water.

Forty-one

Sarah
November 1968

Sarah was in bed in the morning, still feeling shaky from the flu, when she heard the surgery bell ring. People nearly always telephoned these days to make appointments to see the doctor, and then walked in during surgery hours. She went back to her book and relaxed, knowing that Eileen the receptionist would be dealing with whoever it was. Her duty now was to recover from the beastly flu as soon as possible, and that took rest. Melissa would need her, and she had to be in good health to help look after the new baby.

After a while, she heard Arthur's footsteps coming up the stairs, coming to check up on his favourite patient, as he always said. She detected something in his hurrying tread that made her uneasy.

The door opened. She saw his face and knew instantly that something terrible had happened. He moved across to the bed, his mouth slightly open, eyes bewildered and red, skin blanched.

She pushed her hands into the mattress to sit upright, saying, 'What is it, darling?'

He came over and dropped on to the bed, pulling her forward awkwardly into his arms. She stiffened, but then put her arms around him. There was a pause.

'Sarah, there's something I have to tell you. You'll need to be very brave,' he said after a while. 'As brave as you've ever been.'

Sarah didn't feel brave, she was terrified. She began to shake.

'Darling, there's been an accident. Melissa.'

'What – what – what are you saying?'

She could feel herself beginning to pant, her heart speeding up, her forehead furrowing into painful folds. She wanted to push him away, get out of bed, run to her daughter, make it all right.

'I'm afraid Melissa has had an accident.' Now he was sobbing into the shoulder of her bed jacket.

'How – why – what do you mean?'

His tears terrified her. This man who had never cried before in her presence.

'What's happened to Melissa?'

'She's dead.' Arthur's voice was muffled in her shoulder.

She pushed him quite sharply away from her. 'What did you say?'

'Melissa has died.'

'Melissa has died? How?'

Unbelievable. Her daughter dead? She began to shake.

She took him by the shoulders with her trembling hands, digging her fingers into him, feeling a kind of rip inside her as her heart was damaged beyond repair. She wanted to hit him. There were no tears just this aching shock that lodged inside her stomach like a cold ball.

'Why is she dead? What happened? What has that man done to her?'

She realised she was shouting and Arthur's head was rocking

back and forth. She was shaking him and he did not resist, his eyes screwed shut. His hands came up and covered hers on his shoulders. She stopped the dreadful shaking, let go of him and fell back on her pillows, darkness peeling consciousness from her mind.

'Sarah?'

She could hear him calling. Then he pulled her upright, swung her legs over the side of the bed and pushed her head between her knees. She wished he wouldn't. The darkness had been welcome.

Sarah sat feeling dizzy her head still down. Not knowing how to be in a world where her child wasn't. She knew she should ask, make sure, make it clear, but she thought she would say nothing. If she ignored the world then Arthur and everything would leave and she could push this terror away from her to somewhere distant where she didn't have to feel.

Now Arthur was beside her telling her this terrible thing about her daughter. Her beloved Lissy Lamb with her little hoof for whom she had crossed an ocean.

Bravery, yes, that was needed but it seemed inadequate. There was no room for the thought that Arthur had lost Melissa too. She started to sit up, and she felt Arthur's hand tense and then relax, his arm curving around her shoulders as he pulled her against him. Her arms came up around his neck. Not looking at him she pressed her face into his shoulder that shook from time to time with sobs coming from so deep within.

She asked, dreading his answer: 'What happened?'

'The police just came. I thought it was about one of the patients. They told me Melissa had died. Darling, you're going to have to be very strong.'

'Why did she die? Was it something to do with the baby? Is the baby all right?'

'Yes, darling, the baby is absolutely fine. Completely safe. It's just that we didn't realise Melissa wasn't very well in herself. She did something irrational and dangerous early this morning which I'm afraid was fatal.'

'What did she do? What went wrong? She seemed fine when we saw her.'

Her strong husband, used as he was to the realities of disease and death, was crying helplessly now. She could detect his guilt and it flowed into her as well sending her mind hunting wildly for clues. As doctor and nurse surely they should have known something was wrong? At that moment they were both suspended, dangling above an abyss of guilt, grief and blame together like the corpses of betrayers glimpsed in newsreels.

Pushing her hot face harder into his shoulder, she said, 'How?'

'What did you say?' He hadn't heard her.

'What did she do?'

'I believed from Miss Smith's letter that she might have a touch of the baby blues, but it didn't seem serious and I wanted to get you better so you could go and help. But it was clearly much more serious than we understood or it came over her very quickly.'

'What came over her? What are you talking about?'

'I'm so sorry, darling, but I think it must have been puerperal psychosis.'

The words hissed between them. Sarah gasped. He was still

talking.

'She didn't seem to have done anything on purpose at all. She was found in the lake. She couldn't be saved. The police said it must have been an accident in the end. We are going to have to be very strong.'

She hadn't cried. She couldn't cry. Once the dam broke she knew she would drown. A voice in her mind told her that many and many a mother had survived far worse. Every home was full of the echoes of children who'd never flown the nest. Now she and Arthur had joined that uncountable commonplace army of bereft parents.

Her back straightened and into her mind came the baby girl left behind. Something to hold on to like a pale perfect lifebuoy bobbing on black waves among the wreckage. Damson. Her shattered mind sent out little feelers towards the motherless baby girl.

The tears came then and Arthur silently passed her his damp handkerchief. She wept in great gasping torrents, on and on and on. Held quietly, mutterings of meaningless comfort transmitted from him to her.

'Where was the baby?' she sobbed.

'The pram was on the edge of the lake with the baby safe inside. That's one of the things that makes me think she didn't mean to hurt herself. She probably imagined she was taking Damson for a walk. Poor darling Melissa.'

She made a decision then not to ask any more questions, to let Arthur tell her what he would. He went over the medical details of what had probably happened to Melissa, and she could feel her heartbeat slowing. She knew about cases like this. Some poor demented mothers took their babies with them. Sarah breathed a prayer of thanks that they were spared that at least.

'You're sure Damson is all right?'

The name, which she'd found strange to begin with, felt comforting and familiar.

They were interrupted by a knock on the door. 'Dr Reeves, I brought up what you asked for. I'm so sorry, Mrs Reeves.'

It was Nurse Gregory from downstairs who did all the vaccinations. She handed Arthur a syringe.

'Do you mind, darling? I think we need to give you something to help you get through this. I don't want you relapsing.'

She nodded, desperate to escape from the all-consuming grief that threatened to derail her completely. There was a prick in her thigh. She sank away into sleep without any dreamy transition.

When she awoke, she lay for a minute or two wondering what was so awful, before the memory of what had happened to Melissa came crashing back into her consciousness. She curled on to her side in a ball trying to understand that she wouldn't hold her daughter in this life again.

After a while she got up shakily and went over to the chest of drawers. She hadn't thought about it for years but she went straight to where it was hidden under seldom-worn blouses at the back of the bottom drawer. The Waffen SS dagger – her trophy. She'd looked it up since to find out who and what her attacker had been. She reached under the soft cotton and silk and her hand touched cold steel. She carried the knife back to the bed and climbed under the covers.

The dagger had a theatrical look. A toy dagger for men who had never grown up, posturing in their black, skull-strewn uniforms and killing for real. She pulled up her nightdress and looked at the scar in the top of her thigh. It was quite white now, a little shiny mark about an inch wide. A wider scar than it should have been because it had never been stitched. She glanced back at her younger self, dealing with smashed limbs and boys dying in her arms without breaking down. But she had loved none of them and everyone else had been in the same boat.

She examined the clip that had held the dagger to the officer's belt and tested the sharp tip with her finger. Along the blade were engraved the words in Gothic script *Meine Ehre heißt Treue*. A torment of remembering Melissa crashed into her and her mouth dropped open in helpless grief. The pain was appalling. A noise came out of her mouth. It frightened her and she pressed her lips together trying not to scream.

It would be so easy to stop the pain. To slip the blade between her ribs and let it out forever. Except it wouldn't slip. It would have to be shoved, and there were no guarantees. A stupidly clumsy way to end her life. But to go to Melissa where she was now and comfort her? There was no certainty though that they would meet.

'No.' She could hear her voice echoing in the room. 'No.' She could not go to that place where Melissa had gone. She had to stay here. For Arthur, for Melissa's baby. For the boys.

She scrambled out of bed to put the dagger back before anyone came in, feeling weak and faint as she did so. Then she lay against her pillows letting the memory of her lost Melissa wash over her. Into her mind came words: 'Lord, now lettest thou thy servant depart in peace.'

Melissa was so young, only twenty. How cruel was it to take her now, away from her baby and her mother as well? She hadn't realised she had any tears left. She lifted the edge of the sheet to wipe them away. Crying was all she could do, she was so weak. After a while, her consciousness eased away from her again and she let it go, thankful for the release.

Forty-two

Damson
April 2009

Damson couldn't move as Hari was still sucking his bottle. She was overrun by wave upon wave of shock, grief and horror. In her mind, she had always placed her dying mother in bed, or possibly in hospital, shying away from the details. Not this tormented scene in the lake.

'Why didn't I guess? Everyone was always so weird about it.' Her voice rose, and Hari's eyes snapped open. She calmed herself.

'I think you know the answer to that. I am sorry now though that we didn't tell you. I don't think your mother did it on purpose. I'm sure in the end it was an accident. That's what the inquest found.'

Her grandmother came over and sat down on the sofa beside her. Damson's eyes filled with tears for the young woman who had died of a frightening disease and very nearly taken her baby with her. Puerperal psychosis crept up at her out of the misty lake like a monstrous thing, dragging her down. Why had no one realised she was so ill?

'Do you think she was trying to kill me as well?'

'No, I don't, not at all. Pauline told me you were safely in the pram, with the hood up and the waterproof cover attached at the sides.'

Hari, replete now, was drowsing dreamily on her lap, his eyes half closed.

'It was a long time ago and she's at peace now.'

'But she was so young. And I never knew her. She must have suffered so much.'

'I know.' Sarah looked stricken.

'No wonder Munty always looked so crushed.'

'He genuinely adored her. He was devastated.'

'Why didn't he stop her? Didn't he notice there was something wrong?'

'We can't know. There such a taboo around mental illness – there still is. He probably just thought she was tired. He knew nothing about childbirth or women. You know how reticent he is, even now.'

'I always wondered why he avoided the lake. I remember when Margaret organised that extraordinary water and light show for the Millennium, he didn't watch it. I found him sitting in his study looking sad. Too bound up in myself then to wonder why.'

Sarah went on, 'When we visited after the birth, she seemed fine, just tired. Then I was ill for a long time and your grandfather insisted I stay quietly at home. We had organised a very experienced monthly nurse for Melissa, as you know, and the plan was for me to go and stay when her month was up and look after you and your mother. But I was still too ill, and Munty had employed Pauline from the village as a housekeeper to allow Melissa to rest. We thought she would be well looked after. It was such a shock.'

'Granny, can you hold Hari, I think he's had enough of his bottle.'

Sarah held out her hands and took the baby, putting him over her shoulder to wind him. Damson put on her wellington boots which were waiting by the door. She turned back to see her grandmother checking Hari's nappy.

'He'll be fine, don't worry about that. Do you mind watching him for me, for a bit?'

'Of course I will. I'd love to. I'm just so sorry about all of it.'

'I always wondered, I suppose. I am glad I didn't know before I had Mellita though. I don't know what I would have done. Something even more stupid probably.'

She could hear her grandmother protesting gently in the background, but she had to get outside, so she opened the door and let herself out, walking fast towards the lake. She found it sparkling in the spring sunshine, neatly landscaped in contrast to the muddy shore and rank grass of her childhood. She glanced at Margaret's fountain. Presumably she didn't know that Melissa had died in the water. Damson didn't believe her stepmother could be as tactless as that.

It would have been November when Melissa had waded into the icy water. Dead grey sky. Cold still air. She didn't know of course. Helpless frustration stoked her anger and she clenched her fists and growled deep in her throat, the sound building and startling her as it came out of her mouth as a roar of 'Hell and damnation. Why didn't anyone stop her? Where were they all?'

She stared at the trees on the other side of the lake, trying once more to rip through the fabric of time between herself and Melissa, standing in that same spot separated only by the years.

Her own behaviour after she had had Mellita had been odd but she had always continued to function. She had wept and raged but had not wanted to destroy herself. Just waded on stubbornly against the muddy tide of her life never letting it overwhelm her. How much worse an experience had Sarah suffered, grieving so bitterly and never complaining. Had guilt made it worse?

Damson might have suffered the loss of a child but at least she knew that Mellita was alive somewhere. Where and doing what? She didn't even know if Leeta had looked at her cache of photographs of Hari online.

She heard someone crunching across the gravel sweep behind her and turned to see Sarah approaching pushing the old-fashioned pram that Margaret had left in the Lodge's porch for Hari.

'Hari could do with some air,' she said. 'I didn't want to leave you alone.'

'Was that my pram?'

Damson could hear herself sounding abrupt.

'Yes, the one your mother put you in for safety on her last walk.'

She took a steadying breath and moved closer to her grandmother. Sarah's arm found its familiar place around her waist. Damson bent forward to pick up the child, careful not to dislodge her grandmother's embrace, straightening to hold him upright in her arms. They looked out over the water.

The swifts nipped insects out of the air to feed their young, diving to break the silvery surface with their sharp beaks. Every year the fledglings slipped away while their parents hunted and flew alone to Africa. Every year the same nesting pairs returned to the eaves of Castle Hey.

Damson lifted Hari higher to watch the little birds whirl and shriek.

Acknowledgements

Thank you to my mother-in-law Elizabeth Young – an early reader and always so encouraging. Thank you to Rachel Hore, whose generous offer of a cover quotation came out of the blue and jolted me back into action. Thank you to Lizzy Kremer for helpful suggestions. Thank you to my beta readers for your invaluable support: Maud Young, Fred Adderley, Marianne Kavanagh, Charlie Keyes, Kate Morris, Helen Walters, Phoebe Frangoul, Deborah Botwood-Smith, Jillian Moore, Michele Gorman and Caroline Driggs. Thanks to Holly Thomas and Steve Gove for editing assistance. Thank you to Monisha Rajesh for essential information. Any mistakes are entirely my own and forgive me if I have left anyone out. Grateful thanks to Lawrence Mynott for the beautiful drawings, and to Alison Eddy for the originality of her cover design. Above all I want to thank my children, Maud, Archie and Tolly Young, who put up with all the hours of writing and editing. To all three of whom this book is dedicated with my love.